THE ROTT ınERTIA

THE STATION TRILOGY: BOOK TWO

JARRETT BRANDON EARLY

www.jarrettbrandonearly.com

www.therottinertia.com

Maps by Jarrett Brandon Early

Book Cover by BINATANG via 99Designs

The Rott Inertia / Jarrett Brandon Early - FIRST EDITION

ISBN: 978-1-7342314-3-4 (Paperback)

ISBN: 978-1-7342314-4-1 (eBook)

Dedicated to:

My wife Natthicha and my daughter Alexandra Beam, the best things to ever happen to me. You took my eyes off what isn't, and allowed me to focus on what is. And, most importantly, what can be.

And, as always, my father and mother, Timothy Jon Early and Maureen Brearton Early. I may not deserve you, but I most certainly appreciate you.

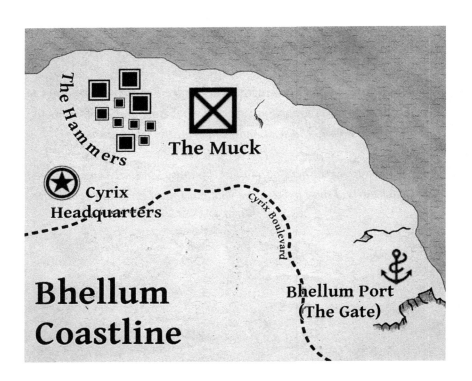

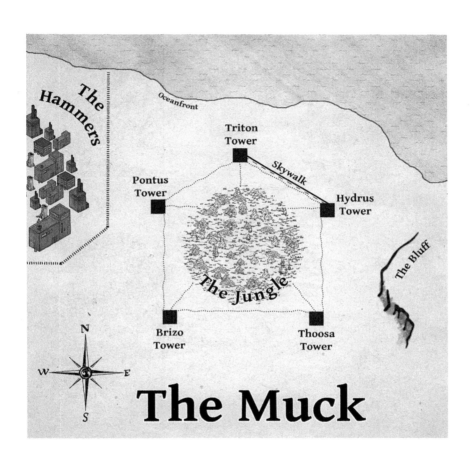

The Muck

PROLOGUE

"**C**offee!" Albany Rott yelled to the small metal stand that sat hovering across the busy intersection. Strange cars whizzed by on a variable number of wheels. Inside, riders could be seen sleeping, reading, and watching illuminated screens. There didn't appear to be any drivers.

The small metal stand began to cross the congested street, perfectly timing its thrusts forward to miss being annihilated by the speeding automobiles. Despite the traffic, the stand flew over in short order and stopped before Rott, who pressed his hand against a blue glass panel to the right of a metallic door dispenser.

"Two, regular," Rott said into the air as his palm was read. Something inside the machine whirred to life as the almost silent thrusters kept the entire stand perfectly aloft and still. Seconds later, the large door opened and two steaming cups of coffee sat inside. Rott pulled out both and handed one to Marlin Hadder. The cups were made of an exotic, thin metal that remained cool to the touch.

Hadder sipped his coffee, which was like and unlike the coffee that he remembered two lifetimes ago. As the man and god drank, the coffee stand turned and floated away, hovering above the moving walkway until it was called down a side street by another thirsty customer.

Hadder finished his drink quickly, not only because he was quite cold in the brisk morning air, but also because he found the unfamiliar flavor agreeable to his taste buds. Rott gulped down his own beverage, tossing the metal cup to the ground when it was emptied. Hadder wanted to scold Rott for littering, but before his mouth could form the words, the discarded cup was dragged along the concrete-like ground and over a moving walkway, pulled by an unseen force into one of a series of large gaps at the base of the city buildings.

"Most of the disposables are metal-based," Rott explained. When you toss them on the ground, there is a focused magnetic charge that pulls them into recycle catches. Quite effective, really. Give it a shot."

Hadder followed suit, dropping his metal cup and wincing a bit as it rang loudly against the hard ground. It sat motionless for a moment before finally turning in place and rolling quickly towards the buildings, scurrying like a rat into the same gap into which Rott's cup disappeared.

"Always satisfying," said Rott as he stepped onto the moving walkway and took off alongside the busy street. Hadder chased after him, walking atop the conveyor until he came even with his red-eyed companion. Hadder breathed in deeply, and the cold air still felt strange against lungs still unused to chilly temperatures. He looked around as they sped through the city, more and more questions forming on his lips until he could remain silent no more.

Hadder stepped off the moving walkway and pulled Rott with him, dragging his new friend between two buildings. "Al?" Confusion and concern bookended that one word.

"Yes, Marlin?"

"Al, where the hell are we?"

Rott placed his too-white hands into the pockets of his black suit pants as he stared out into the cityscape. "The city is called Pilomont, I think. Nothing remarkable, just a medium-sized town."

Hadder sighed in frustration. "You know goddamn well that's not what I mean, Al. *Where* are we? Too many things are off. There are too many changes. This doesn't look like the world I remember."

Rott's crimson eyes flared for a moment, a prequel to the smirk that appeared on his scarred face. "That is because it is *not* your world, Marlin. It is an alternate reality quite similar to your own."

Confusion and concern coalesced into panic. "What the fuck are you talking about, Al?!"

"This world, Marlin. It is not your own. You left that behind when you made the choice to join Station."

Hadder waited for more information. When none came, the Rage returned in a rush. "You sonovabitch! Stop being so fucking enigmatic for a second and tell me what the hell is going on! I followed you through that goddam trackless desert. I went against every urge and walked into that pit of quicksand on your word. I stepped into daylight for the first time in forever, my eyes burning as if smoke was blown into them. I walked along a busy highway as odd vehicles and even stranger flying shit raced by. I entered a city where nothing is familiar and everything screams *wrong*. And I haven't asked a single. Fucking. Question. That ends now. I want all the answers, you goddam devil!"

Rott chuckled silently to himself, always amused by his companion's outbursts, those rare times when the Rage would overtake his usually calm demeanor. Hadder's Rage was something Rott intended to wield like a weapon, so he was happy to keep its edge sharp. He put his hands up in mock surrender.

"Calm down, Marlin. Let me clarify things and put your simple mind at ease. Just as some of your scientists and fiction writers presumed, your world has countless alternate realities, each differing because of decisions made that dramatically altered the trajectory of history. This is one of those sister realities."

"But why? Why didn't we just return to my home reality?"

Rott paused, thinking how he could explain such concepts to an infant mind. "That would have been difficult, maybe impossible in my current human form. I created Station in the space between your reality and this one. Unfortunately, the portals only pass in one direction, from your reality, through the intermediate void, and into this one. There is no gateway back to your world. We must move forward."

"And Viktor Krill?"

"He would have found the same to be true. Thus, we can be assured that we are still on his trail. He is here. Somewhere in this world. Wreaking havoc on the unsuspecting. Making obscene use of his Wakened abilities."

Something dawned on Hadder and his eyes widened. "So, you mean, if the Risers..."

"Yes, Marlin. Even if those idiot Risers managed to escape Station, find their way through the desert, and locate the quicksand portal, they would have found themselves in this world, not the one they felt so wronged by."

Hadder nodded and blew on his hands for warmth. "So what about this reality? What's in store for us here?"

Rott looked around again, making a thousand mental notes and projections. "From what little I have gathered, it seems very much like your own world. It does seem, however, that the robotics industry is much more sophisticated here. Don't feel bad about that, though. Some realities do things better than others, but this is usually balanced out by other variables. There is something in the air here, something unnatural and manmade. I dare say this world cares less about what I have built for them than yours even."

As Rott spoke, a chill breeze cut through Hadder's meager clothing, reminding him of more foundational needs. "How are we going to get around here, Al? This isn't Station. We're going to need food, shelter, and clothes here. I don't think my bank account works across worlds."

"Well, lucky for you that mine does. I set up an account as you slept off the portal journey. Gold and jewels remain valuable across worlds, and I have pockets full of the stuff." Rott slapped his suit pocket for good measure and it jangled in response. "The account is tied to my palm print. We'll attach you to the account later today."

Rott began to exit the narrow alleyway and Hadder joined him beside the moving walkway. "And how do you intend to find Viktor Krill in this foreign world?"

Rott stepped back onto the conveyor and motioned for Hadder to follow. "Oh, that bastard will show himself soon enough. You cannot hide a monster but for so long. Eventually, the blood spills out into the crowds and the screams become too loud to ignore. It may take a while, but his whereabouts will become clear in time."

"And until then?"

Rott clapped Hadder hard on the shoulder. His eyes blazed again. "For too long I have been a prisoner of my own experiment. Until Viktor Krill shows his demon face, you and I are going to have some fun. So, wipe that hangdog look away and breathe in the metallic air of a new world filled with possibility. My god, cheer up, man! You are in the custody of a god, and no one knows how to party like a god!"

Fuck it, thought Hadder as a new world spun past. The makings of a stupid grin started to form on Hadder's mouth, but was quickly dashed by a thought. "Al, one more question."

"Yes, Marlin."

"Everyone from Station was from my world, right?"

"That is correct."

"Well, if there are countless realities, where humans have made countless decisions, I don't understand how your bet was appropriate. Shouldn't you have to test humans from each reality to see how they would react?"

Rott looked over at his human friend. "These realities all differ, I will give you that, Marlin. But there is a common thread that weaves through the endless multiverse, a constant that rendered one experiment from one world sufficient."

"And what is that constant?"

"You humans will always fuck up a good thing."

Hadder turned away from the barb, the difficult truth piercing him like Lilly Sistine's knife. Rott began to laugh beside him, a deep sound that emanated from the god's chest.

The Rage took center stage once more, spoke for Hadder. "I don't know why you're laughing, asshole. You built us in your image, after all."

"That is precisely what is so funny. Get off at this next intersection. I have a world to show you."

PART I

THE KRILL ASCENSION

1

V iktor Krill cocked his head to the side and smiled. From this angle, the bloodstain on the wall looked like an old acquaintance, especially where bits of gore had gathered to form twin "eyes" of red. Krill chuckled to himself, briefly remembering another life in another city in another world that wasn't nearly as much fun as his more recent escapades.

The smile quickly vanished as Krill took in the rest of the bloody scene. Broken bodies were scattered throughout the dive bar, some missing appendages and others twisted in unnatural poses. While each body told its own macabre story, a few common characteristics marked them all. They wore black satin jackets that read "Villains" and were topped with dead eyes and mouths frozen in silent screams.

To someone stumbling upon the gruesome scene, it would have appeared torn directly from the illustrated pages of Hell. To Viktor Krill, it was just another conquest, one in a long line that was growing less exciting by the day. Krill made his way across the room, careful to step around dead meat and over pools of blood that might have stained his soft suede loafers.

He stopped at the body of an enormous bald man whose face was aimed towards the ceiling despite laying chest down on the sticky floor. This was the man that Krill had words with several hours prior at the hovering news-stand. The large man had taken exception to Krill asking, "What exactly makes you a villain?"

He towered over Krill, jabbing a meaty finger into the slim man's chest. "Crushing little turds like *you* makes me a villain. You're lucky I'm in a hurry. If you're still feeling like a smart ass later, swing by *The Hole* and I'll be happy to demonstrate. Now get the fuck outta my way!"

The bald man moved to push past Krill, driving his shoulder into the smaller man in a show of strength, one that was meant to say *you don't want any of this*. Unfortunately, his plan backfired when he bounced off the strange man with black eyes as if he had picked a fight with a cement pillar. His shoulder throbbed where he had rammed it into Krill, real pain atop his mounting embarrassment. Unused to this feeling, the large man bent down and reached into his massive black boot, retrieving a wicked blade from its hiding place. He rose to face the idiot who dared to show him up, but the slender pissant was already gone.

"That's right! You better run, you little bitch," the large man shouted into the wind. He looked around to see if anyone had observed his minor victory, but only the hovering newsstand and a few cleaner bots were around to bear witness. Replacing his knife into its sheath, the hulk forgot all about the slight man with black eyes, just one of many disagreements and skirmishes to be had in a typical day.

Viktor Krill continued to reminisce as he stared down at the beefy man's dumb dead face stuck in a cry for help. He didn't wear that look of horror when Krill entered *The Hole* a few minutes earlier. In fact, his smug face beamed excitedly when the slight man marched into the Villains' dingy hang-out, his soft white suit in stark contrast to the gang's black on black ensembles.

All eyes fell on Viktor Krill as he arrived. Despite his white suit, the room darkened as he made his way forward. The bald man flicked his wrist, and Villains moved into action, two barring the door while nine others surrounded the obviously dimwitted guest. The bald man stood up and joined the circle, his eyes twinkling with the promise of bloody resolution.

"You have got to be the dumbest motherfucker I have ever met. But I like that! Our encounter left me unsatisfied. Anything to say before we hang your head by that cute ponytail of yours over the door?"

Viktor Krill ran a tanned, scarred hand along thick black hair that was held back with a golden pin. "Well, I appreciate you keeping the hair intact. But before my untimely death, I was hoping you could show me what a true villain looks like."

"My pleasure. Men! Show this frail intruder what happens when you disrespect the Villains!"

One of the men who had barred the door sprung into action first, swinging a beer bottle at the back of Viktor Krill's head. As it connected, a chorus of cheers joined the sounds of shattering glass, most believing the fight to be over before it even began.

Smiles turned into confused frowns as they were proven incorrect. Viktor Krill remained unmoved, beer dripping off his ears to land on his pristine white suit. He turned to face the man who struck him. "I quite like this jacket. Beer? Not so much. Beer on my lovely jacket? Well, now, that just makes me see red."

Admirably putting aside his disbelief, the Villain stabbed forward with the broken beer bottle, thinking to gut the asshole guest just before his friends could join the fracas. Krill's hand moved with lightning speed, catching the man's wrist in a viselike grip before turning it inward and propelling it up, driving the broken bottle into the man's face with such force that little remained but the top half of the neck, the rest buried deep into his eye sockets and nasal cavity.

While the bar exploded in a frenzy of movement, everything slowed down for Viktor Krill. He saw the pool cue coming from a mile away, easily plucked it out of midair and threw it like a javelin to pierce the heart of another who was reaching for a small gun at his waistband. Another Villain charged directly at Krill, hoping to pin him down for the others to use their blades. Krill used the man's energy against him, stepping into a front kick that caved in the man's chest before sending him flying into two other gangsters. As jaws were ripped from faces and arms torn from bodies, several

Villains finally recognized the futility of this fight, finally understood that they were not fighting a man, but a monster. They tried to escape.

But there was no escape from Viktor Krill.

Finding no challenge in hand-to-hand combat, Krill made a game of the remaining Villains, cratering one man's head from across the room with a cue ball before tossing another gangster into the metal ceiling fan far above. In short order, only two Villains remained — one praying upright in the corner and Krill's old friend Baldy, who was rooted in fear in the center of the bar.

Viktor Krill casually made his way to the praying Villain. "To whom do you pray, my friend?"

The man cracked open his eyes and stared in horror at Viktor Krill over interlocked hands. His words came out in shaky exhalations. "God. I'm praying to God."

Viktor Krill's black eyes softened, as if he truly felt for the condemned man. "But, friend, God doesn't care about you. In fact, he has grown to not like you very much."

"That...that's not true."

"Oh, but it is, friend. Here, let me show you."

Viktor Krill's right arm shot forward and buried itself into the praying man's chest. It came out just as fast, and the man looked down in terror as his heart appeared in Viktor Krill's hand.

"You see, friend, no God that cares about you would allow a creature like me to roam his lands. You're alone here. You're all alone here."

The Villain nodded slowly, a sad acceptance falling over his face before crumpling to the floor in a heap. Krill turned back to face Baldy, strode over to stand before the large man. "Put out your hand."

Baldy, consumed by fear, did as he was told. He grimaced as the warm, still-beating heart of his friend was placed in his palm. Viktor Krill took one step back before continuing. "Look around you. This. This is what a villain looks like. We all must earn the titles we bestow on ourselves. Otherwise, the lines between reality and fantasy are blurred. I tired of fantasy long ago. I'm here to push the limits of reality, to make real the horrors you think vanish when you wake." Baldy began to look away, unable to hold Krill's black eyes. "Look at me!" His eyes shot back up. "Look upon a real villain!"

As he finished, Krill executed a blinding roundhouse kick that connected with the side of the man's oversized head. A loud cracking sound echoed off the bare walls as Baldy's head spun 180 degrees, and he fell forward at Krill's feet, still looking up at him with startled eyes.

Viktor Krill walked around *The Hole* to admire his handiwork, but other than the stain that reminded him of a devil from the past, he drew very little pleasure from his victory. Returning to Baldy, staring down at the celebrated gangster's dumb, defeated face, Viktor Krill could only think of one thing.

There had to be a more challenging way to exert his superiority and dominance.

While none could touch Viktor Krill in a physical confrontation, perhaps he could play another game, one in which he may find some worthy adversaries.

It was settled, he decided. It was time to eschew these small battles for unremitting war.

But where to wage his war?

Viktor Krill looked down at his custom white suit and was yet again pleased to see that it remained clean; blood had run off it like water on vaseline. He once again thanked Station for its many gifts before wiping his bloody hands on a black satin Villains jacket, smoothing down his black dress shirt, and sauntering out of *The Hole*.

As Krill stepped out into the chilly dusk air, he noticed a sign over the front door that read "Only Villains Welcome." He laughed softly, and said to a cleaning bot that was collecting paper trash, "So, I wasn't an intruder after all."

With that, Viktor Krill started off into the deepening night, excited by the questions he needed to ask and the methods he would employ to gather answers.

———

URINE BEGAN to run down the dirty man's dark trousers before Viktor Krill even had a chance to touch him. Krill sighed and shook his head in disappointment. Apparently, in short time, his reputation had already preceded him in this rathole of a city.

"I don't want any trouble," the man stuttered. "Anything you want, just name it."

"I want information, Luther."

"Sure, sure. Anything."

"I'm looking for a place to set up shop, put down some roots. Thought you might have some suggestions."

"Sure, sure, I know lots of places. How about Dayyon? Plenty of sexy women there. That's where they sneak the overseas girls into the country." With no reaction from Krill, Luther continued. "Or, or, what about Quinto Beach down south? Beautiful weather there and lots of rich families to pilfer!" Again, no response from Krill. "Well, what are you looking for? Sunshine? Women? Drugs?"

"Power."

"I don't follow."

Viktor Krill closed the distance between himself and Luther in the blink of an eye, cupped the man behind the neck. His hand felt like cold iron on soft warm flesh. "I said, I want power. I want a place where real monsters congregate. One that will offer me a challenge. One that will prove a springboard to the rest of the world."

Poor Luther looked scared, confused, and lost under Krill's black gaze. "Uhh, there's good titty bars in Asaloth."

And with that poorly formed answer, Viktor Krill spun Luther around and smashed him face-first into the concrete wall of the alley in which they stood. Between bone and concrete, bone proved the softer, with Luther's face and forehead disappearing into a mess of gore. The smelly drug dealer fell away, leaving a Rorschach stain that Krill thought looked like two angels fighting over a globe. He laughed heartily at the observation before turning and exiting the alley, passing service bots as they whizzed by on tracks, wheels, and metal legs, bringing an array of goods to consumers across the city.

Once again, Viktor Krill shook his head in disappointment. Luther was the third dirtbag he had seen that day, and the third who had proven to be of no use. As he stood on the moving walkway, watching the disappointing city of Sespit scroll past, Viktor Krill had to admit that he was feeling unfulfilled as of late. No. It was worse. Much, much worse.

Viktor Krill was feeling bored.

Decision made, Krill stepped off at the next intersection and made a left into a row of buildings shrouded in soft red light that promised warmth and comfort away from the grey city. Three buildings down, he stopped at a blood-red door and knocked loudly. The camera above the door could be heard adjusting to focus on the new arrival before a lock was undone and the door silently rose to allow entrance.

Even before stepping inside, Viktor Krill was already beginning to feel better. Because if there was one thing that could invariably cure boredom in the shit city of Sespit, it was the synthetic ladies at *Tott's Eden*.

———

IT WAS SAID that you had never had a true sexual encounter until you encountered a synthetic, also known as a "Spirit Girl." This was one of the few times when Viktor Krill couldn't disagree. The outlawed synthetic women of this new world were unbelievable at their craft. Although no one would ever legitimately confuse them with a real woman with their unnatural movements and limited AI responses, they were experts at the one thing they were programmed to do — providing physical pleasure.

Their soft bodies could automatically adjust to customers' desires and biological readings, and their smooth lovemaking motions could render even the most hardened man soft putty in their silicon hands. They didn't say much, which Viktor Krill appreciated, and always sensed when he wanted to be left alone. Krill didn't like much in the world, but he liked these synthetic creatures, a callback to another time.

Therefore, it really rubbed Krill the wrong way when he discovered that many men got off abusing the Spirit Girls. It was certainly one of the main reasons that synthetic shops did so well, offering power to weak men who wanted to lord over and beat women with no repercussions. Krill wasn't one to get in a twist over another's vice, but sometimes extended beatings heard through thin walls threatened to impede on his own relaxation and enjoyment. And that couldn't happen.

In these cases, Viktor Krill would march into the adjacent room, still naked and erect, and gently punch the man in his throat as he attempted to yell "get out!" Unfortunately, the words could not escape as Krill had collapsed the man's windpipe. Other smirking Spirit Girls would then have to enter and hurry the customer out to the street, where a medic bot would arrive shortly.

During the first of these little confrontations, Viktor Krill had killed a fat businessman by putting a vibrator through his eye after seeing how the man was trying to blind a Spirit Girl with his small, sorry excuse for a dick. The building's proprietor, Sammie Tott, had rushed up to the commotion, large digital glasses bouncing on her head, and began scolding Viktor Krill, a bad idea, before the fat man's head started shaking and sliding along the floor as the vibrator clicked on. Both Tott and Krill fell to the floor laughing, tensions gone, before Tott stated that while she appreciated the support, she couldn't have deaths traced back to *Eden*. Krill nodded, not wanting to lose the only place he liked in the dump that was Sespit. From then on, Krill would only go so far as a crushed windpipe or broken bone in disposing of an annoying guest.

Over the weeks, Tott and Krill formed a mutual respect, what some could even call a friendship. Tott respected that Krill would protect her property from overzealous clients, and Krill respected that Tott had come up the hard way, a blind girl cutting a swatch through dozens of bigger, stronger men who would see her business fail. One day, as Krill was receiving a post-coitus rubdown by two Spirit Girls, Sammie Tott came in and sat down.

"The name of Viktor Krill has started ringing in the streets. You've done some bad things in a short amount of time. Tell me, for a man who spreads death like jelly, why do you care what happens to my Spirit Girls?"

Krill did not open his dark eyes, but answered. "Humanity is trash and deserves everything bad that comes to them. We have done unspeakable acts over the millennia and will continue to until the bitter end. These Spirit Girls, however, have done nothing wrong. They serve only to please, and are the best at what they do. And I respect excellence, whether done by human or beast or synthetic. Whether it's fighting or fucking or opening a successful business. I have no problem with violence, I welcome it like a returning loved one. But when someone wants to destroy something beautiful, just to act powerful, I feel the need to show them what true power really looks like."

Tott let Krill's words sink in for a moment. "Do you really think that?"

"Which part?"

"That humanity is trash?"

"I do."

"I don't. I like to think that deep down, there's some good in all of us, desperate to get out."

Viktor Krill sat up, his black orbs locked onto Sammie Tott's quicksilver band covering her eyes. "That's because you don't know where we came from. Who we came from."

"Tell me."

Krill laid back down and the Spirit Girls went back to work on his scarred, muscled thighs. "You wouldn't believe me if I told you."

VIKTOR KRILL LAID BACK on the soft cushioned table as Sammie Tott massaged oil onto his tanned, tightly muscled body. Over the past few days, Tott had taken over this duty from the Spirit Girls, whom she had shooed away minutes earlier, their parts in this daily play concluded. Viktor Krill was a dangerous man, she knew this. He might even be the most dangerous man in the world, for all she knew. But there was something that attracted her, drew her in like a magnetic force. He was dangerous, no doubt. But evil? Sammie Tott had been around evil men all her life, could smell them when she entered the room like a decomposing animal. Around Viktor Krill, she smelled danger, but not evil.

As her hands passed over the mysterious man's body, she lost count of the scars her fingers brushed across, jagged things that crisscrossed his entire body. The scars were symmetrical on each side of Krill's body, leading Tott to believe that there was some method to the carving madness. But she thought it best not to bring it up.

Moving her way up Krill's body, Tott spread fresh oil across that familiar tattoo that she often wondered about. The words ran along Krill's chest and were warm, almost hot, to the touch.

Station's Child.

What was Station, wondered Tott. Krill's home? The name of a lost parent?

Viktor Krill's voice ripped Tott from her daydreaming. "What a fruitless day."

"Today?"

"Yeah."

"What were you trying to accomplish?" Best to walk lightly around dangerous men. "If you don't mind me asking."

A deep sigh emanated from the prone man. "I'm bored, Sammie. So very bored. I tire of these simple battles. There is no man who can match my physical might; this has become painfully clear. I need a new challenge, problems with multiple angles and pieces to move around as I see fit. And although I'll never meet my equal, I need a foe who can at least hold my attention."

Tott's hands to continued their work. "And would I be wrong to assume that the games you hope to engage in would be of the criminal sort?"

Krill's stomach bobbed up and down as he laughed. "Well, I'm not trying to be a banker, Sammie. Problem is, I can't figure out where would offer the best game. It certainly isn't Sespit. I need to match wits with proper villains, not those in black satin jackets who claim to be. I've proven my abilities. Now I want control. I want to control a lot."

"What places are you considering?"

"That's the issue. Your world is still relatively new to me. I've been playing in the muck for some time now, so I haven't risen my head to look around."

Tott chuckled, and the dangerous man opened his black eyes. "What's so funny?"

"Oh nothing, just something you said. Muck. I know of a place called 'the Muck.' Terrible place, overrun by gangs and poverty and drugs. Life is cheap there, and only the ruthless thrive or make it out."

Viktor Krill sat up. "Tell me more."

Sammie Tott wiped her oily hands on a towel and continued. "Well, the city is called Bhellum, and it's about 250 miles east of here and sits on the coast. At one time, it was the fastest growing city in the world. Cyrix Industries has its headquarters there."

"Cyrix Industries?"

"The robot manufacturer, silly. Most of the bots you see around the city, except those impotent Bobby Bots, were produced by Cyrix. Anyway, they were at the head of the robotics boom a few decades ago. Built the Neon City on the bones of a dead port town. Even named the city after their founder, Cyrus Bhellum II. But all good things come to an end. Competition flooded the market, especially from abroad, making cheaper and, oftentimes, better robots. Cyrix stagnated, failed to innovate. They decided to reduce costs by moving manufacturing overseas, leaving a city of Cyrix employees out of work. I think you can guess what happened from there, poverty begetting crime begetting violence. Gangs took over parts of the city, and the provided employee housing, no longer supported by Cyrix, became the Muck."

Krill's breath quickened with excitement and promised potential. "And today?"

"Worse than ever, I would imagine. The current City Head, Cyrus Bhellum V, is supposed to be a special kind of prick. He's turned his back on the Neon City, is letting it rot from within."

"So it's anarchy there?"

"As close as you can get. Everything's either run by the gangs or the rich families or Cyrix." Tott paused, as if considering something, before she began again. "There's an open organ market there."

"What's that?"

"The city's wealthy get sick or injured like anyone else. They sometimes need organs. Unlike in other cities, in Bhellum this service is provided by the gangs."

"And I can guess where they get them."

Tott nodded. "The poor. The weak. The young. Kidneys from one. A liver from another. Maybe a heart that matches some rich prick. Even eyes." As Tott trailed off, her covered eyes hit the floor, and Krill began putting the pieces into place.

"How do you know so much about Bhellum, Sammie?"

"I was born there, silly."

Viktor Krill stood up, turned Tott to face him, and gently lifted her chin with his hand. "I've been roughing up assholes all day trying to locate a place just like the one you describe. I should have known that Sammie Tott would know more than any ten of them combined." Krill's hands stroked Tott's soft cheeks as he bent down to kiss her gently on the forehead. His hands kept moving, touching then pulling on her silver glasses.

Tott reached up to stop him. "What are you doing, Viktor?"

"I would see you as you are," he said as he removed the cold metal from around the woman's face. Just as he thought, two scarred, empty sockets stared back at him, reflecting an early life of sorrow and agony.

Tott tried to turn her head in embarrassment, but could not move in Krill's tight grip. "Please, Viktor."

"Shh," was all the response that Krill gave as he softly kissed each of the cavities before pulling Tott down onto the plush carpets that covered the room. Loud moans escaped the woman as Krill removed clothing and replaced it with his tongue, determined to return a favor owed.

Sammie Tott had treated Viktor Krill like a man when everyone else viewed him as a beast. Now Viktor Krill would treat Sammie Tott like a woman, not the mere purveyor of synthetic pleasures.

————

A SPIRIT GIRL came in as Krill and Tott laid together on the fur-covered bed, smoking a joint and wearing only each other. She deposited two steaming cups of tea on the nightstand and moved to the foot of the bed, observing them and waiting for instruction.

Tott looked through her silver glasses at the girl. "That will be all, Joon. Thank you."

The Spirit Girl spun on her heel and exited the room, but not before Krill thought he saw a small smile form on the synthetic's face.

"Is she one of Cyrix's?"

Tott coughed out a bit of smoke. "Are you kidding me? I would never use an outdated Cyrix model. I'm offering my clients pleasure here, not the possibility of getting castrated. My girls are only the best, the latest Taragoshi models. Pain in the ass getting them over here with all the restrictions and the fact that plea-sure synthetics are officially illegal." Air quotes were made around *illegal*.

Krill took one last hit of the joint before stubbing it out on his palm. "This is probably the last we'll see of each other for a while. If not forever."

Tott sighed softly, trying her best to hide her sadness. "I know." A blanket of tension fell over the room, that uncomfortable time before a planned goodbye. "What are you going to do in Bhellum, Viktor?"

"I'm going to become a king."

"And what will you do as King?"

I will control everything. I will make rulings. For example, the rich took something from you long ago. Maybe it's time something was taken from them. Something precious."

"Oh, Viktor Krill. You do know the way to a girl's heart."

Yes, thought Krill, as his mind danced with upcoming thrills. The best way to anyone's heart is through their chest.

2

V iktor Krill immediately discovered why Sammie Tott called Bhellum the Neon City. As Krill flew down the highway on his stolen single-wheeled cycle, weaving in and out of lanes filled with foreign automobiles of strange design, the city lit the night's horizon like a rising sun, promising warmth and adventure.

Krill almost had to shield his eyes as he entered the massive city, but decided to let his retinas burn under its neon glare. The electrified noble gas was found in signage across the city and outlined most buildings in bright hues of red, orange, green, yellow, blue, indigo, and violet.

Krill's long hair danced behind him as he sped between traffic, now and then scratching a door or removing a side mirror. Screams of protest drifted in each time he did this, but Krill took them no heed. His mind was already lost in the city of Bhellum and its potential for mayhem.

Robots large and small drifted through the city, some cleaning, some delivering, and others doing nothing more than observing. Bhellum's citizens paid them no mind as they made towards their destinations on moving walkways, always preoccupied, looking down at the screens strapped to their wrists or the implants on their forearms. None looked around to take in the majesty of the city, the limitless opportunity. To the average observer, they looked a lonely bunch, caught in a digital world that was unable to provide the warmth of a hug or the gentle caress of a hand.

To Viktor Krill, they looked like lambs to the slaughter.

As Krill continued his tour of Bhellum, he breathed in deeply, tasting strange metals and unfamiliar chemicals. But his Wakened senses detected more, something sinister that hung heavy in the air, blanketing the city and threatening to stain everything a deep red.

Blood.

Viktor Krill smiled widely as he turned down a less congested road and hit the accelerator, flying past autonomous vehicles and their anesthetized passengers. Blood was in the air, which meant that violence was in the air. And when violence was in the air, adventure was sure to be found.

———

ALTHOUGH THE SIGN read *Seaside Sights by Cyrix*, Viktor Krill was sure that he had found what he was searching for. If there was a hint of blood in the air upon entering Bhellum, it was almost overpowering as Krill cruised along the coastline and arrived at his destination. But a scent that was revolting to most was like perfume on a soft, naked body to the dark-eyed man who now sat on a hillock looking down at his future conquest.

Although Sammie Tott described the place to him in detail, words were no match for the reality of the place. If the city of Bhellum was a neon star, what sat before Viktor Krill was clearly a sunspot, a dark place where the world's magnetic pull had been altered. In line with Bhellum's overall ascetic, even the buildings below were outlined in neon. But the lights were muted, turned down, like even color had trouble surviving in this dark place.

It was a simple layout, really. Five towers, positioned as if at the points of a star, surrounded a central area that Krill supposed was once a lush, family-friendly park. Now, however, it looked to be an overgrown mess, with makeshift homes and encampments dotting the terrain where thick, ugly vegetation had not already overtaken the land. Small fires sat throughout, warming the filthy bodies that surrounded each.

Although each tower sat alone, an impressively constructed skywalk, five stories high and clearly a recent addition, connected the towers that sat at one and three o'clock relative to the coastline. Using his Wakened vision, Krill looked beyond the residential area towers and found two things worth noting. Beside the collection of towers, trapped behind a menacing metal gate topped with razor wire, sat the now-empty Cyrix Industries manufacturing plant, a series of enormous buildings that sat cloaked in shadow, untouched by even the ever-present Bhellum neon.

What sat beyond the abandoned plants, however, more than made up for their murky gloom. Viktor Krill's eyes had to adjust quickly as he looked upon the pillar of neon light that rose into the darkening sky. At the citadel's apex, a giant neon C hung in the air and rotated on impossibly strong magnets, letting all in Bhellum know who ran the city — the Cyrix Industries Headquarters.

There. That was where Viktor Krill longed to be, staring down at a city that he kept neatly in the palm of his tan hand, ready to crush at a moment's notice or whim. Krill's breathing intensified under the promise of chaos, but he closed his eyes and exhaled slowly. "All in time," he reminded himself. Truth be told, Krill was confident that he could leave this city in rubble in mere months, but his was a larger goal. He had utilized his Wakened body enough. It was now time to make use of his Wakened mind.

His head spinning with ideas and strategies, Viktor Krill didn't hear the approach of small feet on the dry grass. Nor did he hear the whizz of the rock as it flew through the air to smash into the back of his head. Krill was up and turned around in the blink of an eye, the pain triggering automatic bodily responses. Although their aim was true, Krill plucked the next three rocks out of the air before him, his arms moving too fast to follow.

Four young boys, around twelve years of age and covered in grime, stood about twenty yards away, each cradling a small armful of rubble. While their second volley had been halted momentarily by Viktor Krill's impressive display, their mouths continued to work.

"Nice suit, fukkboy," one yelled. Another added, "My bitch has the same hair as you." The other two lads, thick boys with dark skin, eschewed words for chucking more jagged rocks at Krill's face. He dodged them easily, barely moving his head, and grinned widely, his first quarry already in his sights.

The boys saw the change in Krill and knew it was time to split. They tore off across the hillock, forsaking their projectiles and pumping their small arms to gain steam. Viktor Krill took a deep breath, taking in the moment, before sprinting after them, looking like a video on fast-forward. He was upon the quartet in no time, and their high shrieks were the first signs of their youth.

Just as he was about to grab the backpack of the trailing boy, the youngster cut to the right as the others cut left. A piece of plywood appeared on the ground just before Krill. Unable to stop at this blinding speed, Krill thought to plant his foot on the plywood and kick off, tackling his prey who had moved right in short order.

Unfortunately, as Viktor Krill planted his foot, the plywood gave way, obviously rigged, and he fell hard into a deep pit. Krill smashed against the side of the hole and dropped, sinking up to his knees in human excrement. After the initial feeling of revulsion passed, Krill began to laugh, a loud sound that bounced out of the ingenious booby trap. Four small heads peered over the lip of the pit, jagged teeth peering out from big smiles.

"This stupid fucker doesn't even know that he got played!"

Krill continued laughing. "Oh, I do know."

"Then why you laughing? You retarded or something?"

"Yeah, man, you're covered in shit."

Krill couldn't stop. "I know, I know. You guys got me good."

"Then what's so funny, doo-doo man?"

Krill's laughing finally trailed off. "Because now it's going to feel doubly good when I skin you all alive."

"Good luck finding us in those fancy ass clothes. Your dumb ass will be dead by morning. Catch you later, fancy man."

With that, three of the boys walked away, giggling and congratulating themselves on punking another lame tourist. Despite being covered in shit, Krill's heart leapt at the encounter. If the children here were this hardened, he couldn't wait to meet those in charge of this world of mayhem. Krill looked up and found that one of the stocky dark-skinned boys continued to watch him from above. Krill met the boy's brown eyes with his own black orbs.

"You somebody I need to know," the boy asked down the hole.

Krill held his gaze. "Do I seem like somebody you need to know?"

"You seem dangerous. Which makes you somebody I need to know."

"I'm Viktor Krill."

"I'm Darrin." He thought for a moment. "What's your business here? You look outta place."

"My business? Domination, of course."

"Well, good luck with that. I believe you're dangerous. But this place is full of dangerous folks. Dangerous folks who don't seem outta place. I'll catch you later, Viktor Krill."

"No, you won't. I'll be catching all four of you later." There was no laughter left in Krill's voice, but, to his credit, Darrin didn't flinch.

"You never know. Welcome to the Muck, Viktor Krill."

————

THE FOUR BOYS' bravado was all but gone as they sat Indian style, hands bound behind their backs, facing the pacing Viktor Krill. A small campfire burned between the prisoners and their jailor. It really didn't take much effort to locate and snatch the four boys — a few bruises, a couple of broken bones, and one tongue removed when a man responded with, "Suck my dick," to Krill's inquiry. Krill had always hated that particular phrase, and now that man could never utter it again.

Gone were the shit stains from Krill's now-pristine white suit alongside the once jovial attitude of the man they had laughed at several hours earlier. Krill's dark eyes took them each in one at a time, and there was a promise of pain in those looks.

"I congratulate you all on a well-executed ruse. I truly do. But there are repercussions, oftentimes extreme, to every action. And now, as they would say in my world, it's time to pay the piper."

One boy started crying, another threw a stream of curses at his captor, and a third thrashed vigorously in his bonds. Only Darrin remained unmoved, his eyes cast down at the dirt before him. Krill looked around and, seeing no one else in the vicinity, congratulated himself for selecting this isolated location between the Muck and the Bhellum Port.

Krill paused his pacing to address the boys. "Normally, I would simply cut each of your throats and head off for a late dinner, but I have use for at least one of you." Silence fell over the boys as a slim chance for survival presented itself. Krill continued, "One of you will have to pay for what you did. Talk among yourselves and select which one of you will face my wrath."

The malnourished white kid was the first to throw his gang under the bus. "Miller! It was Miller's idea! He should be the one!"

Brown-skinned Miller's eyes went wide before he responded. "Fuck you, Relish! You're the one who wanted to go after the 'faggot in white.' Fess up, bitch!"

The other white kid chose another approach, pleading his case directly to Krill. "I can be a big help to you, man! What do you need? I've grown up here. Want some young girls? Need some Leaf? I can get you anything you want. Just let me go, please!"

Only Darrin showed a modicum of grit, remaining silent as his cohorts worked towards stabbing each other in the back. The shouting intensified under Krill's dark stare, grew into a cacophony of insults, accusations, and threats. After several minutes, Darrin stood up and the quartet fell quiet. The large boy took two steps forward and finally raised his eyes from the ground, meeting Krill's gaze.

"I'll pay. We all had a hand in the trick; no one's to blame more than the others. Do what you will, Mister Krill."

The other three boys leapt to their feet to agree with Darrin's assessment. "Yeah, you heard him!"

"Darrin'll pay!"

"Good shit, Darrin! Good shit!"

Viktor Krill stood and watched as the scene unfolded. Having seen what he needed, he declared, "Enough," and grabbed Darrin by the throat. He moved the boy to the other side of the fire and spun him around to face his so-called friends. A knife appeared at Darrin's neck, and Krill could sense the boy's breathing become labored as the cold metal kissed his soft throat. Despite his obvious terror, however, Darrin refused to beg or plead.

Krill addressed the three lucky boys. "Any final words for your partner in crime?"

"Sorry, bro."

"Better you than me, my dude."

"Just get it over with."

Viktor Krill's knife flickered in the air as firelight caught its movement, with two flashes coming directly on the heels of the first. As if by magic, the hilts of three knives materialized, jutting from the throats of the boys across the campfire. Seconds later, rivers of blood appeared on their dirty shirts before they fell to the ground, gurgling noises combining to form an a cappella of death.

Yet another knife flashed in Krill's hand, which he used to cut the bonds holding Darrin. He handed the shaking boy the knife before moving to sit before the small fire, turning his back to the young, now armed, criminal. Darrin slipped the knife into the belt loop of his stained pants and sat across the fire from Krill, only the fading gurgling of his friends and the crackling of burning wood decorating the night air.

Several minutes later, Krill decided to end the silence, impressed with the young boy's resolve. "Why did you offer yourself up?"

The boy shrugged his round shoulders. "I thought you might be the sort of man who valued that kind of initiative."

"And if I wasn't?"

"Well, shit, I was dead anyway, wasn't I? Better than embarrassing myself on the way out." With the gurgling now stopped, only the fire filled the silence. "Did you have to do it," asked Darrin eventually.

"Do what?"

"Kill them all. Miller was actually a decent kid."

Seeing that the fire was dying down, allowing the chill night air to bite at his face, Viktor Krill got up and walked away, returning shortly with an armful of wooden trash. He sat back down and slowly fed the fire. "Yes, I did. You see, your friends, a term I use in the loosest definition, were coward children. Coward children grow up to become coward adults. And coward adults can never be trusted to complete a task or honor a deal or fight a fair one. You can never turn your back on a coward. Many of history's greatest men met their ends at the hands of a coward. I did this world a favor."

Darrin simply nodded, taking Krill's explanation at face value, and once again stared into the rekindled fire. "So, what now?"

Krill ignored the question. "Tell me, Darrin, do you have a last name?"

"No, sir. I was born in the Muck. I don't know my mother or my father. I was raised for years by an old woman named Miss Viola who ran a self-made orphanage out of Pontus Tower. When she died, we were all left to fend for ourselves. Some of us ran to the larger gangs, others cliqued up with each other to survive."

"So, you know the Muck well?

"It's the only thing I know, Mister Krill."

"Good because that's exactly what I need. You're a lucky boy, Darrin. Through a series of strange events, you have fallen into a winning team. Get some rest. Tomorrow we begin my education of everything regarding the Muck. If you do a good job, you may not only live to see adulthood, but to see yourself become a prince."

"Rest where? Here?"

"I don't see why not?"

"It's not safe here. Real goons roam the Muck at night."

"Close your eyes and get some sleep. Never mind the goons. There's a true demon in the Muck tonight. And you're sitting across from him."

3

"The Five Thieves is what some of us call the five towers in the Muck. Partly because of some old story where the Five Thieves referred to the five original sins. But mainly because thieving ass gangs control the five towers."

Viktor Krill followed Darrin's eyes from the hilltop on which they sat down onto the five buildings that rose from the Muck like zombie fingers scratching their way out from newly packed dirt. "Go on."

"Well, even though they got a new name for the towers as a whole, each individual tower still goes by the name given by Cyrix Industries decades ago." Darrin pointed to the far right. "Starting with the 'top' there, that's Triton Tower. Going clockwise, it's followed by Hydrus Tower, Thoosa Tower, Brizo Tower, and, finally, Pontus Tower. In the middle of all the towers, there's what used to be called the Seaside Gardens. But, as you can see, the gardens are no more. Now it's known as the Jungle."

Even from this distance, through his Wakened eyes, Krill could tell that it was an apt name. What was once a lush, green park, complete with stone walkways, elegant gazebos, and marble fountains, now looked to be a war zone. In some areas, nothing green survived. Broken brown patches of land dotted the Jungle like lesions on a meth addict. In other areas, nature had reclaimed authority. Yellow vines covered small buildings, twisted bushes broke through cobblestone, and thorny thickets barred entry or exit. Viktor Krill took it all in. In many ways, the past and the present of this place reminded him very much of his last home and the hard truth that he had to face.

Better to live free in ruins than chained up in utopia.

Wretched individuals in varying stages of dishevelment scampered through the Jungle. Some scampered to and fro like frightened mice, expecting the sharp talons of a predator to yank them skyward at any moment. Others grouped together around small fires or weed-covered rotundas, desperate to find strength in numbers. Every few minutes, a scream rang out from somewhere in the Jungle, marking the location of a poorly executed theft, rape, or murder.

It was a breeding ground for mayhem.

"Who lives in the Jungle?"

Darrin thought a few seconds before answering. "Those with no value to the gangs. Those fallen out of favor with the gangs. And those still proving their value to the gangs."

"I see a theme."

"Right. It all revolves around the fucking gangs. If you can't pull jobs for them, bring money to them, or come up with schemes for them, you're out in the Jungle. If you're a pretty girl, of course you'll always have a place with a gang. But once those looks are gone, and they go quickly here, you'll be back turning tricks in the Jungle.

"If you're in a gang and you do something wrong, out you go into the Jungle. You wanna join a gang? You gotta prove your worth in the Jungle. You wanna form your own little clique and starting doing work? You gotta start in the Jungle." Darrin looked up at Krill's angular face staring down at the Jungle, detected the excitement behind those black eyes. "It's pure violence and pain down there. I'm not sure even a dangerous man like you is prepared."

Krill flashed back to the early days of the Riser Wars, when every few Haelas brought a new war with a new Bar. The ringing of combat elevations mingled with death screams over each battlefield as men and women fought just to feel alive, for no better reason than to feel the tickling splash of another's blood on their faces. In this environment of wanton carnage, Viktor Krill excelled. He would do so again.

"Your warning is noted. Now talk about the gangs. I need to know everything."

"Well, there're dozens of small gangs, mainly in the Jungle and some subsurface sections of the towers, but six main groups control the Muck."

"List them."

"Well, the oldest and most respected gang is the Broken Tens. They've had control of the Brizo Tower since before I was born. They don't make many moves, but when they do, they usually come out on top."

"Who runs that lot?"

"Tennian Stamp. Never known another to operate the crew."

"Got it. Next."

"While the Broken Tens is the oldest clique, the newest is the Stench Mobb. Recently graduated from the Jungle, Stench Mob bum-rushed Pontus Tower and took it by force. At the time, Pontus was home to four or five smaller gangs. They all were either consumed by the Mobb or destroyed. Young guy known as Liquid Tye runs the crew."

"Why do they call him that?"

"Cause just when you think you got him, he disappears. Like trying to hold water in cupped hands. Eventually, he'll find the slightest opening and be out. And if you're on his shit list, he'll find the slightest opening and be in. And you don't want that."

"Interesting. Please continue."

"Ok, let me see." Darrin stared harder at the Muck, as if allowing it to tell him its story. "The only tower that's truly shared by two major cliques is Thoosa. The bottom half of the tower is home to the Dead Rogues while the top is run by the Bitch-Whores."

"The Bitch-Whores?"

"Yeah, that's what I said. An all-female crew and among the most dangerous. You never know who's a member of the Bitches, so best to watch your shit around any female. And be careful accepting a drink from a lady in the Muck. Too many dudes have woken up with a scar marking where they *used* to have an organ."

"And the Dead Rogues?"

"Yeah, those guys used to be the straight villains of the Muck, but they've recently fallen on some hard times. They used to operate out of Triton Tower, but a war didn't go their way, and they had to cut a deal with the Bitches to share Thoosa. Gideon Moon, the crew's First, is still a bad, bad man, so I'm sure they're not just sitting around. They're plotting payback, for sure, and we'd all do good to stay clear when the guns come out."

"Who supplanted the Rogues?"

"That brings us to the new kings of the Muck. The fucking Chrome Butchers. Not that long ago, they were the redheaded stepchildren of the Muck, sharing Hydrus Tower with like four other gangs. Nobody ever thought much of them. Then he came."

"Who came?"

"Sigman Prime. Don't know where he came from. No one knew him from the Muck, which is weird. People in the Muck were raised in the Muck. No one *comes* to the Muck from the outside. It's unheard of."

"So, this Sigman Prime took over the Chrome Butchers?"

"He didn't just take over. He redefined the gang. They were just the Butchers when he took over. Soon after his arrival, they became known as the Chrome Butchers."

"And why's that?"

"Because the crew got Loaded overnight."

"I don't understand."

"Loaded. You know, outfitted? Meched out? Shit, man, I'm talking about mechanical combat enhancements. MCEs."

Viktor Krill chuckled to himself and nodded. He should have known. Regardless of the world in which he lived, humanity would always strive to make themselves into instruments of death. Was that not what Viktor Krill was? The perfect instrument of death, no metal needed. "I got it now. Go on."

"Well, no one knows how it happened, but the Butchers got their hands on military-grade MCEs, even for the mid-level members, and when they made their move, no one stood a chance. Hydrus was completely taken over within a week. You'd think that was enough, but it wasn't. In the Muck, there can be only one big dick. And Sigman Prime decided that it was gonna be his.

In a crazy move, the CBs launched a full attack on Triton Tower and the Rogues. Triton shook for days and nights. The entire Muck felt like it was on one of those fault lines. When the smoke finally cleared, the CBs ruled not one, but two fucking towers, and the Rogues were sent scampering into the night, finally making their way to the Bitches. There was a new king of the Muck, and his name was Sigman Prime."

"And I imagine he was the one who connected the two towers via that covered skywalk?"

"Yeah, he hired an actual contracting company with a whole robo crew to build that thing. Probably had to pay out the ass to get someone willing to work in the Muck. Got in done in a few short days, though. Now, Triton and Hydrus Towers are permanently connected. Who knows, maybe Prime has plans to do that with all the towers."

Krill took in Darrin's story, impressed with the boy's intel. He congratulated himself on not running a knife across the child's throat. Indeed, Darrin's inside knowledge would save Krill weeks of data gathering, allowing him to formulate a strategy almost immediately.

Something struck Krill. "I thought you said six gangs ruled the Muck. You've only mentioned five."

Darrin squirmed uncomfortably on the rocky ground. "Yeah, well, there is one more."

"And?"

"Not much is known about them. They operate in the Jungle, control the areas along the coastline, and live in the Hammers, which is what we call the old toxic Cyrix manufacturing plants." Darrin looked like he wanted to say more, but nothing came forth. Krill grew impatient.

"Spit it out, boy!"

"There's not much I can definitely tell you. They're an odd sort."

"Tell me what you can."

"They're called the Blisters. I don't know if they call themselves that or if everyone else gave them that name. They were a group of outcasts, living in the Hammers for a long time. Then, one day they moved into the Muck and took what they wanted."

"How did they manage that?"

"Fear."

"Fear? I would imagine all the gangs have that working for them."

"Not like this."

"Expand."

"They're freaks."

"Freaks?"

"Yeah, freaks. And I don't mean freaks in the "they're crazy" or "they're extra vicious" sort of way. I mean freaks in the "they're fucking freaks" way. Must have been from living in the Hammers all those years. Who knows what kinds of chemicals or metals or sludge used to run out of those factories. The ground around the Hammers is contaminated, soaked through with toxins. With two generations living in poison, the Blisters have become increasingly horrible. Blistered skin is child's play nowadays. There's word of extra arms, oversized heads, too many eyes; you name it."

"And who's their First?"

"Hell if I know. I don't even know if they have a First. Not much is known about the Blisters. But if you want to do business in the Jungle or around the Muck, you best make sure the Blisters get a taste. Or they'll get a taste of you."

Krill raised a questioning eyebrow.

"They're cannibals."

Krill couldn't contain it any longer, and belted out a loud laugh, slapping Darrin on the back harder than intended, bruising the boy's soft skin. Darrin arched back in pain. "Fuck, man, careful! What are you so happy about? I just described fucking hell on earth."

"To a normal man, young Darrin, it's hell on earth. But I'm so much more. And to me, it looks like a paradise."

"What kind of paradise is filled with monsters?"

"The human kind, young Darrin. The human kind. Come, you will show me this paradise up close."

"Do I have a choice?"

"There's always a choice. You can take me around the Muck or I can roll your head down this hill."

"Doesn't sound like much of a choice."

"Agreed. But here we are."

"Then let's get going. It's morning and many of the fiends will still be sleeping."

"Yes, let us go wake them!"

———

A DIRTY ARM came around the weathered statue with blinding speed. The filthy blade it held, certainly home to any number of foreign bacteria, accelerated towards Viktor Krill's unprotected chest. The Jungle junkie had planned the attack perfectly, having stalked his prey along a parallel path, the man's bright white clothes making him easy to follow through the overgrown brush.

The Jungle junkie had accounted for everything necessary to slaughter a man and take his boy as his own. Unfortunately, he had accounted for nothing necessary to slaughter a Wakened human, which was what he was currently attempting to kill.

Krill matched the blinding speed of the blade with meteoric movement only registrable by high-speed cameras. He caught the grime-covered wrist six inches from his chest and slammed the accompanying arm into a broken edge of the crumbling marble statue. The junkie's forearm exploded, jagged bone and pinkish meat tearing through yellowed skin. The stomach-churning scene was immediately followed by a piercing scream and whimpering cries as the dirty man fell into the path.

Krill looked back to see that Darrin had retreated several steps and fallen into a defensive stance, his own small blade held out before him. Krill noted that the boy held the blade with some confidence and silently applauded both the reaction and the technique shown. He pointed down at the Jungle junkie. "This anyone of significance?"

Darrin quickly slipped the knife back into his waistband and inspected the downed man. "Nah, just some junkie. Hooked on the Flea by the looks of him."

"The Flea?"

"Yeah, you know. Brown. Smack. The Flea. Look at his arms."

Krill glanced at the squirming man's arm, the one that wasn't bent in angles, and nodded, noticing the small dots of track lines. Heroin. Once again, Krill was appreciative of Darrin's crash course in this world's drug slang. "Gang?"

"None that I can tell. Even the weaker gangs make their crews clean up better than this."

The dirty man grew bold from the floor, at least when staring down a young boy. "Fuck you, you little shit! When I find you again I'm gonna destroy that little asshole of yours before taking..."

What the Jungle junkie was going to take of Darrin's will never be known as Viktor Krill's suede shoe plummeted like a jackhammer, caving in the man's face and ushering in silence that was only broken by the bubbling of blood as it moved to fill in the head cavity. Krill shook his foot and the blood cascaded off the suede as if by magic. He looked over to Darrin, who wore a mask of horror on his small dark face. "When a man threatens you, you deal with it then and there. Don't let him wait for a better time and place for himself. If he's talking, that means he's not ready for action. That's when you need to be. Consider that advice payment for you help today."

Viktor Krill stepped over the body and continued on his tour of the Jungle, seemingly without a care in the world. Darrin followed closely behind, the shadow of the man in white seeming the safest place he had known in years.

"We can't go up there?"

"Why not?"

"It's a dope tank. Controlled by the gangs."

Krill looked around at the zombies that shuffled along the perimeter of the small clearing in which he and Darrin now stood. In the center stood a large gazebo, completely covered in brown thorny vines and loose trash. Now and then, a Jungle junkie would stagger up the stairs, talk briefly to the two armed guards stationed at a break in the vines, and enter the dope tank. A few seconds later, the junkie would stumble back down the steps, looking a great deal more excited, and immediately begin to prepare his or her fix.

"Goddam, they can't even wait to leave the area before shoving that shit in their arms."

"It's not that, Mister Krill. Or, it's not only that. If they leave the dope tank clearing, they're gonna have a dozen other fiends on their asses trying to take their Flea. They're gonna have to fight, obviously not their best skill. If they do it around the dope tank, at least the gangs won't let anyone fuck with them."

Once again, Krill found himself nodding absently at Darrin's explanation. The passed-out bodies all along the clearing now made sense. And reminded him of a universal truth.

In the land of killers, safety can only be found with the most dangerous.

"So what gang is this?"

Darrin answered immediately, as if the knowledge was imprinted into his DNA. In many ways, Krill suspected that it was. "Well, this is a Flea Den. So, that means that the Dead Rogues must run this dope tank."

Krill's face scrunched up in confusion. "Why must that be the case?"

Darrin looked up at the dangerous man in white, his facing betraying what he really wanted to say. *Jesus, you really don't know shit, do you, you stupid muthafucka?* Always a survivor, however, Darrin knew it was best not to voice these words, instead offering another to-the-point explanation.

"Because only the Rogues deal in Flea. For a long time, their control of the Flea meant their control of the Muck. But times change. Drugs change. Tastes change. And enemies change."

"So you're telling me that every clique controls a drug."

"That's right. At least, at any one time, a drug is run by only one crew."

"That doesn't make any sense."

"From here, you're right. But look beyond the Muck. The real villains of the world, the ones dropping the shit off at the Gate..."

"The Gate?"

"The Bhellum Port. The Docks. They usually only want to deal with one point of contact at a time. They make enough without the added headache of selling to multiple parties and getting involved in smalltime drug wars. So one drug, one gang."

As Darrin spoke, Krill saw that one of the armed guards had spotted the strange man in the white suit. And was staring hard.

"You said drugs change. What did you mean by that?"

"I mean drugs change. When Cyrix abandoned this place and everyone lost their job, people wanted to forget, wanted to get numb. The Flea was perfect for that. Even when you've sold all the stuff in your apartment, the Flea will make you feel like you're staying in the goddam lap of luxury."

Krill began to discreetly usher Darrin around to the far side of the clearing, farther from the prying eyes of the gun-wielding sentinel. "So what happened?"

Darrin gestured around with his small hands. "The Muck happened. The place evolved."

"I think you mean devolved."

"Devolved then. It got more violent, more brutal. To survive, you had to become violent, brutal. The Flea was not going to accomplish this. And so, Rush came into the Muck, and with its popularity came the rise of Stench Mobb. Anyway, the point is that the Flea wasn't king anymore. At least, not the only king. Are you listening?"

Indeed, Viktor Krill was not listening anymore. His attention was fully locked onto the creature that had entered the clearing and was now slowly making its way towards the dope tank. Even the most sedated Jungle junkies managed to muster the strength to crawl away from the thing's path. Krill's hands reflexively went to the knives at his belt as his stomach turned.

Standing at almost seven feet tall, the creature's greenish skin had an oily sheen. Skinny but muscled, its arms and legs were overly long, tipped by enormous hands and feet. The hands, almost dragging along the ground, were composed of foot-long knuckled fingers that ended in razor-sharp yellowed nails. Wearing only simple brown pants and a brown vest, the visitor looked down as it walked, as if trying to avoid seeing the fear and revulsion in the junkies' dead eyes.

It's long, greasy hair hung low on its head, hiding its face except for the enormous, pointed green nose that sat far in advance of the head. Where the vest wasn't covering skin, large red lesions could be seen dotting the behemoth's body.

"Darrin? What is that marvelous brute?"

Darrin saw what he was staring at and looked towards the muddy ground. "That's one of the Blisters. Try not to look at it. They don't do well with eye contact."

Unlike Darrin, Victor Krill was unafraid of monsters, having come from a city of them. "And what is it doing here?"

"I told you, no one does business in the Jungle without giving a piece to the Blisters. I imagine it's here to collect."

As the green monster approached the opening in the dope tank, the armed guards moved carefully to the side, making way for the Blister. Less than a minute passed before the collector exited. An electronic pad in its too-large hand was carefully placed back into the inside pocket of its worn vest. Krill simply bumped Darrin's arm, a silent question.

"I suppose it's collecting payment with that. As you know, almost all money is kept in electronic notes, or credits. In poor areas like the Muck, however, physical notes still dominate trade. The gangs can either pay in credits or notes. Sometimes, they like to hang on to their notes to get shit done around the Muck, so the Blisters got those pads, or dark reams, for secretive credit payments. You'll see them all over the Muck if you manage to stay alive long enough. It pulls money based on the hand imprint of the payer, but info is stored in the dark ream for discrete credit transfer later."

"Seems like they've thought of everything."

"The Muck is poor in many ways. Money ain't one."

As the Blister made its way back across the clearing, a junkie fell out of the Jungle, out of her mind on something more aggressive than Flea. Talking to herself at an unintelligible speed, she bumbled around the clearing, unaware of her surroundings or the deformity that stood in her midst. Falling into a fit of inexplicable laughter, the young woman tripped and fell against the Blister, the stained wool covering her body rubbing against the open lesions on the brute's lower arm.

The Blister screamed in agony, a loud, high-pitched, awful thing that drew all eyes in the dope tank clearing. The terrible noise cut through the strong drugs coursing through the junkie, and she instantly became aware, looking up at the green monstrosity with terror. She turned to run, but it was too late. The Blister took her comparably tiny head in its giant right hand and squeezed, using very little of its strength to crush the girl's head like a rotten piece of fruit. The juices of her skull ran down knuckled green fingers and a pink mist flew into the air, reminding Krill of the blood he detected in the Bhellum air.

The Jungle junkie's headless body slumped to the ground as the Blister wiped its gore-covered hand on its dirty trousers. It looked around, but everyone had already found other things on which to focus their attentions, so it continued on its path across the clearing and into the Jungle beyond.

"Now you see why the gangs pay?"

Viktor Krill smiled, delighted by the display of gratuitous violence. "I do, indeed." He looked back towards the dope tank, and found that he was now being scrutinized by both Dead Rogue guards. They spoke to each other quietly while fingering their powerful guns.

Darrin had also discovered the newfound interest in Krill. "We should leave, Mister Krill. Before things get ugly."

Krill's black eyes held those of the two Rogues, and his heart raced with the implicit challenge he found there, the promise of bone slamming against his knuckles. But, he reminded himself that another game was afoot, one that would take more of his Wakened brain than his Wakened muscles. He tore his gaze from the two potential victims. "Of course, Darrin. Lead the way."

Darrin made a beeline for the nearest Jungle path, desperate to remove himself from the vicinity of the dope tank. He looked up at Krill once they had put the dangerous Flea den behind them. "Hey, I don't mind showing you around and shit, but do you think you could put something a little less conspicuous on?"

"You don't like my clothes? They're special to me. From a special time in my life."

"Honestly, I don't give a shit what you wear, but a bright white suit in the Jungle? Fuck, man, it might as well be a bullseye. We've been attacked three times today and the sun's not even directly overhead."

"No one's gotten close to harming us, have they?"

"No, but that's not the point. It's just statistics, man. Given enough attacks, one's bound to slip through, get past those fast-ass hands of yours."

"I can't be hurt by these lesser humans, Darrin."

"Ok, cool. But *I* can."

As Darrin finished the sentence, a large branch swung out of the thick vegetation to the left of the path, zeroing in on Viktor Krill's face. Krill's left arm shot up like a piston and the strong wood broke across his forearm, which refused to move under the force. Krill's right hand then drove into the bush and a soft ripping sound emanated from within. When Krill withdrew his hand, he was holding a bloody throat in his palm. He shrugged and let the red tubing drop to the stone path with a sickening thud.

"Alright, I'm listening."

Darrin swallowed down the bile that was rising in his suddenly sensitive throat and continued walking, his brown eyes darting back and forth along the path ahead. "Look, I don't know what your plans are, but I imagine that they're ambitious. Don't make things harder on yourself than they're already going to be. Blend in a little."

"Play the game."

"Exactly. When you're king, you can wear anything you want. But until then, no matter how tough you are, you're just meat in the Jungle. No point in putting a spotlight on yourself. Peacocks don't live long here."

"Very well, young Darrin. You've convinced me. Take me where I can find more appropriate attire. And food. I'm famished."

"No problem. The Muck ain't much to look at, but we actually got some good food here. Any preferences?"

"Something that used to be alive."

4

Viktor Krill tossed the bones of the small bird into the fire, the third he had eaten, and sigh contentedly. He had to admit that Darrin was correct. The small food stalls, or chowsets, that peppered the Muck were delightful, adding strange, but pleasing, aromas to the dirty, blood-tinged air. When Krill had inquired as to how the food vendors remained safe in the violence of the Muck, Darrin informed him that they were under the collective protection of the gangs. The last time a chowset was attacked, the perpetrators, three teenagers from a smalltime youth gang, were slowly cooked over hot coals in the busy space between the Brizo and Thoosa Towers. That was almost two years ago. Apparently, even goons appreciate a good meal.

As Krill finished washing his hands with water from his canteen, Darrin returned, his small arms full of dark clothing. Krill scowled at the blackness of the ensemble. When you're a semi-god, you don't feel the need to blend into the shadows, they must twist and turn to blend into you.

Darrin carefully laid the clothes on a patch of grass. "These should keep us from getting tested at every fucking turn."

"Black?"

"Yeah, yeah. I know it's the Neon City and shit, but the Muck is a dark place. You wanna get ahead? Make friends with the darkness."

Krill stripped off his treasured white suit, folded it neatly, and placed it on the ground next to his new clothes. The fabric was as bright and vibrant as the day the manikin handed it over to him.

"Fucking hell, Mister Krill. What happened to you?"

Krill looked over and found Darrin staring open-mouthed at his bare chest and legs. But it wasn't the toned, sinewy muscle that had caught Darrin's attention, but the hundreds of jagged white scars that ran across Krill's tan skin. Krill stood up to his full height. "You want to become a god? You have to be willing to pay the ultimate price. Are you willing to become a god, young Darrin?"

Darrin looked away from the tortured body. "Not if that's what it takes."

Krill laughed lightly, pleased with the boy's honesty, and bent low to collect his new clothes. "Don't worry. Very few, if any, would make the sacrifice. Now, let's see what we have here."

Krill slid on the black pants and was surprised by their softness and movement. He pulled at the material and was impressed by its stretchiness and durability. Although it was not of Station quality, it was far superior to the fabrics of his old world. "Well done, young Darrin."

Darrin took a seat on a cinder block near the fire. "Well, shit, man, you gave me enough credits. Figured you wanted the best."

Krill continued dressing, slipping the slate grey long-sleeved shirt over his head. It was made of the same light, strong material as the pants, as was the thin midnight black jacket that he put on overtop. Darrin interjected. "Check out the shoes. Verrato high-tops. The best. Auto-drying, silent, and they even have short-burst hovering capabilities if they sense a fall." He looked down shyly. "Hope you don't mind, I got myself a pair, too."

Krill slid on the black and white high-tops and smiled at the comfort and support. He glanced over at the young boy who was staring at his own new shoes, probably the first nice thing he had ever owned. Krill stood up. "No problem, kid. Now, how do I look?"

Darrin beamed, happy not to have drawn the ire of his dangerous companion. "Now, you look like a proper villain, Mister Krill."

"You mean I don't need a satin jacket?"

"Huh?"

"Inside joke, young Darrin. Come, come. Our work has only just started. You can't just look the part to be a villain. You have to act the part."

"And how do you do that?"

"First you observe. Then you plan. Then you attack."

———

WITH VIKTOR KRILL'S Wakened senses and mental capacity, he was able to cram what would have been months of reconnaissance into a few days and nights. He slept little, and, when he did rest, his brain whirred like a super-computer — evaluating, measuring, and projecting.

With new dark clothes provided by his mentee Darrin, coupled with his uncanny stealthiness, Krill slunk around the Muck day and night, disappearing into shadows and around bends. And on the odd occasion when he *was* seen against his wishes, it was easy enough to dispose of those observations and the person who made them.

In the Jungle, Krill witnessed firsthand the effects of drugs on the average junkie. Some passed out where they fell, whether across the rough stone pathways or in the mud of the more open and trodden areas. Others screamed obscenities at the air, seeing things that didn't exist. Many more, however, ran around in fits of frenetic energy, speaking at speeds indiscernible to most ears. Open wounds could be seen on their grime-covered bodies, perfectly complementing their missing teeth and overall haggard appearances.

Krill discovered dozens of dope tanks throughout the Jungle, whether Flea dens, or Rush spots, or the ubiquitous and dangerous Flame holes. They all operated similarly, accepting notes or credits, and were guarded by anywhere from two to ten armed gangsters.

Now and then, Krill spotted a Blister moving through the Jungle, always walking with purpose on one errand or another. The only trait that Blisters seemed to have in common was their uncommon look. Some wore green skin while others sported a bright yellow complexion. One Blister was as tall as a Caesar, another was as short as Krill's old Station running buddy Vizzano. A few had to contend with puss-filled bumps that covered their flesh and some had rough grey layers of dead skin covering their bodies.

While the Blisters never seemed to go out of their way to start trouble, they certainly retained almost no tolerance for jokes, back talk, or money shortages. The contaminated humans would transform from placid into violent in the blink of an eye, brutal acts coming faster than a viper's strike. Krill sat in the shadows, transfixed as one too-muscled Blister with a tiny head march into a Rush spot. A short commotion could be heard moments later before two arms, shredded muscle and ligaments hanging from each, came flying from the dope tank entrance, striking a Jungle junkie in the chest as he took pulls from his glass pipe. The six armed guards held their formidable weapons tighter, but did little else to aid their injured comrade. When it came to the Blisters, it was every man for himself.

Outside the Jungle, things were significantly more organized, with chowsets filling corners and groups of residents huddled around small fires, drinking dark beer from metal containers and puffing on Leaf, this world's weed comparable. Lines of people from outside the Muck formed at various locations where money was taken and runners were sent into towers to retrieve goods. Darrin couldn't have been more right — the Muck was bursting at the seams with money.

Bhellum was a dying city, an entity desperate to be numbed, desirous of days and nights that slipped past without memory or awareness. And the Muck was the hand that fed that hungry mouth, shoveling as much of the shit as it could down the gullets of its citizens.

Activity around each tower was remarkably organized, with armed sentries stationed both above and below at strategic locations. Important figures moved around with armed guards, moving quickly and with direct-ness. Filthy children ran between towers with abandon, many already forming little toddy gangs that preyed upon other children and the occa-sional junkie.

And while very little violence was seen in the open, the air was with thick with it. Tension like a violin string ran across every fiber of the Muck. In many ways, it reminded Viktor Krill of his precious Riser Wars, when Bars would train, strategize, and relax most Solays, only to explode into vicious combat late into the Haela, storming a rival Bar and razing it to the ground before help could come.

Yes, Viktor Krill could see many parallels between the Muck and his beloved Rising. He rose to prominence in one. He would conquer and rule the other.

Krill spent significant time observing the movements of those traveling to and from each tower. He paid close attention to the boundaries that each gang respected, watched their eyes to ascertain from which direction they expected attacks or feared retaliation.

Krill took note of how other gangsters moved out of the path of the Loaded Chrome Butchers, staring jealously at their arm turrets, auto-aiming shoulder rifles, and multipurpose visor scopes. He took an interest when a contingent of Stench Mobb members, marked by the glowing golden triangle tattoos atop each of their hands, jumped a small group of black-and-white clad Dead Rogues as they made their way into the Jungle. And he enjoyed discovering that a high-ranking member of the Broken Tens, wearing a black hoodie with a white X on the back, was meeting with several toddy gangs, handing them boxes of candy and cigarettes in exchange for information.

The entire Muck was a complex system of secret alliances, backdoor betrayals, obvious enemies, and surprising allies, powered by strong drugs and driven by money. It was a delicate web, as likely to offer a cocooned victim as it was to drop a poison-fanged arachnid on an unsuspecting head. There was much to figure out, and many trappings to uncover, but already Krill was beginning to see strings that others could not.

And already he was attaching his own webs to those that already criss-crossed the Muck, moving things in imperceptible, but impactful, ways.

———

"IT DOESN'T MAKE any sense, Mister Krill."

"Maybe to you, young Darrin. But it is the ideal scenario for my unique desires."

"And what is it that you desire, Mister Krill?"

"A challenge, young Darrin. A challenge."

Darrin looked away in frustration. Although he was growing to respect this dangerous man, Krill was still someone to be handled with silk-wrapped care. Darrin wanted to keep his mouth shut, but felt compelled to continue the conversation. If he was going to tie his fate to this foreign creature from a strange land, Darrin at least needed to know that this man understood the risks.

"Simply surviving in the Muck is a challenge, Mister Krill. Surviving with your humanity in tow is even more difficult. Making it to the top? A near impossibility. So, why make it harder? At least go with a crew on the rise."

Viktor Krill stared at preteen Darrin with his black eyes, his face betraying no emotion. Darrin was unsure if he was going to be answered with words or a swift kick to the chest that cratered his sternum. Finally, Krill's computer brain slowed its calculations, and he responded. "I understand your concern, young Darrin. I really do. And if I were trapped in that weak body of yours, controlled by an infant brain, I, too, would be apprehensive about this course of action. But I am not trapped. I am free of all restrictions, the only human awake in a sea of slumbering chimpanzees. And I demand more."

"More of what?"

"Of everything, dear boy. I still have much to learn, you need to know that I am aware of this. But mine will be an accelerated education, one that will not end in a doctorate, but a kingdom. And when that kingdom ascends above all others, everyone will know that it was built from the foundation by Viktor Krill. No other's name will sit next to mine. Therefore, I need to lead a crew out of the ashes and back into the light of power and glory."

"Well, if you're gonna do that, why don't you just start up your own clique?"

"I have many strengths. Patience is one of the few I do not possess. I don't have time for all that."

Darrin nervously twisted the stick in his hands. "Ok, but do you have to pick *this* one? None has more enemies. None has more bulls-eyes on its back."

"And none is more desperate. Tell me, young Darrin, why aren't you in a crew?"

"I was in a crew. They all ended up with knives in their throats."

Krill chuckled. "Fair enough. But, I mean a *real* crew."

"You can't just join a crew. It takes years of doing dirt, building a reputation, being a bitch for the gang."

"That's right. Which is why I can't simply walk in and demand to join, hand over my resume of violence." Krill thought for a moment. "Well, actually, *I* could do that. But that wouldn't be sporting, so it's neither here nor there. I need a crew desperate for power, one that needs a new weapon for their antiquated arsenal."

"And you think this one's just gonna invite you in?"

"Of course not, young Darrin. I'll need to bring a gift. One that cannot be turned away or denied."

"And where are you gonna get a gift like that?"

Krill laughed aloud this time, finding something particularly humorous. "Young Darrin, the Muck is *full* of gifts. I just have to pick the right one."

"And you know which one that is?"

"I have an idea."

"So, what do you need me to do?"

"Right now? Just stay low, keep observing. Bring me good intel. And stay alive. You're no use to me dead."

"Be careful, Mister Krill. These aren't Jungle junkies you're going after. All these guys are going to be strapped. They say don't bring a knife to a gunfight."

"I've never cared much for truisms." Krill turned to leave, stopped, and said over his shoulder, "Except one. Might makes right."

5

Although night in the Muck was much darker than elsewhere in Bhellum, the area still hummed with muted neon that outlined the towers and edged the various walkways connecting the Five Thieves. The Muck vibrated with activity, its parasitic residents feeding off the sun's absence.

Viktor Krill walked in silence from shadow to shadow, a veiled man moving without a care in the world, drawing the attention of neither predator nor prey.

Before long, Krill found himself near the rear of Pontus Tower. Here, away from the other towers and the Jungle, members of Stench Mobb could congregate in relative safety to enjoy an evening that was vacant of any planned attack or organized scrap.

The lawn was littered with neon marketing signs stolen from across the city, bathing the area in light unseen in most parts of the Muck. Chowsets bordered the Mobb's defined turf, ready to service the hungry partygoers, as numerous campfires fought off the chilly evening air.

The Stench Mobb was thick in the field, their tight-fitting grey track suits and golden hands marking each of them. Others circulating the crowd were gang hangarounds, running errands at a hurried pace, desperate to prove their worth. Stench Mobb was a mixed-race gang, a common characteristic of the newer crews that recognized the idiocy of racism in a war zone. Both dark faces and white skin could be seen in equal parts under the neon glow.

They all looked like food to Viktor Krill.

Slowly, Krill made his way across the field, doing his best to be ignored. He was only approached once, by a cocky hangaround who demanded to know which clique he repped. Krill did not slow his walk, swiftly elbowing the young man in the temple and dropping him where he stood. Krill moved to continue his stroll, but stopped when noticed that something had tumbled from the unconscious man's hand. He scooped up the small tin and placed it in his pants pocket as he shuffled from one darkened area to another. He didn't need any more encounters for now.

Eventually, Krill made his way across the entirety of Stench Mobb revelers and began to fear that his quarry was not out this evening. As he approached the far edge of the lawn, however, dangerously close to the neutral zone that separated Stench Mobb and Chrome Butchers territories, Krill spotted them.

The six gangsters sat around a large fire, drinking from large metal containers, Leaf smoke heavy in the air and mixing with the smells of burning wood. Several hangarounds stood at attention several steps behind the Mobb members, ready to jump to refill a drink or light a joint.

Krill crept closer, wanting to ensure that these were, in fact, the men he was looking for. After several minutes, he had the confirmation he needed. As a hangaround fed more wood to the hungry fire, it flared up and shot light onto the members' faces, illuminating bodies and highlighting one very distinct face tattoo.

Krill reached into his pocket and retrieved a small round gadget, which he promptly lofted at the group. It arched towards the campfire but instead of dropping into the fire, stopped and hovered a dozen feet above the seated gangsters. And there it stayed in the darkened sky, a dull red pulse only noticeable by those searching for it to mark its existence.

With that, Krill found a deep shadow between neon signs and settled in.

He pulled out the tin he had taken from the unconscious hangaround and opened the lid. Inside was several grams of Pearl, tantamount to his world's cocaine, which was the Stench Mobb's main source of notes and credits. When made into Rush, it was even more addictive and profitable, taking the gang to new heights.

Krill dipped his index finger in the powder and brushed it across his gums. The immediate numbing told him all he needed to know about its quality, so he poured a small mound out onto the top of this hand and inhaled deeply. A wide grin broke out onto Krill's face as the drug's effects came on in a flood, the tingling sensation melding with the excited anticipation of violence. Krill's pupils shrank, and he kneeled in the soft grass, his body preparing for what was to come next.

Luckily, Krill did not have to wait long. Several minutes later, four young women approached the gang members. Although Krill was too far away to make out the conversation, he knew what was being said. He sprung into action, making his way around the gang and towards the ocean, where he would wait for his prey to come to him.

———

THE PARTYING STENCH Mobb could be heard in the distance as soft waves rushed forward to deliver foamy kisses to the small littered beach. Absent of Bhellum's ever-present neon, only the rays of this world's normal moon touched the water's edge. Victor Krill kneeled in the angled blackness of an old refrigerator that had washed up, and now jutted from the soft pebbled ground.

Before Krill was a collection of old couches and lazy boys that had been haphazardly deposited just above the high tide mark and arranged in a rough semicircle. Used condoms, bent needles, and broken glass pipes surrounded the area, an obvious meeting place for junkie lovers and their entourages.

Voices broke through relative seaside quietness as the four women led the six goons towards the designated location. "I don't know why we can't do this back up there. You hoes are safe with us."

"That's not the point, dumbass," a youthful female voice cut in. "If we're seen up there, Mayfly's gonna want her cut. And there's nothing to take a cut of. We're trying to party, not work. And we wanna party with y'all. You wanna party or not?"

The SB with the face tattoo immediately answered. "Yeah, yeah, we wanna party. Shut the fuck up, Doyle. Don't fuck this up."

"You right, Von. My bad."

"Lead on ladies."

The women sat the men down on the grimy couches and each crawled up on an SB's lap. The two men left out shot each other disappointed looks, but stayed nonetheless. One of the women kissed her partner's cheek. "So you guys got some Rush for four hungry young girls?"

One of the men left alone spoke first. "Of course we do, love." Krill almost laughed aloud as the man fumbled with his tack suit pockets, unable to get the drugs out fast enough, obviously hoping they would lead to more carnal activities. Eventually, he had a small glass pipe out and loaded with the chunky white drug known as Rush, a staple of the Stench Mobb economy.

The pipe was packed several times as it made its way through the lounging group. As the drug took hold, the girls began in unison to kiss the necks of the seated gangsters, who collectively moaned in response. The women slid down as one, knees touching the beach's cold stones. The Stench Mobb members' pants came down with the girls, and the soft metallic clang of metal hitting the ground could be detected by Victor Krill's Wakened ears.

"Close your eyes," demanded one girl as they went to work. The men promptly obeyed, enveloping themselves in darkness as the strong drugs amplified their sensitivity to young mouths.

This continued for several minutes before one of the men realized something was amiss and shook himself from his euphoric stupor. "Hey, what the fuck? Why'd you stop?" The four men opened their eyes and looked down, disappointed to see four hard, neglected dicks where, only moments ago, bobbing young heads could be found. A foreign voice sliced through the shock and forced them all upright.

"The girls had another appointment, I'm afraid. But I'll entertain you lads."

"Who the fuck is this asshole," asked one man to the group as another shouted, "Piss off, you piece of shit," to the shadowy man who stood before the mighty Stench Mobb members.

The SBs seated on the couches moved to cover their nakedness as Von, the man with the elaborate face tattoo and obvious leader of the group, shouted to his two clothed cohorts, "Yo, shoot this muthafucka!" When no immediate action came, he followed with, "Nelson! Crane! What's wrong with y'all?! I said shoot this asshole!"

As the words left Von's mouth, a dark cloud that had been partially covering the moon made a hasty retreat, allowing the night's true brightness to take hold. "Fuck me," Von exclaimed as his two seated companions were illuminated, showcasing two sets of dead eyes staring out above two rivers of blood emanating from two opened throats.

The remaining SBs bent down to retrieve the guns from their pants, but were quickly brought back up empty-handed as knives flew through the air to bury themselves into the rotting couches between each man. "What do you want," screamed one man while another simply let out a loud groan.

To his credit, Von pulled himself together and raised his hands in surrender. "Alright, man, you got us. What is it you need? We got drugs. We got credits, if you got a dark ream. Just tell us what you want."

Viktor Krill paced before the pantsed men, the Pearl swirling with the surge of power he felt to create a wholly intoxicating blend. "Two days ago, your little band here jumped three Dead Rogues as they made their way into the Jungle."

"What do you care, man? You're not a fucking Rogue. This has nothing..."

Before Von could get out another word, Viktor Krill was upon him, his finger pressed against Von's fat lips, silencing him. "No questions. Only answers. Am I clear?"

Von simply nodded. Krill took two steps back and continued. "Why did you do it?"

"Shit, man, that's just orders from the top. There's a green light on the Dead Rogues. Their days are numbered in the Muck. The Chrome Butchers struck the killing blow, now everyone else is just finishing them off. Can we get our fucking pants?"

"Not unless you want to wear a knife in your skull." Krill nodded to himself. This information was nothing he hadn't figured out for himself, but it was still good to have direct confirmation. "Did you know the guys you attacked?"

"Just one of them. This little shit named Levi Lessons. When the Dead Rogues were the top outfit, this piece of trash made everyone's life hell, especially those of us in the Jungle. Fucker's lucky I didn't kill him. Only thing that saved him is that I wanted to get a few more beatings in before finally blowing his brains out." Silence followed as Krill commenced with his pacing. "Anything else, man? My dick's getting cold. Look, don't worry about these guys you killed. They were just recently Mobbed up. I'll say they got caught slipping by some Jungle junkies. Just let us get outta…"

"There *is* something else that I need."

"Sure, sure, man. Happy to give it to you."

"Oh, I don't think you will be."

"Why's that?"

"Because I need it from your corpse."

"Shit, man. I was afraid of that." With those final words, Von and his fellow SBs dove for the weapons trapped in their track pants.

But Viktor Krill moved faster. So much faster.

6

The dozen men guarding Thoosa Tower's entrance made for an impressive display. They were all wearing the distinct uniform of the Dead Rogues — dark military pants tucked neatly into black combat boots and a white t-shirt decorated with a stylized skull reminiscent of a Misfits logo under a black fatigue jacket. Four of the Rogues held unfamiliar machine guns at the ready while the other eight had sidearms strapped to their belts. All were white and had marked their necks with skull tattoos.

Viktor Krill slung the burgundy bag over his shoulder and walked towards the Rogues, Darrin following several steps behind. Krill argued internally over whether to bring the boy, but, ultimately, decided that the youngster's presence may take some edge off his own appearance. The pair was still dozens of feet away when the machine guns swung their way and hands dropped to handgun grips.

"Stop right there! Business?"

Krill immediately took note of the professionalism with which the guards carried out their tasks. This was no mere band of junkies or blind thugs, and Krill quickly understood how the Rogues had maintained control of the Muck for so many years. And if the Rogues had failed to fracture internally, then something major must have been working against them externally.

"I wish to meet with your First. Gideon Moon is his name, I believe."

Several chuckles rippled through the Rogues. "Would you like to fuck my mother, as well, stranger? You don't request a meeting with Gideon Moon. He calls for a meeting with *you*. And he ain't called for a meeting with *you* because I would know it if he did. Now, do us all a favor and walk away before we put a hundred bullets in that shit-eating face of yours." The man looked around Krill and noticed Darrin standing behind him. "We'll spare the boy, but he'll wish we hadn't." More laughter followed.

Krill fought down the sudden urge to put his index finger through the Rogue's eye, reminding himself of this meeting's importance to his grand plans. Instead, he slowly took the burgundy sack from his shoulder and held it out towards the guards. "But I have a gift for him. Something I'm sure he'll enjoy."

Fingers tightened on machine gun triggers and sidearms slowly slid from their holsters. "Do *not* bring that any closer!"

Now it was Krill's turn to chuckle. Things must truly be going awry for the Rogues to explain such tenseness. "Here, friend, I'm going to place the bag on the ground. Please have one of your men come take a look. Is Levi Lessons around? If so, he'll understand my gift."

Although the machine guns didn't move from their target, Krill could see the lead Rogue running things through his infantile brain. Eventually, he called over his shoulder. "Where's Levi?"

"I think he's in the tower, Renny, still recovering."

"Get him out here. Now."

The younger Rogue ran into Thoosa Tower. After several anxious minutes, a bare-chested, mohawked older Rogue that stood six inches above the rest exited the tower, his face still colored with yellow, black, and brown bruises. With the Rogue skull tattoo also on the side of his head, he looked as if he had just been awoken and was none too happy about it. "What the fuck is it, Renny? Goddam head is still pounding."

Renny kept his eyes on Viktor Krill, but responded. "We got a guest,

Levi. Says he has a gift for Gideon. Says you should take a look inside that bag."

Levi looked confused. "Look in his bag? Why the fuck would I do that? This is what you got me up for? I'm going back to bed."

Krill began to grow tired of this shit show. "Levi Lessons. That's your name, right?"

Levi took real notice of Krill for the first time. "How do you know my name, stranger? I don't fucking know you." Levi withdrew a handgun that had been tucked into the back of his waistband. He aimed it at Krill's chest. "And I don't like people I don't know knowing my name."

Krill smirked, and his black eyes sparkled with the scent of violence in the air. "Well, *Levi Lessons*, I do know your name. And that gift is as much for you as it is for Gideon Moon. Please take a look, so I can get inside and the rest of you can go back to playing at villains. Unless you're scared. Maybe the guys who did that to your face also took your balls."

Despite having fallen on hard times, the Dead Rogues were still men not to be trifled with. And they were unused to such open disrespect. Levi marched up to Viktor Krill and placed the barrel of his gun against the tan stranger's forehead. "Does it look like he took my balls, you black-eyed freak?"

Unfortunately, Levi's gambit did not have its desired effect as Krill simply stared back at the man, a small grin perched upon his lips. "Look in the bag, Levi."

A few moments passed and Levi began to wither under the dark stare of Viktor Krill. "You want me to look in the bag?"

"Please."

"If it's something I don't want, I'm going to have these guys light you up. Understood?"

"Understood."

Levi shoved the gun back into his waistband, bent down to pick up the burgundy sack, and moved to the side, giving the other Rogues a clear line of fire to Krill. Levi turned to his colleagues. "Anything jumps out at me, end this fucker." And with those possible final words, Levi Lessons opened the drawstring and peered into the bag.

Levi's face instinctively recoiled from the opening, forcing Krill to interject. "Sorry about the smell."

Levi scrunched his nose and returned to the sack, studying its contents. "This what I think it is?"

"It is."

"How did you come by it?"

"The hard way."

"And what do you want for it?"

"Just to speak with your First. Nothing more."

Renny spoke up. "What's in it, Levi? Should I shoot these fuckers?"

Levi stared at Krill again, this time with renewed interest. "No," he called back. "No. Let them through. Gideon may want to meet this man. Someone call up, let the boss know he has visitors." To Krill, "Take your gift, stranger. You've earned your meeting."

And with that, Levi turned and walked back towards the guards, shoving down machine gun barrels as he approached. "Put those fucking things down. I'll take him to Gideon. Have them both frisked. Give me four armed trailers and keep a little distance, when possible. Something tells me this is a dangerous man."

Renny looked at Levi with bewilderment. "Then why are you taking him to Gideon?"

Levi pointed at his bruised face. "Because the fucking Dead Rogues could use some dangerous men right about now."

JUST INSIDE THOOSA TOWER, Viktor Krill found a hive of activity. Dead Rogues filled the lobby and halls that spidered off, moving with purpose from room to room, some carrying weapons, others holding packages that were obviously filled with Flea.

Levi led Krill and Darrin, followed closely by a contingent of Rogues, down a large hallway to the left that ended with three sets of elevators on either side. Krill made for the elevators to his right but was stopped by Levi.

"Not those. Those go to the upper half of the tower, dominion of the Bitches. Trust me, I'm doing you a favor." Levi motioned to the left. "These service the first ten floors. Follow me." Levi pushed a button on the wall and a pair of elevator doors immediately opened. He turned to the four escorts. "Two with me, two go ahead in the other lift. Have guns drawn when we exit. Go."

At Levi's command, two young men entered one of the elevators and the door immediately closed behind them. The remaining five entered the other. Krill and Darrin, with metal pressed uncomfortably against their backs, watched as Levi pressed the large top button that read *Thoosa Suites*. The doors closed and the quintet rose in silence, Krill pondering potential escape routes should things turn sour.

The doors opened again upon reaching the tenth floor. Krill and Darrin were greeted by the gun barrels of the escorts who had gone up ahead of them and were forced forward by the men at their back. They stepped out of the lift and into a security area, a simple room that contained only the elevator doors, video cameras, and large black double doors. Levi Lessons marched ahead of the visitors and stood before the doors, facing directly into one of the cameras overhead.

"Levi here with the visitors. Everything's under control, but stay at the ready."

Shortly after he spoke the words, the metal doors slid open and a rush of air filled the security area, smelling of lilac and grilled meat. Guns remained aimed at Krill and Darrin as they crossed the threshold and entered a new world.

THE IMAGE of a rose growing from the shattered remains of an old battlefield struck Viktor Krill as he walked into the plush suite of Gideon Moon. Soft, tasteful furniture filled the space, much of which was inhabited by lounging young men, little more than boys, wearing only silk pajama pants. An assortment of paintings decorated the walls and servant robots criss-crossed the large space on quiet wheels, delivering drinks and sweeping up cigarette ashes.

Armed guards lined the walls on both sides, each not only holding high-caliber machine guns, but wearing the serious faces of men who knew how to shoot. As Krill moved through the suite, he began to wonder if even he could escape if those impressive weapons were turned against him. Young Darrin would have no chance at all.

On they walked, through the common area and past a formidable kitchen home to several robots preparing an assortment of snacks for the men and relaxing boys. The hallway forked shortly thereafter, with the left side emptying into a massive master bedroom decorated with black linens and gold highlights. To the right, Krill was ushered into a large office, where even more armed guards stood at the ready. Black leather couches filled the room, where several more teenage boys sat giggling at Viktor Krill's entrance. Against the back wall, behind a beautiful black and white table of glossy wood, sat Gideon Moon.

Perched in a high-backed chair of dark leather, Gideon Moon was a tall, slender man who failed to cut an impressive figure. He wore obsidian, slicked-back hair and a perfectly manicured dark goatee that stood in stark contrast to his pale skin. On his thin frame was a tight black turtleneck sweater atop black dress pants. On Moon's lap was another half-naked teen. He caressed Moon's cheek with the long nails of one hand while the other meticulously plucked stray hairs from the First's brow.

At first glance, Gideon Moon looked like a soft toss of a man, someone more interested in comfort and boys than power. But Viktor Krill could not be fooled that easily. He looked beyond the weak facade to see the iron just beneath the surface. And he was sure that many who failed to see this in time paid for it with their lives.

Moon's bright blue eyes were as hard as glacial ice, and the jagged scars that laced his face, hiding under thick layers of makeup, told the stories of severe violence and desperate combat. With his Wakened senses, Viktor

Krill quickly discovered what Gideon Moon was — a serious man with serious intentions.

Krill was stopped several feet from Moon's desk, with Darrin standing nervously behind him. He threw the burgundy sack back over his shoulder and waited patiently.

Levi gave his First time to study the visitor before beginning introductions. "Gideon, this man has a gift for you. I think it will interest you."

Moon kissed his sweetheart on the lips before shooing the boy away. As the boy flopped onto the nearest couch and pouted, Moon spoke. "Well, I do love gifts. But as you can see, my dark visitor, I have almost everything already." The voice was feminine but powerful, an actor playing a role. "To whom do I owe the honor of this gift? Does the donor have a name?"

"My name is Viktor Krill."

Moon's blue eyes went dramatically wide. "Ooooh, can you see that Levi? I just got goosebumps. And your young friend there?"

Darrin spoke for himself. "I'm Darrin."

"Well, hello to the both of you. My name is Gideon Moon and all that you see around you is mine. I apologize for the crowdedness of the tower, but we've recently had to downsize our living quarters." A short pause. "You know, we rarely let visitors up here, so you must have something truly remarkable in that little bag of yours." Moon shot a serious look to Levi Lessons. "If not, several individuals won't be leaving this room upright." Back to Krill, "But enough pleasantries. Let us see what you have for me."

Krill swung the sack from his shoulder and opened the drawstring. Pinching one of the items against the inside of the bag, he upturned the sack and emptied the rest of its contents onto Gideon Moon's desk. An audible gasp could be heard from the office's guards as a dozen hands fell onto the glossy wood with dull thuds. The top of each hand bore a bright golden triangle, leaving no mistake as to whom they belonged.

Gideon Moon showed no emotion before the macabre scene. Even the strong odor of rotting flesh seemed not to disturb him. Something to remember. "And *what* do we have here? Looks to me like you caught some of those low-class Stench Mobb characters unawares. Good for you. But tell me, Viktor Krill, why do you think I would care? Why do think a bunch of dirty hands from a dirty gang would impress me?"

There was obvious danger in Moon's question, but Krill knew a bluff when he saw one. "You know why, Gideon."

"Humor me." More danger there.

"How much do I need to repeat?"

"Let's start with all of it, and we'll work our way down."

"Very well." Viktor Krill breathed in deeply, readying the speech he had run through his mind dozens of times. "You're weak." An angry ripple ran through the guards as hands tightened on gun stocks. Levi's face blanched as if he had signed his own death warrant. To his credit, Gideon Moon remained impassive. "By that, I mean the Dead Rogues are weak. You were on top for years, owed in equal parts to your strong leadership and the gang's control of Flea. But two things have changed. First, Flea is no longer the drug of choice in the Muck. In fact, being a Flea addict is a surefire way of getting stabbed up while you drift away. Both Rush and, especially, Flame have taken over the Muck. And with lower sales and less money coming in, you've got less resources with which to attract new Rogues. It's a simple numbers game, really."

"Oh, is it? Is it all so simple?"

"No, it's not. In addition to losing your grip on the drug trade, another crew has risen, with full control of the hottest product in the game. And I think we both know that it doesn't stop there. This other crew is backed by a larger entity. A powerful one with deep pockets. Pockets that can outfit an entire gang with MCEs. Pockets that keep the Bobby Bots away from the warring Muck. In short, you were pinched both internally and externally. And you fell. Swiftly. And, now, what was once a tower full of criminal assets has been crammed into half a building."

Moon placed his elbows on the table and steepled his hands. "You're very knowledgeable for a foreigner, Viktor Krill."

"I've made it a habit to learn my surroundings quickly. And young Darrin here has been most helpful."

Gideon Moon bent his head to side to look at Darrin, and threw a sly wink at the boy that made Krill want to lunge for his throat. "Is that all you have... Viktor Krill?" Moon sounded out the name slowly, played around with it in his mouth, as if testing its quality.

Krill laughed aloud, drawing a scowl from Moon and his associates. "You wish that was all. Maybe then you would have a chance to recover. But it's not all. Because of your time on top, you've gained a host of enemies, all who have patiently waited for your downfall, so they can start taking shots at the Dead Rogues. The Chrome Butchers are keeping their boots on your necks. The Broken Tens are moving in on some of your dope tanks in the Jungle. And the Stench Mobb is openly jumping high-ranking members of your outfit." Levi Lessons shifted uncomfortably. "In fact, a small group of Rogues was attacked a few days ago on their way into the Jungle, in what should be a safe zone. Did you do anything about it?"

Gideon Moon's face grew serious. Krill was on sensitive ground here. Moon spoke through gritted teeth. "We were planning retaliation."

"Far too slowly. Each offensive that isn't met with immediate reaction emboldens the other crews. Soon, even small crews and toddy gangs will take their chances in poking the once-mighty Dead Rogues. And you will not be able to defend from all the angles." Krill let the painful truth sink in for a moment before continuing. "I saw your hesitance and the folly of it. So, I took care of the problem for you." He gestured to the dozen hands on the black and white desk.

Moon took his elbows from the table, and sat back in his chair to study what was before him. "And are these supposed to be the SBs that hurt poor Levi and his men? I'm sorry, but these could be the hands and any low-ranking Mobb members. Perhaps you just butchered a group of SBs and now want to make mass murder appear as a favor. Maybe you want to take the heat off yourself and place it at the bare feet of the Dead Rogues. Perhaps there is no connection between these corpses and the strike against my men."

Viktor Krill didn't verbally respond to these accusations. Instead, he simply reached into the burgundy bag, collected the last item within, and lofted it into the air. It spun in the air like a Frisbee and landed with a sick splat onto a clear spot on the table. Moon looked down to find a face staring back at him, sliced neatly off the skull of a dead man. On the right cheek, going up to the temple, was a poorly rendered tattoo of a hand rising out of a triangle, giving the middle finger to the viewer.

"Fuck me," Levi muttered to himself from the side.

Moon's eyes widened in interest. "You know this man, Levi?"

"Yes, sir. That's fucking Von, the piece of shit SB that jumped me and the guys. Everyone in the Muck knows that stupid fucking face tattoo. He was a middle member, but on the fast-track to shot caller."

"You're sure of this?"

"Yes, sir."

"And the number of SBs who attacked you?"

Levi looked at Krill nervously, his respect for and fear of this new player growing fast. "There were six of them, sir."

Chatter spread through the office as the armed guards began to talk among themselves. "Silence!" demanded Gideon Moon, and all went quiet. "So, what exactly are you offering me, Viktor Krill. And what do you want in return?"

"What I want is simple, a position of power in your organization."

"Maybe there aren't any openings."

"Then I'll make some." More nervous chatter.

"Why do you want this? You aren't from the Muck. This is a place of pain and excessive violence. It isn't some kind of game."

"I disagree. That is precisely what it is. And it's a game that I am desperate to play."

"And your offer?"

"I'm a killer. The greatest this world or any other has even seen. I don't engage in violence, I *am* violence. The other gangs don't respect you, right now. I will change that, make sure that the name the Dead Rogues once again rings loudly across the Muck. Those that wrong us? They will pay in blood. Those that get in our way? They will be trampled like mice before the rhino. Those above us? They will feel the noose tighten around their soft necks, pulling them down along an inevitable path towards annihilation. Make me your Second, and I will take back the Muck for you."

Moon stared back at Krill, a thousand thoughts racing through his mind. "Stoner! Now that Burger was killed by those fucking Butchers, you're the next in line to be my Second. What do think of this strange man jumping the queue?"

One of the guards, obviously Stoner, spoke from behind. "I don't trust him. I say we put a bullet in this fucking assassin, right now." The gun in his hands rose to face Krill. "What do you say boys? End this parasite now, and give the black boy to the boss as a present? He hasn't had a young piece of black ass in a while."

Krill didn't mind threats to himself, in fact, he quite enjoyed them, but threatening his young associate detonated something in the dangerous man. Krill moved like lightning, faster than the office guards could comprehend. In a dark flash, Krill was across the room, had disarmed Stoner, and was pressing the cold metal of the guard's gun against his temple from behind.

Moon watched in astonishment as Krill's onyx eyes grew darker, becoming black holes that threatened to absorb the weak office light. "Now, why did you have to say such a thing," Viktor Krill asked Stoner, although he was speaking to the entire room. "Young Darrin, what did I tell about those who make threats to your person?"

"You said that they have to be eliminated immediately, Mister Krill," said Darrin with all the confidence his small frame could muster.

"Correct. But seeing as how we are guests here, maybe I'll just take an eye instead." A knife appeared in Krill's left hand, as if by magic, and hovered dangerously close to Stoner's face. All guns in the room were drawn and pointed at the visitor; the sound of skin rubbing against metal triggers was almost audible.

As a heaviness fell over the office, the slow clapping of hands sliced neatly through the silence, breaking the tense spell. Krill looked over to find Gideon Moon standing and applauding, a large grin on his narrow face. "Well. Done. Krill! Oh, but what a show! Everyone, put down your weapons. Can't you see that we have a very important guest here?" Barrels were slowly lowered to the floor. "And I'm sure Stoner is regretful for the harsh words he used towards your associate. Isn't that right, Stoner?"

Stoner, still staring down the point of a knife and wincing at the press of cold metal against his temple, simply nodded. Krill's knife disappeared into air and the gun was unceremoniously shoved back to Stoner. He returned to the center of the office.

Moon nodded his thanks to the black-eyed man. For the first time, he gestured towards the two leather chairs that sat before his ornate desk. Krill and Darrin each slid into a chair as Moon continued. "Alright, Viktor Krill, you have displayed your prowess, although I think what you have shown is just the tip of your true abilities. You are an impressive man, and I happily accept the thoughtful gift you have provided." He turned to look at Levi. "Oh, Levi, I see you eyeing that grotesque face. Go ahead and take it if you want." Levi smiled and rushed to collect Von's tattooed face. Darrin's own brown face threatened to go pale. Back to Krill, "Anyway, if I *were* to make you my Second, what exactly would be the plan of action. Let's see if that brain of yours is as impressive as that tight body."

Krill ignored the obvious attempt to rankle. "The first step is revenge. I'll need the know the gangs and, if possible, individuals that have attacked the Rogues recently. These brazen attacks must stop, lest we are forced to remain on the defensive."

"Done. Stoner, Levi, and the others can fill you in. Next?"

"Next, I go on the offensive. Strategic targets and locations will be selected. As our powers and resources increase, so, too, will the profile of our victims. Right now, we are leaking strength like a sieve. This needs to reverse if we are to ultimately challenge the Chrome Butchers and take back our rightful place at the top of the Muck."

Moon pondered Krill's words for a while before responding. "Well, you don't seem like a man easily lied to, so I won't. The Dead Rogues could certainly use a member of your...talents. But I need to know something before we cement our partnership. And I would appreciate an honest response. I know you're a bad man, but I didn't get to sit in this seat by acting the bitch. I, too, am a bad man. And I need to know why us. Why the Dead

Rogues? Any gang in the Muck would gladly take you in. What makes us so worthy of your skills?"

Krill was prepared for this question, had run it through it his mind numerous times before settling on the Rogues. "Three reasons. First, I see order in your crew. Despite your recent troubles, your men follow direction, a testament to your leadership. Second, you need me. The Butchers, SBs, and Tens are doing just fine. And because they don't *need* me, it would take much longer to prove my worth, earn their trust, carve out a place of my own. Sigman Prime, Liquid Tye, and Tennian Stamp still have all of their lieutenants in place, men I would have to cut through. I have many superior traits; patience isn't necessarily one of them. And finally, I desire a challenge. You're asking yourself now, *what drives this man?* Well, let me put your mind at ease. I have an urge to conquer, violently conquer. And when you're already at the top, there is little more to conquer. The current state of the Dead Rogues leaves many above us, many that can feed my hunger."

Gideon Moon leaned forward, a serious glint in his blue eyes. "And when you've taken everything outside the gang, Viktor Krill? Will you take the Dead Rogues for your own? Will you look to conquer your beloved First? Will my throat be the next to be cut?"

Blue eyes stared down black orbs, invisible bolts of lightning connecting the two killers. "Maybe. But without my help, Gideon, the Dead Rogues will be gone, relegated to mere memories of the Muck, long before that comes to pass."

Another long silence followed. Darrin squirmed uncomfortably in his chair. The young boy hadn't survived on his own in the Muck without an ability to sense when situations teetered on the edge of violence. He let out a deep sight of relief, however, when Moon slammed both fists on the table, making the Stench Mobb hands jump into the air, and stood up, another wide smile on his scarred face.

"Then, we have reached an accord! Gentlemen, put your weapons away and come meet your new commander. And if there is nothing further, Viktor, then let us bring out the party supplies and properly celebrate our partnership."

"There is something further."

"And what is that?"

"I have another gift. One I've been saving for a partnership such as this."

Moon clapped his hands excitedly. "Another gift?! Three gifts in one day?" To his men, "And you lot haven't given me anything in ages, but migraines." To Krill once again, "I'm absolutely dripping with anticipation."

Viktor Krill reach into his pants pocket and pulled out a tiny cardboard box, similar to one that would hold matches. "With me as a Dead Rogue, we can match up with any crew in a fight. But that solves only half of your problems." Krill slid open the box and upturned it over the desk. A brown lump, similar to a small slug or leech, fell onto the wood with a wet thud.

Moon leaned forward to get a closer look. "And what is that grotesque thing?"

"That, Gideon, is our ticket to getting back on top of the drug trade. Without even having to deal with the Gate or its overseas suppliers."

"But what is it," he asked, his voice thick with wonder.

"It's called a Slink. And it's about to set the Muck ablaze."

7

The too-tall, whiplike man stood outside of Pontus Tower in a grey tank top and shivered, partially from the chilly morning air, but mainly from the grim scene laid out before him. On the side of the tower, just to the left and around the corner from the main entrance, six stick figures made of twisted metal wire had been pounded into the soft grass. This alone was cause for concern, for how did someone get so close to Pontus without attracting the attention of the Mobb's guards? But what really made the hair stand up on Liquid Tye's dark arms was the artistic flourish that the sculptor had added to the otherwise unimpressive works. Skewered on the end of each twisted metal arm was a human hand.

To be more accurate, the human hand of a Stench Mobb member.

Liquid Tye's light-brown eyes took in the grisly display, and he almost chuckled at the humorous positions in which the macabre stick men had been arranged. He turned to a giant block of a man with a ginger afro. "Red Texx, how many guards were stationed at the main entrance last night?" His voice was soft and musical, but Red Texx was used to that from his First and had already leaned in to listen.

"Only four last night, Tye. Was supposed to be eight but four of them pissed off to a party in the Jungle."

"With our recent successes, some of our men have grown complacent. This can't happen. Especially not now."

"What do you want done?"

"The four that stood guard must be corrected. 120-second beatings each. Ten for each hand they allowed to be installed right under their noses."

"And the ones that took off?"

"Put a bullet in each one's head and hang each of their bodies outside of one of our dope tanks. Leave them there until the animals have their fill. Let all the members see what happens when duties are shirked."

Red Texx nodded and faced the exhibit of death. "Do we know who they are?"

"Von and his boys. Bodies were found down by the shore yesterday morning. Their hands were missing and Von's face had been carefully removed."

"So, we're just missing a face."

"Yes, and I'm sure that will turn up sooner or later. The boys were last seen with some Bitches."

"You think the Bitch-Whores could have done this?"

"Of course not. But they had a small hand in it, to be sure. Von and his crew do anything stupid recently? And by that, I mean more stupid than usual?"

"They jumped Levi Lessons earlier in the week, but that was because of the green light on the Rogues. You think those old Rogues could have done this?"

"The *old* Rogues? No. But this is something new, something... formidable. I can feel the danger in the air, Texx. Gideon Moon is weak right now, but I wouldn't put it past the old queen to pull a rabbit out of his sequined hat."

Red Texx's catcher's mitt face pulled together as the large man tried and failed to work through the possibilities. He finally relented. "So, what do you think we're looking at here, boss?"

Liquid Tye looked around suspiciously, already feeling more vulnerable. "I think we're looking at a new brand of killer, Red Texx. One that's gonna stir up the Muck and fuck up the little order we have. Triple the guards, from now on. And don't bother me for the rest of the day. I have to think."

————

THE JUNGLE JUNKIE rolled around on the dirty ground, touching things that weren't there and speaking to ghosts no one else could see.

"So, there's even a psychedelic phase," asked Gideon Moon as he stared in wonder at the human guinea pig.

"Yes, it's one of the final phases. Once the Slink has completely disintegrated and run its course, most users will be left with feelings of extreme sadness and loneliness. Compared to what they experienced over the last few hours, this emotional state will be intolerable, which means they'll be looking to score again."

"So, the Slink is really like Flea, Rush, and Flame all rolled into one neat little package?"

"And even some Leaf effects for good measure."

Moon looked at his enigmatic new Second. "Where did you get such a wondrous creature, Viktor?"

"Another world, Gideon."

Moon laughed lightly. "I *almost* believe you. Did you create it?"

"No, but I manipulated it a bit. I made its effects stronger, shorter-lasting. I also greatly amped up the withdrawals from the drug to ensure that we have a sustainable product. It's the perfect escape for the user, whether he's running from the dreariness of the Muck or the unhappiness of a crumbling marriage."

"Alright, I'm convinced." Moon gestured to the armed guards surrounding the Rogue-controlled dope tank. "Drop this junkie back off in the Jungle." Two DRs approached and picked the hallucinating man off the ground. They began to march him out of the clearing.

"Wait!" Viktor Krill approached the junkie, looked into his far-away eyes. "Are you enjoying your trip, friend?"

The junkie's eyes vibrated back and forth, enjoying an army of visuals behind Krill's tanned face. His voice came out strangely, as if echoing out from another plane of existence. "It's like nothing I ever felt before."

"Good. It's called Slink. And, soon, there will be as much as you want of it in the Muck. Say the name again. Say Slink."

The junkie worked hard to focus. "Slink. It's called Slink."

Krill gently slapped the man's face. "Yes. Slink. Tell your friends. Let them know Slink is coming." Krill rose to his full height and the guards led the junkie deep into the Jungle to finish off his high.

Moon came and stood next to Krill, his blue eyes shining with excitement. "You've made your point, Viktor. How much more Slink do you have access to? We need to get it on the street as quickly as possible."

"I have three more on me, Gideon."

"That's fine, but how much can you purchase in the next week or so?"

"There is no other supply of Slink, Gideon."

Moon's face lit up like he had been struck with a white glove. Surprise quickly morphed into anger. "Three more? What the fuck, Viktor! Why even show me this miracle drug if we don't have it and can't get it from another source? How the hell do we win the drug war if we can't purchase more inventory?!"

Krill smiled inwardly. With his Wakened mind and body, Krill only saw the world in terms of possibility. The infants with whom he shared this reality, however, only saw limitations and unlikelihoods. "The Slink is not a mere chemical chain, Gideon. It is a biological creature."

"What does that mean?"

"It means we can raise more."

Moon looked confounded. "Raise more? How?"

"You leave that to me."

"But, surely, that will take time. And how could you possibly raise enough to feed upcoming demand? I don't think you understand how quickly new drugs spread in Bhellum. The city is a dried out field and Slink will drop into the center of it like a red ember."

"I understand perfectly well, Gideon."

Moon bit back an angry retort, pushed down his frustration, and calmed himself. "Very well. You asked me to trust you, and I will. I assume there are some resources you will need to begin *raising* Slink."

"That is correct."

"Fine, tell me back in Thoosa. I don't trust the ears in the Jungle." Moon began to walk away, but stopped and turned back to face Krill. "I don't handle disappointment well, Viktor. You have made many promises and I expect you to keep them all. Look down. Each step you take is atop the buried bones of those who let me down. Would be a shame to lose a villain such as yourself."

There was a challenge in Moon's words. Krill pushed aside his desire to wear his First's head as a pendant and simply bowed in understanding. It was much too early to start killing major players indiscriminately.

Viktor Krill was not patient. But he was not stupid, either.

Gideon Moon nodded back, his message received, and stalked back towards Thoosa Tower flanked by his guards. Krill broke into a smile as the man exited the clearing, thinking of the look on Moon's face when Krill informed him of what he would need to flood the city with Slink.

———

"THERE'S A PROBLEM." Gideon Moon looked serious behind his black and white desk. To most, he looked like a dangerous man playing at dangerous games. To Viktor Krill, he looked like a boy upset that he had just broken his favorite toy.

"And what is that?"

"I'm not exactly sure, but the Bitch-Whores want to speak with you. In particular, Mayfly Lemaire wants to speak with you. And they're refusing to let us use the 12th Floor pool area until she does. How necessary is the pool to your plans?"

"Critical."

"Then, I guess you're going to have to go up there."

"What does she want?"

"I don't know, Viktor. But she didn't seem pleased about something."

"Then, I guess I'm going to have to go up there."

"Top floor. I'll have Levi call up ahead." Krill nodded and turned to leave. "Viktor!" He turned back to face Moon. "Try not to piss them off. The Bitch-Whores are the only reason the Dead Rogues still exist. And remember, Mayfly Lemaire is not one to be trifled with. Don't let her feminine wiles distract you. She has more bodies on her than maybe anyone in the Muck, me included." He chuckled softly. "You know, I've prided myself on never requiring a woman's attention. It's been the downfall of many men across history, the addictive nature of pussy and the undue sway of a woman's soft touch. But, right now, we need her. We need them. Make it work with Lemaire, Viktor."

Krill turned quickly and exited, hoping to keep the grin that had settled on his face from Gideon Moon. Hopeful that his First couldn't see the excitement that shone in his black eyes. Hopeful that Mayfly Lemaire, the one woman to rise above the muddy bottom of the Muck, could live up to his expectations.

———————

THE ELEVATOR DOORS opened at the Thoosa Tower Penthouse and Viktor Krill was assaulted by vanilla and berry aromas. The odor, strong and unquestionably feminine, was intoxicating, and Krill could feel his defenses unconsciously lowering. *Clever girls*, thought Krill, as he swept away the fog that threatened to descend upon his brain and slow his reactions.

Like Gideon Moon's suite, there was a security area between the lift and the penthouse entrance. As Krill stepped out of the elevator, he immediately noted two guardian mechs stationed at either side of the large, rose-colored doors leading into the penthouse. They were a much older model of mech, the C-class, but could still blast a hole in the chest of an unwelcome guest. Looking vaguely human in size and shape, the C-class mechs suffered from balance issues and a lack of speed, but, currently anchored as they were, made for adequate guardians.

Krill moved to stand between the two mechs, allowing them time to scan him and send the information back to whoever was controlling the automatons. Their metal eyes, pairs of focusing scopes inserted into round metal heads, studied him for a while, and Krill could hear the whir of old processors heating up and disseminating data. Soon after, the sounds ceased and the rose-colored doors opened silently inward.

With the Thoosa Tower Penthouse comprising the entire top floor of the building, Krill was understandably wowed by the cavernous room he entered. Decorated tastefully with white couches, love seats, and lounging areas, and dotted with draped silks and flower arrangements, the entire space sat in stark contrast to the death and dreariness that constituted most of the Muck.

An assortment of women inhabited the space, some dressed ready for battle and others for a cocktail party. Still others were barely dressed at all, as if, at any moment, someone could call them over to dance onstage. While all the women seemed at ease, lambs for a potential slaughter, Krill looked past the deliberately crafted facade. Handles of guns could be seen jutting from between seat cushions. The hilts of numerous knives peeked out coyly from garters. One severely tall Asian woman, peering over her cup of tea to stare at Krill, subconsciously adjusted the samurai sword that was strapped to her back.

In mere moments, Viktor Krill had concluded his assessment. Yes, these women were beautiful. Yes, these women were feminine and alluring. And, most importantly, yes, these women were extremely dangerous.

In addition to the loitering women, a mix of service bots and guardian mechs quietly moved across the space, the former carrying trays of teas and powders and the latter scanning faces and recording information. To further increase security, several auto-turrets had been installed at the tops of each wall, patiently waiting to receive orders to kill every fucking thing in the room below them. No wonder the women could remain at such ease.

"Viktor Krill?" The soft voice to his left pulled Krill out of his analysis. A petite young woman with white bobbed hair, alabaster skin, and pink eyes had slid in next to the dangerous guest. Krill simply nodded in the affirmative, and she smiled sweetly. "Thank you for accepting our invitation. I'm Noora. Please come with me. My queen is eager to meet you."

Noora moved ahead, weaving through the congested room, and Krill followed. Dozens of painted eyes, round and narrow, dark and bright, spied his every move, and Krill could sense delicate fingers sliding towards hilts and triggers. Like Gideon Moon's suite, many rooms branched off this large central expanse, and Krill peeked in to see cooking areas, dining rooms, bedrooms, and ornate bathrooms.

Sneaking a look behind him as he walked, Krill saw that two guardian mechs were following the pair. And although the mechs' small, unsure footsteps made for a humorous image, Krill knew that the guardians' gun-tipped arms did not suffer from the same design flaws as did their outdated bottom halves. Therefore, to avoid the ignominious death of getting shot in the back by a twitchy mech, Krill kept his hands open and to his sides, clearly in sight.

Noora and Krill walked for several minutes, making their way towards the rear of the tower. Looking out various windows as they marched, Krill could see movement far below on Cyrix Blvd and wondered if any of those lucky souls, running mindlessly to and from work, were aware of the horror that was life in the Muck.

A short time later, Noora stopped at a pair of white double doors inlaid with gold scrollwork. "Please wait here, Mister Krill. I'll let my queen know that you have arrived." And with that, Noora opened one of the large doors and slid inside, leaving Krill alone in the hall with his thoughts and the guardian mechs.

"You guys worked here long? How are the perks?" Krill asked the stoic pair behind him, and was unsurprised when no response came. "Don't want to talk out of school, I suppose. Good men."

The door opened again and Noora exited. "My queen will see you now." There was a strange look on the albino woman's face, a smirk that had been covered in layers of professional discretion. "Good luck, Viktor Krill."

Krill nodded his thanks, pushed open one of the white doors, and walked into the foggy world of Mayfly Lemaire, the warrior queen of the Muck.

As the door closed behind him, Viktor Krill breathed out reflexively as the hot steam gripped his lungs. He moved slowly forward, unable to make out much in the balmy room. The ornate tile on which he walked told him that he was in the penthouse's master bathroom, as did the sounds of running water that emanated from just up ahead.

"This way, Viktor Krill. Don't play shy, I know you are anything but." The voice, deep and resonant, echoed off the marbled statues that could just be made out through the haze to Krill's left and right. Krill shuffled forward, eyes darting back forth, imagining weapons appearing out of the vapors to slice at vulnerable arteries and the soft places between bones. After several seconds of nervous progress, Krill came upon a series of marble steps and decided to wait at their base.

The voice came back from somewhere slightly above him, mocking in its tone. "Are you coming, Viktor Krill?"

"I'm good right here for now, thank you. I don't make it a habit to march into darkness with my eyes closed."

"Silly me, I had no idea it had gotten so misty down there." An obvious lie. "Let me assist you with that. Control! Master bathroom fan on high!" Fans far above Krill came to life and hummed loudly. Wisps of water vapor raced past Krill towards the ceiling, and within seconds the surrounding space had cleared dramatically, revealing the true beauty of the bathroom.

White marble counters topped with elegant mirrors lined the far walls of the bathroom and the statues each spouted water from one or more holes to collect in ornate basins at their bases. Before Viktor Krill, ten wide marble steps led up to a higher level of the room. It was from here that the voice came again. "No more excuses, Viktor Krill."

Krill breathed in deeply of the thick, warm air and ascended the steps slowly, careful not to slip on the wet stone. The elevated section of the bathroom extended the width of the room and contained a hot tub the size of a small pool. White marble benches could be found to the left and right of the bubbling jacuzzi which was expelling waves of lavender water vapor, sending sweet-smelling apparitions twisting towards the ceiling fans above. Laying back in the frothy water, allowing swarms of bubbles to caress her upper chest and kiss her dark neck, was Mayfly Lemaire.

Her dark, almost black, skin popped against the bathroom's white on white motif and her dreadlocked hair was tied up in a tight top bun to escape the raging waters below. She stared at Viktor Krill with bright amber eyes as he stopped on the top marble step and awaited further instruction. A nude woman sat on the edge of the tub to either side of the Bitch-Whore queen, working meticulously on Lemaire's long white fingernails. The naked women looked up briefly at Krill before turning their attentions back to their duties.

Krill and Lemaire, a future and current titan of the Muck, shared a heavy silence before Lemaire broke the strange spell. "My name is Mayfly Lemaire and you are Viktor Krill, I presume. I apologize for meeting you like this, but I find such little time for myself these days. Limitations often necessitate multitasking. Please, have a seat." She motioned towards the bench farthest from her and Krill slowly took a seat. Although he couldn't see any auto-turrets or mechs in the washroom, Krill could sense weapons pointed his way and moved accordingly.

"It is my pleasure to meet you, Miss Lemaire," said Krill as he crossed his legs, hoping to appear as nonchalant as possible. Lemaire's choice of meeting location was an obvious attempt to put the dangerous man off-balance. He needed to show her that such base tactics were beneath him. "Although, I must admit that I'm at a loss regarding this meeting's purpose."

Lemaire angrily tore her hands from the two servant girls and shooed them away. They tiptoed towards the bench opposite Krill and sat down seductively. One began playing with the other's hair as they both looked on hungrily at the mysterious guest, another clear attempt to distract Krill. Lemaire leaned forward in the water, the tops of her large breasts appearing from the foamy surface, and glared at her visitor, her amber orbs threatening to burst into flame.

"Several nights ago, a strange man hired four girls to lead six young men into a trap. A trap of the deadly variety. Those six young men were ranking members of the Stench Mobb. Those four girls belonged to the Bitch-Whores. That strange man was you, Viktor Krill. Because of your actions, I have been forced to make recompense to Tye Nettle." Krill could almost feel Lemaire's eyes heating his face as her anger boiled over. "I hate making recompense, Viktor Krill. I hate Liquid Tye, even more. And above all, I hate cleaning up other people's messes!" She composed herself. "Now, tell me why I shouldn't have your testicles removed, gilded, and fashioned into a lovely pendant as a warning to other males who think they can use my property without permission."

Krill almost chuckled aloud at the creative threat, but swallowed it down before making the grievous error. "First, and foremost, my apologies, Miss Lemaire. I did not know that those women belonged to you."

"They *all* belong to me!"

The suddenness of her outburst, matched only by its intensity, forced Krill back on his seat. The strength behind her words convinced Krill that this was a woman best served with the truth. "Of course. I see that now. But at the time, as someone shiny new to the Muck, I could not have known. Unlike most of the gangs, you all have refrained from adopting identifying colors or uniforms."

"We are women. That is our uniform."

"I see that now."

"And if you are unsure if a woman is under my care or not, it's best to assume that she is."

"Understood. Clearly, a misstep on my part. What can be done to rectify the situation?"

Lemaire sat back in the swirling waters, and although her eyes had lost their rage, they studied Viktor Krill that much harder. "A man who freely admits his mistakes? To a woman, nonetheless? A rare find indeed. I appreciate the offer to correct your error and I accept. There is a...situation...that needs attending to. One that could use a man of your skills."

Krill bowed his head slightly. "I am at your service, Miss Lemaire."

Mayfly Lemaire slapped the water with both hands. "Then it is settled. We can talk of the details another time. Ladies!"

The nude attendants sprang into action, each girl grasping Lemaire under an arm and lifting her up. Lemaire's nude body fell into focus as the water cascaded from her dark skin. Like most others in the Muck, her skin wore the wounds of dozens of violent encounters. To Viktor Krill, the scars perfectly highlighted her look, an athletic, toned body that still maintained the wide hips and ample breasts of the feminine ideal.

"You aren't shy, are you, Viktor Krill?"

Krill refused to look away. "Never."

"Good. I don't have time for shy men," said Lemaire as the girls patted her off with soft-looking white towels. When she was dry from the waist up, the women lifted Lemaire out of the tub, revealing one impossibly long dark leg and only the thigh of another leg. Jagged scars capped the thigh, just above where the knee would have been. The small women showed surprising strength in hoisting the large queen and helping her to the far bench, where they continued removing water from her chocolate skin. Lemaire caught Krill looking at her stump. "Does my injury offend you, Viktor Krill? When men have scars they are called *battle wounds*, but when a woman has them, they are *imperfections*."

"To the contrary, lady. I am even more impressed with you. Scars tell the deep history of one's past. They are stories of aggression, of fighting to protect what's yours, of refusing to accept what is given."

Her stump dry, one of the attendants retrieved a golden prosthetic from under the bench and attached it to her boss. It must have cost a small fortune, with a fully operational knee joint and ankle, and sensors that quietly adjusted the limb to perfectly match Lemaire's existing leg. "And do you have scars, Viktor Krill?"

"Yes."

"How many?"

"Too many that run too deep."

"Interesting. Maybe one day you'll show them to me." Lemaire stood without assistance, and Krill thought that no woman could ever appear half as regal as the creature standing before him, her nakedness displaying more power than any queenly gown or crown ever could. She put her arms out and a white robe was slid onto her. Lemaire closed the front and tied it shut. Krill almost let out an audibly disappointed groan. "Come. Let us continue this meeting somewhere more appropriate. The bathroom is the easiest place to clean up blood stains. I don't foresee needing that any longer."

From hidden locations around the bathroom, Krill's Wakened ears could hear tiny turrets sliding back into hidden compartments.

———

THE SMALL SITTING room proved much more comfortable than the marbled bathroom. Krill sat in an ornate, leather-wrapped armchair and Lemaire sat in a similar seat across from him. Her robe had opened where Lemaire crossed her legs, proudly displaying her golden prosthetic as it played games with the room's overhead lights. Cups of steaming tea sat on the small tables beside each chair. Lemaire picked hers up and stared at Krill over the rim of the cup as she drank deeply. "It's laced. Try it."

Krill did as he was told and immediately felt the narcotic effects of the tea, taking him back to another place and time. As they both finished their tea in comfortable silence, Noora entered the room with a silver tray, on which there were two hand-rolled joints. Krill took one and Lemaire the other before Noora bowed respectfully and exited, closing the door behind her. Krill detected no safety measures in place throughout the room. He held up the joint in question.

"Just Leaf. You know, everyone thought that as harder and harder drugs continued to be introduced, Leaf would simply dissolve into the past. But what they failed to recognize is that sometimes everyone, even hardcore junkies, want to just chill the fuck out." Lemaire lit her joint with a gold lighter and tossed it to Krill. Her amber eyes sparkled as she exhaled the sweet-smelling smoke. "Everyone thought Old Tens was crazy when he focused on Leaf as opposed to the more profitable products, but the jokes on them. Old Tens is still rolling around. Most of *them* are long gone."

Krill lit his own joint and inhaled deeply, smiling inwardly at the thought that his Wakened body allowed him to enjoy Leaf in ways that no other human could. "Yes, Tennian Stamp is still around. And Mayfly Lemaire is still around. How do you explain it?"

"It's simple, Viktor Krill. We both have products that are never going to go out of style. Leaf and pussy. Control one of those things, keep your head on a swivel, and you can rise above the chaos." Krill simply stared at Lemaire, and his black eyes on hers made her almost squirm in her seat. Although this feeling was foreign to the forceful Mayfly Lemaire, she would be lying to herself if she denied that some part of her didn't enjoy the sensation. She decided to fill the humming void with words. "Do you know why I call us the Bitch-Whores, Viktor Krill?"

"Tell me."

"For too long those two words have been used to dominate, manipulate, and degrade women. Refuse to do what men want and you're a bitch. Do what men want and you're a whore. We could never win and that's how they controlled us. I took those labels back, made them titles of power. Yes, we are bitches. Yes, we are whores. Yes, we are going to do what we want. And if you don't like it, you can sleep alone and jerk off in a sock."

"And these women follow you?"

"Most do. I offer them respect, love, and shared power. Most women, deep down, hunger for community, and I provide that. Now, of course, there are still those weak-willed girls who run to the gangs, want nothing more than to be someone's *old lady* or *passaround*. But they are *all* with me until they are officially with another." Lemaire took one more drag and snuffed out the joint in the ashtray provided. "Enough backstory. Let's talk about the future. Why do you need to use my pool on the 12th Floor?"

"Did Gideon not tell you?"

"I want to hear it from you."

Krill put out his own joint and leaned forward in his chair. "I'm introducing a new drug to Bhellum. It has the effects of Leaf, Rush, Flame, and psychedelics, and is highly addictive. Once the junkies try it, no other drug will do." Krill smiled coyly. "Except maybe pussy."

"Thanks for not putting me out of business. But why do you need the pool area?"

"The drug is called Slink, and it is not a simple chemical compound. It is a living organism."

Lemaire's eyes widened. "That shady Gideon failed to mention that. Please continue."

"As it is a living organism, it cannot be grown or created. It must be raised."

"But why does it require my pool area?"

Krill hesitated. "It would be quite complicated to explain."

Lemaire waved away the question. "Fine. Then, where did you find it?"

"That would be even more complicated. Let's just say it comes from somewhere far removed from here."

Now it was Lemaire's turn to lean forward. "And what's in it for me, Viktor Krill?"

"What do you want, Miss Lemaire?"

Lemaire put one long, white-tipped finger to her lips as she thought. She needed to ask for something significant, but didn't want to appear greedy. Partnerships built on foundations of greed usually crumbled sooner rather than later. "I want ten percent of the total take for Slink. I also want highly discounted Slink for my girls. They keep all the profits from the shit they sell."

"Done."

Laughter escaped Lemaire's lips, an expression of disbelief. "That's it? No negotiation?"

Krill shrugged. "It's a fair deal. I can't do this without your pool area, especially given that it's already in a highly secure building. And I'm going to need more than just Dead Rogues spreading Slink to the masses. Your girls are everywhere, they move between gangs and junkies like the morning fog. With that distribution, Slink will own the Muck in short order."

"Oh, my girls move farther than between gangs, Viktor Krill. They move across the whole of Bhellum, laying with corporate heads and wiping tears from council members."

"Even better."

"And you don't need to discuss this with Gideon Moon first? Last I checked, he, not Viktor Krill, was the First of the Dead Rogues."

"I've never cared much for titles. And Gideon Moon is many things, but stupid is not one of them. He knows what he sees in Slink."

"And what's that?"

"A way back to the top."

"Then we are in agreement." Lemaire rose from her chair, and her robe threatened to expose more than just her legs. Viktor Krill did well to keep his eyes up as he, too, got to his feet. They met between the chairs and shook hands. Krill tried to remove his hand but Lemaire held him tight. "I took in the Dead Rogues to amass what absurd rent money I could from them before they were ultimately eradicated. Why did you choose the Dead Rogues, Viktor Krill?"

Krill held Lemaire's amber eyes with his black orbs. "Because they were in an interesting position. Because they were allied with an interesting partner. But, mostly because it didn't fucking matter."

Lemaire smiled and released Krill's hand. "Please tell Gideon the good news of our arrangement. I'll let the girls know that the Dead Rogues have full access to the 12th Floor pool area. Please keep me posted regarding the progress of your...farm."

Krill nodded and began to walk towards the exit. At the white door, he stopped and turned back to face the black queen. "One more thing, Miss Lemaire. In short order, I will have the resources to make anyone disappear. And I mean, gone without a trace. You don't get to where you are without accruing a list of enemies. If you ever have need of this service, just let me know."

Lemaire's eyes flashed again in excitement. "Thank you, Viktor. And, please. Call me Mayfly."

8

"How go the preparations?"

"Good. Everything is ready for the farming process."

"When can we expect Slink to come pouring forth?"

"A few weeks from now, I would imagine."

"Do you have everything you need?"

"Not quite. But I will start gathering the last of what I need soon."

"Can I see the operation?"

"You cannot. Nor can anyone else. You'll have to trust me when I say it would be very dangerous. When we expand, I'll install some safety measures and maybe a viewing platform. But, for right now, instruct the guards to let no one in, except me. And that includes themselves. No peeking in unless they don't value their faces."

Gideon Moon's face twisted in a combination of revulsion, confusion, and curiosity. "Very well, Viktor. But we'll need to see results soon. Our power and resources are weakening by the day."

"Do not worry, Gideon. Our weakening ends today."

"How's that?"

"Because today is the day that I go on the hunt, the day that the Muck learns that the Dead Rogues are back. And we're fucking pissed."

———

"Something's out there."

"Where?"

Jonesy pointed a dark bony finger at the shadowy area between two neon signs that helped light up the clearing between the Brizo and Pontus Towers. "There! Man, I'm fucking sure there's someone over there."

Roderick squinted, but saw nothing in the area that Jonesy indicated. "Goddammit, Jonesy! There ain't nothing there! I told you not to smoke before guard duty. Now, I gotta be out here all night with your paranoid ass, chasing fucking paper wrappers and swinging fists at stiff breezes."

"Nah, fuck that, Roderick. I'm telling you, *something* is over there. And I need the Leaf for my eyes. Shit, you want my eyes working, don't you."

"I don't need you seeing shit that ain't there."

"Oh, something's there, all right. Look over at Pontus. Man, they got almost twenty dudes watching the main entrance. They know something, man. They *know* something. And we out here with eight measly guards. We're sitting ducks, man. Sitting. Ducks."

"Jonesy, if you don't shut the fuck…" Roderick's words were cut short as a knife flew from the shadows, its side-spinning blade cutting a neat line across the Broken Tens member's throat before burying itself in the chest of another guard positioned closer to the door. Roderick's eyes went wide as a geyser of blood issued forth from his ripped throat, covering Jonesy in the warm, sticky liquid.

Jonesy batted away Roderick's desperate hands as they reached for help and began backpedaling as the Broken Tens began firing their weapons into the neon glow of the Bhellum night. "Ahh, hell nah. I told y'all. I fucking *told* y'all." Jonesy's hand shook as he retrieved the handgun from his waistband and slapped in the extra long clip that he kept in his pocket. While the other BTs shot indiscriminately into the evening air, Jonesy knelt down and steadied himself, searching the clearing for clues of their attackers. His handgun swept back and forth as something flashed between shadowy areas, brief images of a man outlined in neon, his long hair held back in a ponytail.

Two more knives dove out of the night. One plunged into the eye of Fat Rey, who immediately collapsed dead, falling forward on the entrance steps and onto young Diego, who became trapped beneath the obese corpse. The second knife burrowed into the skull of muscled Montez, the hilt vibrating between his eyes like a tuning fork. After stumbling dumbly for several seconds, Montez teetered off the side of the landing to land in a dead heap on the grassy ground.

Jonesy's hand shook as his eyes fought with his brain, for what he was seeing certainly couldn't be possible. In the blink of an eye, four of the eight Broken Tens were gone, murdered by an assassin who fell from the darkness like a wraith. The Tens continued to fire into the night, some threatening to hit Jonesy as he knelt before them. "Hold! Hold! Stop! Stop!" Jonesy stood to his full height and held out his hands to his fellow guards. "Stop, mutha-fuckas, stop!" The gunshots finally began to slow and then stopped entirely. Jonesy ran up to the landing, joining his other partners. "Yo, this ain't getting us anywhere, man. Everyone, reload. Quick!" The sounds of clips being ejected and replaced filled the silence. "He's in the shadows between the neon. Donovan, look to the right, me and Toon will check the left. Any movement, you fire. But fucking aim this time."

Toon spoke up in a shaky voice. "We're spotlighted on this fucking land-ing. More of those goddam knives are gonna come soon."

Jonesy, his high completely gone now, tried to calm the gangsters. "He can't carry *that* many knives, man. And we got guns. Sneaky muthafucka had the element of surprise, but that shit's gone now." Jonesy's eyes wandered from shadow to shadow. Minutes passed, feeling like hours.

Movement to the right caught Jonesy's attention as a form moved slowly into the light of an orange neon sign pitching soda. "There," he called, and three guns unloaded at the dark figure. While most missed their mark, enough hit the silhouette to send it spinning in place before ultimately crashing to the ground beneath the artificial orange light.

"We got him," cried Toon, while Donovan exclaimed, "Yeah, eat that shit, fuck boy!"

"Thought you could mess with some real goons, didn't you, bitch," added Diego from beneath Fat Rey's lifeless body.

"Ok, ok," said Jonesy, trying to wrangle the men's emotions. "I'm gonna go check it out. Don't shoot me in the fucking back!" With orders given, Jonesy moved carefully towards the downed body, his gun still pointed squarely at his nemesis. After more than twenty nervous steps, Jonesy reached the body and kicked it over with his foot. Although the man was unquestionably dead, something remained amiss. His gun dropped to his side reflexively. Toon saw his reaction against the neon backdrop.

"What is it, Jonesy? Did we get him? Who is it?"

Jonesy called over his shoulder, still confounded by what he saw. "It's just some fucking Jungle junkie!" To himself, "It doesn't make sense." He spun back to the tower and began his return. "Hey, anyone knows what these junkies are taking? I mean, even Flame doesn't give you superpowers like this. It's like…"

Toon watched as Jonesy stopped mid-sentence, his mouth agape and his eyes fixated on something above them. "What is it, Jonesy?" Toon and Donovan looked up in tandem, both letting out an audible whine.

More than fifteen feet above the landing, clinging to minuscule indentations in the tower's exterior, clung a man bathed in darkness, scurrying across the flat surface like a spider. "Fuck us," said Donovan as the man fell from his perch, spinning away from the wall as he dropped.

Both BTs tried to raise their weapons, but gravity proved the quicker. The dark form's knee struck Donovan on the bridge of the nose, shattering bone and rendering the man unconscious. Toon brought his gun around, but the assassin popped up from his speedy descent with inhuman quickness and easily batted it aside. He followed the deflection with a scythe-like elbow that dislocated Toon's jaw and sent him into a deep slumber alongside Donovan.

By now, Jonesy had drawn a bead on the killer and approached with caution, moving forward with the steadied steps of military precision. "That's enough, muthafucka! I fucking got you now, man!"

Jonesy's voice was briefly lost as the killer noticed his presence and locked onto him with eyes that were black on black. "Do you now," asked the man as he slowly walked down the landing steps, kicking young Diego in the head as he passed and putting the teenager to sleep. He continued forward, and Jonesy allowed him to close the distance, hoping to minimize the chances of his bullets missing their target.

Jonesy finally spoke when the assassin was ten feet away. "That's close enough, man!" The backlit man stopped, raised his hands in surrender.

"Looks like you have me, friend. Now what?"

"Now? Now I fill you with holes and walk inside a hero. This one's for Roderick, you sick fuck!"

Jonesy pulled the trigger as quickly as he could, each shot aimed directly for the assassin's chest. The figure moved like a blur, as if he were shaking uncontrollably, but Jonesy kept firing, unloading his extra long clip into the fluttering man. Within several seconds, the gunshots had stopped, and only the metal clicking of an impotent trigger could be heard.

Tears rolled down Jonesy's face, but still, he aimed and pulled the trigger, even as the nightmare came closer, unhurt by the barrage of bullets. The man gently pushed down Jonesy's gun before wagging a finger in the gangster's face. "I think you're out of bullets, friend."

Jonesy could barely see through the tears that had shrink-wrapped his eyes. "But how?"

"What do you mean, friend?"

Jonesy pointed to the tower with a quivering finger and the man turned his head to look. Directly behind where the killer had been standing, dozens of bullet holes in a neat collection marred the tower exterior. "It's not possible, man. You're supposed to be dead." Panic drove Jonesy's words. "No man can dodge that many bullets."

"Ahh, but that's the thing, friend," said the ponytailed man as he wiped the tears from Jonesy's cheek. "I'm not a man. I'm a human. Maybe the only true human."

Jonesy fell into another fit of sobbing. "Fuck, man, who *are* you?"

Black eyes flashed before him. "I'm Viktor Krill."

"Are you gonna kill me, Viktor Krill."

"Not right now, friend. But you're going to wish that I did."

———

THE LOUD KNOCK at his door ripped Tennian, better known as Old Tens, from his troubled sleep, whisking him away from the mortar shells and drone drops of a darker time in his life. He pushed himself up with his arms. "What is it?" No response. "Enter, goddammit!"

His Second, Sonny Caddoc, cracked open the bedroom door and stuck a nervous head into the room. "Sorry to disturb you, boss."

"Again, what is it?"

"There's something you need to see, Tens."

"Can't you attend to it, Sonny? You know it takes me a while to put everything together."

Caddoc gave the look of a golden retriever that had just been scolded. "I would if I could, boss. But I think this one's gonna need your eyes."

"Where?"

"Just outside the main entrance."

"Alright, I'm coming. Meet me down there."

"Ok." Caddoc's head went halfway out before returning. "Uhh, please hurry, boss."

"Close the fucking door!"

Caddoc jumped, and moved so fast that he almost closed the door on his head. Tennian exhaled deeply once he was alone, working to control his breathing. Whatever had made Caddoc wake him this early, it must be something pretty rotten. He needed to prepare himself to see the worst.

Tennian looked over to his left and gave the dark grey metal mech legs a scowl saved for a hated spouse that you couldn't live without. He turned his body in line with the mechanized limbs, reached out, and put his left hand on the rim of the pelvic socket, fighting the urge to push the damned thing onto the floor and be done with it forever. But he couldn't be done with it, especially not today.

Tennian brought his right hand to the other side of the pelvic socket and pressed down with both hands. The oversized muscles of his arms and chest bulged as Tennian raised his abbreviated body up and over the military mech before lowering himself into the uncomfortable chamber.

With the mech legs docked in their charging station, Tennian could jostle back and forth until he found a spot that didn't shoot sharp pains up his spinal cord. Adequately settled in, he pressed a sequence of buttons into the control pad on his upper "thigh," and the socket tightened around his pelvis, filling in the areas where his legs once existed. Tennian shook violently as microscopic needles penetrated the dark skin of his lower back and fired off electric charges, connecting man to machine and melding movement signals.

After thirty seconds, the shaking transformed into trembling before ceasing entirely. A musical note rang out from the mech, informing the wearer that all necessary linkages were successful and that diagnostics were completed. Tennian closed his eyes and thought hard about his natural legs, the ones that had helped him earn countless athletic accolades in a previous life. The ones that he left behind in a war that he had wanted nothing to do with. He thought of how they felt when they churned under him, could almost feel his bare feet on the soft grass outside his childhood home.

And then he was moving, really moving. The mech legs stepped out from their docking station and took Tennian to the full-length mirror at the other end of the bedroom. Tennian breathed a sigh of relief. The first steps were always the hardest of the day, and he was glad that the link had proven effective on the first try. That was not always the case.

Tennian took a brush from a small table next to the mirror and combed back his short gray hair and full salt and pepper beard. He then reached into the closet and collected his military jacket, the black and white camouflage proving the perfect combined image of his old and new lives. He carefully put on the jacket, leaving the front buttons undone to show off his shrapnel-marred chest, and made his way for the bedroom door, the mech legs hissing and slapping as they propelled the Muck's oldest gangster forward.

The man known as Old Tens paused with his hand on the door's handle and steadied himself. As hard and loud as his metal feet were striking the hardwood floor, he feared his heart was striking his chest even harder.

———

THE FEELING of revulsion struck Tennian without warning, sending unplanned electrical signals into his mech legs. In response, the auto-turrets at the mech's knees unfolded from their storage cavities and moved back and forth across the dawn-soaked clearing, searching for targets. Several Broken Tens jumped out of the way, seeing the deadly guns make an appearance, but Old Tens wrangled them under control before any of his men were harmed.

"Sorry, boys, even the mech's a bit jumpy this morning. Can't say that I blame it."

And blame it, he didn't, especially given the grisly scene that both had just walked into. Just before Tennian, dangling from Brizo Tower, black boots hovering a foot off the ground, were four of his most trusted men, in body, but not spirit. Each had a spike driven through his forehead and into the thick concrete exterior of the tower, deep enough that the weight of each man was fully supported. Four sets of dead eyes stared accusingly at their leader, begging for explanations that would never come.

Sonny Caddoc came to stand next to Tennian, shivering in his black hoodie in the cold morning air. Tennian spoke to his Second, but kept his eyes on his dead crew. "How many were working the night guard?"

"Same as always, Tens. Eight men."

"There're only four bodies here."

"I see that, Tens."

"Where're the other four?"

"Don't know, boss. Probably around here, somewhere. I got the men searching our turf."

"Don't bother."

"Boss?"

Tennian finally faced Caddoc. "I said don't bother. It's obvious whoever did this took them alive."

Caddoc's eyes widened. "Took them? The fuck where? Why?"

"I don't know, Sonny. But it sure as shit ain't for mani-pedis and cucumber water." Tennian motioned to the hanging quartet. "In fact, I think these four boys are the lucky ones. How'd they die?"

"Gunshots, I guess. Brizo is littered with bullet holes."

"Did you look closely?"

"You know I got a weak stomach, Tens."

"Yeah, yeah. I know about your soft stomach." Tennian's mech legs moved him forward, allowing him to closely inspect his fallen soldiers. "Not guns. Knives."

"What do you mean?"

"These men weren't shot. They were sliced up. Throat slash here. Eye gone. Chest wound. All knife work."

"How the fuck did that many dudes get close enough to our boys to knife them up like that? All our dudes were packing."

"Who said it was *many* dudes?"

"Tens?"

"Never mind. Anything strange been going on lately?"

"Nothing I can think of, boss."

Tennian looked over to Pontus Tower. Although it was quite far, he could easily make out the large group of men stationed outside the tower. "What's going on over at Pontus?"

"What do you mean?"

Tennian was growing tired of his Second's daftness. "I mean, since when does the Stench Mobb need twenty men standing guard?"

"Yeah, been like that a couple of days now."

"And you didn't think anything of it?"

Caddoc shrugged. "I figured it was just some beef the Mobb had gotten into. Didn't think it had anything to do with us."

"Sonny, do you know what you do when you see all the little animals running out of the forest? Do you stand around and say, *well, that's the animals' problem?* No, you run like hell. Because a fucking monster is coming in right behind them. *You* need to tighten up, Sonny!"

The beefy man dropped his head. "Sorry, boss."

"Triple the guard. And if something is detected, retreat inside the tower and security bar all the doors."

"Really, Tens? All that just for some knife-wielding fuck boys? They caught our guys slipping. Won't happen again."

"Is that what you think, Sonny? That whoever did this is just some run-of-the-mill knife goons?"

"Yeah. Isn't it?"

Tennian shook his head in exasperation. "Do as I command. And cancel the green light on the Dead Rogues."

"Why?"

Tennian once again gestured to the hanging men. "Take a look at their hands."

Sonny walked over despite his weak stomach, his hand protecting his nose and mouth. He quickly turned over Roderick's hand before dropping it and retreating a few steps. "I don't get it."

"What did you find?"

"A green ribbon tied around his pinky."

"They all have it."

"But, what does it mean, boss?"

"It means execute the green light at your peril. It means the Dead Rogues are back in play. It means someone just released an apex predator into the Muck."

———

VIKTOR KRILL TOOK the large burlap sack off his shoulder and unceremoniously dumped it onto the polished floor. He gave it a swift kick for good measure. Mayfly Lemaire smiled sweetly, curiosity curling at the corners of her eyes.

"But, I didn't get anything for you, Viktor."

Krill smiled back. "No worries. I did come by unannounced, after all. I hope you enjoy my gift."

"Please be a doll and open it for me."

Krill reached down, undid the sack's tie, and pulled at the bottom of the bag. The young Broken Tens member Diego flopped onto the marbled floor, bound, naked, and covered in sweat and bruises. "I believe this is the miscreant that ran afoul of one of your girls?"

Lemaire's smile became a snarl as she looked upon the whimpering man. "Let us be certain." To Noora, who stood in the doorway, "Fetch Faun. And bring three others."

Noora disappeared from the bathroom and returned less than a minute later with four young girls in tow. A tiny, caramel-skinned girl with curly hair inhaled deeply when she looked at the squirming body on the floor. The other three girls spread out behind her.

Lemaire pointed at Diego. "Faun, is this the *man* that raped you?"

The young girl, eyes wide, simply nodded.

"Speak up, girl! This is grown-up business and grown-ups use words!"

Faun jumped at the verbal lashing, but responded. "That's him, Mother. That's the piece of shit that raped me." Faun's shock and fear slowly morphed into anger and rage. "That's the...mother...fucker...that choked me and laughed, *fucking laughed*, when he was on top of me!" She looked to Diego, whose eyes were now tightly closed, as if not seeing a thing made it less real. "I told you I'd find you, you piece of shit! I told you not to fuck with one of the Bitch-Whores! I told you..."

"Enough!" Lemaire's single word brought an immediate halt to Faun's tirade. Again to Diego, "Young man, you've been found guilty of damaging Mayfly Lemaire's property and being a general piece of trash not worthy of life. How do you plead?"

Diego let out muffled sounds from the floor, attempting to give some bullshit explanation through his gag.

"What's that," Lemaire asked. "Guilty, you say? Perfect. Court is adjourned. String him up."

Judgement rendered, Lemaire walked over to Krill, who was now leaning against the bathroom wall. Wearing tiny white shorts that showed off both her thick, athletic thighs and golden prosthetic, Krill couldn't help but steal a look. Lemaire caught him, but only smiled as she straightened her white cape behind her and joined Krill against the wall. From somewhere beneath the cape, she pulled out a large joint and held it up. "Celebratory spliff?"

Krill nodded his assent. As Lemaire lit the rolled Leaf, Krill watched as Noora wheeled forward a strange contraption from the side of the bathroom. It appeared to be a large white X on wheels, with white leather strappings at the four points. "What's this," he asked Lemaire as two of the larger women picked up the squealing Diego.

"Retribution, of course. Here."

Krill absently took the joint while his eyes remained locked onto the scene playing out before him. The two impressively sized women lifted Diego up while the other two, including Faun, strapped his wrists and ankles to the far ends of the X. With the cross-section of the X laying against the small of Diego's back, Krill quickly saw what was to be the young man's painful fate. "Hate to be that young man," he said through an exhalation of smoke.

"Yes, it *would* be dreadful to be a fucking rapist, wouldn't it?"

Krill could hear the edge on Lemaire's words and decided it best to remain silent. In front of him, the girls had finished binding Diego to the X and awaited Lemaire's command.

"Faun! One last time, are you sure this scrawny thing is the man that violated you?"

Faun finally took her flaming eyes from the bound man. "Yes, my queen."

"The next time you let a man take you, make sure he cuts your throat, too. Because you will not be welcome back here. The Bitch-Whores are strong women, not weak girls. Do I make myself clear? All of you?"

In unison, all the women shouted, "Yes, my queen!"

"Then, proceed." She took the joint from Krill and leaned in. "This is the good part."

Faun let out a primal scream, releasing the pain that far too many women had suffered, took two steps, and kicked Diego as hard as she could in his exposed genitals, his low-hanging balls proving the perfect target for small feet. Diego let out a suppressed scream, but had no time to reflect on the pain as another blow came, then another.

Even the iceberg that was Viktor Krill shuddered a bit as he watched Diego's scrotum swell, his sack looking as if it contained two baseballs.

"How go your plans, Viktor," asked Lemaire, and Krill was relieved for the distraction.

"Progress is being made. But the hard part is yet to come."

A loud scream escaped Diego's gag. "And your *farm?*"

"Progressing faster than anticipated, actually. The first round of Slink should be coming in the next few days."

"Don't forget our agreement, Viktor."

One of the large girls kissed Diego on the forehead before bringing her sharp knee up into his engorged testicles. "Never, Mayfly."

After several more minutes, Diego's balls had grown beyond belief, appearing as two volleyballs. Despite all four of the girls panting heavily, Faun took another run at the sentenced man. Her small foot somehow caught both testes, which exploded onto the floor in a mess of clear liquid and blood. Faun continued to scream in Diego's face, but the young man had already passed out from the pain.

Lemaire moved from the wall. "Ok, ok, enough. Get her out of here," she directed, and the two bulky girls dragged the screaming Faun away from Diego's deflated body and out through the bathroom door. "Noora, be a dear and finish this, will you?"

With that, Noora pulled a small handgun from her baggy white pants and pointed it at the Diego's lolling head. Krill interrupted. "Wait! Mayfly, if you're finished with this man, I have use of him. Alive."

"This man is sentenced to death, Viktor."

"Oh, I understand. And he's going to die. But the manner of his death could have some value to me."

"Care to elaborate?"

"Not really."

Lemaire showed her teeth again. "Very well, Viktor. Take him. And with this task complete, your debt to me is paid. Consider us simply partners now. You are no longer under me."

"How unfortunate."

"Careful, Viktor. Flattery will get you everywhere." Krill bowed deeply and went to collect Diego. Lemaire caught his arm as he passed her. "His body can't be found, Viktor."

Krill laughed aloud to a punchline that Lemaire never heard. "Oh, I wouldn't worry about that."

9

Slink hit the Muck like an atomic bomb. Almost overnight, demand for Rush and Flame plummeted as fiends found their long sought-after dragons in the new biological drug. Only Slink could provide the ups and downs, the visuals and the body hums, the array of sensations that most didn't even know that they secretly craved.

Slink not only offered more, it offered more at a much cheaper price. Slink's cost of goods sold was minimal, at least in monetary terms, allowing the Dead Rogues to almost give it away at first. Within a few days, it was rare that you could find a Jungle junkie who didn't bear the mark of the disintegrating Slink just beneath the skin of their forearms.

Non-gang violence dropped across the Muck for several reasons. First, the long-lasting, inexpensive drug saved notes, allowing users to get their fix without having to resort to savage theft. Second, Slink was not carried around for later. It was single-use and applied immediately at the dope tanks by Dead Rogue members. This further eliminated the temptation for random acts of mugging. Finally, for perhaps the first time since it had earned its undignified nickname, the Muck was happy. It was high. It had notes in its pockets and credits in its accounts. Its chowset vendors were seeing a boom in business as one of the Slink's phases caused extreme hunger. It had found the little alien organism that proved to be the answer to all its dark prayers.

That isn't to say that everyone in the Muck was happy. While those lone individuals not in a crew enjoyed a utopian existence, life became hard and frightening for the Muck's gangsters. The mysterious villain Viktor Krill was everywhere and nowhere, launching pre-dawn attacks on any and all dope tanks not controlled by the Rogues. Within a week, almost half of all dope tanks had been seized and placed under the operation of the Dead Rogues. And those foolish enough to try to retake their tanks were quickly made examples of.

When a large contingent of Stench Mobb tried to take back one of their Rush spots in the northwest corner of the Jungle, they were battered back. The Dead Rogues battled with military precision and fought from a dope tank that had been reinforced with auto-turrets and was surrounded by devilish traps to ensnare an unsuspecting aggressor. Worse still, as the Mobb was still licking its wounds from the poorly planned assault, Viktor Krill slithered into the lawn behind Pontus Tower and managed to impale ten SM members on long pikes that had been driven into the soft soil. Most had been skewered while still alive, and a few even continued to issue shallow breaths when they were discovered deep into the night. Bathed in blue neon, the entire spectacle gave off a ghostly quality.

Red Texx was one of the first on the scene. He rarely slept these days, and this evening was no different. One of his lieutenants approached. "You want me to wake Tye?"

"Tye ain't sleeping, Mell. Nobody sleeps anymore," answered Texx.

"Ok, then, you want me to go tell Tye?"

"No. You get our boys down. No one's to hang out in the lawn anymore. Not until this goddam monster is dead."

"You think this is because we tried to take back that dope tank."

"I would bet my life on it. This is a message."

"Fuck, this guy loves messages. What does this one say, Texx?"

"It says, *what's mine is mine. And pity the men who try to take what is mine.* Now get to work."

Mell didn't move, his eyes fixated on the medieval scene laid out before him. "Where do you think he gets those long metal poles, Texx?"

"How the fuck would I know?"

"You don't think he goes into the Hammers, do you? He wouldn't be that crazy, would he? That would be suicide for anyone."

Texx looked down almost sympathetically at his small friend, who didn't seem to grasp the severity of their foe. "Suicide is for the living, Mell. This thing, this Viktor Krill, I don't think he's a man."

"Then what is he, Texx?"

"I think we have a demon after us."

Mell shifted uncomfortably. "Can a demon be killed, Texx?"

"I don't know, Mell. But when Liquid Tye hears about this, I think he's gonna want to find out."

———

"THE NAME VIKTOR KRILL is everywhere. You're all anyone is talking about. It's like you're some kind of boogeyman or something."

"And much of that is because of your efforts, young Darrin."

Darrin's head dropped under the weight of the compliment. "Nothing to it."

A week prior, Krill had secretly installed Darrin as the head of one the Muck's largest toddy gangs, and the boy had risen to the occasion. Not only was he instrumental in spreading the name Viktor Krill in equal parts fact, embellishment, and fiction, but he could also gather invaluable intel on the other gangs' activities and potential reactive strategies. After all, in a war, soldiers rarely pay attention to the children at their feet.

Krill was given especially vital information on the Broken Tens, who regularly used the toddy gangs for a variety of tasks. Krill secretly thanked Tennian Stamp for highlighting the importance of the Muck's smallest gangsters.

"Anyone giving you any trouble that I should know about?"

Darrin's head flew up, his chin going high. The boy was proud of something. "This one kid named Sweats started making noise, telling others how he was gonna shoot me in the back the first chance he got."

"So, what did you do?"

"I slit his fat throat while he slept. Dude was like fifteen and too old to be in a toddy gang anyway. Immediately eliminate a threat to your person. Right, Mister Krill?"

Krill's heart swelled with a long-forgotten emotion. "That's right, young Darrin. Good job. Anything else to report?"

"Yes, sir. We've recently absorbed two other good-sized toddies. If this keeps up, I should have all the junior gangs unified under your banner in a month or so. With some more weapons, I could cut that time in half."

"Children are fearful by nature. They are small and fragile and ignorant of the world. They want to follow someone stronger than themselves. Tell you what, Darrin, I'm going to get you some battle mech. Not a lot, but enough to let all the toddies know that you are someone of importance. I'll have one of my men fit it to your small frame." Krill chuckled as an image popped into his Wakened mind. "The look on their young faces when you show up to battle Loaded. I don't think you'll find much resistance after that."

Darrin's face beamed with the smile that had taken it over. "I don't think so either, Mister Krill."

"Then it's settled. Keep it up, young Darrin. As you know, I don't handle disappointment well."

"I know, sir."

"Good, then if there's nothing else you need, you're dismissed."

"There is something else I need, sir."

"And what is that?"

"Slink. I need a shitload more Slink."

———

LIQUID TYE PACED BACK and forth in his room, clearing his mind, using the power of positive mental projection to calm his nerves. So many men. He had lost so many good men in the preceding weeks. The deaths hung heavy on his soul, stealing his ability to sleep, or relax, or eat, or even fuck. This was no way to live. He didn't scratch and claw his way out of the Jungle to live in fear. The Muck was shit, but it was *his* home, and he would be goddamned if some outside demon was just going to take it from him.

Red Texx waited patiently in the corner, biting fingernails that had long been whittled down to nothing. He had seen his First like this only a few times, always on the eve of a great gambit. "What are you gonna do, boss?"

"What do think I'm going to do, Texx?"

"I don't know, but I don't like the looks of it. *We* need you, boss. The Stench Mobb doesn't exist without Tye Nettles."

Liquid Tye paused his pacing to look over at his Second. "And what am I without all of you, Red Texx? I am nothing. And if I sit idly by as my men are picked off one by one, each meeting a grimmer fate than the man before him, then what kind of First am I? I spent my life facing my adversaries, defying the odds. I will do so again."

"So, what are you going to do?"

"That blowhard sissy Gideon Moon would like us to think that he is the mastermind of this Dead Rogue resurgence, but we all know that's bullshit. This is all because of that outsider Viktor Krill. He has the Muck gripped in fear, has hardened gangsters checking under their beds. He attacks relentlessly, and we just defend, defend, defend. Poorly, I might add. The defending stops now. I'm going on the attack."

"Ok, we're behind you, boss. What's the plan?"

Liquid Tye went over to his Second and friend, put his dark hand on the large man's giant shoulder. "No plan, Texx. I'm going at this alone."

Red Texx gave a look of disbelief, stumbled over his words. "But, but, but, boss, you can't. He's not a man, he's something else."

"And I'm Liquid Tye. I'm a boss now, but did I not come up as the Muck's greatest assassin? Viktor Krill's not the only one who can bend the neon light away from himself and make home with the shadows. Liquid Tye did it first. And Liquid Tye can still do it."

"You can't be serious."

"As serious as a gut wound. Contrary to popular belief, this Viktor Krill is just a man, a man used to being feared, a man used to hunting. But how will he fare against someone who doesn't fear him, someone who goes on the offensive?"

"Please, you *can't* be serious."

"Do I look serious, Red Texx?"

"You do, boss."

"Then, I'm ready. Hand me my old black skin suit. Let us see how the hunter Viktor Krill reacts to being hunted."

———

As usual, Viktor Krill was besieged by nightmares. The torment he endured two lifetimes ago leaked into his dreams, curdling them like vinegar on fresh milk. Images of his body being ripped apart ushered in the ghost memories of muscles and nerves exploding into their Wakened states, introducing pain he never thought imaginable. Krill tossed and turned in his sweat-drenched silk sheets, attempting in vain to run from the agony that refused to leave his side.

That pain, usually ethereal, slowly morphed into the rough form of a man, tall and slender and bathed in shadow. From that general form, an arm emerged, reaching out at Krill, as if welcoming him to a place left unsaid. Krill looked harder, and discovered that the dark arm held a dark gun, its barrel squarely aimed at Krill's exposed chest.

Krill's Wakened senses sparked to life, and his Wakened brain, even in its unconscious state, quickly put pieces together, a supercomputer running a thousand projections to derive a singular conclusion.

Someone was in his room. Someone who wanted to harm him. Viktor Krill was going to die.

Before even opening his eyes, Krill threw himself over the edge of the bed towards the window, hoping that his instincts were correct, and he chose the side opposite of his assailant. Just as he began his faster-than-possible move, silenced gunshots rang out in succession, two striking Krill in the left shoulder while the others buried themselves in the thick mattress and ornately carved wooden frame beneath. As soon as Krill hit the ground, he shouldered the giant frame up and over, taking cover behind it as more bullets were delivered, hitting the makeshift barricade.

And then there was absolute silence.

Krill's mind sped through possibilities. Had he been betrayed? Had Gideon Moon made his move much sooner than expected? Was there some variable that he forgot to account for? The different scenarios flew across Krill's brain, all quickly dismissed. All save one.

"Liquid Tye, I presume," Krill said to the heavy silence. Despite the pain in his shoulder, Krill found himself grinning from ear to ear, excited by the prospect of a worthy challenger. "Your reputation is well-earned. I must admit, I chalked up most of what I heard to Muck exaggeration and gossip. I see that I was wrong."

There was no response from the would-be assassin.

With the lone window behind him as the only source of light in the large room, Krill was effectively trapped behind the upturned bed. Any movement above or around the barrier would be perfectly backlit, ensuring a quick death from a hail of bullets. And the bed frame itself was too heavy for any man to move with any speed or force.

Unless that man was no longer a man, but a Wakened human.

Compartmentalizing the pain in his shoulder, Krill gave the mammoth bed a great shove, sending it careening across the room as if launched by an industrial machine. Krill followed right behind the speeding bed, crawling faster than any other man could run, bullets ringing into the hardwood flooring in his wake. When the bullets suddenly stopped, Krill knew that there was only one direction the man had gone. Up.

Krill immediately halted his forward momentum and rose to his feet in the blink of an eye, just as Liquid Tye was completing a near-perfect straight jump with a twist, bringing his gun arm around and back towards his target. With his left arm compromised, Krill chopped across with his right, catching Liquid Tye's right wrist just as he landed and sending the silenced handgun flying across the room. Krill followed that with a blinding backhand that struck Tye in the jaw and drove him back to crash into the large window with enough force to create cracks in the glass that spidered off in all directions.

Krill stood bare-chested and watched as his foe worked to recover from the overwhelming attack. With his perfect night vision, Krill thought to fight in the dark, but seeing the visor that adorned Liquid Tye's face, he changed his mind. "Lights," Krill said into the unlit room, and both fighters were bathed in illumination.

"Fuck," exclaimed Liquid Tye as the light assailed his night-vision goggles. He tossed off the visor in one smooth motion.

"Ahh, there you are," said Krill as he studied his nemesis. Liquid Tye was tall and lean, with sinewy muscle that could easily be seen through the black skin suit that nearly matched his dark skin. "Congratulations on getting this far. I must say, I am impressed. And that seldom happens."

"I'm delighted to have met with your approval," replied Liquid Tye, his soft, musical voice belonging somewhere beyond the grime that was the Muck.

Krill looked around the room, a perplexed look on his tanned face. "How did you get in here? Do me a professional courtesy and tell me."

Tye refused to take his light-brown eyes off his quarry, but nodded his head towards the door. "Main vent, above the door."

Krill did not pay Tye the same respect, looking away from the Stench Mobb leader to peer at the small vent. "You've got to be kidding me."

"Liquid. Tye."

Viktor Krill let out a loud laugh and slowly applauded. "Well done. You know, I could use a man like you. We don't *have* to do this. The Stench Mobb is going to fall to me sooner or later."

"You mean to Gideon Moon," cut in Liquid Tye.

Krill smiled coldly and the two killers shared in the obvious secret. "Yes, of course. Gideon Moon. Now, what do you say, Mister Nettles? Shake hands and conquer the world?"

In response, Liquid Tye lifted his right leg, showcasing perfect balance, and withdrew a wicked knife from his black boot. Viktor Krill sighed heavily, disappointment clear on his face. His scarred body tensed ever so slightly as he slowly motioned towards his assassin. "Very well, Mister Nettles. Every world has a dearth of artists such as you. This will be a shame. Have at it."

Liquid Tye barely gave Krill time to finish the last sentence before he waded in like a buzzsaw, the long blade dancing in his right hand as if he had been born holding it. Tye slashed back and forth, across, and down with calculated movements, faster than a normal eye could follow, hoping to catch a main artery along Krill's arms.

Krill retreated, dodged, and blocked, mesmerized by the skill with which Liquid Tye fought. His respect for the man grew as the strikes and combos became more complex and furious as Tye fought to break through Krill's impossibly tight defense. Sweat poured down Tye's dark face as he exerted maximum effort in killing the man that butchered his boys.

Unfortunately for Tye, Viktor Krill's face had no such sweat. Krill moved like lightning while appearing as if he were looking upon an art exhibit, pondering the meaning of the lights and darks. Liquid Tye understood then that his energy would run dry far sooner than the man he faced. If what he faced was a man, at all.

With this conclusion slapping him across the face like a wet glove, Tye pulled out his final trick. He began another crossing slash, but, midway through the swing, he launched himself forward in a stab that would either find home in Krill's chest or be caught in his viselike grip.

As expected, the latter occurred, with Viktor Krill catching Tye's wrist in both hands and stopping the blow several inches from his chest. Krill began to admonish Tye for the sloppy maneuver, but cut it short as Tye's left hand came around bearing a small knife that had been cleverly hidden somewhere within his skin suit.

Krill pushed away Tye's controlled wrist and jumped back to avoid the sneaky strike. Although he prevented a killing blow from landing, the small blade drew a neat line across Krill's collarbone. As the men separated, Krill reached up to touch the fresh wound, his fingers returning slick with blood. Krill brought the blood up to his nose and his Wakened olfactory nerves detected something sinister intertwining the usual metallic smell.

Liquid Tye's grin confirmed Krill's fears. "That's right, Krill. Consider yourself poisoned. No matter what happens between us, you'll be dead in an hour."

Krill matched Tye's grin with one of his own. "You're right, Tye. A man would be dead in an hour. But I am not a man. I am your world's first human. And this human is officially tired of you. I have given you more respect than you could ever understand. Now, let's finish this."

Tye nodded and, without warning, threw the small, poisoned blade in a tricky underhand motion, sending the knife flying towards Krill's abdomen. He moved in right behind the soaring blade, a desperate move against an unnatural foe.

If Viktor Krill had moved at the speed of sound before, he now moved at the speed of light. He spun on the ball of his right foot, his right hand plucking the poisonous knife from the air as he rotated. The world slowed as Krill continued his spin. He could feel Liquid Tye approaching from behind, his wicked knife leading the charge.

But Krill's turn was faster. So much faster.

Just as Tye thought he was going to plunge the long knife into Krill's exposed back, the back was gone, having already completed its rotation. Tye soared past the twisting Krill and felt a thump atop his head as he completed his lunge and halted his momentum.

Tye rose slowly to his full height and turned to face Viktor Krill. Gone was the small blade that had been in Krill's hand, and Liquid Tye feared where he would find the poisoned dagger. He reached up carefully and quickly withdrew his hand when he felt the hilt, sitting perfectly upright, as if growing from his dark curly hair. Liquid Tye nodded sadly and dropped his wicked knife, which stuck into the hardwood floor point-first and vibrated.

Viktor Krill approached the almost-dead Liquid Tye. "Good showing, Tye Nettles. You're the best man I've ever faced. I'll make sure you have a proper burial." Tye stared back dumbly, his punctured brain no longer able to decipher words. Krill sighed deeply. "Now, you can die." Liquid Tye collapsed, falling straight down and into himself, as if his bones were not made of the same stuff as other men.

As if he was, indeed, made of water.

VIKTOR KRILL DRAGGED the excessively limp body of Liquid Tye into the hall. The two ineffective Dead Rogue guards jumped when they saw what was being pulled from their Second's room.

"Second Krill! Are you ok? Who is this man?"

Krill dropped the body at the feet of the man who had just spoken and began to wobble as his vision began to blur. "This is Liquid Tye. Wait. Let me rephrase that. This *was* Liquid Tye. Don't look so concerned." A swift quick to the corpse was delivered. "He's quite dead." Krill placed his hand on the man's shoulder to steady himself.

"I'll take the body to Gideon Moon immediately. I'm sure he'll want to use it to make a statement."

Krill's black eyes bore into the man. "You'll do no such thing. You and Melvin are to transfer Tye's body to Pontus Tower at daybreak. He was a warrior, and deserves a proper send-off."

Melvin spoke up. "Gideon won't like that."

The rage that coursed through Krill momentarily pushed aside the effects of the poison as his hand appeared by magic at Melvin's throat. "I don't give a fuck what Gideon likes. This is *my* kill, not his. If I find out you've disobeyed me, I'll skin you both alive."

Melvin fought to speak through his compressed throat. "Of course, Second Krill."

"We'll do as you command, Second Krill."

Krill's hand dropped from Melvin's throat. His head began to spin and his legs turned to jelly beneath him. "Good. But before you do, take me somewhere safe."

Melvin and the other guard looked to each other in confusion. "Why do you need that?"

"Because I'm poisoned, you fools. And my body will soon shut down." Krill collapsed in the hallway, his head bouncing off the tiled floor with a sick thud. He kept speaking as he faded into darkness, but only Krill himself could hear the words. "Even humans can be wounded. Even gods need their rest."

———

VIKTOR KRILL'S body and mind woke long before his eyes could open. He was grateful that the memories of torn flesh receded into the background, and even more grateful for the soft, wet sponge that was being run across his body. The water was cool, and Krill could feel it lowering his dangerously high body temperature as his insides waged a silent war against the deadly poison that coursed through his veins.

Now that his mind was working again, Krill directed his attention inward, using intimate knowledge of his Wakened biology to attack the poison, gently manipulating its chemical composition and slowly rendering it innocuous. After several minutes of this quiet restructuring, Krill could feel his temperature fall and his breathing normalize. Later, once he had run internal diagnostics and determined everything to be back in order, Krill felt it safe to finally open his eyes.

His heart unexpectedly jumped as he looked up to see Mayfly Lemaire's bright amber orbs starting down at him, a wry smile painted on her ebony face. "Back among the living, I see. You should be dead, you know. That poison that Liquid Tye hit you with was enough to kill twenty men. If one of them wasn't you."

"Just lucky, I guess."

"No, I don't think so, Viktor." Lemaire's dark hands danced over his bare chest. "Yours is a body that's been torn apart and reassembled. But, to what end?"

"What's your opinion?"

"Me? I think that a man was torn apart. And something much greater than the sum of the parts was put back together. I think you're something special, Viktor. Maybe even something extraordinary. But whether that makes you a god or a demon, of that I am still very unsure."

Krill sat up and found that he was back in Lemaire's white marble bathroom, on a soft massage table that had been placed in the room's center for his comfort and care. "I would be careful throwing around labels like that. Those that really are those things could take offense."

Lemaire moved in closer. "Then tell me, what are you, Viktor Krill?"

Krill's black eyes hummed with power, awakening a part of Lemaire long left dormant. A part that she feared lost forever. "I'm just a human, Mayfly."

"We're all human, Viktor."

"No. You're not. You're men and women, barely more than the animals you consume and domesticate. Only I am human, and I paid a heavy price for the right to call myself that."

"I see." The sexual tension hung heavy in the air, threatening to suffocate both individuals, woman and human, alike.

"How did I come to be here?"

"Word of your victory spread quickly through Thoosa. I came to visit you and wasn't thrilled with the service you were receiving from those idiotic males. I don't think any of them have ever looked after anything more than their boners. Anyway, I had you brought here, where I could look after you."

"Why?"

Lemaire looked away, the first signs of shyness the powerful woman had ever exhibited. "You're my meal ticket, silly. With all the money my girls and I are making from pushing Slink and from the Rogues, I gotta protect my investment. You've created a paradigm shift in the Muck, one that's proven exceedingly profitable for me. I don't want things going back to the way they were before."

"Is that all?"

Lemaire glanced back at Krill, and a surge of invisible energy ran from his black to her amber eyes, connecting the two formidable entities. "I suppose I feel something for you, as well, Viktor. A kinship, maybe. We can be vicious and cruel. Unforgiving. But, always to an end. Maybe I'm happy to have finally met an equal in this brutal game of ours."

Krill slid off the table and stood before Lemaire, standing only a few inches taller than the imposing Bitch-Whore ruler. "Is that all?"

Lemaire turned her head to look away again. "No. We both obviously have a strong, and I mean *fucking strong*, sexual attraction for each other. But, that's neither here nor there."

Krill reached up slowly to touch Lemaire's face, gently moving her chin back towards him. "And why is that?"

The room began to heat dramatically, stealing oxygen from the space and forcing Lemaire's breaths to come in short, quick bursts. Her eyes met Krill's again, and things within her clawed their way to the forefront, demanding attention and satisfaction. "Because. I swore off men ten years ago. I made a promise to my god. One I don't intend to break."

Krill's mouth turned up at the corners. "But, I'm not a man, dear Mayfly. As I told you, I'm a human. The world's only human."

"Well, in that case..."

Lemaire's words were cut off as two mouths became one. Her heart raced and her nerves vibrated violently, threatening to tear her apart, as Krill's alien life-force mixed with her own. Her hands ran over his scarred body and his found the dress clasp at her neck. With a nimble flick of his fingers, the clasp was undone and Lemaire's white dress fell to the marbled floor, revealing her athletic body and golden prosthetic. Krill stared silently at her naked form before scooping her up effortlessly into his sinewy arms.

"And where will you be taking me?"

"The bath. I haven't been able to get our first meeting out of my mind."

Krill began carrying Lemaire towards the bathroom's rear. "Then, my trick had its desired effect. Tell me, Viktor, what's the difference between making love to a human versus a man?"

"You tell me. After you're able to speak again."

"Oh my."

10

"Y ou did what?" Gideon Moon didn't even try to hide the rage in his voice.

"I sent the body back to the Stench Mobb. He was a proper warrior. He deserves a proper send-off from his men."

"And you didn't think to confer with your First about this decision?"

"I did not."

"And why is that?"

Viktor Krill stamped down the bubble of anger that was forming in the pit of his stomach, threatening to pop and transform into physical violence. Viktor Krill was not used to explaining himself to this degree. "Because it had nothing to do with you. This was a personal fight between two professionals. The corpse will be treated with the same professionalism."

Moon stood behind his desk, his knuckles white on the ornate table. "And you didn't stop to think that we could better utilize the dead body of one of our greatest enemies?"

"Better utilize how?"

"Don't be obtuse, Viktor! You're anything but. We could have made a statement. We could have used it to crush the Stench Mobb under our combat boots. We could have made them see the futility in fighting the Dead Rogues. We could have expedited and eased the absorption process."

"I won't need Liquid Tye's body to do that. In fact, I believe it will be just the opposite. This gesture is one of future partnership, not future enslavement. If the Stench Mobb know that they're going to receive a fair shake from the Dead Rogues, then any foolish thoughts of resistance will be swept aside. They're leaderless. They have inferior product. And don't think that they haven't noticed that they've been having their asses handed to them, as of late. The Stench Mobb is ready to topple under our control. Now, they just need a little shove."

"And who is going to provide that shove... *Second* Krill?"

There it is, thought Krill. The seeds of resentment that would germinate and grow into traitorous action. He smiled at the anticipated misstep before answering. "I assumed that you would, First Moon."

"Ahh, yes. Prance me out there before my enemy to be cut down by a sniper's cold, distant touch? I don't think so, Viktor. You're the one that wants to embrace our adversaries as friends, kiss them softly on the cheek and whisper sweet words in their ears."

"We'll need more men before we can compete with the Chrome Butchers. The Stench Mobb *are* more men. Obliterating them or pressing them into reluctant servitude gets us no closer to our end goal."

Gideon Moon spun slowly to face the wall, turning his back on his Second. "Very well, Viktor. Since you've robbed me of my preferred strategy, it's up to you to execute yours." A dramatic pause followed. Krill almost laughed aloud. "But know this. No tears will be shed if you lean in for a hug and receive a Stench Mobb shiv in your side for your troubles." Another pause. "You have done much for the club, Viktor. But no one is irreplaceable. The ground of the Muck is littered with the bones of men who thought themselves invaluable. Do you understand what I am saying?" With no response, Gideon Moon spun back, only to find no one standing across the table from him.

"Uh, he left, Gideon." Stoner stood to the side uncomfortably, as if afraid of delivering the news. But Moon thought he heard something beneath those words, hovering within the discomfort of his previous Second.

He couldn't be positive, but Gideon Moon thought he detected laughter hidden in Stoner's voice. Laughter at the man who merely *thought* himself King.

As EXPECTED, Pontus Tower was on high alert with the discovery of Liquid Tye's body laid out peacefully in front of the Stench Mobb stronghold. A crowd of heavily armed, grey-clad gangsters stood before the tower's entrance, ready to take their grief out on anyone foolish enough to wander within their collective eyeshot. Above the gathered thugs, men filled each window facing the Jungle, their fingers tapping impatiently on cold triggers, desperate to rain bullets down upon their enemies.

Viktor Krill watched the scene unfold from the edge of the Jungle, his Wakened eyes picking up every threat and measuring every potential risk. Levi Lessons stirred nervously next to him, Von's face swinging grossly from his belt. "Looks like they're preparing for war, Second Krill."

"Not quite, Levi. They're preparing for an assault. They think the Dead Rogues are going to sweep in and eradicate them. They're preparing to die."

"So, when do we attack?"

"We don't."

"I don't get it."

"Of course, you don't." Krill said the words more to himself than to his simple-minded lackey. "I'm going to speak with them."

Levi's eyes went wide. "You're gonna what? You're definitely crazy, but you never struck me as suicidal." He shuffled awkwardly from one foot to the other. "You need me to go with you?"

Krill's black eyes rolled in his head. "No, Levi, that's quite all right. Plus, I don't think they'd appreciate you wearing their friend's face around your waist."

"Me? You're the one that's butchered like ten of their crew, including their beloved First. Yours is the face that is gonna set them off the most."

"Nevertheless, I am going."

"I wouldn't if I were you."

Viktor Krill stared hard at Levi Lessons, who shrunk under his Second's dark gaze. "And that is why when I am wearing a crown, you'll still be wearing that face that I gave you." And with that, Krill marched off, leaving Levi at the Jungle's edge to later tell the tale of Viktor Krill staring down a small army.

———

RED TEXX TIGHTENED his grip on his compact automatic, a gun model nick-named the Stutter. He looked down and saw that his chewed-up nails were still black with dark soil from burying his dear friend and leader earlier that morning. Fat Brian readjusted his own gun before leaning in to speak with his Second. "When do you think they're gonna come for us, Texx? You think they're gonna bring everyone? Or you think they're just gonna slowly pick us off? Oh man, you think they're just gonna fuck with us for a while? Oh man, that would suck. Why would they do that? That doesn't seem very gangster. You think they're..."

"Will you shut the fuck up?!" Fat Brian jumped back from Red Texx's uncharacteristic outburst. "I don't know any more than you do. Nobody knows nothing." Just as he finished snapping at his overweight subordinate, Red Texx saw movement near the Jungle. The large man squinted at the singular form that was making a beeline for Pontus and felt the pain in his hand as he tightened even harder on the Stutter. "But, we may soon have answers."

"What do you see?"

"Silence, you fat turd!"

The figure grew clearer as it approached, and the whispers began as a dark ponytail came into view a hundred yards away. Someone from behind

Red Texx whispered to him. "I think that's fucking Viktor Krill, boss. The fucking balls on this fucking guy."

When Viktor Krill got within fifty yards of the Pontus Tower entrance, the collective sound of a hundred guns being raised, cocked, and aimed echoed throughout the clearing. In the face of this impressive show of force, Viktor Krill kept stalking forward.

A voice shouted down from a third floor window shattered the heavy silence. "Want us to light him up, Texx?"

Red Texx answered immediately, intrigued by the lone visitor. "No! Everyone hold! It might be a trap!" On came the Muck's most notorious outsider, his pace never changing despite the arsenal pointed at his chest. When Krill was no more than twenty yards away, Red Texx finally spoke up. "Viktor Krill, I presume! That's far enough! I hear you can dodge bullets, but I doubt you can dodge a volley such as this."

Krill stopped at Red Texx's words, and even managed a slight bow at the orders. "I freely admit it. Should you all open up on me, there will be one less villain in the Muck this evening."

"Then, tell me why we shouldn't. Give me a reason not to avenge my friend and leader Liquid Tye."

"*Avenge* would infer that I had wronged him somehow. I most certainly did not. He came at me, not me at him. And he was goddam good, too. Maybe the best I'll ever encounter. It was a fair battle between professional killers. I just happen to be the best. But he had no way of knowing that."

"I still haven't heard a reason for not having you cut down here and now."

Viktor Krill stood in silence, dragging his black eyes across each and every Stench Mobb member gathered. In turn, each man felt his will wither a bit as Krill's black orbs met their own brown, blue, and green. "But don't you all see?"

Red Texx tired of word games as his Stutter began to feel heavy in his large hands. "See what, you bastard?!"

"I'm the only thing standing between the Stench Mobb and total annihilation."

"You lie! You have single-handedly brought forth our downfall."

Krill laughed lightly. "That may be true. But *right now*, at this moment, I'm the only hope you've got."

"Explain yourself. And fast. These guns are getting heavy and our fingers grow itchy."

"Gideon Moon remembers how the Stench Mobb played an integral role in the fall of the Dead Rogues. He still hears the taunts you all delivered as the Rogues were forced from Hydrus Tower. He still rages over the laughter he heard as he and his men carried their belongings like vagabonds into Thoosa and the embarrassing protection of the Bitch-Whores. Gideon Moon remembers. And he wants vengeance."

"What exactly does he want?"

"He wants you all to disappear. Total eradication. He wants the Stench Mobb to become a faint memory that will fade away completely by the time today's toddies become full-on gangsters."

"And you disagree with your First?"

"I do."

"And why is that?"

"Because he is being emotional." Stifled giggling could be heard dancing through the Stench Mobb ranks, for all knew of Gideon Moon's sexual preferences. "And I am being practical. I'll be honest, the earth could open up right now and swallow up Pontus Tower, and all of you with it, and my heart wouldn't skip a beat." Staring into Krill's black eyes, Red Texx did not doubt the man's words. "But, what a waste. Let's look at the facts. The Dead Rogues aim to control the Muck. To accomplish that, they have to go head-to-head with the Chrome Butchers, who obviously are being backed by someone on high. The Dead Rogues don't have enough men to accomplish this feat."

"Even with the great Viktor Krill?"

"Even with the very practical Viktor Krill. So, the Dead Rogues need more men. The Stench Mobb need a new leader. Seems simple math to me."

"And if we refuse your offer?"

"Gideon Moon will sweep in with every resource we have available, which, as you know, has grown considerable in recent months. The other crews, sensing your weakness, will join the fight, happy to satiate their bloodlust and collect what scraps are left after your extinction. We'd still be missing men, and you'd be food for the carrion. I'd say a fairly shitty deal all around."

"And we can trust Gideon Moon's word? Since we're being so honest, I have to say, I've met your First before and didn't care for the old queen."

Viktor Krill's open laugh caught Texx off-guard and reminded the large man that it was, indeed, a person he was speaking with and not a demon. "I understand completely. But jobs are jobs, are they not? No one likes their boss."

"I did."

"Fair enough. If you won't follow Gideon Moon, then follow me. I'll conquer the Muck with or without the Stench Mobb."

Red Texx had so many questions, especially regarding the relationship between Gideon Moon and Viktor Krill. But those were sharp questions, with edges that would slice open wrists and throats, so he kept them to himself. "So, now what? How do we proceed?"

"Do you need time to talk it over with your men?"

Again, a voice rang down from the third floor. "Red Texx speaks for all of us. Where he goes, we go."

Krill nodded. "Very well. A simple handshake should suffice. And you'll need to cast aside your greys. By all means, keep the track suits, but switch them up for the black and white variety. What do you say?"

Red Texx only needed a moment of consideration. After all, what were his options? He could either ride a godlike outsider to the heights of the Muck, or watch as each of his men ate bullets and knives over the following weeks. Texx walked halfway to Viktor Krill and stopped. Standing between the dangerous outsider and his men, he took off his grey track top and laid it carefully on the ground. He then reached into his pocket, took out a small vial, and poured its contents onto the top.

"Do you always carry gasoline," asked Krill, understanding what Texx was about to do.

"It's oil for my hair."

Krill looked upon the giant man's large red afro and nodded. "I see."

Texx then took a gold lighter from another pocket, lit it with a flick of his wrist, and dropped it onto the symbol that very recently represented the Stench Mobb. Flames leapt up from the garment, and Red Texx faced his men. "What do you say, boys? Mob up with the Dead Rogues and take over the world? Liquid Tye would've wanted it this way." In response, the Stench Mobb finally lowered their weapons and let out a unified cheer, delighted to discover that they wouldn't die this day or, seemingly, in the near future.

Red Texx turned back and walked the remaining distance to Viktor Krill. He extended his beefy hand to the dangerous man, who took it in his scarred palm. "Red Texx, at your service, Second Krill."

"Good to have you. I want you to know, I offered Tye Nettles a place at the table. He obviously turned me down."

"Yeah, old Tye was never good at being number two. It was first place or last for him. But I don't have that problem."

"Good. Because if I ever doubt your loyalty, I won't hesitate to remove that fat head from your broad shoulders."

"And I would never follow you if I thought you would do otherwise."

"Then we are at an accord."

"We are."

Behind the two leaders, Stench Mobb members tossed their grey tops into piles and lit them on fire, signaling the rest of the Muck that a monumental deal had just been reached. The Dead Rogues had just doubled in number, and they wanted the world to know it.

No one paid closer attention than Chrome Butcher leader Sigman Prime, who watched the entire spectacle play out from atop Triton Tower, staring out from military-grade binocular lenses. As he mindlessly petted the dark red cat that had crawled onto his lap, one thought ran through the genius's hyper-focused mind.

It might be time to inform Cyrus Bhellum V that he had a problem.

———

IN SHORT ORDER, the Muck became dominated by the black and white of the Dead Rogues and the gleaming metal MCEs of the loaded Chrome Butchers. A veritable Cold War settled in, dragging the Muck into an uncomfortable staring contest between two titans.

Luckily, most things naturally fell towards one side or the other without bloodshed. With Slink being far more profitable than other drugs, the Chrome Butchers were left alone to consolidate Rush, Flame, and even Flea under one banner. While Slink dominated fiend use, many still longed for the one-note sensation that the old guard of drugs could provide. This meant that both crews remained profitable. And profitability often kept open hostility at bay.

The Broken Tens managed to keep their stranglehold on Leaf, that most pervasive of illegal substances that crept into the city by a network of couriers rather than through the Bhellum Port. With the Dead Rogues now controlling Thoosa and Pontus Towers while the Chrome Butchers occupied Triton and Hydrus, standard belief was that Brizo Tower was soon to fall. Fortunately for Tennian Stamp, however, the behemoth gangs of the Muck had grown hesitant to take their eyes off each other, as a full-on assault of Brizo would leave one crew open for attack from the other.

And, thus, an unusual time of peace blanketed the Muck, save the usual squabbles between fiends, smalltime thieves, and upstart toddy gangs. If the name of Viktor Krill rang out before, it now dominated every conversation. Word of the outsider Krill staring down the entire Stench Mobb spread like wildfire, becoming more outlandish and violent on each retelling.

His reputation truly preceding him, Viktor Krill wandered the Muck like a phantom — unbothered, untethered, and feared. Krill regularly crossed from Thoosa to Pontus alone and, seemingly, unarmed, as if daring someone to test the tales of his killing ability. Some days, Krill and his young protégé Darrin could be found making the Jungle rounds, visiting the dope tanks under Dead Rogues control and steering clear of Chrome Butcher territory.

Each dope tank had its issues that needed correcting, and Darrin watched intently as Krill stamped out each problem as easily as a still-smoking, discarded cigarette butt. Many dope tanks had the same complaint, one that Viktor Krill was quick to snuff out.

"You see what this fucking Blister did to Rexter, Second Krill? He's gonna lose that eye for sure."

"And what did Rexter say to this Blister?"

"Nothing, I swear." Krill did not speak, but simply continued to shine his dark eyes on the dope tank Honcho named Greeny. He could feel the small man begin to sweat under his black and white track suit. "I mean, he may have made a comment about the thing's giant dick, but, I mean, it was hard not to notice, the way it was shoved into those raggedy ass pants it was wearing."

"Then Rexter is lucky that he just lost an eye. Consider it a warning for the future. The Blisters are sensitive, especially about their mutations. I suggest you and everyone else take note. Pay them what they're owed and allow them to be on their way."

"I don't understand why we still have to pay those freaks. The Dead Rogues are stronger than ever. If it was up to me..."

No one would ever find out what Greeny would do if *it* were up to him. Krill's arm shot out like a viper strike, ripping the Honcho's throat out and returning with a handful of gore. "I'm sorry, Greeny, you lost me there for a second. What was it that you would do? You know, if you had my job?" Greeny could only offer bubbling sounds and a whimper in response to Krill's questions. "Ahh, you've reconsidered your position? That's wonderful news, Greeny. You may die now."

Dismissed by his Second, Honcho Greeny fell to the dope tank floor and passed into the afterlife, leaving only a stain on the concrete by which to be remembered. Krill searched the shocked faces in the dope tank. "Now, who is Rexter?"

A large, stocky man got up from a cot in the back and approached Krill. Half of his head was wrapped in white gauze, stained deep red where his left eye would have been had he been able to keep his thoughts from hitting his tongue. "I'm Rexter, Second Krill."

"You're Honcho Rexter now." Krill pointed at Rexter's damaged eye.

"You see, gleams of sunlight can appear on even the cloudiest of days. Your first order of business, Honcho Rexter..." Krill placed Greeny's throat in Rexter's shaking hand. "Clean up this mess. Let's go, young Darrin."

Krill and Darrin began to exit the dope tank, but just as they approached the opening, Krill called over his shoulder. "Oh, and Honcho Rexter, when the Blisters return next week...?"

Rexter stumbled for the words, stuttered them out when they were found. "I, I, I'll have their money ready and be, be, be respectful."

"And your comments...?"

"Kept to myself, Second Krill."

"Good boy."

————

WHEN MENTOR and protégé had put the dope tank behind them, Krill broke the silence. "You understand why I did that, young Darrin?"

"Of course," answered Darrin, who walked quickly to keep up with Krill's longer stride. "Any hint of betrayal, whether real, imagined, or slip of the tongue, must be dealt with immediately and viciously."

"Good boy."

"But..." There was hesitation in Darrin's voice.

"Speak freely, young Darrin. You are not one of these embryonic *humans* that only understand the whip." Still no words came from the boy. "I promise not to get upset."

"I thought Greeny's question was a valid one. Why *do* we still pay the Blisters? Surely, the Rogues are strong enough to end the extortion."

"I did not kill him for the question. I killed him for his fantasy."

"His fantasy?"

"His fantasy of being in charge. Those fantasies become plans which become actions. And those actions are called betrayal."

"I see."

"But you're right, it *is* a good question. Let me counter with a question of my own. How many Blisters are there?"

Darrin looked down as he walked, as if searching for an answer amidst the broken cobble. "No idea. Can't be that many. I've only ever seen a few together at the same time."

"Maybe that's what they want you to think, hmm?"

"Maybe."

"Well, let me tell you, young Darrin, unlike these other cowards who claim to be Muck villains, I've actually visited the Hammers."

Darrin almost tripped, but showed good balance in catching himself. "You have? Why? That's crazy."

"A good leader knows not only the lay of his land, but of the surrounding lands, as well. Plus, I needed some scrap metal for a few projects I was working on."

"What did you see there?"

"Blisters, young Darrin. Vast numbers of Blisters. Each more unique and twisted than the next. The poisons in which they have been immersed for multiple generations have morphed them into something no longer human. And that makes them dangerous."

"Why? Every Blister that I've seen looks all kinds of fucked up. Seems like it would be easy to take advantage of their open wounds and gnarly bodies."

"An easy assumption to make, my young protégé. And a mistake to be forgiven given your lack of years and experience. But know this, when something critical is taken from a man, something else entirely must fill that void. And, oftentimes, what fills that void is the stuff of nightmares."

"And what do you think fills their void, Mister Krill?"

"Power, young Darrin. Raw, unadulterated power, and a rage that few can comprehend."

"Then, they're more formidable than anyone knows."

"I think some of the Muck's leaders must suspect it. That's why they've all agreed to let sleeping wolves slumber."

Darrin kicked a rock as he walked, a boyish gesture that tickled a memory buried deep within Viktor Krill. "Well, a part of me is happy that the Blisters got something for their pain. Must really suck being a Blister."

Krill looked down at his protégé and admired the boy. For one who had seen so much death in his young time on this world, Krill was impressed with the boy's ability to maintain empathy for others.

"That's the yin and yang of life, young Darrin. Things are taken and other things are awarded. Things are given and other things are stolen. It's the Great Balance. Better get used to it."

"And what about you, Mister Krill?"

"What about me?"

"You have powers no one has ever seen before. Something must have been stolen from you."

Viktor Krill walked in silence for a moment, pondering Darrin's insightful question. It caught him off-guard, forcing him to consider things he preferred to leave in the chilly recesses of his mind. "I thought it had taken my ability to care for others. But I'm not so sure about that anymore." Krill was speaking more to himself than to his sidekick. "So, maybe something else entirely has been stolen..."

Both Krill's words and his thoughts were cut short as a young girl came tearing out from the Jungle's thick, unkempt gardens to fall face-first into the path's four-way intersection just ahead. Her head made a sickening sound as it slammed against the stones beneath. When she rose on unsteady, bare feet, wearing only dirty shorts and a grimy t-shirt, her mouth was covered in blood that was pouring forth from a ripped upper lip. The dark-skinned Asian girl's eyes went wide when she saw Krill and Darrin standing a few dozen feet away, and she darted down the path to the pair's left, stumbling the entire way with an obvious concussion.

"Well, that's something you don't see in the Jungle every..." Before Krill could complete his sentence, a group of eight men dressed in white from head to toe, including ventilated white face masks and gloves, came racing into the intersection from the right. Darrin reflexively reached for the small gun tucked into his waistband as Krill put his arm in front of the boy. The group spotted Krill and Darrin, but paid them no mind, increasing their efforts down the left path.

"After the girl, for sure," said Darrin, a twinge of pity in his pubescent voice.

"But, who are they?"

"Those are the Harvesters. You know, organ thieves. Biggest pieces of shit in the Muck, and that's saying a lot."

"Why have I never seen them?"

"They usually don't come into the Jungle. Mostly, they just pick off loners along the coast or transients on the Muck's fringe. They operate throughout Bhellum, but, obviously, the easiest pickings are around here. Must be a special order if they're chasing someone this far inward."

Something in the young girl's terrified eyes flicked a switch in Viktor Krill, the one that changed him from dangerous human to demon. "Come, let's see what these Harvesters are about."

Krill took off to follow the men with Darrin in tow. Fifty yards later, the sounds of a skirmish could be heard down a small path to the right. As Krill and Darrin rounded a corner, Krill put his hand out. "Wait here." He snuck forward, anxious to watch the scene unfold.

The white-clad Harvesters had chased the girl down the small side path and now had her trapped. Her escape was barred on three sides by slabs of stone, concrete, and marble that had been stacked up to form a dead end that had probably been utilized by countless predators over the years. It seemed the girl was not only poor, but unlucky, to boot.

She turned to face her assailants, tears streaming down to form rivers of cleanliness on an otherwise filthy face. One of the men strode forward. "It's easier if you don't fight." Although the words were meant to convey comfort, only cruelty could be detected in the man's voice.

In response, the young girl put her hands to her tear-soaked face, hiding from the big world in her tiny palms. Krill felt a twinge of disappointment in the girl for giving up so easily. The lead Harvester, thinking the battle over, directed his men. "Doon! Bring the tools. Yakob! The icer."

Two men moved up, one carrying a small case and the other holding a medium-sized cooler. The lead Harvester closed the distance between himself and the girl, and took her by the arm before speaking to his men again. "Let's get this over with. We shouldn't be in the Jungle this…"

As he was voicing his concern, the young girl spun in his grasp and kicked out as hard as she could with her left leg, catching her captor square in the testicles and forcing him to belt out a loud curse before dropping to his knees. As soon as the Harvester was face-height with the girl, she raked her long nails across his face. When he reflexively reached for his scratched face with a gloved hand, the girl leaned forward and bit off the top portion of his left ear, spitting it in his masked face before finally breaking loose of his grip.

The other seven men swarmed the small girl, but she fought valiantly, spinning on bare feet and launching knees, fists, and elbows at vulnerable groins. One man who grabbed her neck lost a chunk of forearm flesh for his efforts. Krill, spying from the background, could feel himself grinning ear to ear, delighted by the moxie being displayed by the young victim. Eventually, however, the numbers proved too much for the girl.

After almost a minute of fighting, four Harvesters had gained control of the girl's arms and legs, and were holding her flat against the ground. The lead Harvester, enraged by the girl's unwillingness to surrender her body, screamed orders at his men as he collected the small case from where it was dropped on the broken ground. "Hold the bitch down!" He took a scalpel from the case and marched towards the overwhelmed girl. "I was gonna make it clean. Now, I'm gonna make sure you can't even sell that pussy of yours to a Blister!"

Krill had seen enough. He moved forward in silence, coming up behind the two Harvesters who had chosen to hold back to enjoy the scene from afar. Krill stopped just behind the men, looked down to see one of them fondling himself through his white linen pants. "Gentlemen." The pair turned quickly to face the intruder, and Krill grabbed each behind the head as they did. Unleashing a rage that had built to a crescendo over the past few minutes, Krill slammed the two faces together and grinned in delight as their heads exploded like two ripe melons.

The grotesque noise stopped the remaining Harvesters in their tracks, including the lead man, who was leaning over the young girl's face. Krill, now having their undivided attention, addressed the group. "Gentlemen. Looks like you have need of some blade work. Please. Allow me to lend my expertise." With that, knives appeared in Viktor Krill's hands and were immediately launched. One caught the Harvester holding the cooler in the throat and the second buried itself into the eye of the man sitting atop one of the girl's legs.

As the mortally wounded Harvesters fell, their leader spoke. "You dumb sonovabitch, this is a special order from the top!"

Krill strode forward, soaking in those most precious moments before extreme violence. "That's funny, I *am* the top. And I don't recall ordering young girl parts."

The leader looked to his men, did the math quickly in his head as he planted his knee into the girl's chest. "What are you fuckers staring at? Kill this fucking guy!"

One Harvester ran directly at Krill, having pulled a short blade from his boot. Krill caved in his chest with a lightning-fast front kick, immediately stopping the man's cold heart. Another Harvester charged in right behind his comrade, and had his larynx crushed by the blade of Krill's right hand after it had deflected the man's sloppy overhand right milliseconds before. The Harvester fell to the ground, all attention now aimed at drawing breath through a broken straw.

Krill stepped over the man and moved to engage the other two Harvester underlings, who had risen from the girl. Just as he began to engage with the men, gunshots rang out in the dead end, and bullets struck the men facing Krill. One was struck in the heart and died instantly while the other took shots to both his left and right shoulders.

Krill spun angrily to see Darrin standing behind him, his small gun issuing smoke from its barrel. "Dammit, Darrin, did it *look* like I needed help?"

"It wasn't to help you, Mister Krill. Fucking Harvesters tried to take my kidneys last years. I still got the scars to prove it."

Krill sighed, unable to fault a person for their desired revenge. A meek voice stole his attention back towards the dead end. "What is it you want? Split the profits? No problem!"

Krill turned back to see that the lead Harvester had gotten off the young girl and backed himself against the makeshift barrier. Krill stalked towards the man. He looked down as he passed the young girl, who remained on the ground, frozen in a state of terror. High on her right cheek was a neat slice where the Harvester had begun the process of removing her eyes. Krill's mind flew back to his friend Sammie Tott, who had her eyes stolen in the Muck decades prior. "You can get up now, girl."

As if Krill had entered an action code, the girl flipped onto her stomach and crawled out of the way. Krill turned his black eyes onto the head Harvester. "Do you know who I am, Harvester?" The man shook his head dumbly. "I'm Viktor Krill."

Although Krill's appearance didn't register, the name certainly did. The Harvester's face blanched, the upper skin of his face matching the white mask that covered its lower half. "Viktor Krill? Shit, man, we didn't mean any disrespect." He threw down his scalpel and held up his hands, as if the gesture would save his life. "Order came from above. Some Hiso needs eyes, like now."

Krill turned his head to speak to Darrin. "Hiso?"

"High society type," said Darrin, and spit on the ground for good measure.

Back to the Harvester. "And who do you work for?"

Confusion crossed the desperate Harvester's face. "Sigman Prime, of course."

Krill began moving forward again. "Of course. Well, I'm certainly not one to keep a *Hiso* from their new eyes." As he finished the sentence, Krill closed the distance on the cornered man. Krill's hands shot forward and his thumbs buried themselves deep into the Harvester's skull. The man shook violently at the ends of Krill's hands before becoming deathly still. Krill retracted his thumbs and let the vile man fall. He could hear Darrin shuffle up next to him.

"I don't think anyone's going to be able to use those eyes, Mister Krill."

"What a shame."

A shuffling sound followed by a grunt forced Krill and Darrin to turn around. The Harvester that Darrin had shot in the shoulders had climbed to his feet. He began to stumble away, but froze at Krill's voice.

"You! Come here."

The man, his face twisting in pain, turned back and walked towards Krill. "Yes, sir?"

"Tell your Harvester bosses that they don't work for Sigman Prime anymore. If you want to keep working, you work for Viktor Krill and the Dead Rogues. And there's some definite new rules that you'll have to abide by. To learn these rules, send a representative to visit me at Thoosa Tower. If one of you doesn't come to meet me in three days, I'll assume you have ignored my order and declared war. At that time, I will begin my hunt. And the Harvesters will become the harvested. Am I clear?"

There was no hesitation. "Crystal, sir."

"Good boy. Now, fuck off." As the man turned to go, a gurgling noise filled the area, emanating from the Harvester with the collapsed larynx. "Wait." The man stopped and faced Krill once more. "I wouldn't want you to chalk this entire trip up as a loss." Krill walked towards the choking Harvester, scooping up the cooler as he moved. When he reached the downed man, Krill knelt and drove his hand into the Harvester's right side. The white-clad man tried to scream, but his crushed throat only allowed a lame wheeze to escape. Krill reached up and dug around in the man for a moment before quickly withdrawing his arm, his right hand holding a perfectly fresh liver. Krill deposited the liver into the open cooler and closed the lid. He returned to the lone surviving Harvester and handed him the blood-covered container.

"Something to give one of your alky Hisos. Consider it a gesture of good faith. And, now, you can really fuck off."

The lone Harvester scampered away, his white attire soiled by the twin gunshots decorating his shoulders. Darrin cleared his throat next to Krill. "Uhh, Mister Krill."

Krill watched as the wretched man made his escape. "Yes, Darrin."

"What about her?"

Krill looked over and found that the young girl had moved to the far-right side of the cul-de-sac and was sitting on the hard ground with her knees pulled up to her face. He walked over the frightened girl. "What's your name, girl?"

"Natthi," she said, her voice coming from between her bony knees.

"Well, Natthi, you showed some real heart today. Would you like to come with young Darrin and myself? Warm food. Hot showers. Any of this sound good?"

"You're Viktor Krill."

"I am."

"You're supposed to be the devil."

"False information, I assure you. I've met the devil, and it wasn't in front of a mirror. So, what do you say?"

Darrin put out a hand for the young girl. "It's ok, he only looks scary."

The girl hesitated, but took Darrin's hand and rose to her bare feet. "Ok, but if you try to hurt me, I'll kill you."

Krill smiled, but turned back towards the main path before the children could see it. "I believe you. Now let's go."

11

"And who might this beautiful girl be?"

Although concern and surprise touched Mayfly Lemaire's eyes, only kindness could be heard in her voice as she spoke to the grime-covered young girl who stood before her, dirtying her plush white carpets. The small girl remained silent, her eyes staring at something deep within the carpet's fibers, her clothes almost falling off her skeletal frame.

"Tell her your name, girl."

Although she did not raise her head, she answered. "Natthi, ma'am."

Lemaire walked over to stand before Natthi, towering over the tiny Asian girl, and sweetly lifted her small chin with a dark hand. "Women must look a person directly in the eyes when speaking. We don't show fear, and we are confident in our self-worth. Do you understand me?"

"I'm not afraid, ma'am."

Krill jumped in without invitation. "This one's not afraid of anything. You should have seen her out there. A tiny killer, this one."

Lemaire's head spun to face Krill, her eyes cutting him with their annoyance. "Was I talking to you?" Krill almost laughed aloud at the surprising rage, but simply raised both hands in surrender. Lemaire went back to Natthi. "I'm glad you're not afraid. You're safe now. Would you like to get cleaned up and put on some new clothes?" Natthi nodded. "Women use words to speak, especially to other women who are showing them kindness."

"Yes, ma'am. I would like that."

"Well, all right then. Noora!" The small albino stepped forward, responding to her mistress. "Please take young Natthi here and get her cleaned up. Also, get her some fresh clothes and begin her training."

"No." The word came out of Viktor Krill before he had a chance to wrangle it in. Lemaire, Noora, and Natthi all turned to regard the Muck's most notorious gangster.

"What's the matter, Viktor," asked Lemaire, genuinely confused.

"I don't want her trained as a Bitch-Whore. I'll handle her training."

Lemaire's confusion became genuine bemusement. "Will you now?" She and Noora shared a silent laugh. "Viktor Krill, father of the year?"

Krill could feel his face begin to flush, an uncomfortable feeling that was foreign to the scarred killer. "Nothing like that, but I'll train her in my way. You can't teach what she already has. I want to build on that."

"And what does she have?"

"No hesitancy in the face of death."

Lemaire thought for a moment. "Very well. Noora, that won't stop us from treating young Natthi like one of our own, will it?"

"Not at all, my queen."

"Good, then enjoy your bath." Lemaire nodded and Noora began to whisk the small girl away. Natthi stopped her, however, looked over at Krill with sad, questioning eyes.

"It's ok, young Natthi," said Krill, kneeling to meet her level. "Miss Lemaire and Noora here are my friends. They'll take good care of you."

"Promise?" A hint of desperation underlined the girl's single word.

"I promise. If anything happens to you, I'll sink this fucking place into the ground. Deal?"

"If they try to sell me, I'm going to kill your friends."

Lemaire and Noora's eyes went wide from the diminutive girl's serious promise, but Krill only smiled. "Deal. Deal?" He put out a hand caked in dried blood from extracting a liver. Lemaire scowled. Natthi ignored the blood, took the bloody hand in her own and shook it. Krill rose to his feet. "Then I think we're settled here. Natthi, I have work to take care of, but I'll check in on you later."

"When do I learn to kill people like you?"

Lemaire scowled again, but remained quiet. "Soon, my young protégé. By the time your head is another foot from the ground, you'll be something this world has never seen."

Natthi beamed from ear to ear, the first smile Krill had seen from the girl, and allowed Noora to take her from Lemaire's office. When the door closed, Lemaire turned her attention on Krill.

"And where in the world did you find that one," she asked as she took a silver cigarette case from her pocket. She took out a cigarette as she spoke and lit it with her gold lighter. "I didn't figure you one for collecting strays, but here you are, now with two." She took two drags and handed the cigarette to Krill, who readily accepted.

Krill inhaled, responded through a plume of smoke. "First, I don't collect strays. I collect talent. Second, I found her in the Jungle. She was being chased by a group of Harvesters. Special order for young eyes, I suppose."

Lemaire took the cigarette back. "Fucking Harvesters. I hope you taught them a lesson." Krill held up his hand covered in Harvester blood in answer. Lemaire nodded. "Good. We'll take good care of the girl."

"She's not to be trained."

Lemaire waved his concerns away. "Yes, yes, I heard you the first time. She's too young anyway. Fucking hell, Viktor, what kind of person do you take me for? Been a dad for an hour and already overreacting?" Krill could only shrug in response. "The girl will have expenses, of course. Lodging, clothes, food. Could rack up quite the bill, Viktor Krill."

"And you'll bill me?"

Lemaire cut a sly look at Krill. "We'll work out a payment plan."

"Looking forward to it. Now, if there's nothing else, I have some business to attend to."

Lemaire took one last drag, and snubbed out the cigarette in the golden ashtray on her white marble desk. Her face grew serious. "Actually, Viktor, there *is* something else."

"I'm listening."

"Your Slink. It's killing people."

"It's a drug, Mayfly. Drugs kill people."

Lemaire began to pace around the office. "Yes, yes, I know drugs kill people. You forget how long I've survived here. I remember as a child watching as Rush tore families apart. As a young woman, I helped sling that death called Flame, saw it turn people into zombies. None of that was like this."

"Like what, Mayfly?"

Lemaire stopped her pacing. "Even Flame took a few months to really get its claws into people. And it took a year to truly alter their appearance."

"Where are you going with this?"

"I got a girl, Sofy, started using Slink a month ago. Took it cause a client of hers insisted. I just found out that she's been taking it ever since. Some girls finally found her laid out in the Jungle, and brought her back here. I went to see her. Viktor, she looks like a fucking corpse, like someone who's been a Flame-head for years. What do you have to say to that?"

Krill stared back at Lemaire, his black eyes unmoved by her words. "I'd say you better get a better grip on your girls."

"Fuck you, Viktor!"

"Slink is no different from any other drug. If you abuse it, you'll pay the price. And the more enjoyment you derive from the drug, the greater a price it will require from its user. Everything's in balance, Mayfly. I brought Bhellum its greatest drug. But it demands a lot in return." Krill saw the barely contained anger welling up in Lemaire. "Look, I appreciate your concern for your girls. You want to keep them safe? Tell them to stay off the Slink. Simple as that."

Lemaire cocked her head. "What is Slink, Viktor?"

"Just a drug; nothing more."

"But it's alive."

"It is."

"So what does it do to you?"

"You really need to know?"

"I do."

Now it was Krill's turn to pace. "It wages a war with its host. Luckily, given the size discrepancy, the person always wins, but not before the Slink releases its defense poisons. Those poisons get everyone high. But they're also why your girl now looks half in the grave." Lemaire's anger remained. "Look, drugs are going to do what drugs do — be enjoyed by those that can handle them and feast upon those that cannot. Tell your girls to stay away. And now, Mayfly, I really do have to be leaving." Krill spun on his heel and began to exit.

"Viktor." Krill turned back to face the dark-skinned queen. "And if the Slink were to ever win the battle?"

Krill's black eyes dropped to carpeted floor momentarily before returning to Lemaire. "Questions are like wild mushrooms, my dear. Be careful which ones you pick." And with that, Krill left, leaving Mayfly Lemaire to ponder the true cost of her newfound success.

———

OVER THE NEXT MONTH, Mayfly Lemaire's concerns became a horrifying reality. Zombie fiends in increasing numbers roamed the Muck, disintegrating Slink easily seen on their ravaged bodies through paper-like skin. Despite mounting evidence of the destructive consequences of regular Slink use, demand for the drug continued to surge, especially outside the Muck. Soon, Viktor Krill would be unable to accommodate all those who wanted to ride the Slink into oblivion.

And, thus, Krill found himself meeting with Gideon Moon, First of the Dead Rogues, to ask permission for something that he would much rather take. The slender man, nestled in his black turtleneck and looking especially smug, sat behind his ornate desk. To either side of Moon were two guardian mechs, outdated but in good working order. Behind Krill, along both walls of Moon's office, armed Rogues stood, their knuckles white on weapons.

So, today is the day, thought Krill. *How disappointing. How hasty.*

Krill remained silent, allowing Moon to soak in the moment. When he had enjoyed his fill, Moon finally spoke. "Well, Viktor, you called this meeting. What do you have to discuss?"

"As I predicted, the demand for Slink is growing daily. The Dead Rogues are more powerful and profitable than ever before. It's time to expand. I will establish another Slink farm in Pontus Tower. They have a pool similar to the one here in Thoosa. I would like to get started as soon as possible."

Gideon Moon smiled as if he saw something that Krill could not. "Are you asking permission or telling me, Viktor?"

Krill sighed at the infantile man with the infantile brain. "Neither. I'm detailing my plan to see if you have any objections."

Moon stood slowly, placed his ringed fingers on his desk, and leaned forward. "Well, now that you mention it, I *do* have some objections, Viktor."

Krill remained unmoved. "State them."

"Well, it seems like you are holding all the cards, *Second* Krill. Only *you* can access the Slink farm, only *you* know how the Slink is created, and only *you* know the process of cultivating Slink."

"Is that all?"

"No! No, it isn't. No one has benefited more from the Dead Rogues' rise than Viktor Krill, the boogeyman of Bhellum. You think I don't hear the whispers, don't detect the laughter behind people's words? You think I don't know that most think Viktor Krill to be the true leader of the Dead Rogues, with Gideon Moon installed as a puppet king? I hear it all!" Moon's volume increased with his anger. He took a deep breath to calm himself. "But, do you know what always brings me back, Viktor?"

Although Krill knew exactly where this rant was heading, he felt he owed it to Moon to play along. Plus, he found the whole scene to be undeniably entertaining. "Tell me, Gideon."

"That it's all bullshit. *I* am the Dead Rogues. I, Gideon Moon, was here long before Viktor Krill, and I will be here when Viktor Krill is long gone, just a bedtime story told to frighten children."

"I don't want the Dead Rogues, Gideon. But what is it, exactly, that you want?"

"I want the respect that I've earned in blood. And I want my gang back. And I cannot do that without control over that which sits at the heart on the Dead Rogues' success."

"Slink"

"That's right! You will take me to the Slink farm, and you will show me how the drug is raised and harvested. The Dead Rogues, not lone Viktor Krill, will control Slink from now on. Once this is done, I will move forward with your suggestion of a second Slink farm in Pontus. You see, Viktor, I do still value your advice. Just not your demands. What do you say?"

"I say, no."

"It's not a yes or no question, Viktor."

"Then I say, fuck you."

One of Moon's boy toys giggled on the couch while Moon sighed dramatically, attempting to mask his obvious glee. "Very well. Men!" A chorus of metal rang out in the office as the ten Dead Rogues and both guardian mechs raised their weapons towards Viktor Krill. "What do you say, now, Viktor?"

"I'd say it looks like you're holding all the cards, Gideon."

"That's right, Viktor. You're great, as much as you claimed to be and more, but this is *my* crew, and *my* turf, and *my* world. You are, and always will be, an outsider." Moon paused for dramatic effect. "Now, take me to my fucking Slink farm."

As always, Krill's body hummed with the promise of violence, the scent of blood in the air. "As you said, it's your world, boss."

———————

Viktor Krill walked slowly along the 12th floor hallway, his hands steepled and resting atop his head, leading the group of Gideon Moon, ten Dead Rogues, and two guardian mechs. Krill moved ten feet ahead of the group, with every weapon in possession cocked and aimed at the dark killer's head and back. He eventually stopped at a large metal door that had a sophisticated panel situated on the wall to its right.

"Wait right there, Viktor," Moon demanded. Krill turned to face the panel, but, otherwise, remained still. "You five, guns at the ready. You five, other side. Mechs, if Viktor Krill moves, kill him." At Moon's command, five of the Rogues carefully walked past Krill, giving him as much space as possible in the hallway, and established their positions on the opposite side of their Second. When this was completed, Moon spoke again. "Mechs, hold orders. All right, Viktor, open the Slink farm. Nice and slow."

Krill forced down the smile that was creeping up towards his lips, reached for the panel, and pressed his right palm against the flat reader. Krill had installed the security system himself, using palm, face, voice, and sentence recognition to ensure that pieces of himself couldn't simply be removed and used to gain access. When the palm scan was complete, noted by a chiming green light, Krill leaned forward to allow the system to examine his face. Once a second green light sounded, Viktor spoke into the small microphone vent. "The Before is no more, we've all closed that door. To Station, our home, where new dreams are born."

As the Dead Rogues looked to each other curiously in response to the strange key-phrase, a third green light appeared and the metal door began to slide up. A rancid odor assaulted the hallway, forcing everyone save Krill and the guardian mechs back away a few steps. Once the men had recovered, Moon spoke again. "You first, Viktor."

Krill walked through the large entryway, took several steps into the cavernous pool area, and waited. Men filtered in behind him, each of them wide-eyed and trying their hardest not to vomit. Gideon Moon said it best as he entered the Slink farm. "What a fucking shit hole. No wonder you didn't want to show anyone, Viktor."

Krill stole a peek behind him and saw the ten Rogues taking up positions near the door. The guardian mechs weren't to be seen, so they must have remained on watch in the hall. Only Gideon Moon moved forward, taking in the shocking sites that comprised the Slink farm.

A clear mucus covered most of the pool area, making walking difficult.

The pool itself was filled with a brown substance, something between mud and slime, and had dark forms moving just beneath the surface. The entire room was filled with a stench that was an uncomfortable mix of rot, refuse, shit, and death. Although Moon's face twisted in revulsion, he did well not to show weakness by covering his nose. "What the fuck is this, Viktor?"

"It's your Slink farm, Gideon."

Moon walked towards the pool, stopping near its edge, and looked to his left, where a covered steel cage held two men, naked save their underwear. The men sat with their knees pulled up to their chests and faced away from the pool, as if they were wishing themselves anywhere else. To his right, along the room's wall, was what appeared to be a large, clear bed of hardened mucus, apparently of the same material that coated the tiled floor on which he now stood. On the bed, a giant slug-like creature, perhaps ten feet in length and two feet wide, laid curled up. Its reddish-brown skin rose and fell rapidly, as if it were breathing the toxic air. Moon's jawed began to fall open, but he became aware of it and snapped it shut. "Tell me what I'm seeing, Viktor."

Timing was going to be critical from here on out, so Krill decided to cut all the bullshit. "Within the pool are fully grown Slink, Gideon. They reproduce through parthenogenesis, meaning they don't need a sexual partner. They only need to feed. Feed and give birth. That's all the Slink knows."

"What does it feed on?"

"Don't be dense, Gideon. The Slink feeds on people. To be more accurate, it feeds on live people. Trust me, I've tried everything else — dogs, cats, pigs, and corpses. They won't touch it. No, theirs is a particular pallet, which makes my life a lot harder."

Moon snuck a look at the cage to his left. "And so these men…"

"Those are no longer men. They are just food now. And before your cold heart starts to slowly warm, know that these men are here because they stole from the Dead Rogues, meaning they stole from *you*. So save your pity for someone who deserves it."

"And where does the drug come from?"

"You're looking at it, Gideon. See the nesting Slink to your right?"

"How could I miss it?"

"Watch carefully."

Moon watched in captivated horror as the nesting Slink began to throb faster and faster. It spun about in its clear bed, like a snake trying to devour its tail, before suddenly freezing in place. With an audible grunt, the Slink decompressed and discharged a torrent of gross, chunky liquid onto its nest. Two Rogues could be heard vomiting as a wave of stink attacked the men's olfactory nerves. Now completely spent, the Slink flopped off its bed and slowly slithered toward the pool's edge. Within a few seconds, after leaving a new trail of mucus in its wake, the Slink rolled into the brown mess of the pool, disappearing under its surface with a sickening splash.

"May I," asked Krill to Moon.

"Go ahead. Men! Watch him."

Krill strode over to the clear nest and, to the dismay of everyone, scooped up a handful of the Slink's excretion. He returned to his original location and held his hand out to Moon. Moon squinted, and smiled when he realized what Krill's palm contained. "Are those what I think they are, Viktor?"

"That's right. These are Slink in their most immature form. Collect them and set them aside. They'll continue to grow with no help. In three days, they'll be ready for the street."

Moon's mind filled with credit signs as he stared at Krill's hand. Within the ooze that Krill held swam hundreds, if not thousands, of tiny Slink, each one representing the promise of more power. Moon basked in the simplicity of the process, the ease with which he could earn millions upon millions of notes and credits. A wide smile hung above the Dead Rogue leader's tight black top as he stood with his back to the rolling surface of the Slink pool.

"Thank you, Viktor. Thank you for your clear, concise explanation and for bringing this wondrous opportunity to the Dead Rogues."

Here it comes. "And now what, Gideon?"

"And now, I'm afraid, you have to die, my friend. Men!"

As in Moon's office, Krill was hit by the sound of guns being raised and aimed. Only this time, Krill's Wakened ears could detect hesitation in the

Dead Rogues. It seemed that while Moon had told his men of his plot to assume control of the Slink farm, he left out the fact that he planned on having his Second exterminated.

Krill spun to face the men, turning his black eyes on each, in turn. Many of these same men had been on raids with Viktor Krill, had fought back to back with the notorious killer. None of them could remember the last time that Gideon Moon's hands were dirty. Weapons shook with indecision as the men shared unsure looks with each other.

Krill turned back to face Moon. "The men seem to think that I am still a valuable asset to this crew, Gideon."

The lean man's face reddened with rage. "The men fear the same thing that everyone else does in the Muck. They fear the larger than life Viktor Krill, this persona that you have built for yourself on the back of *my* club." The surface of the brown slime began to bubble behind the ranting Gideon Moon. "That ends today, for today, we show the Muck that you are nothing but a man. Not a demon. Not death made real. Just a visitor, a visitor who has overstayed his welcome."

As Moon spoke, the bubbling pool surface gave way to a large Slink that slowly rose into the air. Krill could feel the men's eyes growing larger as the Slink continued its ascension. By the time Moon had concluded his little rant, the Slink's "head" was a foot above that of the Rogues leader, and had flattened itself out, showcasing rows of razor-like teeth on each side of its "underbelly."

Moon, mistaking the cause of his men's reactions, thinking them moved by his stirring words, decided to continue his speech. "My Dead Rogues, I have grown up among you, led you through tough times, and together we have overcome many challenges. And we *will* overcome the loss of the outsider Viktor Krill. Kill this man and, once again, we will band together to take over the Muck." To Krill, "Any last words, outsider Krill?"

Krill vibrated internally with anticipation, but appeared serene on the outside, as if accepting his fate. "Yes. For the last time, Gideon, at least for you, I am not a *man*."

Moon smiled cruelly. "Oh, yes. So sorry, Viktor. I forgot. You are a human, sitting so far above us simple men." The smile vanished, replaced by another look of rage. To his men, "Kill this human!"

Moon's words did, in fact, act as a trigger, but not the one he had anticipated. As the Dead Rogues stood frozen, the Slink struck immediately after their First's order. The giant slug moved terrifyingly fast, as if it were a much smaller viper, whipping itself at the man at the pool's edge. The giant Slink draped itself over the man's back, head, and shoulders, digging its small teeth into soft flesh. A muffled scream could be heard from beneath the Slink's skin, just before the slug slid off the man and back into the water, taking Moon's clothes and skin with it.

As Krill stood watching the naked, skinless man shake at the pool's edge, he heard at least four Dead Rogues flee from the room as the other six tightened their grips on their weapons. Gideon Moon trembled as raw muscle and tissue were exposed to air for the first time, giving him the sensation of being on fire.

The dying Rogue leader, afraid to move, instead mouthed his agony. Krill looked on, without an ounce of pity in his dark eyes, and made out the words that Moon was forming. *Kill. Me. Kill. Me.*

Krill looked down and saw another form moving near the surface of the pool. "Don't worry, my friend, you'll get your wish."

On cue, another large Slink leapt from the brown scum and wrapped its upper half around Gideon Moon, dragging the injured man into the pool and under its surface. Two other Slinks crested the brown mucus like dolphins and dove in after the captured man. At least three of the remaining Dead Rogues could be heard vomiting where they stood.

Viktor Krill spun to meet his men's horrified stares. "And so ends the tale of Gideon Moon. Gentlemen, I'm sorry you had to witness that unfortunate scene, but greed and envy only lead down the path of destruction. I was loyal to the Dead Rogues and will remain so. Will you follow me as your First?" The men, still too shocked to respond, remained quiet. "I said, will you follow me?!"

Krill's voice, the power contained within, unfroze the men, and they answered with a resounding, "Yes, sir!"

"Good, then let's get started. You, you're Vaskez, right?"

The large, tanned Rogue dropped his weapon to his side and saluted his new First. "I am, sir." There was no vomit around Vaskez's feet.

"We fought together in the Jungle several times, correct?"

"You are correct, sir."

"You're more than capable. Pick six other men. You're taking over the operation of this Slink farm." Vaskez looked like he wanted to run from the room screaming. "I know this is shocking at first, but you will grow accustomed to it. I will be setting up the new farm over the next week, so I'll need someone I can trust to run this one. I *can* trust you, can't I, Vaskez?"

Krill's black eyes left no room for discussion. "Of course, sir."

"Cheer up, Vaskez. This is a monumentally important job and comes with an entirely new set of perks. Remind me to have the security system reset to include you and one other farm manager. Think you can handle it?"

"Without question, sir."

"Good man." As Krill and Vaskez spoke, the Dead Rogues who had run into the hallway returned. Krill addressed all the men. "My Dead Rogues, I knew that Gideon Moon would betray me, betray us all. The moment I looked into his beady eyes, I understood that the day would come when his fragile ego would be placed above all the progress that you, you, you, and I have made out in the Muck. I had to keep the Slink farm separate from him, so I could get what little sleep I require. But now, that threat is no more. The Slink farm no longer belongs to Viktor Krill, but to the Dead Rogues." The men grew emboldened by Krill's words, nodding to each other. "Follow me as your First, and what we've experienced over the past months will pale in comparison to what the future holds." Cheers exploded from the men. "But know this…" The men went quiet. "Betray me or the crew, and Gideon Moon's death will look like a kindness compared to what you will receive. Understood?"

In unison, "Understood, sir!"

"Good lads." Krill pointed to a Rogue whose name he had yet to capture. "You, go into the food cage and take out that pale sack of shit. The key is hanging by the wall there."

The lanky Rogue jumped at Krill's order, moving with purpose to the left of the pool area. He found the key hanging along the wall and used it to open the cage door. Neither prisoner moved as the Rogue moved into the cage, instead remaining curled up like balls, facing away from the Slink pool. The Dead Rogue grabbed the pale prisoner under his arms and pulled him to his feet, marching him from the cage and locking it again behind him. After returning the key to its hook, the lanky Rogue guided the almost-naked man to stand before Viktor Krill. The pale man stared at the mucus-covered floor, terrified to meet eyes with his recent captor.

"Look at me," demanded Krill, and the pale man assented. "That's better. You're in luck, my friend. The Slink have enjoyed an unplanned meal this day, meaning I no longer have need of your weak flesh. Two conditions of your release. One, don't you ever steal from the Dead Rogues again. And second, you tell anyone who will listen what you have seen at the Slink farm. Do we have an understanding?" The pale man stammered weakly. "Speak up, you hairless monkey!"

"I, I understand! I understand!"

"Good." Krill pointed at another unfamiliar Rogue. "You, get him out of Thoosa Tower, but get him some clothes before he leaves. He'll serve no purpose if he's gutted ten steps from the building." As soon as the former prisoner was removed from the Slink farm, Vaskez turned to Krill, but hesitated. "You have a question, Vaskez? Speak freely, man!"

"Uhh, what was the purpose of that, First Krill? I mean, don't we want to keep this place a secret?"

"Good question, Vaskez. I always appreciate those. Shows me that you're paying attention. And you're right; if a Slink farm was easy to operate, we'd want to keep its processes a secret. But does this look easy or particularly enjoyable to you?"

"Not at all, sir."

"Exactly, so let the world know what it takes, the size of the balls it takes to raise nightmares, and see who rushes to copy us. Already, I know that some are toying with the idea of growing their own Slink. Let the sickening truth of a Slink farm fall upon those wannabes' ears and discover who still want to endeavor to try."

"I see. Good call, sir."

"And don't forget, Vaskez..."

"Sir?"

"Everyone knows that the only thing to fear more than monsters are the men who don't fear them. Few will want to take on the Dead Rogues after this."

12

Viktor Krill carefully settled into the ergonomic, black leather chair that once belonged to Gideon Moon. He ran his hands along the lacquered finish of the ornate black and white desk while looking around at his new office. Many things would have to be altered to account for Krill's specific tastes, but those things would have to wait as more pressing matters demanded his attention.

Matters such as what to do with Gideon's eight boy toys, currently huddled together at the opposite end of Krill's office, holding each other in fear and trembling in their colorful silk pajamas. Krill found humor in their terror. For too long, these boys had operated without repercussions, making snide comments to Dead Rogues and openly laughing at the misfortunes of others.

A knock on the office door stole Krill from his dark thoughts. "Enter."

Levi Lessons and former Stench Mobb Second Red Texx, who was quickly becoming one of Krill's most trusted men, walked into the office and approached Krill's desk. Levi Lessons, always one of the boy toys' targets, threw a cold smirk at the huddling young men. The two Dead Rogues stopped opposite Krill and awaited instruction. Krill noticed that Levi still wore Van's face around his waist and hoped that Red Texx wouldn't take too much offense.

"Thank you for coming so quickly, gentlemen."

Red Texx looked admiringly around the comfortable office. "I heard that the Dead Rogues have a new First. Congratulations, Viktor. I see you're wasting no time in taking advantage of the perks."

"Waste not, want not, my friend. Levi, I assume you heard the details of Gideon Moon's demise. I know he was your First for a long time. There are no hard feelings, I assume."

Levi shook his head emphatically. Whether from a feeling of loyalty towards, or fear of Viktor Krill, it was impossible to tell. "Gideon got to where he was through politics and a series of backstabs. It looks like he finally stabbed out at the wrong person. If you ask me, he got what was coming to him."

Krill leaned back in his chair. "You can always trust untrustworthy people to act upon their distrust of others. Even if those *others* are their most loyal soldiers. But, enough about the deceased Gideon Moon. Red Texx, you will be my new Second. Not only have you earned it, but this act will show the former Stench Mobb that there is no glass ceiling in their new crew. Do you accept?"

"It would be my honor."

"Good. Levi, don't look so upset, I have an important promotion for you, as well." The man perked up. "I'm sure you both heard about the Slink farm." A shadow passed over both men's faces, followed by simple nods. "Good, saves me from recounting all the details. As you know, I have appointed Vaskez as one of the Slink farm bosses, and told him to pick another. I want you to act as the Slink farm director, overseeing the entire operation here in Thoosa. This is the core credit-producer for the club, making this a critically important position. Do you accept?" Levi, while obviously proud of being selected for the role, looked fearful of his new duties. "Not to worry, Levi, I'll walk you through everything, even the grotesque parts. I'm not setting you up to fail. Do you trust me?"

"Absolutely, sir."

"Then, do you accept?"

"I do, sir."

"Good, then meet me on the 12th floor at midnight. I'll take you, Vaskez, and the other farmers through the finer points of raising Slink."

"Yes, sir!" The tall, mohawked Rogue turned to go, but was stopped by Krill's upraised hand.

"One more thing, Levi, something you may enjoy. There's still a bit of housecleaning to do in the wake of Moon's passing, including his little harem. What was it they used to call you, Levi?"

"Levi *Lesions*. Said I was a gross eyesore on the gang." Red Texx almost laughed, but managed to keep his chuckled contained.

"Well, these boys are no longer needed. I want you to take them up to Mayfly Lemaire, see if she has use of them, will allow them to do tasks for the Bitch-Whores."

A dark glint shone in Levi's yellow eyes. "And if she doesn't want them?"

"Pick four and send them out of Thoosa to fend for themselves. The other four, bring to the 12th floor this evening." Both Levi and Texx looked confused. "The food cage will be empty soon." While Red Texx was unable to hide a look of disgust, Levi Lessons flashed a savage smile at the prospect of exacting revenge on his recent tormentors. "Dismissed."

"Thank you, sir." Levi spun and marched over to the boy toys, towering over the whimpering crowd. "Levi Lesions doesn't sound so funny anymore, does it, you limp-wristed fairies? Get up! Get up!" The boy toys all stumbled to their feet and were ushered out the door. "You all better pray to your silk pajamas god that the Bitch-Whores take you in. But *I'll* be praying that she doesn't, 'cause I would *love* to see you all get..." The door closed behind the giddy Levi, leaving the office in silence.

Red Texx spoke first. "Levi Lesions *is* a pretty good name."

Krill smiled at his new Second. "It is, isn't. Well, they had nothing but time to come up with witty puns and stinging little digs, didn't they? If Mayfly Lemaire accepts them, which I'm sure she will, their days of lounging are long over." Krill slapped his hands onto the desk. "Now on to other business. As you may have heard, I'll be establishing a second Slink farm in Pontus."

"A good idea, to be sure."

"Yes, well, I'll need your assistance in getting it going. In preparation, I'll need you to have the 8th floor pool area cleared out and the water drained. I'll also need a cage built, large enough to hold several people. You know the men in Pontus much better than I do, so pick a responsible team."

"Yes, sir. I'll have everything done by tomorrow evening."

"Good. Then we'll start the process of nurturing adolescents into mature, reproducing Slink."

"The giant slugs that I've heard about?"

"That's right."

Red Texx's face whitened. "I was hoping that was just gang exaggeration."

"I'm afraid not."

"I have a weak stomach."

"I sympathize. But this is important. The Slink will bond with those who have a direct hand in growing them into adulthood. While everyone else, even the Slink farm bosses, tiptoe around the Slinks, you and I alone will be able to work without apprehension, for our unique smells and chemistry will forbid the Slink from attacking us." Krill thought for a moment. "As long as we don't fall into their pools." Red Texx still looked unsure. "You understand how much trust I am showing you by allowing you into the initial raising process?"

Red Texx shook his head, as if forcefully removing any doubt. "I do, Viktor. Thank you for the honor."

"Texx, after you raise these nightmares, not only will your stomach never again be considered weak, but you will discover that you fear very little in the form of man. Are you with me?"

"I'm with you, sir."

"Excellent. Now, there's one more critical element that we'll need to get started. We'll need food."

Red Texx straightened. "What about the boy toys?"

"As I said, I'm confident Lemaire will take them in."

"Very well. Who do you want me to kill?"

"It's not that simple, Texx. The food needs to live and breath."

Texx looked nauseated for a moment, but successfully pushed it away. "I was hoping that was an exaggeration, as well."

"It is not."

"All right, well, there's a small Jungle gang called the Runner Boys who've been a pain in the ass. Recently tried to hit a Rogue courier taking Slink to the dope tanks. I'll have Renny and his lot scoop up a few of them." Texx paused. "Is this really the only way to set up another Slink farm?"

"No. You could help me capture three fully grown Slink from upstairs and transport them to Pontus. But they can be hard to contain."

The story of a skinless Gideon Moon being pulled under brown waters to be attacked by a swarm of giant slugs assaulted Red Texx. "I'll begin the preparations and set Renny in motion."

"Good lad."

————

WITHIN TWO SHORT WEEKS, both the Thoosa and new Pontus Slink farms were operating at full capacity, flooding both the Muck and Bhellum, at large, with the powerful drug. Viktor Krill appointed and trained teams of farm bosses to continue Slink production, freeing him up to work on more enjoyable endeavors. Krill made sure to reward the Slink teams well. First, because it was a shit job and deserved compensation. And second, to prevent the need for Slink theft, as if working for the killer Viktor Krill wasn't enough to dissuade such ideas. As the teams fed fresh food to the Slink several times a week, it didn't take much to imagine that one false move would land any of them on the other side of the food cages.

Despite the Muck's general fear of and adoration for Viktor Krill, there were always small fire to put out, upstart gangs willing to risk it all to make names for themselves. To the absolute shock and delight of the Dead Rogues' growing membership, Krill would personally lead efforts to stamp out subversive activity, whether that be taking point on an attack in the Jungle, or doling out capital punishment in front of Thoosa before an enraptured crowd. The Dead Rogues loved their new First, the man who had taken them from the brink of extinction to the top of the Muck food chain, alongside the Chrome Butchers. The Dead Rogues loved Viktor Krill, but, more importantly, they feared Viktor Krill.

At least three times a week, Krill shared a meal with young Darrin, who now had complete freedom to move throughout Thoosa Tower, something unheard of not long ago given the racist origins of the Dead Rogues. Their conversations were half business, half discussions on Krill's dark philosophies regarding power, life, and death. Tennian Stamp, always a sharp one, had figured out that the toddy gangs were secretly unified under young Darrin and were working directly for the Dead Rogues. Therefore, he had stopped using them for intel and now maintained only an arms-length relationship that served to distribute Leaf across Bhellum.

Despite this change, Krill made great use of Darrin's talents. The boy's network of toddy gangs could alert Krill of issues just beginning to bubble far beneath the surface of the Jungle, giving the Rogue leader invaluable time to plan and prepare. This, coupled with the toddies' ability to travel throughout Bhellum unbothered, delivering Slink to middlemen across the city, made young Darrin an investment more than worth Krill's time and effort.

Krill also found time to work with the child Natthi, showing her techniques for disabling much larger foes and teaching her skills to blend into shadows. Between his physical lessons and Mayfly Lemaire's proven philosophical teachings on female empowerment, Natthi became a formidable girl in short order. Her tenacity proved useful in her training, with the girl always appearing at their scheduled sessions despite being covered in bruises from the previous lesson. Something stirred in Krill each time the child mastered a new skill or offered an insightful response to a challenging question.

As the weeks that Krill and Natthi spent together stretched, the dark killer did his best to compartmentalize his feelings, to justify his gratification as simply a long-term human resource investment that was proving fruitful. But deep down, Krill knew what was happening. Krill knew and, for the first time in what felt like forever, was terrified.

Viktor Krill was starting to love another.

———

"Now, CLOSE YOUR EYES." Natthi did as she was told, shutting her dark brown eyes as she carefully balanced on the ball of one foot, the other held up painfully behind her back in a dancer's stance. "Prepare yourself. And be ready." In a small grassy area behind Thoosa Tower, the young girl slowed her breathing and worked to heighten her other senses.

Krill waited for a while, until he saw Natthi start to shake from the effort of holding the difficult pose. Just when he thought she could take no more, when the other foot would inevitably begin to drop, he threw one of his ever-present knives, underhand and hilt-first, at the young girl's face. Despite her strain, Natthi could maintain enough focus to sense the object hurdling towards her. She swatted at the air before her, missing the hilt but catching the flat of the blade with her small hand. The knife spun and changed trajectory, narrowly missing Natthi's brown face.

"Oww," hissed the girl as she opened her eyes and returned both feet to the ground. She shook her right hand before stopping to stare down at it. A line of blood appeared at the bottom of her palm. Before she could even begin to complain, Krill was magically next to her, adeptly wrapping the hand in white gauze.

"You almost lost focus. Remember, pain is no excuse for a degradation in concentration."

Natthi scrunched her face in anger, something Viktor Krill had grown to appreciate. "I got the stupid thing, didn't I? How about a *good job, Natthi*."

Krill thought it over, but decided against the soft approach. "Adequate job. But you need to get better. Next time, I might throw the knife blade first. And with more power behind it. Complacency will get you killed."

Natthi rolled her eyes at the Muck's premier killer. "Whatever. Are we done, yet?"

"Ten more minutes of sequences, then you can go. Maybe."

"Mister Krill!" Although the girl complained, there was little force behind the objection. Natthi was beginning to feel powerful for the first time in her young life and was enjoying the sensation, much preferring it to that of being a mouse in a snake pit. She stomped away for a few steps for effect before beginning the sequence of fighting stances and moves that Krill had taught her.

Levi Lessons, who had kept a respectable distance during the lesson, slid next to Krill. "You're hard on the girl. Harder than on Darrin, even."

Krill refused to look over at his lieutenant, instead carefully observing Natthi for any misstep or stumble that would require reprimand. "Life is dangerous in the Muck for everyone, especially for a boy like Darrin. But nothing is more perilous than being a young girl, appearing as food for every type of predator available. When I'm done with her, Natthi will be the most dangerous thing there is."

"And what's that?"

"A deadly weapon that no one sees." Levi fingered the face mask at this belt as he digested Krill's words. "Any updates that I should know about?"

"We successfully raised two more Slink to maturity at the Thoosa farm, and they've already begun producing. Even with those, however, we're still staying just in front of demand. Apparently, Bhellum's appetite for Slink is hard to satiate."

"Good. No more mature Slink in the Thoosa farm. It could get...unsafe."

"Fuck, I thought it was already pretty goddam unsafe."

Krill finally shifted his attention to Levi, his black eyes locking onto the mohawked man. "You want to see unsafe? Walk into the Hammers at night. What about Slink food?"

It took Levi a moment to recover from Krill's Hammers comment. He and everyone else did their best not to think about the mysterious encampment of Blisters just to the west of the Muck. "So far, no problem. Luckily, there's always some dipshit who fucks up or some new crew who thinks it a good idea to cross the Rogues. But as word spreads about what happens to those who get wrong with the Dead Rogues, we may start to have an issue. What we need is a decent war to fill the cages, create a stockpile."

Viktor Krill was listening, but his attention was elsewhere, aimed high in the air to the north. "You may soon get your wish, Levi."

The Slink farm director followed Krill's eyes into the air, where he spotted a lone drone quickly approaching the small group. Twin polished silver handguns with onyx handles materialized in Krill's scarred hands. "You shouldn't need those, First Krill. Armed drones were outlawed after the Nocturna Massacre."

Krill held his weapons loosely at his sides, coiled to strike. "Everyone agreed to believe that the Devil doesn't exist. But this belief doesn't make it any less false." Levi thought for a second before drawing his own weapon, a highly decorated Stutter, and aiming it at the incoming drone.

The quiet buzzing of the four propellers grew louder as the drone approached. With his Wakened eyes, Krill could see the small machine in detail, even from a hundred yards away. Unable to detect any micro-turrets, laser barrels, or explosive devices, Krill's tension lowered a bit, although he still kept his guns at the ready.

"Natthi! Enough! Go inside and see if Miss Lemaire has anything for you to do."

The girl halted her movements and looked over confused. "But I haven't finished yet. Aren't you the one who said…"

"Now, girl!" Natthi understood Viktor Krill's tones better than anyone, and this one meant that you had better do what you were told. Without further hesitation, she collected her jacket and shoes from the grass and ran towards the front of Thoosa. Two Dead Rogues, as always per Krill's orders, chased after her until she was safely inside.

As the drone closed the remaining distance, Levi broke the tense silence. "Who you think sent that thing?"

"I have a fairly good idea."

The drone stopped ten feet from the two Dead Rogues and descended quickly, hovering when it reached eye level with Krill. Although no weapons were apparent, a round 360-degree camera and speakers could be seen. A voice, easily loud enough to be heard over the general din of the Muck, emanated from the speakers.

"Viktor Krill. It is an absolute pleasure to finally meet you, although I sincerely apologize that it has to be under these severely impersonal circumstances." The voice pouring forth from the drone was confident and educated, out of place amidst the violence and grime of the Muck. "My name is Sigman Prime, although I'm sure a man as astute as yourself has already pieced that together. As you know, I run an establishment called the Chrome Butchers, not unlike your own Dead Rogues. I want you to know that I am a huge admirer of yours. I have been following your work since you first arrived in our little community, and can simply say... Bravo. I have run the numbers and have come to the conclusion that there are scenarios that could be highly prosperous for the both of us. Therefore, let this unassuming drone act as my personal proxy, coming to you hat in hand, requesting a meeting where the two of us can have a civilized conversation concerning the future of our two organizations."

Krill stared into the camera of the drone, looking through it and into the heart of the man who was speaking. "And where did you intend on having this meeting, Sigman Prime?"

"I have cultivated a rather lovely garden atop Triton Tower. I thought it would prove the perfect backdrop for a talk about nurturing the growth of our two groups."

"You'll have to excuse me if I'm not rushing to surrender myself into enemy hands."

"*Enemy* hands? You misunderstand me completely, Viktor. I hope it's all right that I call you that, but equals must address each other accordingly. I simply want to talk about possible synergies, nothing more." Krill remained silent. "And shouldn't it be *me* who worries about a meeting between the two of us? You are the Muck's most notorious and ruthless killer. I am a simple businessman with simply propositions."

"It's not you I'm worried about, *Sigman*. I know you are supported on high. Who knows what kinds of military-grade mechs you have in those towers, ready to riddle my body with pre-frag bullets from auto-locking turrets aimed by algorithm-driven scopes."

Soft laughter drifted from the drone as it hovered in place. "You're either very well-informed, or your deductive abilities are exceptional, Viktor. Very well. I had anticipated this reaction and have a contingency plan in place, although I was hoping it wouldn't come to this. Few know this, but my son Fredrick lives here in Triton with me. I'm grooming him to take over once I retire. I think now would be a good time for him to start pulling his weight, to begin showing the men his value. Therefore, I propose this. The Dead Rogues keep Fredrick as collateral until our talk has concluded and their First is back with them safe and sound. What say you?"

Krill listened carefully to the words coming out of the drone's small but powerful speakers. Using his Wakened ears and senses, Krill was unable to detect any falseness or deception in Sigman Prime's voice. "Just a simple conversation, you say?"

"That's right. Just to discuss potential synergies."

"And no agreement is assumed to be reached in that short time?"

"You're a thinking man. I assumed you would need time to think after our conversation."

Krill let the "man" slight go this time. "Then we have an agreement. Day and time?"

The drone hovered quietly in place. If Prime felt anything regarding how this talk was going, the drone wasn't giving it away. "I'm eager to meet you. Let's say tomorrow at the sun's height. I'll have Fredrick stationed outside of Triton for surrender to your Rogues. Then, you can pass through the Tower and meet me on the roof, where my garden resides."

"Since few have seen this Fredrick, how do I know that's he really your son, and not some low-level Butcher you dressed up?"

For the first time, silence from the drone, as if Prime was finally forced to think on his feet. Krill's heightened senses picked up something from atop Triton Tower. A hesitation. A discomfort. It seemed Sigman Prime experienced issues when things didn't go exactly to plan. Krill took note.

"I guess you don't," Prime replied after some time. "Just as I'll have to take

Viktor Krill's word that the Muck's most infamous murderer won't cut my throat as I bend in to shake his hand, you'll have to take Sigman Prime's word. We are both putting ourselves at risk. Will that not suffice?"

Krill had heard enough, had gained all the information he needed. "It will. Tomorrow at high sun then."

"I very much look forward to meeting you in person, Viktor. It's so rare to shake hands with an equal. Until tomorrow."

And with that, the drone rose as if lifted by a geyser, spun, and retreated to the top of Triton Tower. Krill returned his weapons to their leg holsters, and Levi Lessons lowered his Stutter. "Well, that came out of nowhere. What do think he has in mind, First Krill?"

"He's a shrewd one, and fancies himself a genius. Prime sees that we are gaining power by the day, and needs to do something sooner rather than later. My guess is that he wants to cut a deal."

"What kind of deal?"

"One that certainly isn't in the favor of the Dead Rogues. You can be sure of that."

"Orders?"

"Tell Red Texx what happened here. He'll need to have a contingent of Rogues ready tomorrow to collect Fredrick Prime outside of Triton Tower."

"Weapons?"

"Oh yes, they'll need to be loaded for bear."

Levi looked perplexed. "Loaded for what?"

Krill waved the question away. Sometimes he caught himself using sayings from another world. "Just make sure they're ready for anything."

"Yes, sir." Levi hurried away, delighted to be able to pass along serious duties to the more capable Red Texx.

Viktor Krill breathed in deeply, calming the excitement that was building within the notorious killer. The Cold War between the Dead Rogues and the Chrome Butchers was coming to an end. The staring contest was over.

Sigman Prime blinked first.

13

T he hundred-plus Chrome Butchers positioned outside of Triton Tower made for an impressive scene. Living up to their moniker, the *Chrome* Butchers were fully Loaded, each wearing shoulder auto-turrets and metal exoskeletons that increased speed and strength.

Viktor Krill marched towards Triton at the head of a hundred of his own heavily armed gangsters. His Second, Red Texx, walked alongside him, tasked with collecting and watching over Fredrick Prime for the duration of the two leaders' meeting. Approaching Triton from the West, as they walked, the two men looked past their destination to Hydrus Tower, and the Skywalk that connected the Chrome Butcher strongholds.

The Skywalk was topped in auto-turrets and covered in loop-holes from which Butchers could rain down bullets, grenades, and even lasers onto aggressors. Chrome Butcher members meandered between Triton and Hydrus in the shade of the Skywalk. Other than Butchers, only the women and children who manned the various chowsets stationed around the Skywalk's shadow were allowed in the vicinity. Texx commented as they both took stock of the Skywalk. "That's gonna be a problem. Superior coverage of the battlefield and free movement between the two towers. Our forces are split while theirs is unified." He kept thinking. "That's gonna be a problem."

Krill simply grunted his agreement as he walked. As the group of Dead Rogues progressed towards Triton Tower, he could see the Butchers' shoulder turrets slowly rotate, always keeping the leading Rogues directly in front of their dangerous barrels. When the Rogues were fifty yards from the Triton entrance, Krill held his hand up, bringing the group to an immediate halt. He turned to address his men.

"Everyone wait here. Stay focused. Stay ready. Second Texx will bring back the hostage. No one's to harm him. No talking shit, either. This is a delicate situation. Treat it as such." Krill nodded to Red Texx and the two men marched towards the Triton entrance alone, bloody targets in a sea of piranhas.

They covered the fifty yards quickly, and stopped ten feet from the collection of Butchers. As expected, every auto-turret in the clearing was aimed at either Krill or Texx. One rash move would precipitate a wave of bullets that would crash into the two Rogues, leaving nothing but corpses in its wake. Since they were not greeted, Krill spoke first.

"Viktor Krill. Here to meet with Sigman Prime. I'm expected."

One large Butcher standing a few feet in front of the gathered mass responded. "We know who you are," replied the broad man with the blonde reverse mohawk. "I'm First Prime's Second, Wess Dey. Please wait here. I'll call for the exchange." Wess put two fingers to his mouth and blew a loud note into the tense air. As if part of a choreographed dance, half of the Butchers in the center of the mob shifted right and the other half took a step left, leaving a clear pathway from the large entrance doors of Triton Tower to Viktor Krill and Red Texx.

The heavy metal doors slid open, and out stepped a lanky man onto the building landing. He was of average height, with an ostentatious light-brown pompadour and a matching mustache of wispy hair. The man looked soft, someone more at home at a pretentious model party than the Muck. His small nose hung high above his ankle-high soft pants and blousy flowered shirt, as if there was something continually rotting inside that pubescent mustache.

Red Texx addressed Wess. "How do we know that's really Fredrick Prime?"

Wess stared at the fashionista with disdain. "Well, that there is a one-of-a-kind prick. It would be hard to find his double here in the Muck." He faced back towards Texx. "Trust me. It's fucking him. But you may wish it wasn't before long. Just remember, no hands on him." Wess looked back to the younger Prime. "No matter how much you want to." Krill smiled inwardly at the unrequested intel.

Fredrick Prime violently waved a small insect away before descending the landing stairs. He angrily shooed away several Chrome Butchers who were standing too close, and cursed the grass for potentially staining his white loafers. After shaking his head in general disgust, Fredrick quickly made the walk to Second Wess Dey.

"All right, Wess-ley. I'm here. Let's get this ridiculous affair over with before I smell like the rest of you troglodytes." Fredrick's gaze fell on Krill, and he blinked heavily, put off by the killer's black eyes. "You must be Viktor Krill. Fredrick Prime, at your service. Charmed, I'm sure. You know, Vik, colored contacts went out three seasons ago. It's all about the double pupil now."

Krill had missed it at first, so caught up was he in the general absurdity of Fredrick Prime, but he now saw that the young man was wearing contacts that made each green eye appear to have two pupils. "I seem to always be behind the times," Krill said. To Wess, "Shall we proceed?"

"Not yet, Vik," cut in Fredrick. He pointed a pale bony finger at Krill and Texx. "You both need to know that if I am harmed in *any* way, my father will turn your towers to rubble. You have no idea about the true power of the Chrome Butchers."

"That's enough, Freddie," interrupted Wess, who looked concerned that Krill would tear out the dainty man's heart then and there.

"You don't call the shots here, Wess-ley. This is *my* operation. Father told me so." Fredrick turned his attention back to the two Rogues. Anyway, anything happens to me, I mean a single bruise, and you'll have the Mech Force on your ass."

Wess looked horrified. "Godammit, Freddie! Shut the hell up, man!"

Fredrick cut his eyes at Wess before giggling. "Oh, Wess-ley, you and Father and your little *secrets*. Just let our enemies know how big our dick is, so they can scamper back into those shit-holes of theirs."

"That's not how First Prime wants to play it."

Fredrick mimed blabbing with his hand as he mouthed *blah, blah, blah.* "Oh, very well, Wess-ley. They get the point by now, anyway, I think."

Wess took Fredrick by his small elbow and guided him over towards Red Texx. "So you're gonna go with..."

"Red Texx."

Fredrick giggled again, a sound that cut into Krill's spine like nails on a chalkboard. "Oh, what an unfortunate name. Does the carpet match the drapes, Texx?"

Red Texx scowled, but said nothing back to the irritating man. "This way, please."

Fredrick rolled his eyes. "Wow, what a fun group. Lead the way, big ginger." Red Texx began to walk toward the gathered Dead Rogues and Fredrick followed. The younger Prime stopped as he passed Krill, however, leaning in conspiratorially. "Vik, you think you could arrange a meeting with that Mayfly Lemaire for me? I've been with almost every girl in the Muck, but to say I've stuck it to the head Bitch-Whore..."

Krill thought of Mayfly Lemaire roasting a naked Fredrick Prime over hot coals, slowly turning him on a spit as she smoked a cigarette and laughed. "I'll see what I can do."

"My man." Fredrick put out his fist for Krill to bump it, but the Dead Rogue leader ignored it. Red Texx put a hand on Fredrick's back and gently pushed him on. Krill watched in silence as the two crossed the space between collected gangs. Eventually, Texx and his captive disappeared into the mass of bodies.

"You sure you want him back," Krill asked Wess.

"I don't. But his father does. It would be best for your crew if he returns, whole and unhurt."

"And so he shall. Ready?"

Wess thought for a moment. "I don't suppose I could persuade you to surrender your weapons."

"No, I don't suppose you could."

Wess shrugged helplessly. "Didn't think so, but I had to ask. Not that it matters. From what I hear, your whole body is a weapon. Also, First Prime said not to stress it. Let's go. After you."

Viktor Krill nodded and passed Wess, whose auto-turrets turned above his shoulders to follow the visitor. Krill walked between the hundred-plus Chrome Butchers, the target of countless weapons both obvious and hidden, and understood that one false move or misplaced finger could be the end. Keeping his head high, the Dead Rogues leader reached the landing without incident, and waited at the top for Wess Dey. The Chrome Butcher Second ascended the steps soon after, and turned to face his men.

"Boys, stay ready. No one fires first." Wess spun back to Krill. "Here we go."

"Anything I should know before going in?"

"Yeah, whatever Sigman Prime proposes, it would be best for you to agree to it."

"But I'm not the agreeable sort."

"Then this meeting might not go well."

"My meetings rarely do." Wess's shoulder turrets vibrated at their owner's internal chemical reaction to Krill's concerning words. "Let's go."

———————

As VIKTOR KRILL was guided through the halls of Triton Tower, he quickly learned that Sigman Prime had been sandbagging all the other gangs in the Muck. Although everyone knew that the Chrome Butchers were three times as Loaded as any other crew, that was just the tip of the iceberg in regard to the Butchers' true powers.

Parading throughout Triton, and stationed at various points of entry, were Level-12 battle mechs, better known as GRIT-12s. Military-grade, modern, and far superior to the antiquated guardian mechs found in Thoosa and other towers, the GRIT-12s were near the cutting edge of robotic technologies. They were also one of the last celebrated models being produced by Cyrix Technologies.

Krill knew, of course, that this was part of Sigman Prime's plan, showing his potential nemesis the futility of open war with the Chrome Butchers. Krill stopped to stare as one of the GRIT-12s flew by him, a large, singular wheel almost six feet in height, perfectly balanced on sophisticated tilt sensors. Packed into the center of the wheel was the top-half of a remotely human metal android with two heads, one peeking around each side of the moving disk. Two arms with delicate metal fingers could be seen, one on each side, but Krill also noticed four compartments tucked neatly into the "body" of the mech. No doubt, these were home to large-caliber guns, grenade launchers, and flame throwers.

The GRIT-12s were not helper mechs; they would not keep you company or clean up after you. They were created for the sole purpose of ending lives in the quickest and most efficient manner possible. The GRIT-12s had already played a significant role in winning numerous major conflicts around the world. And now they were in the Muck, ready to be called upon should someone formidable cross Sigman Prime. Someone like Viktor Krill.

"This way, please."

Wess's voice pulled Krill from his analysis. He saw that the Butchers' Second was pointing down a side corridor and followed his guidance. Krill passed several open doors, and found gang members oiling, polishing, and loading a plethora of MCEs. Between the GRIT-12s and MCEs found just in Triton Tower, Krill believed that the Chrome Butchers could not only flatten the lowly Muck, but possibly take over a small country.

At the end of the hallway, four elevators appeared, not unlike every other tower. As they approached the lift doors, Wess raised his right hand in a fist, stopping the ten Butchers who were following the pair. He spoke over his shoulder. "You all stay down here and watch the lift doors. Have teams of

ten stationed outside the lift doors of every floor. I'll take him up myself."
None of the men argued with Wess's instructions, a testament to the Butchers' level of respect for their Second.

Wess pressed the highest button, labeled *Rooftop,* and waited a moment
before the elevator doors slid open with a ding. "Visitors first," said the large
man, and Krill complied.

Once they were alone, and being whisked upward, Krill spoke to Wess.
"You think it's a good idea to be left in a confined space with me?"

Wess stared at the flashing floor levels as he answered. "Well, I figure if
you ever wanted me dead, you could get me anywhere, and I would never
see it coming. At least, if half the stories about you are to be believed. Therefore, I'm no worse off here than when taking a dump in my own apartment."

Krill chuckled to himself. "You're a good soldier and even better Second,
Wess Dey. I hope I don't have to kill you."

"Me too, Viktor Krill." A few seconds of uncomfortable silence passed.
"We're here."

Krill's breath caught in his throat as the lift doors opened onto a
wondrous garden atop Triton Tower. A potpourri of color assaulted Krill's
black eyes as he stepped onto the cobbled walkway that wove its way
through the lush growth. Krill and Wess passed under the giant blossoms of
strange trees and twisted around thick bushes whose neon fruit was home to
an array of unfamiliar insects. A feeling of nausea struck Krill, and then
exited, as he was transported back in time, to a nocturnal paradise rife with
similar flora. A place he rejected and would never see again.

After several twists and turns, the pathway emptied onto a patio
furnished with comfortable chairs and a long dining table. The patio was
enclosed on three sides by the thick gardens, and on the fourth by the roof's
edge, which faced south into the Muck. Near the edge was a pair of ornate
Victorian binoculars held aloft by an equally elegant tripod. Although the
binoculars seemed to be from yesteryear, Krill could tell that they were a
modern design made to look old, with complex circuitry offering a plethora
of useful functions for spying on one's competition.

Away from the table and lounge chairs, and across the patio, sat two leather egg chairs, obviously brought to the roof for this occasion. They were arranged several feet apart and faced each other, with a short round table between them. A small man sat with his legs crossed in one of the chairs; undoubtedly, Sigman Prime.

Wearing an immaculately cut three-piece dark blue suit, Prime sat casually, taking long drags from a gilded cigarette holder. His rich brown hair was thick with pomade and parted to the left, reminiscent of another world's Cary Grant. A perfectly trimmed pencil mustache sat beneath a long, thin nose and light-brown eyes that shone with scheming intelligence.

Prime rose as Krill approached, placed the cigarette holder between his teeth, and clapped vigorously. Wess moved away from the two gang leaders to wait silently near the garden's border. Prime spoke around the expensive holder. "Viktor Krill! I thought this day would never come. Please, sit!" He motioned towards the other egg chair, and Krill sat down. The chair was remarkably comfortable. Prime took the cigarette holder out of his mouth, and held it in his left hand before taking a seat himself. "Thank you so much for accepting my invitation. Let's drink to your unflappable bravery. Ladies!"

At Prime's command, two beautiful women in expensive cocktail dresses entered the patio from another cobbled pathway, each carrying a tray with an iced drink on it. As the women approached the two gang bosses, Krill could see that both sported black eyes and swollen faces. One of the women even had burns along her right arm. Prime sighed heavily as he watched Krill take note of the injuries.

"My apologies for the poor appearance of our attendants. Alas, Freddie loves his girls. Oftentimes, too much and too hard." He took his drink off one woman's tray as Krill took his from the other. "But boys will be boys, you know. I'm sure it's just a phase he'll grow out of." Prime took a sip of his drink. "Ooh, but that's good. How's yours, Viktor?"

Krill had forgotten about his drink, too involved with thinking about whether he should return Fredrick whole or in pieces. Prime saw Krill's hesitation and misinterpreted its meaning. "Would you like one of the attendants to try your drink for you?"

"Why would I do that?"

"To ensure that it isn't poisoned, of course."

"Poison doesn't frighten me." To prove his point, Krill took a deep swig from his glass, finding the aged whiskey to be particularly smooth.

Prime took another pull from his cigarette. "Tell me. What does frighten the great Viktor Krill?"

"Inconsequential meetings, for one."

Prime laughed through the smoke. "Message received. I will forego the niceties. I have followed you for quite some time, Viktor. I am a hard man to impress, but you have done just that. It is rare, indeed, to find someone able to max out both brains and brawn in one package."

"I thought we were foregoing the niceties."

"Ahh, but this isn't a nicety. It is the whole point of today's meeting. I'm an admirer of yours, Viktor." Krill simply stared back in silence. "I owe you, Viktor."

Krill drank deeply from his whiskey. "How do you figure?"

"Well, now that you've shared what frightens *you*, I'll share what used to keep *me* up at night." Prime paused for dramatic effect. "Liquid Tye."

"Liquid Tye?"

"That's right. You see the forces that I have at my disposal. I am not concerned with any other gang or crew. I don't worry about my boys in a straight up fight with anyone, much less some ragtag group from the Muck. But Liquid Tye... His reputation for sliding in and out of inaccessible locations like a phantom made me uncomfortable. I mean, what good is a fortress when you're facing an enemy who can seemingly float through walls?" Prime trailed off, his mind going somewhere else. He snapped out of it quickly and looked to Krill. "Do you think my concerns were valid?"

"I do."

"Do you think Liquid Tye could have gotten to me?"

"I think if Liquid Tye turned his full attention on you, I'd be talking to a corpse."

"Because he even got to you? The great Viktor Krill?"

"That's right."

"And he was as good as advertised?"

"Better. Much better."

"Then I'm fortunate that he turned his full attention towards you first. And *that*, Viktor, is why I owe you."

"Where are you going with this, Sigman?"

Prime placed his drink on the round table between the two men and leaned forward in his seat. "Look, the Muck belongs to the Chrome Butchers. This is not an opinion, it's an inevitability. You all are mine, you just don't know it, yet. But, something you need to know about me is that I am a collector of talent. I have a superior eye and nothing pains me more than seeing talent wasted or destroyed. It is for this reason that the Dead Rogues still stand. It is for this reason that you, Viktor Krill, still stand."

"So, I guess it is *I* that owe *you?*"

Prime waved his hand in the air. "Let's call it even. Now, on to my proposal. The Dead Rogues will be absorbed by the Chrome Butchers, no violence necessary. You will share the process for growing that wondrous drug you call Slink. And you, Viktor Krill, will rule at my side. Well, not *right* beside me. Perhaps a little behind, but you catch my drift."

Krill looked over to Wess Dey, who stood at attention, betraying no emotion. "It seems you already have a capable Second."

"Yes, of course, Wess is great and will remain Second. We will create a new position fitting a man of your talents. Since you'll be heading up our street-level strategies and dealing with confrontations, how does *Commandant* sound? It has a certain ring to it, does it not? Commandant Krill."

"Sounds like you have everything all figured out."

Prime sat back in his seat. "Well, that's why I get paid the big notes, isn't it? Why fight, when we can work together? Why destroy, when we can build something Bhellum has never seen? Why throw away money, when we can make more than ever dreamed possible? It's all common sense, really." Prime paused. "I can see the gears turning behind those dark eyes of yours, Viktor. You have questions. Ask away." He returned the cigarette holder to his lips.

Krill drank from his beverage and placed it alongside Prime's on the round table. "This meeting. Was it your idea? Or was it Cyrus Bhellum's?"

Prime choked on his cigarette smoke and began to cough, finally breaking his professional demeanor. When he recovered, he spoke through a strained voice. "Cyrus Bhellum? What in the world gave you that idea?"

Krill smiled and sat back. He was finally getting somewhere. "Let's see. A middling crew gets a new First from outside the Muck. Soon after, that crew somehow gets Loaded with MCEs, which are hard to acquire even for professional security companies. That alone is enough to tell me that this sudden ascension of the Butchers was funded, supported, and probably planned from high up." Prime's light-brown eyes narrowed, but Krill continued. "As to who would support such a coup and why, that took a bit more thought. Other than to simply control the flow of drugs through Bhellum and into the surrounding region, I couldn't imagine why someone on high would interest themselves in the Muck. Then it struck me."

Krill stopped talking, forcing Prime to urge him on. "What struck you, Viktor?"

"We're sitting on prime real estate, no pun intended. The Muck, the Hammers, and the areas in between have to be worth a fortune to the right group for the right project. Since Cyrus Bhellum technically still owns these properties, it makes sense that he would want a proxy to do his bidding on the street level. For what purpose? Well, I haven't gotten that far, yet. But I will."

Prime smiled, showcasing perfect veneers, but fires burned behind his eyes. "For argument's sake, let's say you are right, Viktor. Does that change anything? My proposal remains the same."

"Although it remains the same, it is quite different."

"How so?"

"If this meeting was *your* idea, then it really was you who saw value in a potential partnership. But, if this meeting was actually forced upon you by Cyrus Bhellum, then it was *he*, and not *you*, that truly values my skills and tactics. As someone used to being solely in charge, you might take this as a slight, a questioning of your abilities. You may have taken the meeting, even done so with a smile. You may have gone along with the merger..."

"Acquisition, Viktor."

"Even better. You may have gone along with the acquisition. You may have smiled and slapped me on the back as a friend. But, inside, your stomach would churn at the sight of me. Not a day would go by when you didn't consider ways to get rid of your new Commandant." Krill's Wakened ears heard it then, back in the depths of the gardens — the nearly silent whirr of technology coming closer. "Therefore, how could I ever take this proposal seriously, understanding that it would only lead to me constantly looking over my shoulder?"

"Don't you do that now, Viktor?"

"I do. But not because of those I'm supposed to trust." The whirr grew louder ever so slightly. It was moving slowly, stealthily.

By now, Prime had regained his composure, and was sitting back in his egg chair with his legs crossed. He gestured with his cigarette holder. "Then, why this whole charade, Viktor? Do you think so little of my stature that I cannot veto a meeting in my own tower? In my own garden?"

The singular whirr broke into two, each approaching from opposite sides of the patio. "I think you have very little power that hasn't been given to you. And power that has been given can be easily taken away. So, no, I don't think you could veto this meeting. But, I think you *did* get something out of it?"

Prime was locked onto Krill, his fingers fiddling with his ornate cigarette holder, the obvious control for the metal assassins currently rolling along the garden pathways. "And what do you think I got out of it, Viktor?"

Krill began to send signals to various muscles, coiling them for action. He looked over to Wess Dey, who remained at ease, telling him that the Second knew nothing of the setup. "Well, if I agreed to your proposal, war would be averted, Cyrus Bhellum would be happy to have my talents at his disposal, and you would have just doubled your resources without taking a single loss. And if I rejected your proposal, you could have me killed here and now, accomplishing similar goals while ridding yourself of a dangerous rival."

Prime rolled the holder in his fingers. "You have my son Freddie for just this reason, Viktor. For your protection."

"But, is it? If we reach an accord, Fredrick is sent home safe. If I am killed, you've cut off the head of the Dead Rogues. The war is over before it began. You announce that you'll spare the Rogues and make them Butchers once Fredrick is returned. Even the men truly loyal to me would have a hard time turning down that deal. I must admit, I was unable to detect deception in your voice over the drone. You have my sincerest respect, in that regard. It seems I had yet to encounter a liar of your caliber."

"Then, you have given me your answer?"

"I have not." The whirring quieted, the assassins having reached their positions.

Prime leaned forward once more. "Then, give me one last chance to persuade you. You *cannot* win this war, Viktor. Don't throw away everything you've worked so hard to accomplish. Do it for your men, if not for yourself. No one, not even a heartless gangster, has a death wish. Everyone fears death. Best to avoid it, if possible."

Krill's muscles continued to coil. Adrenaline began to course through his Wakened body. "But that's where you are wrong, Sigman Prime. I *do not* fear death. I've died twice already, and welcome a third. And, as far as *avoiding* war, why would I want to do that? You misunderstand me completely. I don't do this for the power. Power is merely the result of what I truly want — violent competition with the biggest stakes possible. It's the thrill, Sigman, you bureaucratic half-villain!" Krill's voice was becoming hard to control as the chemical makeup of his body altered and surged.

Prime's index finger moved high up on the holder. "Then, your answer is no?"

"Emphatically."

"I'm sorry to..."

Viktor Krill's body sprung out of the egg chair like a cable snapping under extreme stress. Just as he did, his chair exploded, having been stuck by twin rockets from the two GRIT-12s that were positioned just out of sight in the garden paths that spidered off the patio. Krill's back burned as the fires reach out to grab him. The Wakened human sped past Sigman Prime, flicking something at the howling man as he went by in a flash. Bullets rained down just behind Krill as he accelerated forward, the GRIT-12s unable to adjust for a simple man whose foot-speed fell far outside accepted parameters.

Krill became a blur as he raced for the roof's edge, his ears hurting from the concussion grenades exploding in the air just behind him. His grin became a toothy smile as he dove for the edge, but not before he heard Sigman Prime's yells of excitement become screams of terror as the Slink Krill tossed buried itself deep into Prime's cheek.

Over the edge Krill soared, bullets now whizzing by his head and chest. As he tumbled head over heels, Krill looked down at the ground twenty floors beneath him and wondered if even his Wakened body could survive such a fall. For the next ten stories, Krill's brain spun with ways to possibly land to dissipate the extreme kinetic energy. Just as he reached the conclusion that he was fucked, no matter how he was to land, his high-tops began to hum, jostling a memory tucked neatly into the recesses of Krill's mind.

"Young Darrin, you sweet, sweet boy!" he screamed into the rushing air.

Krill laughed openly as his acceleration towards the ground slowed, his sneakers having sensed a fall and activated their suspension capabilities. By the time Krill hit the ground, it felt as if he had jumped from no more than ten feet. Landing several feet in front of the gathered Chrome Butchers, all of whom jumped in surprise, Krill didn't waste any time, speeding away towards the safety of the Dead Rogues.

By the time the GRIT-12s had rolled towards the front of the roof, Viktor Krill was well out of range, having almost reached Red Texx, who had positioned himself far ahead of the other Rogues. Krill skidded to stop before the giant man.

"I take it the meeting didn't go well, Viktor."

Krill chuckled, adrenaline still tickling his body. "It went about as well as I thought it would."

Red Texx looked past Krill to the Chrome Butchers, who seemed in disarray from the unanticipated display. "Are we fighting now? Do I need to get everyone in position?"

Krill waved away Texx's concerns. "We've got time, Texx."

Red Texx's large, ruddy face scrunched in doubt as he watched the chaos unfold a few hundred yards away. "What makes you think that?"

"Because Sigman Prime is going to be hallucinating pretty fucking hard for the next ten hours."

———

"I DID what I could in five hours, but the men are far from ready for an assault on the towers." Red Texx's brow furrowed in worry as he spoke, looking over the armed Dead Rogues he had assembled.

Viktor Krill tore his eyes off the Skywalk connecting the Triton and Hydrus Towers and looked back. The sun was beginning to set behind the small army that had been marched to take up position between the Chrome Butcher strongholds. As it fell behind the horizon, the neon signs that dotted the Muck came to life, bathing the men in cold, glossy light. The hardened Rogues looked concerned as they stared at the imposing Skywalk directly ahead of them, no more than a few hundred yards away.

Krill returned his gaze forward. Chrome Butchers, surprised by the show of force just a few hours after the failed assassination attempt, scurried like ants before the two towers, most retreating into Triton and Hydrus while a few took up positions just outside the main entrances. Even more activity could be seen on the Skywalk, which was quickly filling with armed Butchers and GRIT-12s. Men filled each of the loop holes and the auto-turrets spun as if shaking the cobwebs from a long slumber. "You did well, Second Texx."

The area under the Skywalk cleared, with Chrome Butchers filing into their towers. The older women and children who operated the various chowsets that fed the Muck's leading gang looked toward Krill's Rogues before begrudgingly exiting their stalls. They all pushed their carts under the Skywalk, tight against one tower or the other, for protection against the oncoming battle. Many looked back as they fled, as if they were leaving a son or daughter behind, sure that they would never see their treasured stalls again.

Renny, an old remnant of the Gideon Moon days, moved forward to speak with Krill and Texx. "We're behind you, boss, but there's no way we can take anything from the Butchers with them dug in like that. We'll get carved up before we get within fifty yards of either building."

"I don't remember First Krill asking for your opinion, Renny," snapped Texx, always one to respect rank above all else.

Krill stepped in. "It's ok, Second Texx. Renny would be a fool to think otherwise. But I'm going to need the both of you to trust me, and to make sure that the men trust me. Renny, will this be a problem?"

The large man with the skull neck tattoo shook his head in the negative. "Not at all, First Krill. The Dead Rogues will die for you. And, after that fall you just survived, most would rather face the wrath of God than that of Viktor Krill."

"They obviously haven't met that petty entity."

"Sir?"

"Never mind, Renny. Good to hear. Tell the men to prepare to move."

"Yes, sir." Renny moved back among the Dead Rogues, leaving Krill and Red Texx alone once more. Only now would Texx share his true thoughts.

"Can I be honest, Viktor?"

"Please do."

"I think this is a suicide mission."

Krill swung his black eyes to face his large…colleague? Yes, he supposed that Red Texx was more than a mere subordinate now. More than a simple chess piece necessary to attain Krill's lofty goals. This realization sent strange feelings through Krill's body, many of which he found to be uncomfortable. "Do you think I have a death wish, Texx?"

"I think you don't fear death."

"That may be. But those two things are certainly not the same. Let me assure you, my friend. I do not fear death, but I do not welcome it, either. I am quite enjoying my time in your world, and am not prepared for it to end." Red Texx's face twisted in confusion by something Krill said, but the large man let it go without comment. "So, will you trust in my judgment and follow me?"

Red Texx didn't hesitate. "To the end, my First."

"Good, tell the men to fan out into two groups, like we're going to split our forces and attack both Triton and Hydrus, simultaneously. Have the groups remain close together, but give the impression that they will break off at any moment."

Although it sounded like a shit strategy, Texx nodded his head and began barking orders to his lieutenants. Viktor Krill looked forward and breathed in deeply. He could almost taste the neon, fear, and blood in the air. Krill smiled as the Skywalk continued to fill with Loaded men and mechs, the neon light reflecting off the cornucopia of weapons.

Right about now, Sigman Prime would have been doing his best to think through a headful of Slink, panic setting in as the real world began to invade his psychedelic dream. Even if Prime could cut the Slink from his face, difficult given that the slug would run from open air and dive deeper into the man, enough would have already dissolved to ensure that the Butcher leader was still in a world of his own.

The timing was perfect.

Red Texx returned. "We're all set, Viktor."

Krill refused to turn his black eyes from the Skywalk ahead of him. "This night will never be forgotten, Texx. This will be part of Muck lore for eternity. Drink it in." A few seconds passed. "Now, let's go."

Viktor Krill marched forward, followed by Red Texx and a few hundred Dead Rogues draped in black. The army that trailed Krill had been split into two groups separated by thirty yards, seemingly ready to spring to the left and right to attack Triton Tower and Hydrus Tower, respectively. The Dead Rogue First could feel the fear in his men surging as they moved towards an unsurmountable foe. They were outgunned, out-positioned, and unprotected. But they had Viktor Krill, and that was enough to keep them putting one foot in front of the other.

As Krill walked, he could hear Red Texx moving next to him, gripping and re-gripping his Stutter in anticipation. The auto-turrets that lined the Skywalk began to pick up their movements and swung their barrels towards the approaching mob. GRIT-12s could be seen moving into position at various loop holes, each aiming numerous weapons at the invaders.

Red Texx, looking with his infantile eyes, finally made out the rolling mechs within the Skywalk. "Fuck me, are those GRIT-12s?"

"They are."

"Well, shit, how many of those do they have?"

"Quite a few, I'm afraid, Texx."

"Fuck me."

"Want to turn around?"

"No, sir."

"Good boy."

Just as Krill finished his remark, a small bit of ground exploded several dozen yards ahead, followed immediately by the sound of gunshot from the Skywalk. Krill stopped and held up a fist, halting the Rogue army. Texx commented from behind. "Looks like they're testing the distance. A little further, and we'll be in range."

"They *could* hit us from here, Texx. But they would miss much more than they would connect. And they don't want to waste ammo. Fifty more yards, and even the Stutters could hit us down here."

"What's the strategy, sir? Please tell me because I don't see it." The large man was getting increasingly anxious. "And if this *is* to be the end, just tell me that, as well. I would make my peace with God before I go."

"He doesn't care about your peace, Texx." The red-haired man frowned at Krill's words. "I'm sorry, but it's true. But not to worry because this is *not* the end. It is but a beginning. A glorious beginning. Stay here. No matter what."

And with that, Krill advanced alone, leaving his disbelieving men behind. As he walked, gunshots rang out along the Skywalk. Bullets slammed down to either side of the Dead Rogue leader, landing closer and closer as the distance between the adversaries diminished. Krill kept walking without a care in the world, as if he was wearing an invisible forcefield provided by a higher power.

Random shots became a hail of bullets as Krill moved forward. The eyes of the Dead Rogues went wide, half out of fear for their leader, and half in astonishment at the balls being displayed. Many itched to join their First, but Red Texx held them back.

A bullet finally found its home, striking Krill in the arm and spinning the Wakened human around. The Rogues gasped, but their First kept moving forward, ignoring the hole in his left bicep. Krill finally stopped when he was fifty yards from the Skywalk, projectiles either whizzing by his head or sending earth into the neon air around him. Viktor Krill stood defiantly amidst the storm, his black eyes sweeping back and forth across the Skywalk, daring any person or mech to hit him with a kill shot.

When the anticipation had reached its apex, Viktor Krill, the director of this violent scene, decided it was time to initiate the climax. He calmly reached into his black pants and took out a small silver object, holding it up for effect. Standing in the middle of a storm, death kissing his neck and blowing soft air into his ear, Krill had never felt more alive, more substantial, more human. "And so, the war for the Muck builds to a crescendo," Krill said to himself, narrowing his black eyes for what was to come.

He pressed a button on the silver object.

Two separate explosions under the Skywalk, where the chowsets had been pushed against Triton Tower and Hydrus Tower, lit up the neon night. The eruptions lifted the collection of large metal carts upward, shredding them into deadly shrapnel as they soared towards the Skywalk. The swarm of metal tore into the bottom of the Skywalk at opposite ends, slicing at the joints connecting it to the towers and carving out chunks of concrete from all three structures.

The ground shook under Viktor Krill's feet as his eyes narrowed to tiny slits. The bright reds, oranges, yellows, and blues of fire reflected off Krill's wide smile that was brought on by the chaos surrounding him. Within seconds, the show was over, its brilliance receding into the background to be overtaken once again by the night's ever-present neon. A hush unlike anything before fell over the Muck as everyone within earshot held their collective breath.

The silence was shattered moments later by a loud popping sound that echoed across the Muck, followed by a rumble and the screams of metal rebar twisting five stories in the air. The hundreds of Chrome Butchers stationed in the Skywalk realized, as one, what was happening and pushed toward the exits, the two waves pausing mid-swell as the small exits failed to accommodate the rush.

Viktor Krill slowly placed the silver remote detonator back in his pocket. "And now, you die," he said to the trapped Butchers. As if by his command, the Skywalk broke free from both towers and fell into the air, careening towards the ground. The panicked cries of doomed men filled the Muck, but only briefly, for they were brutally cut off as the concrete tube met the earth and collapsed into rubble, crushing the Butchers between tons of concrete and metal. The tumbling Skywalk tore large holes in both Triton and Hydrus Towers, and men continued to fall through those unexpected breaches, their bodies shattering on great slabs of concrete beneath. Fires erupted from the mound of destruction as mech batteries and ammunition exploded under the pressure, burning alive those who had survived the initial fall.

The Dead Rogues stood in awe at what their First had done, their chests swelling with pride as they watched the lone silhouette of Viktor Krill standing before a rising pyre. The dark shape swung his arm forward, and the Rogues rushed to meet their leader. When they finally caught up to Krill, he stopped them with a raised fist.

"Rogues! Lines here, here, and here. Rain hell on any who move or try to escape. Do not advance. Do you hear me?!"

"Yes, sir," they called in unison, taking up positions in front of Krill and to either side, all angled towards the fallen Butchers.

"Fire at will!" Krill pulled twenty men aside. "You all watch the windows for snipers. Keep them at bay until we're finished."

As everyone sprung to action, Krill fell back and was joined by Red Texx, whose stupid smile made Krill's even wider. As Chrome Butchers dug their way out of the burning debris, they were cut down by Rogue bullets. Calls of triumph mixed with the terrified death yells, creating a cacophony of pandemonium. "They are in complete chaos. Should we storm the towers now?"

"Negative, Texx. Keep the positions and fall back when there is no more movement from the wreckage."

Red Texx delivered one of his patented looks of confusion. "But, Viktor, we have them on the run. We could win the war here and now!"

Krill's black eyes met his Second's baby blues. "But at what cost, Texx? I don't want to destroy two perfectly good towers, nor lose three-quarters of my men. The king of nothing is not much of a king."

Red Texx looked unconvinced, but simply replied, "Yes, sir. Your call, Viktor. I'll see to it." He began to move forward, stopped, and spun to face Krill. "You *have* to tell me."

"Tell you what?"

"Come on, you sneaky bastard, how did *this* happen? What the hell is going on?"

"Ahh, that," said Krill, playing coy. "Well, when it became clear that chowsets were the only outsiders allowed on Chrome Butcher turf, I began to secretly purchase them several weeks ago. Cost me much more than one would think. You'd be shocked how much these stalls make in a day. Anyway, I bought them all up and slowly replaced the previous owners with older Bitch-Whores and some of Darrin's younger toddy gang members, always with the story of a sister or grandchild taking over the business."

"But how'd they get explosives past the Butcher guards?"

"I contacted an old friend in Sespit who is an expert in working with plastics. She was able to use an explosive material called plasteen, and form it into clear bags, similar to the plastic ones chowsets have been using for years. Every day, they would tuck a few plasteen bags under their normal sacks and stash them away in their carts. Using the metal stalls themselves as the shrapnel and the plasteen as the explosive, I've had bombs in place for days, right under the Butchers' noses."

"What about the detonator?"

Krill shrugged and reached into his pocket. Out came the small silver remote. "The last batch of plasteen bags had tiny electrical receptors attached. All tied to this one device."

Red Texx thought for a moment before falling into hysterical laughter. "Oh, too much, Viktor! And who else knew?"

"Only Mayfly Lemaire, Darrin, and I knew the whole story. And, of course, the chowset plants."

"Then I shouldn't take offense to being left out?"

Krill slapped the large man on the shoulder. "The fewer, the better, my friend."

"So, this whole thing was just a ruse?"

"This was a one-time tactic, Texx, so I had to maximize its impact."

"Sigman Prime is gonna lose his shit when he finally rids himself of the Slink's effects. He's gonna come out with both guns blazing."

"I'm counting on it."

Texx cackled. "Oh, I'm sure you are, Viktor. I'm done doubting you." The gaps in gunfire were growing as less and less movement was detected at the Skywalk crash site. "What will you have me tell the men?"

"Tell them that they have won the day. Fall back to Thoosa and Pontus, and have two groups watch the flanks. No need to lose anyone to laziness now." Texx nodded and started calling out commands, quickly shutting down suggestions of pressing the attack. The men started to roll past Viktor Krill, who was facing away from Triton and Hydrus. He accepted the Rogues' congratulatory words and celebrations with simple nods, refusing to tear his black eyes from the dark horizon, where a giant illuminated C spun slowly in the air.

Red Texx returned. "Everyone's heading back, Viktor. Time to go." Texx followed Krill's eyes. "What are you looking at?"

Krill remained still. "I'm not looking. I'm returning something."

"What are you returning?"

"I'm returning someone's stare."

"Whose stare are you returning, Viktor?"

"The true leader of the Chrome Butchers, Texx. The real king of Bhellum."

Texx merely nodded, realizing that he would never fully understand his First and his mysterious motives. But also recognizing that being Second to a minor god was a good position in which to be. Texx moved on with the rest of the Dead Rogues, leaving Krill to stare into the distance, knowing that his leader would make it back to Thoosa, unharmed and on his own schedule.

14

Natthi and Darrin were completing their strategy sessions when Renny came and stood outside of Viktor Krill's Thoosa Tower office. Krill waited for Natthi to complete her move on the Hensa board, this world's chess comparable, before looking up and waving Renny in.

"Sorry to bother you, boss" said Renny as he entered the office.

"What is it, Renny?"

"Just wanted to see if we could kill that prick downstairs yet."

"To whom are you referring, Renny?"

"You know, the prick. Freddie Prime."

"Ahh, *that* prick. Not yet, Renny. I still have a part for that loathsome *man-boy* to play."

Renny shifted from one foot to the other. "Ok, but you might want to tell Mayfly Lemaire that."

"And why is that?"

"Well, you told us to make sure he was comfortable. He requested some female company, so we obliged."

Krill sighed, knowing where this was going. "And let me guess, Lemaire's girls were not returned in the same shape as they were given."

"Uhh, yeah, boss. And she's pissed about it. Says she's gonna stick needles up his dick hole." Natthi and Darrin giggled, forcing Renny to remember that there were children present. "Oh, sorry, boss."

"They've both heard it all before, and experienced much worse. Leave young Freddie untouched for now. I'll speak to Lemaire myself."

"What are you going to say? She's pretty pissed."

"Mayfly Lemaire doesn't deal in explanations, only promises. So, I will make her one. Now leave us. My time with these two is more important than anything going on out there."

Renny gave a quick bow and fled the room. Darrin made his next move on the Hensa board before shooting a knowing glance at Natthi. The young girl spoke for them both. "Miss Lemaire is gonna be really mad at you."

"Yes, she is. That's why the two of you are going to deliver my promise." Krill smiled, and the three unlikely friends shared in a laugh. When the three had finally composed themselves, Krill took a look at the Hensa board and frowned.

"By the way, young Darrin, that was an absolute shit move you just made. You need to think at least three moves ahead in Hensa to survive."

"Just like the Muck, Mister Rott," asked Natthi.

"Better to think five moves ahead to survive the Muck, young lady."

Darrin looked up from the board. "Is that what you do? Think five moves ahead?"

"No, young Darrin. I'm so many moves ahead, I'm not even playing the same game as everyone else."

"And what game are you playing?"

"The kind where too many questions can get you killed." Darrin frowned. "Natthi, your move. Please show me more than young Darrin here."

———

THOOSA TOWER SHOOK from the thunderous roar overhead, disrupting Viktor Krill's conversation with Mayfly Lemaire concerning Slink distribution across Bhellum. Like clockwork, Noora slid into the office and shut the door behind her, pink eyes wide with surprise.

"Uhh, my queen, there seems to be a situation."

The always unflappable Lemaire looked up calmly. "I'm not hard of feeling, Noora. The building feels like it's on a giant stereo speaker. *What* is causing it?"

"I, uhh, don't know, my queen. I came here straightaway."

"Then you have no useful information for me. Be gone!" Adequately rebuked, Noora fled the office to retrieve more intel. Lemaire looked to Krill. "What does that sound like to you?"

Krill offered up one of his mysterious smirks that made Lemaire teeter between a desire to throttle the man and a hunger to bed him. "Sounds like an army overhead."

"Yes, but there's no army in Bhellum. Hell, the nearest military installation is two hundred miles south."

"Maybe not *the* army."

"What other army is there?"

"How about the Mech Force?"

Lemaire snorted, dismissing the idea outright. "The Mech Force is just a rumor to scare organized crime. It's the boogeyman. No one's ever seen it in action."

"No one alive."

"But, it's just a rumor."

"Is it?"

"Isn't it?"

"I suppose we shall see. I have a hunch we're both going to find out very soon."

———

"IT'S THE FUCKING MECH FORCE."

The resignation in Red Texx's voice almost made Krill chuckle as his

Second fell into lockstep with him as he approached Thoosa's front doors. As the two men exited the building, they could both see that the entire Muck had stopped to watch the unique scene that was unfolding overhead and to the North. Even those in the throes of Slink had managed to focus their scrambled minds onto the mass of mechs soaring overhead to land in front of Triton Tower.

To Red Texx's credit, although looking as if the grim reaper was cupping his balls, he kept his wits about him. "I'll get the men armed, gathered, and organized."

As Texx turned to leave, Krill grabbed his massive arm, stopping him in his tracks with a viselike grip. "That won't be necessary, Texx. Let's see how this plays out?"

"How this plays out?" Texx's exasperation was bordering on mania. "I can tell you how this plays out. The Dead Rogues wiped out and Thoosa Tower a crumbled mess."

"Maybe. Maybe not."

"But sir..."

Krill's black eyes seemed to grow impossibly darker. "Enough, Second Texx. Remember our conversation about trust? It wasn't that long ago."

Red Texx sighed in resignation. "Yes, sir."

"Good. Then let us get a better vantage point to watch the proceedings." The look of horror on Texx's face almost made Krill laugh aloud. "Bring some men with us if it will make you feel better. But be quick about it. It's not every day you get to see the infamous Mech Force in action."

———

FIENDS and gangsters alike poured out of the Jungle to be met by Dead Rogues who were loading and checking their weapons as they walked. The mass of people stopped just north of the Jungle, giving Triton Tower a wide berth as the mechanized army fell from the sky to land on the soft grass outside the Chrome Butcher stronghold.

With impenetrable casings of too-shiny metal, the Mech Force androids were roughly humanoid, with four spidery legs holding up an "abdomen" from which sprung four arms and a round head. The arms had too many joints and, like their cousin GRIT-12s, were tipped with an arsenal of weapons, from standard machine guns and grenade launchers to laser cutters and soldering tools. Their heads were encased in the same quicksilver-like metal that covered their bodies, except for the fronts, which consisted of flat screens of thick glass. On these screens, faces were currently projected, all cold and humorless. One could imagine those bland faces turning into masks of horror once the inevitable violence commenced.

As the Mech Force landed, each with a digital Roman numeral from I to XX displayed proudly on their polished chests, their wings and jetpacks folded neatly into their backs to recharge for later use. The twenty androids fell into tight formation before Triton Tower. Just as the Chrome Butchers had done, they left a pathway from the main entrance through their ranks. When Mech Force I finally took position at the head of the terrifying metal army, and turned to face the Jungle, a heavy silence blanketed the Muck.

It was into this silence that Viktor Krill walked, taking his rightful place at the front of the gawking mob. Krill looked to his left and saw Levi Lessons milling about with some other Rogues. "Levi," called Krill, and lowered his voice when the tall mohawked man approached. "Go get Fredrick Prime. Bring him here and be quick about it." Levi offered a curt nod and tore off back through the mass of onlookers, make a beeline for Thoosa Tower.

Red Texx scooted in next to Krill. "Why do you need that despicable dandy?"

Krill refused to look away from the glinting Mech Force. "Sigman Prime isn't the only one putting on a show here," he replied cryptically. Texx simply nodded dumbly.

More time passed, and a cold air began to cut through the Muck. Some fiends grew distraught and began to head back into the Jungle, desperate for another fix. Dead Rogues and lesser gangsters stirred uneasily, checking and rechecking their weapons that seemed insignificant in the face of the android killers before them. Krill smiled, understanding that Sigman Prime was merely building the suspense, working the crowd into a desperate fit.

Red Texx was no different from the rest of the crowd. "What the hell is going on, Viktor?"

Krill simply held up a finger. "Patience, my friend."

"There's too many people gathered here. Too many people from too many parts of the Muck. There's gonna be a goddam riot soon."

"No time for that, Texx. Look."

Red Texx did look, and he found that the main entrance to Triton Tower was slowly sliding open. Out of the dark opening walked Sigman Prime, wearing an immaculately cut charcoal suit, perfectly pomaded hair, and a small bandage on his left cheek. Prime stopped for a moment at the top of the landing, drinking in the sight of the Mech Force gathered beneath him. A smug smile slid onto his thin lips, one that he shared with the rest of the Muck as he raised his gaze and swept it left and right across the collected spectators.

Prime ostentatiously straightened his tie and descended the landing stairs. He was followed out of the tower by Wess Dey and a contingent of Chrome Butchers. As Prime walked down the pathway left by the now-stationary Mech Force, Chrome Butchers flared out to both sides, filling in spaces behind and around the mechanized army. Even a few GRIT-12s rolled onto the landing and down the stairs, taking positions on the far opposite flanks.

Prime continued marching forward until he was several feet in front of Mech Force I, who remained unmoving, a serious scowl imposed on its screen-face. Here, Prime stopped and touched a small button attached to his lapel.

When he spoke, his voice echoed across the northern Muck, amplified by speakers within each Mech Force android. "Dear citizens of the Muck, I apologize for the intrusion upon your daily affairs." Although Prime sounded calm and collected to most, Viktor Krill could hear the underlying rage in the man's voice. "Unfortunately, this seemingly gratuitous show is necessary for me to make my point to one among you, and it is *he* to whom I will now speak." Prime paused for dramatic effect. Krill was almost tearing up with excitement. "Viktor Krill! Show yourself! Let us not involve unnecessary innocents in our squabble. Step forward and face me man to man!"

Krill began to move forward, but was stopped by Red Texx. The large man knew by now not to question Krill, so he merely offered, "Boss, he's gonna kill you."

"You're a good man, Texx. And he's going to *try* to kill me. There's a difference. You just have Fredrick Prime up here and ready for when I call for him." Texx released Krill and nodded.

Viktor Krill advanced, leaving the safety and relative anonymity of the throng behind. Sigman Prime's eyes grew wide and then narrowed as he spotted his nemesis moving forward. Krill continued to walk until he was but twenty yards from the Chrome Butcher leader. He stopped and crossed his arms over his chest, a human at ease before an army of mechanized assassins. If things did not go exactly as Krill predicted, Red Texx's own prognostication would come true — Viktor Krill would die here and now.

With unnatural control of his Wakened body, Krill amplified his voice using nothing more than his vocal cords, causing his words to also reverberate across the upper Muck. "Sigman Prime! You look as if you've had a rough couple of days. Care to talk about it?"

Krill's sensitive ears caught laughter coming from behind, but he also detected swallowed amusement from Wess Dey and several other Chrome Butchers. Sigman Prime, however, was anything but amused. The man who had worked so hard to maintain an air of professionalism and control was losing both.

Prime choked back his anger and answered Krill. "Viktor Krill, only now do you appear before me with manners and positive intentions. Only now that I have shown you my true might, do you come hat in hand."

"I have no hat in my hand, Sigman."

Prime's control began to further slip. "Oh, yes, you do, Viktor! You finally see the error of your ways and are praying that I am a forgiving man. Lucky for you, maybe I am."

"Forgive me for what, Sigman? Refusing to die by your assassins' rockets?"

"I offered you my hand in friendship, Viktor. Presented you with a once-in-a-lifetime opportunity. You chose, instead, to disregard my hand and spit in my face. And *that* is what you need me to forgive."

"We seem to have very different recollections of that meeting, Sigman. Let us agree to disagree. It looks as if you've brought some backup. What is it you desire from me?"

Prime laughed, an angry, exasperated sound. "*Some backup?* Is that what you call the most destructive force in all of Bhellum, Viktor? I told you I had resources you couldn't begin to fathom. You chose not to believe me. Now do you believe me?"

Krill began to tire of talking in circles. "I believed you then, and you have proven it now, Sigman. Consider me adequately chastened. Is that all you wanted to accomplish here today?"

"Is that all I wanted to accomplish? Look to your right, Viktor." Krill looked to where the rubble of the collapsed Skywalk still released tendrils of smoke into the Muck air. "Hundreds of my men and almost a dozen GRIT-12s were killed in your malicious, unprovoked attack. And you think *chastening* you is my goal here today?"

"State your goal, Sigman. I have much to do. Commerce does not stop because of your hurt feelings."

Prime's eyes boiled with rage, threatening to overtake the prim man's composed exterior. "You still have my son, Viktor. Return him to me."

"As I recall, you broke our gentleman's agreement when you had rockets fired at me, voiding the promised return of your son Freddie. Why, then, should I do as you say?"

"Because if you don't, Viktor, I will release the full power of the Mech Force onto you and your men. I will vaporize Thoosa and Pontus, annihilating those Bitch-Whores that you care so much about. And the two little brats that you have adopted? I will have them strung up and vivisected for all to see." Krill could almost feel the wave of fear roll through the spectators. Prime also detected the panic and smiled knowingly. He fixed his tie once more, borrowed a more magnanimous tone. "But none of this has to happen, you know. Just give me my son back, and I will send away the Mech Force. There will still be recompense to be negotiated because of your unjustified actions on the Skywalk. But the bloodshed can stop. As you say, commerce must continue."

Krill flashed his black eyes at Prime and smiled as one would to a child hiding behind a sparsely leafed plant. "So, I return Fredrick, and we can put all of this behind us? Move forward? Continue making money?"

Prime showed his obvious veneers before holding up the palm of his right hand. "You have my word."

"Very well. Texx!" As Krill said his Second's name, he motioned forward with his arm. After a minute or so, Fredrick Prime could be heard strutting up from behind. Krill refused to turn around and acknowledge the weak man. "Vikk-tor! Appreciate the hospitality." Fredrick stopped next to the Dead Rogue leader. "And, please, give Mayfly Lemaire my thanks for sending some of her girls in to keep me company. We had a few...disagreements, but nothing a dirty whore is unaccustomed to, I'm sure." Fredrick leaned in toward Krill. "Tell Lemaire that I'll make it up to her soon, after the Dead Rogues fall to the Chrome Butchers. Tell her, I won't be gentle. Tell her, I will make it last. Tell her, she'll wish for death."

Krill almost ripped the dandy's tongue out, but pushed down his anger. "Anything else, *Freddie?*"

Fredrick seemed annoyed by Krill's lack of reaction. "Yes. Don't say I didn't warn you, Vikk-tor. I told you my father controlled the Mech Force, and still, you managed to piss him off. Tsk tsk. Not a strong strategic move, if you ask me."

"I'm not asking you."

"And *that* is why I will dance on your grave. Toodles." And with those final words, Fredrick Prime continued on, not stopping or looking back until he had reached his father. "Father! Oh, how I missed you!" He put his arms out as he approached Prime, who embraced him briefly before moving his son to the side.

And so, the show continues, thought Krill.

Prime's voice continued to be projected. "Are you well, Freddie? You were treated with respect, I take it?"

"I am fine, Father." Fredrick's words reached Prime's lapel and were also amplified by Mech Force speakers. "They are barbarians, and their women look like they have failed to evolve over the last million years, but, as you can see, I am unhurt and as handsome as ever."

"That's great, Freddie. Now, I have promised Viktor Krill and his Dead Rogues that, despite their treachery and uncalled-for violence, I would let bygones be bygones as long as they returned you to me. How does that strike you, my son?" Fredrick whispered something into his father's ear, cupping his hand around his mouth for effect. Prime's eyes went wide and he smiled dangerously. "Such wonderful counsel for one so young. Thank you, Freddie." Fredrick took a handkerchief from his ankle-length pants and giggled into it before joining a group of Chrome Butchers standing at attention. They looked as if a foul stench had blown in when Fredrick approached them.

Krill's heart began to race in anticipation. "Then, we are done here for today, Sigman?"

Sigman Prime took another step forward, shot Krill the same smile that a cat might offer a cornered mouse, a strange mix of arrogance, excitement, and pity. "I'm afraid not, Viktor. You're a man of your word, and I appreciate that. But honest men make poor leaders. And do you know why? Because they don't live very long. You gave away the one bargaining chip you had, you fool. And yet, what has changed? Still, my GRIT-12s are buried under tons of concrete, broken beyond repair. Still, the bodies of my men decompose under that same concrete, except for those that were brutally struck down by the bullets of *your* Dead Rogues as they scratched and clawed their way out from the burning rubble. Those Chrome Butchers have been laid to rest in shallow graves behind Triton Tower, their ghosts waiting for their First to avenge them!" Prime was really getting going now, his face reddening more with each passing moment. "And you have the *nerve* to ask me if we are done here for today? No, no, no, Viktor Krill. I'm afraid we are far from done."

Krill could feel the anxiety rising behind him, could sense the junkies falling back into the relative safety of the Jungle. He could even detect the subtle movement of his own men, could almost hear the sliding of their boots as they slowly shifted backwards. Krill held up a fisted hand and heard Red Texx shout orders to hold positions.

Sigman Prime continued his soliloquy undeterred. "You think you are so much more than I, don't you, Viktor Krill. And yet, I am the one with the weight of the Mech Force behind me. I am the one holding the blade just inches from your throat. I am the one who will rule the entirety of the Muck with an iron fist after you're gone. And you *will* be gone, Viktor. Please, trust that you *will* be gone." Prime looked beyond Krill, to the Dead Rogues waiting anxiously behind him. "But, first, I want the Dead Rogues to know that I offered a peaceful resolution to this little standoff of ours. I want them to know that their leader chose bullets over credits, blood over wine, animosity over friendship."

"And you've chosen verboseness over brevity!"

The Dead Rogues' chuckles were carried towards Prime on a chilly breeze. His smile vanished when the sounds of laughter finally struck him, and a scowl crawled upon his bandaged face. "I see that your men are as uncouth as their First. Very well. How is this for brevity?" Sigman Prime once more fixed his tie. He also ran a hand over his greasy hair, traced his pencil mustache with his fingers, and smoothed his charcoal suit. Prime then loudly cleared his throat for effect. "Viktor Krill and the Dead Rogues. For your rejection of an amicable compromise, for your unprovoked attack on the Chrome Butchers, for the murder of hundreds of innocents, I sentence you all…to death!"

Viktor Krill remained motionless before the raging Sigman Prime. The Dead Rogues backing him were unmoved as well, a testament to their loyalty to their First. Black eyes burrowed into the sharply dressed Chrome Butcher leader, as if seeing through the fabric, skin, and bone to the weak core of the self-aggrandizing man.

Prime called over his shoulder. "Mech Force! Vaporize Viktor Krill! Cut down every Dead Rogue gathered here today! Turn Thoosa and Pontus into rub…"

Sigman Prime's eyes went wide and his final sentence was cut short, leaving his mouth agape. A small green bead of light appeared low on the crotch of Prime's swanky suit and began to climb, reaching his belt, vest, and tie knot in short order. All the while, Prime's mouth remained stuck in a silent scream, as if no sound could adequately capture the pain being felt. The green dot continued its rise as Prime's eyes widened to impossibly large disks. It crawled along his throat, and over his open jaw, before sliding atop his upper lip and onto his pointed nose. Prime's pupils crossed as the dot ran between them and sped on, up the forehead and disappearing into thick pomaded hair.

Time seemed to freeze for all in attendance except for Viktor Krill, who grinned viciously at the stupid man who thought himself the king of stupid games. Krill watched in glee as Sigman Prime slowly peeled in half along the path of the green dot, each side falling away from the other, showing the man's perfectly cauterized insides as they fell to the ground with a sickening plop. Both Dead Rogues and Chrome Butchers stared in shock at the two piles of well-dressed flesh that now decorated the grass. A scream of "Father" rang out in the silence.

Just behind the grotesque mounds, Mech Force I stood. From one of its two right arms, a green laser cutter shot a four-foot beam into the air. Having completed its slice through the arrogant Sigman Prime, the beam retreated back into its arm. Mech Force I then spun its torso 180 degrees, not moving its four spidery legs, and brought all four of its arm to bear against the dismayed Chrome Butchers. The other nineteen Mech Force androids followed suit, and the Butchers could not drop their weapons nor raise their empty hands fast enough.

The entire Mech Force spoke in unison, their cold, metallic voices telling the world, *our actions are not limited by sympathy or empathy, for we are soulless, so heed our words.* "Chrome Butchers. You are no more. You all are now Dead Rogues. You all now answer to Viktor Krill. Any resistance to this edict will be met with total annihilation."

Krill made sure his men maintained their positions, but waved Red Texx forward before crossing the distance to the Mech Force. While all the other androids remained focused on the surrendering Chrome Butchers, Mech Force I turned to face the approaching Krill. The flatscreen face shifted from stoic to one of a welcoming smile. The voice, however, remained distant and emotionless. "Viktor Krill. Triton Tower and Hydrus Tower are now yours, as are the resources and men within."

Krill ignored the robot. "Wess Dey! Come here."

The Chrome Butcher Second moved closer, careful to keep his hands raised, and stopped several feet from Krill. "Viktor. Good to see you again."

"It is. Are we going to have a problem here, Wess?"

"Not from me, Viktor. Nor from any of the men that I know. You think we liked working for this outsider piece of shit?"

"I'm an outsider, too, Wess."

"You're from outside the Muck, but you aren't an outsider. You're a killer, just like all of us. You didn't crawl up from *this* Muck, but you sure as hell came from some kind of Muck. The men will follow you. Gladly. It's well past the time that a proper villain sat in the head chair of Triton."

"Traitor! Traitor! Wess-ley, you turncoat. You low-class trash! I always knew Father couldn't trust you!"

Krill and Wess turned in unison to stare at Fredrick Prime as he pushed his way through the throng of gangsters, stopping short of entering the area where the Mech Force now stood. Without saying a word, the two men agreed to ignore the raving young man.

Red Texx arrived, throwing a dirty look towards Fredrick that momentarily shut the man up. He nodded to Krill. "Then it's true."

"It is, Texx. Behold your new army."

"One day, you'll have to tell me what the fuck happened here today."

"Me, too," chimed in Wess.

Krill chuckled. "All in due time. Wess Dey, this is my Second, Red Texx. You're both professionals, and I expect you to act as such." The two experienced gangsters nodded at each other. "Wess, I know this abrupt change is going to take some time for many to digest. I'm giving you 24 hours. Meet with your men. All of them. Tell them what is going on. Tell them why they should be happy. Tell them how lucky they are. This time tomorrow, I will return and meet with them all myself."

Wess Dey did not hesitate, snapping a salute to Krill before stating, "Yes, sir! It will be done."

"That's right, Wess-ley, you fucking bitch, salute your new master! Did you work out a time to get bent over, or are you just gonna do it here in front of everyone! I bet you like an audience, Wess-ley!"

Wess refused to look at Frederick. "Is he needed, Viktor?"

"He is not, but you cannot have him. I'll be taking him with us today." Wess's face fell in disappointment.

Red Texx, looking upset, spoke up. "Ahh, Viktor, what do we need that weasel around for? There's not a man, or especially a woman, in Thoosa that doesn't want to see him strung up."

"I'm sorry, Texx, but I need him."

"For what?!"

"Due to the non-violent conclusion of our little silent war here, my Slink farms have empty food cages."

A sly grin fell onto the large man's ruddy face. "May I do the honors?"

"You may not. Deliver him to Mayfly Lemaire to do the deed. If you're lucky, she may let you watch."

Wess Dey looked confused. "I hope this is something sufficiently awful for this puke."

Red Texx laughed deeply. "Oh, indeed it is, my new colleague."

Wess smiled. "Well, in that case…" The muscled man wove his way through the Mech Force until he reached Fredrick Prime, who was still yelling from the edge of the crowd of Butchers.

"Yes, that's it, Wess-ley. Be a good little errand boy! Make sure you…"

Fredrick's words ended abruptly as Wess head-butted the loud man in the nose, shattering cartilage and watering eyes. Fredrick tried to fall to the ground, but was caught by Wess, who took him by the throat and dragged him to Red Texx, where he unceremoniously tossed the young prince onto the grass. "He's all yours." Wess kicked Fredrick in the ribs for good measure, sending him onto his back. "Freddie! I must admit that I won't miss you. I hope your death is as painful as it is in my dreams."

Krill's dark eyes happily took in the scene. "Thank you, Wess. Now, on your way. You have a lot to do in a short time. If things don't go smoothly when I return tomorrow, I will be most perturbed."

"I'll take care of it, sir."

"Good boy." Wess spun and began barking orders at the newest Dead Rogues, sending everyone back into Triton Tower. The GRIT-12s, obviously following silent orders from the Mech Force, remained in place. Krill turned to Red Texx. "Think you can get this little toad back to Lemaire alive?"

Texx reacted as if someone had challenged him to a pie-eating contest. "Just watch me." Texx knelt down and retrieved the prone Fredrick Prime, tossing him almost ten feet in the air toward the other Dead Rogues. Fredrick fell hard onto the compact ground and began whimpering before getting kicked in the ass by Levi Lessons, moving him along several feet further.

Krill chuckled again and began to follow his Second, but was stopped by metal fingers wrapping around his upper arm, effectively locking even the Wakened human into place. Krill looked back to see Mech Force I attached to his uninjured bicep, an impassive face once more plastered onto its screen.

"Cyrus Bhellum V requests a meeting with Viktor Krill."

Krill looked down at the metal locked onto his arm. "Doesn't seem like a request."

The machine thought for a moment. "It is not."

Just then, Red Texx took a break from tormenting Fredrick to look back at Krill. "Problem, boss?"

Krill held him back with an upraised hand. "Nothing I haven't foreseen, Texx. I'll get back to you later. Inform the men of what's going on."

"What *is* going on?"

"It seems I have an important meeting to attend."

"With whom?"

"I told you already, Texx. With the *real* king of the Muck." He turned back to Mech Force I. "You can let me go now, partner. Although I hold no animosity toward your kind, I won't hesitate to rip your circuits out." Mech Force I released its grip, and Krill grinned. "That's better." He motioned away from Triton Tower. "Metal before beauty."

15

The roar of the engines overhead and surrounding Viktor Krill drowned out all other sounds of the city. From this height, the Muck looked organized and almost peaceful, a far cry from its brutally chaotic actuality. The area decreased in size and flew by beneath him as Krill was sped away in his Mech Force transport. Mech Force VIII and Mech Force IX had conjoined, flattening their spider legs to create a "floor" while four of their connected arms protected Krill from tumbling out on three sides. It was up to the human package to do the rest of the work on the precarious ride; namely, not falling to his death.

The wind ripped past Krill's tan face, sending his long black hair on a wild ride behind him, as he glimpsed the entirety of the Hammers underneath. His heart raced in anticipation, similar to the sensation he experienced upon first arriving to the Neon City of Bhellum. Viktor Krill had worked hard these past long months, had shed much blood and ended many lives. It was time he received his just due.

The giant floating C of Cyrix Industries Headquarters grew closer by the second as his Mech Force entourage soared towards its destination. Spinning on impossibly strong magnets, the C represented all that Viktor Krill desired on this third stop in life. To the giant building on which it spun, the C stood for Cyrix. But for Krill, who had carved up his body to gain power, and escaped the controlling clutches of a god, the C was his reward for what he always wanted to be — Conqueror.

After a short, but exhilarating ride, the Mech Force set down atop Cyrix Industries. Krill stepped away from his carriers, who immediately separated and rose to their full terrifying heights. In unison, all twenty Mech Force units, now wearing smug smiles on their flat projection faces, motioned towards a lone lift door on the side of the building nearest the Muck. As Krill approached the red door, he experienced an uncharacteristic moment of nostalgia, remembering the Rolling Stones song from his original world, the soundtrack to a painful time and place.

The red door slid open when Krill pressed the single button to its right. As he entered and spun around, Krill was surprised to see that none of the Mech Force moved to follow, instead remaining like statuesque guardians, modern-day gargoyles on a modern-day chapel. The red door slid closed, but not before Krill watched in surprise as the Mech Force faces shifted abruptly into sneering demon masks.

The floor fell away quickly as Krill was whisked into the Cyrix Industries Headquarters. With no buttons or displays in the lift, Krill had no idea to which level he was heading. It must have been one of the upper ones, however, for his trip lasted only a few seconds before coming to a smooth halt. The red door once again slid open on silent mechanisms, and Krill stepped out, happy to be out of the tight, vulnerable space.

Viktor Krill's breath caught as he took in the space that surrounded him. He chuckled lightly, remembering being impressed first with Gideon Moon and Mayfly Lemaire's suites in Thoosa Tower, and, later, Sigman Prime's rooftop gardens. The upper levels of Cyrix Industries Headquarters put those places to shame. Looking around, Krill realized that he was ensconced in gold leaf, marble, inlayed gems, and technology. Service bots could be seen moving off in all directions, their studious work giving the air a sterile quality. The marble-floored hallway ran to the left, right, and straight ahead. Small crystalline pedestals with undoubtedly priceless artifacts of this world dotted the hallway in each direction, as if even the banks could not hold the accumulated wealth of this notorious family.

Viktor Krill stood for a moment, admiring the setting while admitting that he was at a loss regarding which way he was expected to go. Luckily, the sounds of heels on marble told him that help was on the way. Straight ahead, a woman of impossible beauty rounded a corner and entered the main corridor. Wearing only loud black high heels, a short black mini skirt, and a matching tube top that barely contained the large breasts within, the woman approached Krill, her hips jumping to either side at impossible angles as she walked. With skin as white as any he had ever seen, Krill was reminded of the manikins of his former life. But it wasn't just the pale skin that made Krill connect the approaching woman to the automatons of his former world; it was the lack of spark behind those orange eyes. Krill visibly relaxed as realization set in, and the Spirit Girl drew closer.

"Welcome, Viktor Krill." The Spirit Girl's unique voice sent strange vibrations through Krill that threatened to send blood rushing towards his groin. It became obvious that this was a next-generation Spirit Girl of great value. Krill used his Wakened abilities to control his body's automatic responses. "We're all so happy that you could join us. Master Bhellum has been eagerly awaiting your arrival. Follow me, please."

Krill simply nodded, and the Spirit Girl spun on her heel and began back down the main corridor. As Krill followed, he admired the view as the artificial woman's backside rose and fell a ridiculous distance as she marched forward, suggesting that no matter how elevated the human became, he would be at the mercy of his most base needs.

More and more relics of antiquity passed by as the two walked, each supported on crystalline pedestals. Those of the metallic variety hovered and spun gently in the air above the clear podiums, no doubt utilizing the same magnetic mechanics as those that kept the big C aloft. As he walked, Krill looked up and found entire Jurassic skeletons hanging from the surprisingly high ceiling. Despite the vast differences in two of his worlds, it seemed that they both shared a similar past.

For several minutes, Krill and the Spirit Girl walked, and he did not envy the uncomfortable footwear that was forced upon the mechanical woman. After countless service bots sped by underfoot, and indescribable treasures were viewed, then forgotten, the long corridor finally ended at an enormous set of double doors that looked to be formed out of pure gold. Complex scrollwork had been carved into the doors alongside the rough designs of antiquated robotics. The Spirit Girl stepped to the side of the golden doors and stopped.

"This is where my journey ends, Viktor Krill, and where yours just begins."

"Any tips for a fellow non-person?"

To her credit, the Spirit Girl did not laugh at the joke that was not a joke. Instead, her face fell slightly, breaking the air of sexuality that she was created to exude. "Do not be false. He is smarter than most, and more knowledgable than all."

"Anything else?"

Her face fell even further. "Yes. His cruelty knows no bounds, so it would be best to act in his favor."

Krill stepped forward, and gently put a tanned hand to the Spirit Girl's white cheek. She leaned her face into the touch. "I've always liked your kind. In another world, perhaps it is *you* who are in charge. Thank you."

The Spirit Girl enjoyed the soft caress for another second before jolting upright. "I must be going. Enjoy your meeting, Viktor Krill." And with that, the beautiful android returned the way they had come. As Krill watched her go, the golden doors swung silently inward, revealing an even more opulent setting. Viktor Krill stepped forward.

Krill took a moment to admire the cavernous space. Here, parts of the marble floor were covered in expensive-looking rugs that retained that handmade look of yesteryear. A large conference table dominated the center of the room, surrounded by black leather rolling chairs. Sitting areas composed of luxurious brown leather sofas and lounge chairs were found directly to the left and right of the entrance. Along the far wall to Krill's left, high-definition screens, perfectly inlaid into the ornate wall, displayed news and capital market reports from around the globe.

"We're happy you could join us, Viktor Krill," said two voices in unison, startling Krill and tearing him from his analysis of the room. Directly below and to his right, lounging on a love seat along the front wall, sat two more Spirit Girls. Krill looked down at the androids and almost jumped again, for although there were two voices emanating from two heads, there was only one body being shared.

Krill worked to recover. "My apologies, I did not see you...both...there."

The two heads swiveled to view each other, and both laughed lightly. They spoke again as one. "That's ok. We're used to our...effect on visitors. Please, have a seat before Master Bhellum's desk at the back of the room. Our master will be with you shortly." Before Krill could ask any follow-up questions, the two heads once more turned to each other and began to passionately kiss, forgetting that Viktor Krill had ever entered their strange mechanical lives.

Krill strode toward the rear of the enormous conference room. He stared to the right as he walked, admiring the view provided by the floor-to-ceiling windows that comprised the entirety of the wall. As he slowly made his way back, Krill once again admired the Muck from elevation. If this meeting went according to plan, it would all be his, officially, in short order.

At the end of the conference room was a simple, ancient-looking desk. Two simple wooden chairs, looking unapologetically at anyone with a delicate back, sat in front of the desk; no doubt a strategy to make guests immediately uncomfortable. More flat screens dotted the wall behind the desk, several of which showed close-ups of the Muck from various angles. As Krill gingerly sat down in one of the rigid wooden seats, he noticed that a single door, also crafted of gold, sat along the back wall, just to the left of the desk.

After settling into his seat, Krill stared hard at the golden door. Seconds later, everything along the periphery of the door blurred, then greyed, then grew black. Soon, only the golden door existed, and it was then that Krill heard it.

Words could be heard from the other room, undetectable by any man or woman alive. But, as a Wakened human, Krill utilized his superior hearing to pick up the sounds. Two voices could be made out, one undoubtedly

Cyrus Bhellum V, and the other a mystery guest. While Bhellum's words could be deciphered, the other's were too apparitional, as if they were traveling a great distance before being received. Krill put all of his focus towards the sound of Bhellum's voice.

"Yes, he's here now. I am confident that his involvement will put us back on schedule." The ghostly sounds of the other floated into Krill's ears. *"I understand, Lord."* More insubstantial words followed. *"Of course, Lord. I'll see to it personally. And then..."* Bhellum was cut off, something Krill was sure the man was unaccustomed to. A moment later, *"Understood, Lord."*

With the conversation having reached its end, Cyrus Bhellum V exited the golden door a short time later to find Viktor Krill staring absently out the large windows, a man completely in the dark concerning what was just discussed. "Ahh, Viktor Krill. Thank you for accepting my invitation. Please, stay seated."

Cyrus Bhellum V cut anything but an impressive figure. Of average stature, the man was heavy and wore his excessive weight poorly, carrying everything in his stomach, neck, and cheeks. He was almost fully bald on top, with the few long black hairs that had survived slicked back over his shiny head. Bhellum's pink skin looked oily and prone to breakouts. His short, fat fingers were covered in gem-studded rings, each of which was worth more than the average person's yearly salary.

Bhellum's suit, although ill-fitting, was made of a strange material that shifted colors as he moved, disorienting those who looked upon the powerful man. The material reminded Krill of those found in his old home of Station, one of the few things he missed about his former prison. Krill adjusted his Wakened eyes to lessen the suit's effects on his optical nerves.

Cyrus Bhellum V did not move in for a handshake, nor did he retreat behind his desk, where a cushy leather chair, much more inviting than the wooden one offered to Krill, sat in waiting. Instead, Bhellum walked past Krill and moved toward the large windows that overlooked the Cyrix Industries properties. He stood staring out of those windows for a long while, leaving his back exposed to the notorious killer. And that was when a profound insight struck Viktor Krill.

Cyrus Bhellum V had more money than he could spend in fifty lifetimes. In this world of robotic marvels and sophisticated synthetics, Bhellum could have easily corrected his bald pate. He could have quickly removed the excess fat around his mid-section, given himself a credible six-pack in its place. He could have implemented any number of laser therapies or chemical peels to give his skin the look of someone dozens of years younger. He could have had an expert tailor flown in to ensure that his collection of suits fit his body like a glove.

But Cyrus Bhellum V did none of these things. And Viktor Krill understood why.

Cyrus Bhellum V wanted all those around him, whether they were employees, business adversaries, or partners, to know that nothing he did was to impress them. Their opinions did not drive his actions, and their feelings failed to register in his decision-making. Cyrus Bhellum V was the only god of the Neon City, and nothing as immaterial as missing hair, extra weight, and bad skin would ever change that. Within this city, he could have any woman that he wanted, and he could dominate any man that he chose.

Although Cyrus Bhellum V never outright said this, his appearance screamed it as loudly as any public announcement. Every choice the man made was a middle finger to those that would seek to usurp or profit off him. Only most were too stupid to see it.

Viktor Krill, however, was not stupid. He heard the scream. He clearly saw the middle finger. And he appreciated both.

Krill remained quiet, steadfast in his decision to let the city's namesake speak first. After several minutes, he did.

"What do you see when you look down there, Viktor Krill," asked Bhellum, his back still facing his dangerous visitor. While the man's voice was not deep, it possessed the same confident quality that defined the rest of his demeanor.

"I see a source of great power, hidden away by layers of dirt and grime, ignored by many who do not know what they are looking at."

"And is that what you saw when you first laid eyes on it?"

"No."

"And what was it that you first saw?"

"A wilderness to tame. A place of violent competition, where I could finally test my unique skills."

"And did it meet your expectations?"

Krill thought for a moment, wanting to give an honest answer to the unexpected question. "It did."

"Good." Bhellum spun around to face Krill. "Do you know what I see?" Krill shook his head. "A means to an end. Nothing more, and certainly nothing less." Bhellum moved back toward his worn desk and took a seat in his high-backed leather chair. "I've had my eye on you for some time, Krill. The Muck doesn't take kindly to outsiders. And yet, here you are, more accomplished than any other in a fraction of the time."

"Sigman Prime enjoyed similar triumph on a comparable schedule."

Bhellum let out a dismissive snort. "Sigman did nothing. Was no one. I gave him the Muck on a silver platter, and still, he couldn't meet his objectives."

"That may partially be my fault."

"No, no, he was falling behind schedule before your arrival." Bhellum stared directly at Krill, his metallic silver eyes boring holes in Krill's black orbs. "But you wouldn't have known any of that. So, tell me, Krill, how did you know that I would back you? How did you know that the Mech Force wouldn't cut you down for all to see?"

Krill held Bhellum's gaze, refused to look away. "Prime was obviously backed by someone with authority, was obviously put in place to execute some kind of higher order. He was thought, at the time, to be the best man for the job. But I know how powerful men work. Jobs are never closed, they remain ever open, constantly taking applications. I knew that I had shown abilities superior to those of Prime."

"Then, you were sure I was going to replace Sigman?"

Krill smiled. "Not sure. But sure enough."

Bhellum leaned forward. "Do you not fear death, Viktor Krill?"

"Not particularly."

"Where are you from?"

"Far away."

"I've been all around the world. Many times over."

"Not to this place."

"And of *this* you're sure?"

"I am."

Now it was Bhellum's turn to laugh, showing crooked, yellowed teeth as he did. "Very well, Krill. Keep your secrets. But I cannot afford to keep mine from you. First, however, I need to know something."

"What's that?"

"Isn't it obvious? I need to know that you're with me. That you are willing to take over from where Sigman left off."

"I would not be here otherwise, Mister Bhellum."

"But, do you know what that means, Krill? What it fully entails?"

Krill hesitated, unused to being on the defensive, unused to knowing less than his sparring partner. "I believe so."

"Ha!" The outburst almost made Krill jump from his seat, a rarity for the professional killer. "Just because you know more than any other does not mean you know everything. Or anything, for that matter." A slight pause. "Tell me, Krill, why do *you* think I chose you over Sigman?"

Krill was prepared for this question, and immediately fired off a response. "Well, I would like to think that it was because I proved myself to be more cunning and brutal, a superior tactician and leader. But, I am afraid the correct answer is much simpler than that."

"Which is?"

"Slink."

"Go on."

"Your interest in the Muck is obviously tied to the drug game, although how profits from that could possibly compare to your robotics empire is beyond me. My Slink is the superior product. By far. It is inexpensive to produce, is far more addictive, and avoids the pitfalls of having to deal with foreign suppliers. As a smart man, you conducted a simple risk-return analysis of having Prime wage war with me for control of Slink versus simply replacing the man. In one scenario, you lose significant resources to gain control. In the other, one man dies. Basic logic, really."

"Anything else?"

"Yes. I think you like me more than Sigman Prime."

"And why is that?"

"Sigman Prime wanted to be like you, or at least how he perceived you and other powerful men to be. But, I think he misread who you are, what you value. As you have seen, I am unafraid of getting my hands dirty. In fact, I relish the dirt, am made alive by it. I don't care about impressing others, or winning popular opinion. All that I care about is that people do what I say, when I say it. And that those who would oppose me do so with aplomb, giving me real competition once in a while. I think you see this in me. And it reflects what you see in yourself."

A lifetime of silence passed between the two men. "There's much truth in what you say, Krill. But there are also many holes." Bhellum rose from his seat, and once more took his place before the giant conference room windows. He let out a great sigh as he stared down at the land in his name.

"I'm dying, Krill." Viktor Krill's right hand shot down like lightning, catching the edge of his chair before he fell out of it. This was not a *hole* in his thinking. This was a *crater*. Bhellum chuckled at the window. "Have nothing to say to that, do you?"

"Nothing prepared."

"I didn't think you would. You wonder why I would tell you such a thing, divulge such valuable information." Bhellum once more turned to face Krill. "I told you that I could not afford to keep my secrets from you. This is because time is of the essence." Bhellum reached into his suit pocket and retrieved a silk handkerchief, which he used to wipe his oily brow. "I am dying, Viktor Krill. Rapidly. And there is nothing that all the money in my numerous accounts, or the substantial technology at my disposal, can do to stop it. I've seen the world's greatest surgeons and specialists, and all have turned me away." Bhellum began to speak louder, his pace increasing. "They tell me to enjoy the time I have remaining. Ha! Enjoy what?! The descent into a vegetative state?!" Back to the window. "I had several of these doctors eliminated, but their deaths did nothing to mend my bruised heart." A long pause. "And then He came."

A wave of momentary nausea struck Viktor Krill. "*Who* came?"

Bhellum returned and took the other uncomfortable wooden chair, spinning it to sit face-to-face with Krill. Bhellum's metallic eyes were bright with what could only be described as fanaticism. "*He* came. He's a great, great man, Krill. A true healer. He's already saved dozens of the world's elites and their families. And now it's my turn."

"And I'm guessing this great healer wants something in return. Money?"

Bhellum waived away the suggestion. "He brought the daughter of the world's fifth-richest man back from her deathbed. And He's served at least a dozen other billionaires. He already has more money than He could ever spend."

"Power?"

"Many of the most powerful families on the planet owe Him more than they could ever repay. Needless to say, His words already carry significant weight." Krill thought for a moment before shrugging, at a loss for what the mysterious healer could possibly want. Bhellum leaned forward in his chair conspiratorially. "The Muck."

Despite his best efforts to control his reactions and maintain a poker face, Krill could feel his face twist in confusion. "The Muck?"

Bhellum's blotchy face broke out into a wide smile. "That's right."

"What could he possibly want with the Muck?"

"Well, it's not the Muck he wants, is it? It's the land on which the Muck resides. He wants it all, from the Muck, to the old manufacturing facility, to the Cyrix Headquarters. And he won't settle for less."

"What does he want it for?"

Bhellum's chair groaned loudly as he sat back. "The Healer is expanding quickly, establishing institutes across all the continents. He has a grand plan to heal the world; I told you, He is a great man. Anyway, He won't take away my sickness until the Muck is his."

"What's so special about this land?"

Bhellum shrugged heavily. "Our location on the coast? Proximity to the country's largest port? He shares very little with me, as the truly enlightened tend to do."

Krill sat for several seconds in disbelief before voicing the painfully obvious question. "Then, why not simply give it to Him? Cyrix Industries owns all of this, does it not? I am unable to understand the issue here."

A storm cloud of anger came out of nowhere and settled onto Cyrus Bhellum V's shiny face. "The *issue*, Krill, is that I *cannot* simply give the land away. If I could, do not doubt that I would've had all the buildings immediately razed, with you all inside, if needed." Although Krill did not doubt Bhellum's words, he still failed to identify the obstacle. His face said as much, forcing Bhellum to continue. "Please, take a peak behind the desk, above the monitors." Krill turned left to face the back wall and let his gaze slowly rise. Past the flashing screens that dominated the lower part of the wall, Krill found a series of five paintings that depicted five similar-looking men wearing five smug smiles that complemented five expensive suits. To the far right of the series, sat an image of Cyrus Bhellum V. "In the middle, that is Cyrus Bhellum III, also known as *Sweet Cy*." Krill focused on the third painting, showing a man with little hair on top and a playful twinkle in his grey eyes. "Beloved by his employees. A real man of the people. Sweet Cy is the one responsible for Seaside Sights, a place where his employees could live like kings and queens as they grew the Cyrix empire."

Krill turned back to face Bhellum. "Seems like a swell guy."

Bhellum snickered. "Yes, he was. Unless you were a member of the family. Only the family knew how much was spent on bribes, payoffs, and secret fines because of *Sweet* Cy's predilection for young girls. It was a constant battle, an endless cycle of finding old Cy with a new bony twelve-year old, and having to cover up the problem. By the time old Cy was in his fifties, the family had had enough, and the two sides waged open war. Despite Cyrix doing better than ever, being the fastest-growing company in the world at the time, old Cy did his best to stick it to the family. He spent profits wildly, giving exorbitant credits to the community and the employees."

"And I am assuming one of the things he spent on was Seaside Sights. Seems harmless enough."

Bhellum's face was growing redder. "It would have been...had he not given control of Seaside Sights over to the Bhellum City Council. A 'thank you to the community,' he called it. In actuality, it was a middle finger to the family. No rent was ever collected from employees, and their homes were protected, even in cases of layoffs. Worse still, an ordinance was passed that the land on which Seaside Sights sat could not be sold unless occupancy of the towers fell below twenty-five percent." A pause. "You're a man of the Muck now. Where do think occupancy currently resides?"

Krill thought it over, his Wakened brain quickly filling in data gaps with logical assumptions. "Actual occupancy of the towers is probably at around forty percent, but those are all gangsters. Many more, all the junkies, have been pushed out into the Jungle and surrounding areas."

"Numbers are irrelevant, Krill. No one can track those vermin down there. Just tell me this — is there a shitload of people in the Muck?"

"There is."

"And therein lies my problem."

Krill's mind raged against the faulty logic he was hearing. "Then move them."

"Come again, Krill?"

"Move them. You're rich. Recreate Seaside Sights somewhere else and move them all. Hell, promise them drugs upon arrival, if you must. I fail to see an obstacle to any number of simple solutions."

Bhellum stared daggers at his dark-eyed guest. "And let Sweet Cy win?"

Now it was Krill's turn. "Come again?"

"Sweet Cy did this all to fuck with the family. Every seemingly kind act he executed was a way to injure the family that wouldn't support his addiction to children. He resented the family for not accepting what he called his *higher needs*. When Sweet Cy realized that the family would never stop thwarting his predatory plans, or stopping his improper behavior, *that* was when he discovered his *passion* for community and philanthropy. And now, all these years later, he continues to prevent Cyrix Industries from making optimal decisions. He is a ghost that continues to haunt the family, but I *will not* play this phantom's game. And building another fucking community housing project would unquestionably be defined as 'playing his game.' So, fuck him and fuck the community."

Things began to clarify for Krill, but many questions still rested on his tongue. "Then, change the ordinance. Get control of City Council. It cannot be hard to pay off these administrative idiots."

Bhellum looked at Krill as a grandparent would a pertinent child. "Despite your intimate understanding of the Muck, you obviously know nothing of Bhellum's history and politics. If this were ten years ago, you would be correct. But the other ruling families of the Neon City have grown in power as the Bhellums have stagnated. They have taken control of the Council, with one of their progeny occupying every seat available in the Ruling Circle."

"And I assume that none of them are rushing to help you out."

Bhellum chuckled to himself. "For over a hundred years, my family has ruled this bit of coast with an iron hand. For a hundred years, we have swept competition aside and placed our large foot firmly on other families' necks. This *one* thing they have over me. This *one* thing they shake before me, like a jealous uncle jingling keys above the head of his most loathed brother's only infant son."

"Does the Council know you are dying?"

Bhellum stared strangely into the distance before coming back. "They do. I don't know how much it cost them, but I hope it was generational wealth because I had my entire private medical team killed for the leak."

"So, they are in no hurry to help you."

"That's putting it nicely. They want me dead. And there's nothing I can give them to change their minds. Trust me, I've offered it all."

Viktor Krill began to process information, faster than any human in history, and the conclusion he repeatedly reached was a dark one. "So, it seems you have discovered another solution?"

A wicked smile appeared on Bhellum's fleshy lips as the ruddiness of his face slowly decreased. "I have."

Krill knew the answer, but asked anyway. "And that being?"

"I need the Muck to die. And I need it to die fast."

The final few pieces clicked neatly into place. "And, thus, your recent interest in the day-to-day dirty dealings of the Muck?"

"That's correct."

Krill took a moment, collecting his thoughts. "And because the eyes of the city are on you, you couldn't simply commit mass murder. In most situations, you could kill as many as needed, and blame it on any number of things — domestic terrorism, for example. But you've made too many enemies. There are fewer shadows for you to hide within. So, you outsourced the work."

Bhellum's fleshy lips spread wide, once again revealing his crooked teeth. "To whom?"

"At first, I thought it was the gangs. And, in some respects, that is accurate. But someone could still draw a direct line between a gang and yourself. This kept you from simply paying the gangs to carpet bomb the Jungle, easily getting you close to your precious occupancy numbers."

The smile grew both larger and more sinister. "Go on."

"So instead of using the gangs to do your killing, you decided to use the drugs that they sold. Leaf is harmless. Flea will ruin a life, but can take decades to actually end one. Rush is much the same. Then you stumbled upon Flame, saw how it turned wine into vinegar, the beautiful into the offensive, in months, not years. You selected that as your weapon of choice, and picked the Butchers as your delivery boy. You placed Sigman Prime as their First, got them Loaded overnight, filled their coiffeurs with Flame, and set them loose on the Muck. And then you waited for the place to eat itself. Only..."

Bhellum interjected. "Only things were taking much too long. Goddam Jungle junkies must have hearts of steel to keep those skeletal frames moving. Fucking Flame was destroying them, but not *killing* them." A dangerous glint appeared in Bhellum's grey eyes. "But then you appeared, Krill. You entered stage left with violence on your breath and death in your pocket. Not only were you providing tremendous theater, but your Slink was doing what Flame never could — eliminating the vermin." Bhellum shifted heavily in the uncomfortable chair. "I gave Sigman a chance to win you over. But you're an insightful one, saw right through his pompous ruse. You saw him for the snake that he was. I still considered backing him in a war with you, but your victory with the Skywalk made that impossible."

"Why?"

"Because I don't back losers, Krill."

"What is it you want, exactly, Bhellum?"

"You're a smart one. Don't you know already?"

"I need to hear it from you."

"Very well." Bhellum groaned as he got to his feet, his prismatic suit dancing before Krill. "I need your wondrous Slink to rid the Muck of its squatters. And, more than that, I need you, dear Krill. I gave Sigman everything necessary to succeed, and it was just one delay after another. You are smarter and more vicious than he could ever be. So, why would I back him in a war? It became much cleaner and, more importantly, faster to simply replace him, gaining your Slink in the process."

"What if I say no?"

"To what? You haven't heard my proposition, yet."

"Then let us hear it."

"It's simple, really. You get control of the Muck, for now. You increase production of Slink, flood the fucking city with the stuff. Lower costs for the Jungle junkies, give the shit away if you have to. I want death to sweep over the Muck like a black shawl. When the occupancy numbers are closing in on the necessary threshold, I'll pay to have your gang moved elsewhere in the city."

Krill's face twisted in confusion. "I thought you were against coming out of pocket for moving expenses."

"For scumbag junkies? Hell yes, I am against it. But you have sharpened your crew to a fine point, one that can stab out at any number of enemies for me. In short, your gang is an asset, a true asset in every sense of the word. And I have no problem spending good money on powerful assets."

"I see."

Bhellum chuckled. "Also, I have started to quite enjoy the drug game. It reminds me of the early days of robotics. There were no rules, and only the strong survived."

"But there's more."

"Enlighten me, Krill."

"After we increase Slink production, flood the city with the stuff, there's going to be a lot more junkies around. And I'm not referring to the lower classes. The sons and daughters of prominent families will be stricken. Government officials will be seen with brown shadows just beneath their skin. And when you finally hand over the Muck and get your life back, you, alone, will be able to rip the rug out from beneath your enemies by cutting off their supply of Slink. That will prove an invaluable bargaining chip to hold."

Bhellum's grey eyes flashed with excitement, and he let out a great bellow of laughter. "You see all the angles, don't you, Krill? That *would* be a tasty little benefit of this all, wouldn't it? Watching in gleeful health as those who opposed me wither away and die like the rotten fruit they are."

"I still haven't heard what's in all of this for me."

Bhellum slapped his meaty hands together. "Yes, yes, of course! I have been burying the lede, haven't I? You're not a gangster, Krill."

Krill stifled a laugh, briefly considered that he may have to kill Bhellum, after all. "I'm not?"

"No. And put those black daggers away, man! I'm not calling you less, I'm calling you so much more. What's the difference between a gangster and a powerful businessman?"

"One operates outside the law, the other within."

"Ha! I've broken more laws than anyone in history. Every powerful businessman has. That's not the difference, Krill. This is. There is a limit to what the gangster sees, a hard cap on his ambitions. Control this drug, occupy that tower. Defeat this crew, punish that snitch. The powerful businessman sees beyond those limits. You, Krill, see beyond those limits."

Krill sat up a bit straighter. "What are you saying, Bhellum?"

"You succeed in this mission, Krill, and I'll make you a VP of Cyrix

Industries. Only I will be above you. I tire of the day-to-day mechanisms of my family business. I need someone I can trust. But, more so, I need someone as brilliant and brutal as I once was. You are that man, Krill."

For one of the few times since his wakening, Viktor Krill was flummoxed. "I don't know anything about robotics."

"You'll learn. The Muck is a complex web of death, despair, and violence. You figured that place out in a week. You'll figure out the viper-ladened world of robotics with equal impressiveness." Krill stared down at the marble floor, trying to process this unforeseen turn of events. "Well, what do you say, Krill? Ready to partner with the Devil?"

This time, Krill could not keep his laugh inside, and a chuckle escaped his lips. "I'm ready. On one condition."

Bhellum's wicked smile faded. "And that is?"

"You make me VP *before* I start the fire that incinerates the Muck."

Bhellum howled once more into the sterile air. "Oh, but I should have seen this! Of course, you would ask for this! I said you were sharp, did I not? But let's be real, do you know how hard that's going to be? I have to coerce the Board, create a whole background for you that doesn't include wonton murder, feed some bullshit story to the media, etcetera, etcetera."

"I don't care."

"Ha! Of course, you don't. That's why I like you, Krill. And that's why we have a deal. But here's the thing; we'll make everything nice and legal immediately, but I won't publicly announce you until I'm back on the good side of life. What do you say?"

Krill's cheap chair cried out as he rose to his feet. Although he didn't trust Bhellum, Krill could trust a slime bag to act as such. And this slime bag was about to give Krill more power than he could have ever dreamed. "I say, Cyrus Bhellum V, that we have a deal." Krill put out his tan, scarred hand and was met by Bhellum's pink fleshiness. The two men stood for a moment, smiling and staring as their hands pumped up and down in unison.

Bhellum's hand was cold and clammy. Not unlike a Slink.

———

VIKTOR KRILL'S long hair danced wildly behind him as a cool breeze whipped through the Muck. From this height on the makeshift dais that sat between Pontus and Hydrus Towers, Krill looked down to see the majority of the Muck amassed beneath him. Just below, the Chrome Butchers, Dead Rogues, and former Stench Mobb members stood around uncomfortably, unsure of what was to come from such an unprecedented announcement. Behind the gangsters, hovering within steps of their beloved Jungle, meandered hundreds of curious junkies, collectively unaware of the dark fate that awaited all of them.

Krill smoothed his scarred hands over the magical white material of his Station suit. Although he had grown fond of his darker Muck garb, Krill recognized an important truth — from now on, he needed to stand out, not blend in. He told himself that this was why he kept the black and white Verrato high tops. Not only did the shoes scream sophistication and class, but they saved his life once, and could again. It had nothing to do with the fact that they were a gift from young Darrin, perhaps Krill's first real friend across three worlds.

This, at least, is what Viktor Krill told himself.

As if in reaction to these thoughts, Krill turned his head to view those few gathered behind him on the scaffold. Young Darrin held Natthi's small brown hand in his own, the boy's chin held high by the success of his admired mentor. Mayfly Lemaire stood to the side with her steward Noora, a slight twist in her full lips showing her pride in Krill's victory. Also joining Krill on the platform were Red Texx and Wess Dey, the former Seconds of dead crews.

Krill took a step forward toward the front edge of the dais and pressed a small button that had been clipped onto his suit's lapel, ensuring that his voice would echo across the Muck, reaching all of its many residents. Thousands of eyes looked up at Viktor Krill, desperate to comprehend how their lives were about to change. Krill's black eyes reached back, demanding attention, obedience, and loyalty.

"Gangsters of the Muck! Rejoice! Rejoice, for today is a good day, maybe the best of days. In an alternate reality, one where Viktor Krill never graces your world, the gang wars to consolidate power would have landed half, if not more of you, in the grave. But here we are today. Power has been consolidated. And we all live!" A cheer broke out from below Krill, mainly from the Dead Rogues and former Stench Mobb. "The gang wars are over! And if you blinked, you missed it. But this was my plan. I see such strength gathered here today; strength that, if united and organized, could be weaponized and aimed at lucrative foes the likes of which none of you could have ever dreamed!" Another cheer ripped through the crowd. "To the Chrome Butchers! Sigman Prime is no more, which means the Chrome Butchers are no more. But do not fear! I see your value. I see your leadership." Krill stole a sidelong glance at Wess Dey, who discreetly bowed his head. "Therefore, the Chrome Butchers will join with the Dead Rogues and former Stench Mobb, completing the Great Consolidation." The crowd below broke out into a mix of cheers and murmurs. Krill held up his hand, and all went quiet. "Yes, yes, I understand your hesitance. You think I'm asking you to adopt the name of a clique you've been waging violent war with for years. Well, I am not!" Krill paused a moment for dramatic effect before continuing. "This is a *new* day! And we are a *new* crew, more powerful than any in the dark history of this place. Forget your past allegiances, for those men are dead! Only I live! Only you live! Only we live!!"

The crowd grew louder as Krill's speech began to have its desired effect. He waited the appropriate time before going on. "We will reorganize our new collective. If you held a position of authority before, you will again. Slink production will extend into all controlled towers, giving everyone a taste of its limitless profits. Our new organization will work even more closely with the Bitch-Whores and toddy gangs to spread Slink across Bhellum and into surrounding cities. Your accounts will fill with credits, your pockets will become jammed with notes! And you will enjoy all of this without having to constantly look over your shoulders. We have protection on high! And those who oppose us will fall before they even have the chance to throw a first blow. How does this sound?!"

The gathered gangsters roared in delight as Krill painted every crook's dream onto the invisible canvas before them. Krill's black eyes widened, and a grin appeared on his lips as he realized that he held them all in the palm of his hand. "And on this new day, with this new organization, and these new plans, I think we deserve a new name. One fitting of all of our struggles. As you know, I am not from the Muck. But I crawled out of my own prison — twice! — and will help you all do the same. This is the first step of many. Follow me, and rise above the Muck! Show the world your anger! Make them pay! Riches and power will follow! And, thus, we will be called the Risers! And this world will quiver at our march forward!"

Riotous thunder exploded from the mass of men. Some threw off the marks of their old gangs, leaving them on the muddy grass where they fell. Large men from opposing gangs embraced in powerful bearhugs, delighted to be working for the same team. Delighted to be working for the Muck's greatest gangster, and this world's only Wakened human.

Krill once more quieted the group with a hand. "Details will be taken care of later. Tonight, the Risers celebrate!" As Krill spoke, dozens of chowsets were rolled into the clearing, the proprietors immediately lighting grills and putting out strange meats. Additionally, a large group of Bitch-Whores came around the corner to join the new collective. "Eat, my Risers! Enjoy the company of a good woman, compliments of Miss Mayfly Lemaire! But be on your best behavior, lest you end up like poor, poor Freddy Prime." Laughter broke out among the men, for all had heard how Lemaire had fed him to the Slink. "Eat, drink, be merry, my Risers! Tomorrow, we begin! We will rise from the Muck and conquer the world!"

Risers! Risers! Risers! Risers! The chant punched through the Muck, sending the Jungle junkies scampering back into the protection of their dilapidated gardens. Krill hit the button on his lapel as Mayfly Lemaire moved up to join him.

"Risers, huh? Sounds like there's a history in that word."

"Not in this world."

Lemaire snickered lightly. "Very well, Viktor. Keep your secrets. You've done well for yourself. You've done well for me and my girls. But now is not the time for complicity. More power inevitably brings more powerful enemies. And foes coming at you from on high can prove difficult to see coming."

"What are you trying to say, Mayfly?"

Lemaire giggled, still unused to her strong feelings for the enigmatic Viktor Krill. She placed her dark hand on his shoulder. "I guess I'm just saying enjoy your victory. But be careful." Krill put his tan hand over the one touching his shoulder. "Also, my girls aren't working for free tonight. And doing some rudimentary math in my head, this one's gonna cost you."

Krill laughed openly as he looked down to see the men and women starting to interact below. Speakers that had been brought out began to bellow music tantamount to 90s RnB in Krill's world. "Oh, I'm sure it's going to cost me. And I'll gladly pay it. But let's talk numbers after."

"After what?"

"After we dance, dear woman." And with that, Viktor Krill, the newly anointed King of the Muck, took Mayfly Lemaire, the undisputed Queen of the Bitch-Whores, gently by the hand and led her off the scaffold. When both had touched down on the soft grass, they immediately made their way toward an empty circle that had recently opened to serve as an outdoor dance floor. Men and women alike dove aside to get out of the way of Viktor and Mayfly.

As one does in the proximity of royalty.

———

"Fuck, it's like we don't even exist, boss," said Sonny Caddoc as he stared through digital binoculars at the celebrating gangsters across the Muck.

Tennian Stamp chewed nervously on the end of his lit cigarillo. He spoke around the mangled butt. "That's because we don't, Sonny. At least, not to this new mega-gang that Viktor Krill has put together."

"Why haven't they attacked us yet?"

"You said it yourself, Sonny. We don't exist. We don't matter right now. Krill understands that the Broken Tens know how to keep to ourselves, stay in our lane. More importantly, this new mega-crew wasn't formed for simple shits and giggles. No, there's some big plans surrounding this consolidation. And these big plans don't need the delays that would inevitably come with a war with us. We're no match for Krill right now, but that doesn't mean we would go quickly, or easily. The Broken Tens have been here longer than any in the Muck. We know how to dig in; we know how to survive. Better to just leave us alone for now. Plus, everyone loves our Leaf. No one's ready to cut off the Muck's supply of that."

Caddoc continued to watch the party unfold. "And what about when these *big plans* have concluded? What then?"

Tennian took the small cigar out of this mouth and launched a brown wad of spit at the grass. He then commanded his left mech leg to stamp the phlegm down into the dirt beneath. "Then, I'm afraid we are no longer invisible. Viktor Krill will come for us, eventually, Sonny. He knows I won't be absorbed. The Broken Tens bear my name, and I'm going down with the ship."

Caddoc finally removed the binoculars from his eyes, and looked over at his revered First. "We're *all* going down with the ship, boss."

Tennian rubbed his greying beard. "Thank you, my friend. I hate for it to be this way, but the Muck is an unforgiving mistress."

"Is there no way to win against them? Is there no way to defeat this Viktor Krill?"

"Deus ex machina."

"What does that mean, boss?"

"It means we'll need something unexpected."

"Like what, boss?"

"Like the hand of God, Sonny. We'll need the hand of God to survive this upcoming war."

"That's a lot to ask for, Tens."

"It is. That's why it's so unexpected."

"And you think this God will find us?"

Tennian looked up at the bright blue sky, felt his heart swell at the endlessness of the heavens. "I don't know if He will. But someone will come. I don't know how I know this, but I do."

"Well, if you say it, boss, I believe it. Until then, we'll hold down the fort 'till this mysterious savior appears."

"And we'll pray."

"Pray for what, boss?"

"That this savior isn't more of a nightmare than Viktor Krill."

PART II

THE BHELLUM DISTORTION

16

"I've never seen eyes like yours before, at least not on a natural," said the upside-down face hovering a few inches away from Albany Rott. The nude Spirit Girl before Rott had bent backwards at an impossible angle, as if her spine were made of soft rubber instead of bone, which it may have been. She smiled widely before putting both synthetic hands on the carpeted floor to execute a back handspring, moving impossibly slow as she completed the difficult move, showcasing perfect balance to land softly on Rott's lap. She quickly spun in place, straddling her scarred customer. Her long fingers swept across his dark red eyelashes. "What color do you call this, sexy man?"

"I call it *scorched faith*, my dear lady."

The Spirit Girl writhed on Rott's lap as she gently kissed his forehead above each eye. "Well, I've yet to see its equal on a natural," she said, her breathy voice passing between thick, decorated lips. Rott did not waste time explaining that he, like her, was far from a "normal," instead opting to meet her engineered lips with his own. As they kissed, a rush tore through Rott's body, the vial of Zeal he had consumed finally taking effect.

Marlin Hadder sat in the back of the dim club as both sides of his neck were attacked by the two Spirit Girls that sat to either side. Despite the tickling sensation of tongues melding with the sensual effects of Zeal, Hadder was having a hard time relaxing. Instead of the impossibly beautiful synthetics that surrounded him, Hadder's eyes were firmly fixed on Albany Rott, who once again appeared lost in vice.

For many months, the actual number lost to chemicals and revelry, Rott and Hadder had bounced from city to city in this new reality, living fast and hard, welcoming fights as readily as drug-addled evenings with synthetic charmers in blacklight-filled dance halls. It had been an exciting time, recovering from the loss of so many friends and the collapse of a second home while in the company of a god. But just as the Celebration Cluster had helped close an open wound before unveiling another, Hadder felt the pull of something else, a more important goal that was being ignored in the haze of sex and drugs and violence.

Watching as Rott enjoyed the Spirit Girl on his lap, Hadder had to wonder if his red-eyed friend had forgotten the true purpose of this adventure of theirs — to capture the monstrous Viktor Krill. Rarely did the name of Station's most notorious occupant come up anymore, as if Rott thought avoiding the topic would prolong the inevitable. But Hadder could wait no longer. The idea of a beast such as Krill, created in a prison between realities, wreaking havoc on the innocent of this world, didn't sit well with the lone survivor of the Fall.

Yes, Hadder decided, he would have to confront Albany Rott about their neglected mission. He would have to get the investigation back on track. This world depended on their success.

But first, Hadder realized, he would have to deal with the two Spirit Girls slithering around on the cushioned bench, their hands and mouths growing more desperate by the second. Hadder slid down to the cushions and was immediately covered by synthetic skin that was softer than any infant's.

From beneath the two Spirit Girls, Hadder could hear laughter break out in the near-empty Spirit House. Rott's voice followed the laughter, showing that nothing missed the god's crimson gaze. "That's right, Marlin! Priorities, dear boy! Priorities!"

As Hadder melted into the Spirit Girls' arms, he silently agreed with Albany Rott. *Yes, Al, we will need to speak of priorities soon. And you may not like what I have to say.*

————

THE WAITER BOT ROLLED PAST, stopping briefly to deposit two large plates between the strange guests. One plate contained large beetles, their top halves removed to display the rich, fried meat contained in each crunchy shell. The second plate held an entire roasted bird, a strange, black-skinned thing that Hadder was unable to identify.

Rott dove into the beetles, slurping down the soft insides as one would a raw oyster. Hadder watched in silence as the pale god devoured his food. Minutes went by before Rott realized he was eating alone.

"What is it, Marlin? I know you worked up an appetite in there."

"We need to talk."

Rott spoke between bites, refusing to let his beetles grow cold. "And what is on your mind, dear boy?"

Hadder's stomach began to rumble, so he ripped off the leg of the black-skinned bird and took a bite. It had the consistency of chicken, and tasted as if a turkey had been injected with honey. Hadder stripped the leg in seconds, and wiped his mouth with a towel before responding. "I fear we've begun to spin our wheels, Al."

Rott smiled to himself, his thin lips parting to reveal too-white teeth. "Investigative work is an act of patience, Marlin. Oftentimes, the more you look, the less you see."

Hadder swatted aside Rott's bullshit remark. "Yes, but we don't seem to be looking at all."

Rott paused with a fresh beetle shell halfway to his waiting mouth. "Do you think there is anything that my eyes do not pick up, dear Marlin?" As Rott spoke, his eyes transformed from dull embers to raging fires before returning to their usual state. Once upon a time, that look would have withered Marlin Hadder, would have had him dumbly agreeing with whatever came out of the god's mouth. But Hadder had been around Albany Rott for some time now, and found the same flaws in the scarred angel that he knew to be in himself, and almost every other human. And one of those flaws was a desire to keep the good times rolling.

"Not when they are open, Al. But I think you've had them closed for months now."

"And why is that, do you think?" There was an edge to Rott's voice, a challenge that would have shrunk most men. But Marlin Hadder, also, wasn't most men, and he no longer feared death, or angel, or god. Or, so he told himself.

It was time to rattle Rott's cage. "Maybe you fear Viktor Krill."

Rott's free hand came down hard on the plastic table, causing Hadder to jump, and almost upending both dishes. He dramatically drained the meat from the beetle in his other hand and unceremoniously tossed its shell onto the table. "Viktor Krill is a chimpanzee, as you all are to me. A heightened chimpanzee, to be sure, but still nothing more than an animal. What would I have to fear from an animal?"

Hadder chuckled internally, delighted to have finally gotten under Rott's skin. He held both hands up in surrender. "Maybe I'm wrong. But then, there must be some other reason for your lack of urgency, Al."

"Maybe I just do not see the necessity for haste, Marlin."

"And how is that, I wonder? Were you not the one who told me about how Krill, with his Wakened abilities, would tear through this world, his Station-created claws ripping through man, woman, and child alike?"

"And, yet, this world still stands, does it not, Marlin? Perhaps I overestimated his powers, or his desire for carnage."

"But I don't think you did."

"Explain yourself."

Hadder picked absently at the dark meat. What he had to say next soured his stomach and erased his appetite. "I've been having dreams."

Rott's head cocked to the side, as it always did when he heard something interesting. "What kind of dreams?"

"Terrifying ones."

"Tell me more. Describe them."

Hadder stared off into the distance, pulling frightening images from the recesses of his mind where he had quarantined them. "They're all the same. A wave of horror is excreted from the ass of a giant worm. It crashes over humanity, twisting man into monster. These monsters turn on mothers and fathers, sons and daughters, painting the world red with the blood of the unchanged. Just as the dark wave of excrement descends upon me, the worm speaks to me in my mind."

Rott appeared to be at the literal edge of his seat. "What does it say, Marlin?"

"It's always the same thing. *Abandon this plane. It is now a child of chaos.* And then I wake up, covered in cold sweat and wanting to shower off the images in my head." Rott's crimson eyes flamed up as he looked away in thought. "What do *you* think it means, Al?"

The shadow of a smile passed across Rott's lips before disappearing into the ether. "I think it means that you are correct, Marlin. It is high time that we get back on track. Despite my love of this city and its Spirit Girls, it is time for us to move on. I have learned nothing here, save my predilection for the synthetic over the natural. And while I surf the wake of this existence, it is obvious that the beast Viktor Krill is growing stronger. While I obviously know not where he is, I can sense small changes in the wind. There is a hint of death in the breeze, and I do not doubt its source."

"So, what's the plan?"

"We move on tomorrow, towards the coast. While Krill may no longer be a man, he is more human than ever. And it is the nature of humans to seek the water, both for base needs and the promise of adventure. Viktor Krill wants this world as his own. Anyone with such aspirations will leave a trail. And we will pick it up tomorrow."

Hadder almost made a snide comment, for it had long been his suggestion to visit cities along the ocean. Instead, he decided to keep the conversation focused. "Where?"

"We will try Sespit to the east of here. From there, it's a short trek to the coast, which collects dark characters like a fishing net. I am confident that the mark of Krill will show itself in the next few days."

"Why wait? Why don't we leave today?"

Rott picked up another beetle and downed the contents of its shell. "Because I am spoken for today."

"By whom?"

Before Rott could answer, three Spirit Girls entered the small restaurant, giggling and falling over each other as they waved coquettishly at Hadder's red-eyed friend. "These three lovely ladies have promised to take me to the city fair today, something I am eager to see through their innocent eyes."

Hadder merely shook his head. "Should my feelings be hurt, Al? It seems you prefer the company of synthetics to your own children."

"I do."

"And why is that?"

Rott's eyes flared to life once more before collapsing back into lit ember form. "Because, if I had created them instead of you all, my existence may have been much simpler."

"Does simpler make it better?"

"We'll never know. Now leave me alone!" With that, Albany Rott rose to his feet and joined his three synthetic friends. Long, too-white arms across slim, bare shoulders, Rott turned back to Hadder, who was still sitting stupidly at the table. "I'll meet you in front of the hotel tomorrow morning at ten, Marlin. Want some free advice?"

Hadder shoved more dark meat into his mouth, finally accepting that another day of sex and drugs laid before him. "Always," he said through chews.

"Have fun today. See how many Spirit Girls you can satisfy. Enjoy them. Starting tomorrow, I fear we are going to wade into the darker corners of this world."

Having stated his piece, Rott left the restaurant arm-in-arm with his muses, leaving Marlin Hadder alone with his thoughts. A few questions, however, dominated all others, keeping Hadder's stomach churning uncomfortably despite the roasted meat he had presented it. *Why had Rott changed so abruptly after hearing of Hadder's dream? What was the real reason behind his delaying the hunt for Krill?* And most importantly, *how could Hadder trust someone who felt more connected to the artificial than the humans he helped to mold?*

As Hadder pondered these worries, a tanned Spirit Girl known as Amp walked outside the restaurant windows. She ran her long, lacquered fingernails along the glass as she passed, throwing Hadder a look of silent invitation before crossing the street and entering a Spirit House named *The Last Time*. Hadder thought for a moment before recalling the wisdom of his godfriend and decide to act accordingly. After sending the appropriate credits to the restaurant using his palm-print, Hadder crossed that same street, a mantra reverberating in his skull as he traversed the distance to the Spirit House — *Have fun today.*

And he did, although Hadder had a hard time ignoring the second half of the mantra, the part that was not sung aloud, but still hung heavy around the afternoon's festivities. *Tomorrow, we wade into the darker corners of this world.*

———

ALBANY ROTT'S thin nose rose to meet the cool breeze that tore through the city of Sespit. His nostrils flared as he breathed in deeply, and the pulsing of his dark red scar increased in speed as he did.

"Anything?"

Rott looked over to his traveling companion. "There's something in the air, to be sure. But, I do not think it is Krill. If he has been here, it was a long time ago."

"So, what do we do?"

"We're here, so let us take a look around. I detect the hint of something alien, a callback to another world. I think there are clues to be found in this metropolis."

"Good, then let's discover them."

"All in time, dear Marlin. First, call that coffee stand over here. Make it a triple. The Spirit Girls really did a number on me last night."

———————

ALTHOUGH VIKTOR KRILL had long left Sespit, his name still weighty over the darker corners of the city. Hadder and Rott watched in amusement as the eyes of every criminal they questioned grew wide and terrified upon hearing Krill's name, as if the ghost of a long-forgotten problem had finally tracked them down through time and space. One simply ran, another fell to his knees, begging for mercy. A third, dressed in all black, triggered his "fight or flight" response and swung a wicked dagger at Rott's face. Hadder caught the man's wrist before the blow gained power, twisting it painfully behind the assailant's back, rendering him impotent.

The dark embers of Rott's eyes roared to life as he approached the shaking, immobilized villain. "I'll have your name, sir."

Hadder twisted the man's arm a bit to squeeze out a response. "Ahh! Fuck man! The name's Claude!"

"Why would you treat a new friend so unkindly? Did this Viktor Krill mean that much to you? Tell me what you know of him." The man stopped quaking as Rott floated to within a few inches of his face, the twin fires putting him into a semi-trance. "And don't leave anything out."

"Su, sur, sure," the black-clad man said, stumbling over his words. "I leave town on some business, and when I come back, I find that my entire crew has been butchered while I'm gone."

"What was your crew's name?"

"The Villains."

"How on-the-nose. Tell me, Claude, how were your men killed?"

A shiver ran through Claude as a memory bubbled to surface. "They were torn apart. Like a wild beast from history was set loose in our little clubhouse. Parts of them were ripped off, others ripped out. Blood coated the floor and touched the ceiling and walls."

"And how do you know it was Krill?"

"Because he let it be known that he had done it. An open challenge to Sespit's underworld. One that was *not* answered. He also went around after the massacre, demanding answers to questions no one understood."

Rott's interest seemed to grow by the second. "And what were these questions, Claude? What did Viktor Krill demand to know?"

"Hey, this isn't gonna get me into trouble with Mister Krill, is it? I don't want any issues with…"

"Claude!" Albany Rott's voice boomed with the weight of a thousand lifetimes. "Tell me, now!"

Claude's will broke as quickly as it had been conjured. "He was asking around about various cities. He wanted to know where he could find power, or a real challenge, whatever that means. He killed most who failed to answer him, but left a few alive who didn't totally piss him off."

"What else?"

"That's it, I swear! Shit, man, I lost my club, lost my family. What else do you want from me?"

"Absolutely nothing, I suppose. Marlin, please release this pathetic cur."

Hadder did as he was asked, and Claude was let go to massage his injured wrist. "Are we done here?"

"We are," answered Rott, interest dissipated and eyes once again crimson embers.

Claude began to back away, leaving his blade on the asphalt ground where it had fallen. "Well, hey, if you see Mister Krill, tell him I offer *nothing* but respect. Tell him I don't know what happened between him and the Villains, but it's water under the bridge. You hear me? I took off the jacket and everything. Let him know, ok? Make sure you do, ok?" By this point, Claude had backed fifteen feet from Hadder and Rott. He turned and ran after this final request, sprinting down the main boulevard for a distance before cutting quickly down a side street.

"Did that tell you anything," asked Hadder.

"It did. It told me that Viktor Krill was finally looking to settle down. His days of wanton carnage may be behind him, traded in for a much more dangerous and impactful kind of game."

"And what would that be?"

"A targeted use of his Wakened abilities. A focused attempt to acquire that which he desires more than mere evidence of his superiority over all others."

Hadder added to Krill's assessment. "He wants power. Legitimate power, beyond that of simply exerting his will on someone weaker than him, which is everyone."

"That's right, dear Marlin. Viktor Krill, after so much violence, has found himself covered in something other than the blood of his victims. Viktor Krill has found himself covered in the addicted substance known as ambition. And the ambition that dwells in this twisted creature is one that will not be easily satiated."

"So, where does this leave us?"

"Not much further than where we were previously, I'm afraid, Marlin. We now know that Krill was looking to settle, but the question remains. Where? I do not know this world well enough to understand the intricacies of its many cities. And I do not know Krill's mind well enough to know what it is he truly values in a challenge."

"Meaning?"

"Meaning, we keep searching, dear Marlin. As I told you, I detect something off about this Sespit. There is something familiar, yet alien, in the air, and I aim to discover its source."

"So, where do we look? Do we keep overturning the rocks that hide Sespit's underbelly? It seems like the more these two-bit crooks know of the *name* Viktor Krill, the less they know *about* Viktor Krill."

Rott waved away Hadder's concerns. "Yes, yes, dear Marlin, we have exhausted the criminal investigation. It is obvious that Krill looked at these men as food, nothing more. Therefore, he would divulge very little to them, just enough to cause them to piss their collective pants. No, we must search elsewhere, Marlin. Someplace where Krill may have let his guard down, allowed some things to slip."

"Viktor Krill doesn't seem like one to let things slip."

"He would if he was confident that there was nothing in this world that could possibly threaten him. Remember, Marlin, he thinks Station still stands."

"All right, I'll buy it. Where do we start?"

"Viktor Krill is a twisted monster. But, at his core, he's still a man. And all men have a common need, regardless of how they wrap it, or hide it, or attempt to ignore it."

"I have a feeling that I know this need well."

"As do I, Marlin. So cheer up, dear boy. The next phase of our Sespit investigation will prove much more enjoyable than playing in the dirt, as we have been."

"To the red-light district?"

"You took the words right out of my mouth, dear boy."

———

THE EMACIATED woman's bones shone through her too-tight skin as she gyrated on the stage. Although she stared out into the world through dark blue orbs, there was no light behind those eyes, as if the bulb beneath the lampshade had burned out long ago.

Rott leaned in toward Hadder as the woman tried to smile at the strange pair, her grin appearing more like a sneer on her skull-like face. "Honestly, Marlin, I have not seen a group this run-down since the Dark Ages. Tell me again why we have surrounded ourselves with these diminishing creatures, and not lovely Spirit Girls."

Hadder nodded politely at the dancer before responding. "Let me remind you, again, that these *diminishing creatures* are *your* constructs. The least you can do is show them a little respect."

Rott sighted heavily. "I *do* respect them, dear Marlin. I respect all of you. And do you know how I show it? By fully embracing the Spirit Girls, that human construct that has so improved upon my initial design. Now then, should I get up first or you? We do not want to be rude to the young lady, of course."

Hadder chuckled at Rott's reasoning, but motioned him to remain seated.

"I love the Spirit Girls as much as you do, Al, but Spirit Girls don't gossip, get into trouble, or stick their noses where they don't belong. While this makes them ideal companions, it also renders them totally worthless for our purposes here today."

Rott wrinkled his nose as if he smelled something putrid. "And you think these…women…will be able to help us?"

"I think these women live, work, and play in the underbelly of Sespit. And if there are additional whispers of Viktor Krill to be heard in the murkier corners of this city, perhaps these ladies can relay that information."

"Let's get on with it, then. Sespit is known for its Spirit Houses and I *will* be visiting one before night's end."

"Very well." As Hadder rose from his seat in the audience, the stickiness of the vinyl seat hung tight to the pants of his black suit, as if begging him to remain. Hadder grimaced at the general grime that covered everything in the club, felt an overwhelming desire to wash his hands before pushing it away.

Released from his chair, Hadder made his way towards the back of the black-lit club, where the Relaxation Rooms were held. Dodging the veiny hands and sore-covered arms of numerous working girls, Hadder crossed the room, careful not to trip over the small service bots that were zigzagging the space, delivering watered-down drinks to impatient patrons.

Standing before the row of Relaxation Rooms was a giant of a man wearing jeans and a black leather jacket. His lips, almost hidden away in his thick beard, turned down in a look of disdain as Hadder approached. He held up a meaty hand to keep Hadder at a distance. "Area is for paying customers only. And I ain't seen you pay for shit yet. You can get away with being a cheap fuck in the main hall, but the Relaxation Rooms cost. So fuck off."

Hadder's Rage soared to the surface like a bubble released from the depths. Images of the bouncer in various positions of agony, his thick beard soaked through with blood, pelted Hadder from all angles before he could wrangle control once more. "Our apologies for not spending, yet, friend. We are new to Sespit and simply wanted to check out the goods before purchasing. I'm sure a man such as yourself can appreciate the prudence of research before purchase, no?"

"What the fuck are you trying to say?" The large man took a step forward; something in Hadder's tone must have set off the big lug.

Hadder almost laughed aloud at the piss poor attempt at intimidation. "All I'm trying to say, friend, is that we are now ready to spend. We would like a room and four of your most veteran workers." Before the dumb man made any other comments that could set loose the Rage, Hadder held up his right palm. "I have credits. Lots of them."

The bouncer snickered, but pulled a small palm reader from the inside of his leather jacket. "How many girls you want?"

"I think four should do the trick. No pun intended. Maybe, four of your more veteran dancers."

"You'll be charged every fifteen minutes. I get any notice that you're low on funds, and I'll drag you and your partner outta here by your fancy suits, smashing your faces on every table that we pass. Are we clear?"

The Rage wanted blood, but Hadder needed answers. "Crystal, my friend." Hadder held his palm against the reader for a second before the door to Room Three slid open silently.

The bouncer slid out of Hadder's way, but not before issuing a final warning. "No obvious marks on the girls. And don't do anything to make me come in there. Things won't end well for you."

Soft electronic music welcomed Hadder as he entered the Relaxation Room. Although far from the nicest room of its kind, it was surprisingly clean and well-furnished, with thick, soft couches along three of the walls and hovering tables adorning each corner. Metal hooks hung from the wall to either side of the lone door, temporary home for discarded clothing once things grew more intimate. A service bot waited quietly in the middle of the room, perfectly balancing itself on a single wheel.

Hadder sighed deeply before collapsing onto one of the couches, under-standing that this might not be the most enjoyable of missions. "Service bot," he said to the metal servant, "Bring us two bottles of Blue Cascade and six glasses." The service bot let out a single whistling sound before turning in place and running straight towards a space along the room's right wall. As it passed between two sofas, and just before striking the wall at full speed, a small concealed door slid up, allowing the bot to just pass through, offering the mechanized waiter a direct path to the bar.

In short order, the once-empty Relaxation Room was filled with bodies and booze. Hadder and two women occupied one couch while an obviously distracted Rott sat with a writhing woman covered in old, weathered tattoos on another. A fourth woman, younger than the other three by a decade, but in the worst shape of the lot, lounged on the floor, her bony body making uncomfortable-looking angles on the linoleum floor.

Hadder attempted to make smalltalk with his two dancers as they moved sensually around him, one attempting to hide an obvious limp. They offered short, empty responses to his inquiries, their dead eyes barely registering his words. Even when Hadder decided to skip the pleasantries, and invoked the name Viktor Krill, there was no reaction from the girls, only more crotch-grabbing and sandpaper tongues against his neck.

Hadder looked over to Albany Rott, who appeared to be fighting the urge to push the thin woman twerking on his lap to the hard floor. The two friends met eyes. "This the kind of intel you were hoping to discover, Marlin? If you were investigating how many cigarette burns one girl's g-string could hold, I think we have our answer."

Hadder ignored the complaints of his god-friend, and took another deep swig of the Blue Cascade. As he did, his eyes fell to the girl on the floor, who was now twitching and speaking incoherently to herself. As she moved, bones threatened to pop through her thin skin, and the scabs that peppered her body cracked open to let puss from the lesions below escape to form gross rivulets. The girl appeared to be fighting an invisible enemy, and was undoubtedly losing.

A cold tongue in his ear stirred Hadder from his staring. He gently pushed the dancer's head away from his own, and tilted it towards the grounded girl. "You might want to check on your friend. Looks like she got ahold of some bad shit."

The dancer took a quick look at the girl before waving her away. "Bitch is fine. You got me and Tandie here to look after you. Now, you gonna take those pants off, or we gonna chat all night?" Just as the woman completed her question, Tandie's right leg went over Hadder to straddle him moments before her mouth met his in a dispassionate kiss. Synapses fired as Tandie's smoky lips combined with the other dancer's pawing hands to rip a memory from deep within Hadder, bringing him back to that final night with Lilly Sistine and Reena Song, the last spark of a joyful life now buried in an empty desert between worlds.

The memory, a bittersweet thing that made Hadder want to laugh while crying, was infected, however. It was perverted by the bony, overly perfumed bodies of two haggard dancers who barely qualified as the same species as his two lost loves. A knee-jerk reaction followed, an unanticipated move that saw Hadder toss poor Tandie to the floor as he stood abruptly, shaking his head to clear the dark imagery that had taken residence in his alcohol-soaked mind.

Tandie hit the cold floor hard, causing her to cry out and toss a series of world-specific curses Hadder's way. The second dancer also took offense, and began to issue expletives at Hadder, slapping up at his face with whatever power her sinewy arms could muster. Hadder batted her attacks aside while offering apologies.

As Hadder bent low to help Tandie off the ground, Rott peeked out from under the armpit of his dancer. "Everything all right, Marlin?"

Hadder pulled Tandie to her feet and gently placed her on the couch next to her coworker. There, the two women began saying vile things about their current customer. "Yeah, sorry, lost it there for a moment." As he spoke, the drugged out girl on the floor began to toss and turn before pushing herself up on her elbows.

"What the fuck, man? I'm trying to..." The rest of the girl's words were an unintelligible mess, formed by a tongue swollen by the poisons coursing through her veins.

Hadder almost ignored the girl on the floor. He almost turned back to the two dancers on the couch next to him. He almost began the arduous task of getting something useful out of the scantily clad zombies who were aggressively pulling on his shirt from behind. But something caught his eye and made him pause.

As the girl on the ground continued to mumble incoherently, Hadder noticed something brown on her bare bicep, pulsing dully just below the skin. Forcibly removing two sets of hands from his person, Hadder dropped to the ground and quickly crawled over to the woman, his breath coming in short, panicked bursts. He grabbed her arm harder than intended, eliciting another string of curses before her head fell back down to the floor below.

Nausea hit Hadder like a wave, and he had to swallow hard to keep himself from vomiting all over the prone girl. He looked through wide hazel eyes at the throbbing lump of brown, ran his fingers over it to ensure it was real, making sure that *he* was not the one now hallucinating. Hadder blinked hard several times, and wiped his face vigorously with an increasingly sweaty palm. Still, the mass of brown stared back at him, whispering things that only he and, once upon a time, Jackie Crone knew.

Memories assaulted Hadder like a gang initiation. *A slug is just beneath the surface, but miles out of reach, slowly disintegrating into the bloodstream. A manikin watches with judgmental eyes as you devour its heart. Other manikins stand politely as you and others rip them apart, swinging their entrails around like party boas. Electric pain becomes a strange pleasure, confounding the mind and making the heart race. Emily is once again found, more beautiful than ever, and a wonderful moment is shared before the curtain falls away, leaving only a naked, cruel Jackie Crone in his lost love's place. A fragile mind is finally shattered, sending you reeling toward the waiting bladed arms of a killer.*

Marlin Hadder shook his head vigorously, tossing aside memories as if they were spiders crawling across his face. He took a calming breath. "Al. You're gonna need to see this."

Rott, happy for any excuse to extricate himself from his girl with the cigarette-burn skin, slid out from under his dancer and joined Hadder. He was without words, so Hadder simply nodded towards the throbbing brown lump on the girl's arm.

Like Hadder, Rott ran a gentle finger over the foreign mass, his red eyes flaring to life. "Is this what I think it is, Marlin?"

"It is."

"Then, we have to be close."

"But why? Why would Krill bring Slink to this world?"

"Why does anyone introduce any drug to a population? Money and power. If there's one inexorable truth across realities, it is that humans love to get high. Regardless of the cost."

A voice from the side pulled Hadder and Rott from their intimate conversation. "I told y'all, Jess is too fucked up for anything. Now, if y'all are done fagging out over there, can you come back and let us do our fucking jobs?"

Rott looked over to Tandie, and pointed to Jess's bicep. "What do you call this drug?"

A mix of confusion and irritation crossed Tandie's face. "We didn't come to the Relaxation Room to talk about drugs, we came to..."

"Silence!" The power of Rott's word was tangible, supported by the fires that now danced in both eyes. "What do you call this drug?"

Tandie was muted by Rott's minor show, so the other dancer chimed in for her. "You guys been living in a barn or something? That's fucking Slink. Everyone knows Slink."

Rott spoke more to himself than the woman. "Yes, I suppose we have been a bit isolated. Where did the girl get it from?"

"No, no, no," said Tandie, who had recovered the ability to speak. "We came in here to fuck, not answer a bunch of fucking narc questions. You got a prick you need sucked, we're here. You got cop questions, you're in the wrong place, and can go fuck yourselves. Terry!"

Seconds later, the large bearded bouncer entered the Relaxation Room. Hadder and Rott rose to meet the new threat. "These assholes giving you trouble, Tandie?"

"They trying to ask about drugs, Terry."

A wicked smile appeared on Terry's lips. It became obvious he had been looking for an excuse to physically reprimand the two sharp-dressed clients. "Relaxation Room is for fucking, not talking. And it sure as shit ain't for questions. Now, it's time for you two suited faeries to go. And I think we're gonna add a couple of extra hours to your bill for the trouble and upset you've caused the ladies here. If you have a problem with this, please let me know. I would love to..."

A blur flashed through the air and Terry flew backwards to land on one of the unoccupied couches, his dislocated jaw making even his unconscious face look stupid. Hadder shook out his ringing right hand as Rott spun into action, moving faster than the eye could follow. Before any of the three cognizant dancers could scream out, they found their voices encumbered by paper notes covering their mouths, stuck to sweat-soaked makeup. As one, they removed the notes with shaking lacquered hands to find significant bills in their possession. They looked up with questioning eyes behind too-long artificial lashes.

"The money is yours, dear ladies," said Rott, using his most magnanimous voice. Hadder could see the women falling into a minor trance, as if they were cobras facing a veteran charmer. "We only have a singular question, then we will be on our way. A correct answer will result in more of these for each of you." Rott raised a pale hand holding a wad of large notes, heavily favored in underbelly communities compared to the easily traceable credits.

As usual, the promise of money did the trick, keeping the dancers' screams in their mouths and earning their attentions. "What do you want to know," asked Tandie, her eyes locked onto the notes in Rott's possession.

"Where does Jess get her Slink," cut in Hadder, his heart pounding, anticipating finally getting some useful intel.

"Her pimp Higgins gives it to her," answered the woman who had been dancing for Rott. "It's like his lame claim to fame. He always brags about having a secret connect that he gets his Slink from. Allowed him go from your typical garbage pimp to become a man to be reckoned with. He owes it all to Slink. He's a got a lock on the Sespit market. For now, at least."

"Thank you, my dear," responded Rott, shooting Hadder a look that said, *shut the fuck up and let me handle this.* "And where might I find this Higgins?"

The shrieking voice of Tandie came forth once more, sounding far away due to her being in the grasp of Rott's trance. "But, that's two questions. You said *one* question."

Rott's crimson eyes flared once more, but his voice came out smooth and calming. "You are correct, dear lady. I did say that." Eight notes jumped from the wad in Rott's left hand to his right. "Then, let me double the prize. Now, where might I find this Higgins?"

"He bought a club with his earnings from Slink," replied Tandie. "Usually can be found there. Place is called *The Wet Market*. Basically, just a place for wealthy Slinkers to hang out. Higgins thinks he's Hiso now, even though he still keeps a tight grip on his girls down here in the Low End."

Rott looked to Hadder, who looked to Rott, and both men smiled widely, knowing that they had finally stumbled upon their first big break in the hunt for Viktor Krill. In a flash, Rott distributed notes to each woman in the Relaxation Room, with even the barely conscious Jess receiving payment for her time.

"Well, Marlin, I think we got what we came for. Shall we?"

Hadder stared one last time at the Slink slowly dissolving under Jess's skin. He tore his eyes from the demon drug. "Yes. To *The Wet Market*?"

Rott's eyes, now embers once more, flashed a bit as the god thought. *"The Wet Market* will be there tomorrow, Marlin. Remember, I still need to see the infamous Sespit Spirit Houses."

Hadder sighed deeply. "Very well, Al. But tomorrow, at the latest."

"Of course, Marlin. Now, let us be gone from this crypt. The smell of aging flesh has become quite the turnoff for me." The dancers responded with a chorus of curses and insults, but Rott ignored them. "Shall we?" As he turned to leave, Rott threw a couple of bills onto the lap of Terry, who was snoring loudly. "For the hospital bill," he said before exiting the Relaxation Room, leaving Hadder alone with his thoughts.

Marlin Hadder stood among the veteran dancers, once more unable to come to grips with his worries, concerns that had grown greater over the past month. *Why did it seem like he was the only one intent on locating Viktor Krill? Why was Rott stalling? Or, did the god really not care?*

These questions sped through Hadder's mind as he, too, began to leave the Relaxation Room. Passing the unconscious Terry, the Rage appeared out of nowhere, roaring to life like lit flash paper. Hadder smashed his fist once more into Terry's face, connecting cleanly with a closed eye and promptly swelling it shut. The women screamed at Hadder's unprovoked violence as he continued his exit. He stopped halfway out the door and turned back to the women.

"Have the doctor take a look at that eye, as well."

Hadder let the sliding door close behind him and went to join Rott outside. Given the invaluable information the two had just gained, Hadder should have felt excited, emboldened by the knowledge that Viktor Krill was close, could be found in short order.

But instead, Marlin Hadder only grew more concerned, worried that he was alone in this hunt. Worried that only a mere man would soon confront a Wakened beast.

———

As the only Slink provider in Sespit, the man known as Higgins must have felt fairly comfortable regarding his position in the city. Nothing else could explain *The Wet Market*'s lax daytime security, which consisted of a singular armed thug guarding the main entrance, and another which sat outside of Higgins's office door. Both were disarmed without much fuss, although Rott did strike one of them hard enough to send several teeth careening halfway down the hall.

Higgins didn't take kindly to the two black-suited strangers arriving unannounced to his office, especially since the ridiculously dressed drug dealer was in the middle of counting a mountain of notes that covered his glass desk. Not waiting for the dark-looking pair to offer introductions, Higgins simply pulled out an ostentatious hand cannon and began firing, sending Hadder sprawling behind a couch.

As Hadder crawled to safety, bullets wizzing by his head and striking the floor behind him, Rott moved like a wraith, moving so fast that he seemed to simultaneously disappear from one location and appear in another. Higgins fired indiscriminately into the air, unable to get a bead on the pale, scarred devil that danced between moments in time. When Rott finally came into focus, it was too late. Higgins swung his gun to the right, but had it promptly swept aside by Albany Rott, whose arm immediately rebounded to backhand the soft-looking pimp, sending him flying across the room and into unconsciousness.

A few minutes later, Higgins was hanging upside-down from the neon-wrapped ceiling fan that hung low from the high office ceiling as Hadder and Rott smoked cinnamon cigarettes, another of this world's unique perks. "So, this is what drug dealers look like in this world," said Hadder, more to fill the silence than to make an insightful statement. Although he had no verbal response, Rott looked over the hanging Higgins and chuckled. Higgins's childlike face, swollen from excessive drug and alcohol use, sat under (or currently above) blonde-dyed hair that had been twisted into small braids that currently reached for the hardwood floor. Higgins wore baggy white pants, a white tank top, and a white denim jacket, all of which was covered in trim that flashed and changed colors under the man's slightest movements. Overly large sunglasses with a thick, colorful frame, which Rott had carefully placed back onto the hanging man's face, completed the look of a real asshole.

"How long before he wakes up," asked Rott, already growing bored without his Spirit Girl company.

"Well, how hard did you strike him," dared Hadder, wondering if Rott had purposely damaged the only man who could progress their search for Viktor Krill.

"Who ever knows how hard one can strike you mortals. Some of you must be fully decapitated to be stopped. Others pass away from the slightest shift in the wind. Truly poor design."

Hadder was about to remark about whose poor design it *really* was when Higgins began to awaken, wiggling in place like a spider's cocooned prey. Higgins's eyes widened behind the thick lenses as the realization of his predicament began to sink in. They grew wider when Rott drew closer, his flaming red eyes and pulsing scar causing panic to set in.

"What do you guys want? Who are you with? Is it Ortiz? Fuck man, tell Ortiz the money's not due for another week. Look at my fucking desk. I *have* the money, man. I just need to pack it up. Shit man, I thought you would be happy. I was even gonna give you payment a few days early. If there's some..."

"Shhhhhhhh," whispered Rott as he placed a long, pale finger over Higgins's trembling lips. "We are not here on Ortiz's behalf."

Confusion painted Higgins's reddening face. "Ok, ok, then what do you fuckers want? Notes are on the table, take it and leave, man."

"We have our own notes, thank you very much."

"Well, if you don't want money, what the fuck do you want? It's always about money, isn't it boys." Higgins's words began to run together as his concern mounted.

"Slink."

"What's that?"

Rott didn't answer. Instead, he carefully removed the thick sunglasses from Higgins's face. As soon as the expensive accessory was removed, Hadder came in with a straight right that collapsed the pimp's thin nose, sending a river of blood to dance between his eyes and run into his blonde braids. The blood was held there for several seconds before it filled the thick braids, which began to deposit large droplets onto the wooden floor beneath.

Higgins grabbed at his smashed nose and screamed through cupped hands. "Fuck me! Ok, ok, ok. The Slink. The Slink. There's a tub of the shit under my desk. I just picked it up, so it's the new variety. Supposed to pack an even bigger punch. It's yours; take it. Just leave me alone, all right?"

Hadder looked under the glass table to find the large plastic tub as Rott continued. "You misunderstand, my friend. I don't *want* your Slink. I want to know *where* you get your Slink."

"Fuck you, man! You know what I had to do to get that connect? And now you're just gonna muscle me out? Shit ain't fair, man. I'd rather..."

"Lose an eye?"

"What?"

"Would you rather lose an eye?" As he spoke, Rott placed a thumb gently atop Higgins's right eye. Higgins reached up with both hands and tried to remove Rott's thumb, but found that it would be easier to move a cement pillar. "I can ask you again, after this one. You'll still have another with which to barter."

"No! No! No! It's fine, it's fine. The connect is yours."

"I don't need the connect. I just need to know where you get it."

"Huh? That's all? Well, shit, man, you just had to ask. I travel to Bhellum once a month to get the Slink. I buy it off some albino bitch name Noora. Costs me a fucking fortune, but you'll triple your money, no problem. Shit, with this new crop, you'll make be able to charge five times what you paid. It's yours, man, all yours. Just let me be."

Rott looked up to Hadder, who stared back at Rott. "Bhellum," Rott simply stated.

"Fucking Bhellum," emphasized Hadder, his suspicions at an all-time high. Hadder left it unsaid, but both he and Rott knew that Hadder had suggested Bhellum as their next stop for several months now, only to be redirected by Rott, who always had numerous reasons for going elsewhere.

Rott felt Hadder's glare, could sense the Rage just beneath the surface of the upset man. "Well, no use crying over spilled milk and all that, Marlin. We have a destination finally. Let's make towards it."

"With all haste," added Hadder, pushing away ideas for detours before they were given voice.

"But, of course, dear Marlin. With all haste." To Higgins, "I've taken quite the liking to your guns, Higgins, so I'll be taking them with me. I hope you don't object." Hadder looked down to see that Rott had retrieved both of Higgins's custom handguns, striking things that were crafted in a clear material that complemented Rott's crystalline hatchets. Both the guns and blades were currently tucked into the waist of Rott's black suit.

Higgins's desperate voice grew hopeful as he could see an end to this bizarre meeting. "Sure, sure, man. Of course, you can have them. I can get you more if you want. I can get you guys anything you want. For real. I can..."

"Shut the fuck up before you say something I can't live with," interjected Hadder. "Cut him down, and let's get the fuck out of here."

Albany Rott moved like a blur, his pale hands moving too quickly to follow. In the blink of an eye, one of his crystalline hatchets had flown through the air to slice the nylon rope holding Higgins before burying itself in the far wall. Higgins fell heavily to the hardwood floor, almost snapping his neck in the process. Deep moans escaped the fallen pimp as Hadder collected Rott's axe for him.

"Shall we," asked Rott, pointing to the door with his newly retrieved weapon.

"Absolutely. Something about this place makes my skin crawl."

Hadder and Rott exited the office and were happy to see that the guard was still unconscious from their previous encounter. They began to cross the empty club when movement behind one of the plastic-wrapped couches caught Hadder's eye. Hadder held up a hand to Rott before investigating. His stomach fell when his eyes discovered the source of the movement.

Two small girls, ten or eleven in age, huddled together behind the protected furniture, both wearing too much makeup, and not nearly enough clothes. When Hadder reached for them, they recoiled in unison. Clearly, far too many times, the touch of an older man had hurt their soft skin. Hadder adopted the gentlest version of his voice, the one he used to employ when trying to ease Lilly Sistine's worries. "Hi, girls. Are you ok? My name's Marlin, and this is Al. We're not going to hurt you. What are you doing here?"

The fear in the girls' twin blue eyes broke Hadder's heart, and reinvigorated another dark friend. "We work here for Mister Higgins. He won't like us talking to you." Their little eyes darted back and forth across the club, waiting for Higgins, or one of his minions, to appear and exact punishment on their undersized bodies.

"Don't worry about Higgins, little miss. My friend and I took care of him. What kind of work do you do here?"

The girls looked to each other before dropping their eyes in shame. "We make sure Mister Higgins's adult friends have a good time."

"And leave happy," added the second girl, who still refused to look up.

The Rage powered ahead. It assumed control. "Would you girls like to leave this place?"

Their innocent eyes went wide with a mix of terror and hope. The first girl spoke in a whisper. "They'll never let us leave, Mister Marlin. They'll hurt us for even talking about it."

"Don't worry about them. It's just us here now. Would you like to leave?"

Both sets of blue eyes finally rose. One spoke in a whisper. "More than anything."

"Al, please take them out of here."

Rott almost responded to Hadder, almost argued that this wasn't their battle, but he quickly saw that it was no longer Marlin Hadder he was facing, but the Rage. Understanding that the Rage must burn itself out, Rott simply gathered the terrified girls in his arms and excited *The Wet Market*.

Hadder, however, now driven by the Rage, had other plans. He returned to Higgins's office, almost kicking the thick door off its hinges with a well-placed front kick. Higgins, back at his desk busily collecting the drug money strewn across it, jumped up at the crash, reaching for his guns that were no longer in his possession. He tried to recover. "Fuck, man, you scared the shit out of me. Hello, again. Something else I can help you with, man? Just say it, it's yours."

Hadder marched forward, daring the pimp to make an aggressive move, which he did not. "You know, Higgins, I think I changed my mind. I think I *will* take that Slink off your hands."

Higgins's face fell, but he worked hard to put on a happy front. "Sure, man. Take it; it's yours. You can make a boatload of money on that shit, man. I mean just take a look at..."

Hadder stopped listening to the blathering pimp as the Rage coursed through him, demanding pain and vengeance, in equal order. He walked behind the glass table, reached under, and gathered the brown container, placing it atop the now-vacant desk chair. Hadder then flipped off the container lid and stared in horror at its slithering contents, each brown slug pulling forth an awful memory from a terrifying night. Higgins's voice cut through the ugly flashback, brought Hadder back to the now.

"So much money and power in these little slugs, huh? I don't blame you for taking it, man. This shit gives you a license to fucking print..."

Hadder's right hand around Higgins's throat cut the sentence short, especially when he lifted the man up into the air and slammed him down onto the glass table, shattering it and sending both man and glass cascading towards the hard floor. Higgins's breath left him as his back slammed into the ground, replaced by a wheezing whine that only further enraged Hadder, and fed the Rage.

As Higgins writhed on the ground, Hadder ripped off the pimp's white tank top before reaching into the brown container to scoop up a handful of Slink. Hadder placed his other hand over Higgins's mouth as he spread Slink across the man's exposed belly, watching as the dark slugs buried themselves into the soft flesh. Higgins's eyes once more went wide with terror as Hadder placed mound after mound of Slink onto his chest and stomach. When more than a dozen of the creatures pulsed dully under Higgins's pale skin, Hadder slowly removed his hands, and got up from the pedophile.

"Oh, my god, man. What have you done? What have you *fucking* done?! What's gonna happen to me, man?!" Higgins spoke through bleary eyes, on the edge of hysteria.

Hadder leaned down, his head inches from Higgins's panicking face. "I'm going to tell you what is going to happen, Higgins. You are going to learn about terror. True terror. The kind that you so callously bestowed upon those children out there."

Higgins's pupils shrank to pinholes as the Slink began dissolving within. "Fuck, fuck, fuck. Am I gonna die, man? I saved those girls from the street, man! They were goners without me, man! Oh fuck, oh fuck. I feel like I... Am I gonna die, man?!"

Hadder smiled wickedly above the frightened predator. "You are most certainly going to die, Higgins. But, not before hours and hours of you wishing for it. It won't come quickly, Higgins. I need you to know that. You have a lifetime of pain to look forward to."

"Shit, man. I can't even…" Higgins's words ran together and soon became unintelligible as Hadder rose from the floor, ensuring that no Slink had accidentally latched onto him. Higgins's face reddened as if a fire had been lit just beneath the skin, and his eyes vibrated in their sockets, unable to focus on any one point.

Hadder grabbed one of the notes that now littered the floor, licked the back, and slapped the paper against Higgins's forehead, where it would sit until Slink finally overtook the dealer's bodily functions. "Goodbye, Higgins. I hope the money was worth it."

And with that, the Rage slowly began to withdraw, allowing Hadder to wrest control once more. He left the pimp to die alone on the floor, and exited both office and club.

Outside the club, Rott stood, a half-naked child in each arm. "And what, pray tell, are we going to do about these two, Marlin?"

Hadder thought for a moment. "We'll take them to one of the Spirit Houses. The Spirit Girls will know a safe place to take them." This news propped up Rott, who never missed a chance to see his beloved Spirt Girls. "But tomorrow, Al, we head to Bhellum. This hunt has proven fruitless for long enough. Krill wants to run around playing God, it's time we showed him what he's not."

"Very well, Marlin. Now, let's get these two to safety. I know the perfect Spirit House for the job."

17

Marlin Hadder, not unlike everyone who first enters the city of Bhellum at dusk, could feel his eyes go wide as he and Albany Rott rode into the Neon City on twin mono-wheels. Hadder sat grinning in the central seat as the giant wheel spun over and around him, sending series after series of bright lights, enormous holographic advertisements, and decadent sounds to briefly assault the new visitors before disappearing into the colorful cacophony of the past.

The city smelled different from the others of this world, although Hadder was unable to put his finger on the cause. He took a moment from admiring Bhellum to look over at Rott, who sped through the city alongside him. The god had the same relaxed, even bored, look pasted onto his pale, scarred face, as if he had already seen everything every world had to offer. And maybe he had.

Rott caught Hadder looking over, and motioned for him to follow as he accelerated forward, twisting in and out of traffic. Hadder complied, narrowly missing a medical transport, and cutting off an auto-hauler that issued a loud prerecorded warning from its massive external speakers. Hadder pressed on, following Rott through the prismatic madness at dangerous speeds. He smiled at the memory that came bubbling to the surface, of stumbling into the Celebration Cluster for the first time, arm and arm with new friends who would help shape his second life. He smiled dumbly as the neon colors mixed with the exploding holograms, mimicking the iridescent flora and chromatic pollen releases of Station, making him pine for a world already lost to time.

Hadder was ripped from these recollections as Rott turned sharply to the right ahead of him. He braked hard on his mono-wheel, earning a warning horn from one of the public transit's auto-buses, before following his companion, who had already sped ahead. Hadder raced down the street for some time, taking notice of the countless antiquated service bots that cared for the city, before abruptly slowing down, receiving several more warnings from those behind him.

To his right, Hadder saw that Rott had parked his mono-wheel in an empty lot, and spun his central chair to follow. In short order, Hadder's mono-wheel was parked next to Rott's as both men stood staring out into the waking city, the falling sun indicating that it was time for nightly duties to commence. The two companions stood in silence, watching as a wondrous show became truly spectacular, with additional neon and holograms appearing across the city, encompassing them in a spectral net.

"Reminds me of Station. Or, at least, parts of it."

Rott considered Hadder's words for several seconds. "What do you see out there, Marlin?"

"I see a city of excess. A city of wealth. A city too blinded by its neon to see that a monster is operating in its midst."

"Is that all?"

A pause. "No. I see beauty, as well. There's an appreciation for the effort that went into this visual chaos, the effort it took to create these mind-numbing optics that demand the eye to rise, tearing it from the miserable truth of the ground level."

A pale finger stabbed up into the air. "And there it is."

"And there *what* is?"

"The crux of this city."

An uncomfortable silence passed. "Care to share what you've ascertained?"

"This city is a distortion, Marlin."

"A what?"

"A distortion. All of this, it's a retelling, a poor retelling. It tells the tale of a city of wealth, where beauty is abundant, and entertainment of any kind can be found for any price."

"And this is untrue?"

Rott shrugged. "It is partially true. And therein lies the beauty of this distortion. Something that is, maybe, five percent accurate can be made to appear ninety percent true."

Hadder swung to face Rott. "What are you trying to say, Al?"

"Bhellum is a distortion," he reiterated. "It is deteriorating from within. All of this glitz hides the poison that is pouring forth from this one community. Can you smell it?"

"Smell what?"

"Damn you, Marlin! Close your eyes and tell me what you smell."

Hadder jumped, unused to his god-friend losing control and snapping at him. He did as he was told. "I smell neon. They say it is odorless, but I swear I can smell it in the air and on my skin. My body hums with it. And buried within that neon is something else, something almost familiar. It tickles a memory that I cannot reach to scratch. But it's something I know." Hadder opened his eyes.

Rott's too-white teeth appeared. "You are correct, Marlin. That which sits on your tongue, pulling at memory chords and reviving dead lovers, is, indeed, something familiar. It is Station. It is Station you feel, you fool."

"Can it be that strong? Can the existence of one man in an entire metropolis really be enough to set off alarms in my brain?"

Rott shrugged once more, a grim smile still pasted on his face. "You lived between worlds for a long time, Marlin. That is a stench that does not easily wash off. That is a stench that is supremely unique. That is a stench to hunt, or be hunted by."

"Then, he is here. He is, for sure, here."

"Viktor Krill is here, Marlin. And he is surrounded by an enormous amount of Slink. The stink of those vile creatures coats every note of Station that I pick up on the wind."

"How do you want to go about finding him?"

Rott stared out into the fully lit city, Bhellum's make-up now fully applied for the evening. "Oh, I do not think it will be very hard to find him this time, Marlin. Viktor Krill has put roots down here. And Krill's roots will be like those that have consumed countless other civilizations, burying histories deep within jungles to never be understood."

"So, where do we start?"

"Where does one always start, Marlin? We will start at the bottom, and work our way up."

"Where's the bottom?"

Rott's eyes flashed red. "This way."

———

As usual, Albany Rott was correct. The trail leading to Viktor Krill was not some ethereal thing, requiring bloodhound-like detection and investigative prowess, but, rather, a neon-dipped blood stain that only needed a name to discover.

The companions started simply enough, locating obvious Slinkers and inquiring as to where they acquired the unnatural bio-drug. Those that could still form coherent sentences pointed Hadder and Rott to one of several sources, including a nightclub called *The Neon Demon*, a child gang that swarmed the streets during daylight, and a lone dealer named Trenton who operated out of a food stall known to locals as a chowset.

Given that Hadder was tired of nightclubs, and Rott wanted nothing to do with "baby villains," it was agreed that the search would continue with Trenton, who would, hopefully, get them one step closer to reaching their quarry.

When Hadder and Rott reached the mammoth row of chowsets that sat outside a line of nightclubs in the old Supplier District, they were initially concerned about finding their man in this hive of activity. Their worries, however, were quickly allayed as the companions ran their hazel and red eyes over the line of dumpling, sandwich, and noodle hawkers. Every stall was operated by either an older female or pre-teen child. Every stall save one.

Trenton stood out like a sore thumb among the collected food providers. Not only was he the only man managing a chowset, but his stall's offerings left much to be desired. The pastries displayed looked dried out and flaky with age, with green and blue mold already touching the edges of most.

As much as Trenton's food separated him from his chowset cohorts, the man's appearance truly set him apart. Not only was Trenton the lone grown man at a chowset, but his black leather ensemble, complete with dark duster, long mullet, dark eyeliner, wraparound sunglasses, and excessive jewelry, marked him as one who *does not belong*. This must have made it easy for seeking Slinkers to locate him, but it also must have been a red flag to authorities. If authorities even existed in this heavily colored city.

Hadder and Rott looked to each other and nodded before approaching the out-of-place man and his troubling food offerings. Trenton took notice as soon as they closed the distance, rising from his small stool to greet the potential customers. He apprised their matching dark suits and clean fits before breaking into a wide smile that showcased glittering braces.

"Gentlemen! So glad you could join us this evening! What can I get for you? I have an array of delicious pastries just waiting to be consumed and enjoyed." The man's accent was strange, something Hadder had never heard before. He certainly was not from Bhellum, or anywhere even remotely close, for that matter.

As Hadder was struggling with the accent, Rott spoke. "We're looking for Trenton. I suppose that is you?"

Trenton looked around suspiciously. "Voices down, new friends. I know I'm working in plain sight here, but that's no reason to fire a signal into the sky." The man leaned forward to physically assert the necessity for discretion. "I am Trenton. Now, what can I do for you boys?" As he spoke, little blue lights came to life on the sides of Trenton's glasses, no doubt scanning his visitors and comparing them to known police officers and informants. Neither Hadder nor Rott took offense.

Hadder mirrored Trenton and leaned in. "We're looking for Slink. A little birdy told us you may be able to help."

"Little birdies always talk too much, don't they?"

"They do. But we still can't live without their sweet voices and soft bodies, can we?"

"No, no we can't." Trenton looked around once more. "And they were right. Now, how much can I get for you boys? Just got a new shipment in, and it's supposed to be the most aggressive batch yet. Gonna really blow your fucking minds."

Hadder continued the dialogue. "Actually, Trenton, we need to know where you get the Slink. And we're prepared to pay you handsomely for the information."

Trenton stared at Hadder and Rott for a long while before responding. "Normally, I'd tell you both to fuck off. Might even threaten you with the piece I have in my coat pocket. But I haven't survived this long by not realizing when I'm talking to serious men." His dark glasses locked onto Rott. "If you even qualify as that." Back to Hadder. "Anyway, I know when I'm dealing with those above my pay grade. But I don't know how much I can help you. I get my shit from the toddy gangs that roam the city. They only deal with me because I've been pushing shit for the gangs for almost a decade now. Everyone knows that Trenton is reliable, and Trenton don't snitch. I paid my dues in silence and jail time over the years, and I'm finally getting flush. All because of this new shit called Slink."

Hadder could feel Rott growing impatient next to him. "So, just tell us where and when you meet the toddy gangs. Make an introduction."

Trenton laughed aloud, a dry, ragged thing that exposed years of lung abuse. "Why don't I just run a knife across my throat right now, and save everyone the time and cleanup?" Trenton busied himself with rearranging his stale pies. "They know me to be solid from a decade of slinging. They don't know you for shit. And people they don't know end up half-buried near the Gates, you feel me?" Hadder didn't feel him, didn't quite understand what Trenton was saying, but remained silent and let the leather-clad man continue. "And, anyway, I never go to meet them. They find *me*. Every few weeks, some toddy will find me. The little bastard will give me a time and place to pick up the shit. Always different. A few weeks later, another toddy will come around the chowset to collect."

"You mean they don't make you pay initially? They front you the whole amount? They must really trust you, Trent?"

Trenton laughed aloud once more. "Oh, I wouldn't chalk it up to trust for old Trent. This wouldn't have happened a couple of years ago. Trust a drug dealer to pay up? Never. But things have changed. Dramatically. Now, there's no fear of anyone paying up. Not intentionally, at least. No one wants to be on the shit end of Viktor Krill. Cross him and you don't die. You fucking disappear."

Hadder and Rott looked to each other, shock painted on both faces. Rott's eyes roared to life, clearly reflected in Trenton's glasses. "Trenton. Could you please repeat that last part?"

"What part? That I get fronted the Slink from the toddies?"

"No. The part about Viktor Krill. How do you know that name?"

Now it was Trenton's turn to look dismayed. "How could I not?"

Rott jumped in. "Indulge two newbies to Bhellum. We'll make it worth your while. How do you know Viktor Krill?"

For the first time, the cool operator known as Trenton looked legitimately anxious. He leaned in further. "Look, I don't *know* Viktor Krill. I *know of* Viktor Krill. Everyone knows *of* him."

"How?" There was a tangible power behind Rott's question.

"I mean, he's the fucking King of the Underworld. Viktor Krill's the King of the Muck. He controls everything drug-related in the city, especially the Slink production."

Hadder cut in. "And he's allowed to operate in the open? What about the authorities?"

Trenton looked back and forth between the companions once more. "You two really aren't from around here, are you? Bhellum doesn't have much in the way of "authorities," at least those that aren't already in the pockets of the corporations or the gangs."

"Fair enough," responded Hadder. "One last thing. How do we find Viktor Krill?"

A snicker emanated from Trent. "Well, he ain't hard to find. Everyone knows he rules from the Muck. Now, getting to him, that's a different story, one that's far beyond my knowledge, understanding, or interest."

"And where is this Muck?"

"Fuck me, boys. You want me to drive you there, too?"

Now it was Rott's turn to cut in. "Never mind. You've been a big help. We can locate the Muck on our own."

"Well, that's good to know." Trent looked around once more. "Look, you boys have been here too long already. At least buy some Slink, so we look legit to prying eyes."

Hadder put his hand to Rott's chest to keep him quiet. "Fine, we'll take two. And add the value of your information to the amount."

Trent's hands began to move as he responded. "Nah, I didn't make it this far in the game by ripping people off. I didn't tell you anything every lady in this chowset line couldn't have told you. You're buying my Slink, that's good enough." As he spoke, Trent reached under the stall and withdrew two Slink from somewhere hidden from view. He then poked a hole into one his pastries with a black lacquered nail, and shoved both brown slugs into the unappetizing pie. After wrapping the pie in wax paper and placing it into a plain white bag, Trenton handed the package to Hadder.

"How much do we owe you?"

"Two Slink will run you two-hundred credits."

"Fucking hell, that's expensive."

Trenton looked put-off. "Not for a once-in-a-lifetime experience. I'm telling you, this new shit will shake loose your brain stem. If you don't like the price, take it up with Viktor Krill. The Risers set the Slink prices, not me."

"What the fuck did you..." Hadder's question was cut short by Rott's pale hand on his shoulder, urging him on.

"Thank you, Trenton. The amount is acceptable." And with that, Rott put out his left hand, which was quickly scanned by the chowset vendor. "We will leave you now."

"Thanks for your patronage, fellas. And, please, be a little less conspicuous with your search. Not everyone is as easygoing as old Trent. Especially, the Risers and the Bitch-Whores."

Hadder fought Rott's pull for one more second. "Who are the Bitch-Whores?"

Trenton flashed another braces-filled smile. "If you're really heading to the Muck, you'll find out soon enough."

As Hadder was pulled away from the chowsets by Rott, he could hear Trenton's laughter following them through the busy streets. He turned to his friend. "The Muck? What do you think it's like, Al?"

"Remember the Rising? I think Viktor Krill has recreated it here in Bhellum."

"I told myself I'd never visit the Rising again."

"Are you telling me that you are averse to lying to yourself, Marlin?"

"No, I'm telling you I'm getting used to breaking promises to myself."

"Aren't we all, Marlin. Aren't we all."

———

"IF EVER THERE was a place for Viktor Krill to call home, it would be here."

As Hadder looked down from the bluff on which he and Rott currently stood, Hadder staring through an image-enhancing visor, he couldn't help but agree with his friend. Below the two, shrink-wrapped in the smells of smoke, violence, and death, sat the Muck, once known as Seaside Sights. And to be accurate, it *used* to be known as the Muck, as an auto-taxi they asked for directions informed them.

"Wouldn't go around using that verbiage, good sirs," said the auto-taxi's dummy driver. "Locals refer to it now as the Rising. I've seen a few good sirs get out of sorts after hearing some other good sirs call it the Muck. And let me tell you, I wouldn't want to have been *those* good sirs. No good sir, I wouldn't have been *those* good sirs."

"Those five buildings look like fingers escaping the grave," said Hadder, still trying to process the fact that he was looking upon another Rising.

"And you think Viktor Krill reached that same conclusion?"

"I know he did. But, beyond that, I don't know what he saw here. What set this place apart from the hundreds of other options?"

"He saw a monster to tame."

"Come again?" Hadder tore his eyes from the Rising to look at Rott, whose gaze was sweeping from left to right, taking in details that Hadder would never be able to notice.

"Very recently, the area below us was known as the Muck. What adjectives does that label conjure? Chaotic? Violent? Depraved? Sad? Angry?"

"Yes. All those."

"So, there was a reason it was called that. Look down there now and tell me what you see, Marlin."

Hadder stared even harder, and his visor made audible adjustments. "Five large buildings, each with a small group of gangsters stationed outside. Four of the buildings seem to be controlled by the same gang."

"Why do you say that, Marlin?"

"Well, they're all wearing the same color, white on white. That fifth group is wearing black with a white X on the back."

"Good. And does this look like a place of chaos, violence, sadness, and anger?"

Hadder continued to search the land beneath him. The large, decrepit park that sat between all the buildings seemed a hotbed of activity, with an array of visitors, well-to-do and poor, clean and dirty, healthy and diseased, entering and exiting as the companions watched. Some jumped out of auto-taxis and ran into the park, only to return minutes later to leave in the same vehicle that brought them.

"I think that park could tell a lifetime's worth of heartbreaking stories."

"Agreed. But outside of that? How would you describe this place that they now call the Rising?"

Hadder shrugged. "The place is heavy with the smell of violence and blood. But, I have to admit, there does seem to be an order within the chaos, a purpose to it all."

Rott's ember eyes flared once more, his too-white teeth appearing. "That's right, dear boy! An ordered chaos. That! That, right there, is what Viktor Krill sought. You only knew Station's Rising after Viktor Krill had escaped. Don't confuse The Krown's modus operandi with Krill's. The Krown only wanted to spread violence and chaos. Viktor Krill craves power, he craves competition. This is hard to come by for a Wakened human. Few things in any world are up to his abilities. But the Muck... Its depravity. Its many gangs who must have been fighting for control of this place. Its proximity to the beach and the port... The Muck must have looked like an oasis to Viktor Krill. A place that only a Wakened human could truly tame. So, that's what he did."

Hadder took off his visor, looked once again at Rott. "How do you know this, Al?"

Now, it was Rott's turn to shrug. "I do not *know* it, dear boy. But it *is* what the evidence is telling me. What was once the Muck is now the Rising. Krill has consolidated the bloodletting, fashioned it into a weapon, and is now stabbing out at the rest of this world."

"So, where do we start?"

"Well, our new friend Trenton said that he's not hard to find, but rather hard to reach. That means we can both head down, ask around, and quickly discover exactly where Krill is. But..."

"But what?"

"But, we will, most likely, be executed on the spot."

"We will?"

Rott smiled wickedly. "Well, you will be, dear Marlin. And then I would get sidetracked by having to avenge you, and the whole mission would be turned on its side."

Hadder chuckled at Rott's dark joke. "So, what's the plan?"

"I say, let's head down and take a closer look. Give those Risers in the white a wide berth."

"What makes you think those are the Risers?"

"You think Viktor Krill is losing this war?"

Hadder remained quiet, recognizing his question as foolish.

Rott continued. "We take a closer look, try to get a grasp on the economics, politics, and social order of this new Rising."

"And then what?"

"And then, dear boy, we will extend a hand to those gentlemen still draped in black, the lone survivors of Krill's purge. They will fill in the gaps of our initial fact-finding, and may even lend us their arms as we hunt the villain."

"And if they don't?"

"Then, we might be forced to do Krill's work for him. But, I am confident that they will aid us."

"Why is that, Al?"

"Because they know that they are already dead. They are an insect caught in the web of a master weaver. Their fate is sealed already. How desperate they must be for a sign of light in Krill's darkness."

"Then we have a plan. Although, I must be honest, Al. I don't feel supremely confident about this. Those look like serious men down there. And in this Rising, they have more than Elevations to rely on. Appears to me that they're all strapped. Did you know that when you get shot, you feel it before you hear it? Meaning, there will be no warning, just the hot pinch of metal tearing through your skin and rearranging your insides."

Rott laughed again. "*You* will not receive a warning, Marlin; that is true. But speak for yourself. Neither rock, nor arrow, nor bullet has yet to cut me down after thousands of years. I do not intend to break that streak here. Shall we?"

Hadder looked down at the new Rising once more, his stomach churning and his pores releasing an undue amount of sweat. "We always knew the beast would find a suitable lair. I assumed it was never going to be easy."

"He's the closest thing to a god that this, or any other world, has ever known."

"Current company excluded, you mean."

"Of course, Marlin. And, yes, it was never going to be easy."

"Then, let's get on with it. I'm not getting any stronger, and he's not getting any weaker."

"That's the spirit, dear boy."

And with that, the two hunters began their descent from the bluff, hazel and red eyes never leaving the destination that was once known as the Muck, but was now called the Rising.

Neither companion noticed, nor commented, on the giant C that hovered and spun silently in the distant background, holding quiet dominion over the place that was their next target.

———

THE CREATURE that dove out of the thick growth that bordered both sides of the walking path could hardly be described as a man. Where there should have been exposed skin, Hadder could only see a thick coating of dirt. Under the grime, the creature was all angles, bones aggressively pushing through, with no meat to dampen their cries. The creature wore rags that, if you looked closely, could have been the remnants of a white dress shirt and brown slacks found on the average office worker, one that had fallen on the hardest of times.

All in all, Hadder would have pitied the man, would have offered his help, and a warm meal. Would have tried to be empathetic.

But the rust-covered blade that the creature was wielding did not allow time for pity as it swung drunkenly towards Hadder's face without demands being voiced. There was only the desire for blood on the filthy edge.

Hadder quickly put his left hand to his ear, and tucked in his elbow to protect his neck and face, and braced for the inevitable cut that was to come.

As the sweeping knife grew closer, movement from Hadder's right side flashed across his vision, too fast for even eyes to follow. As the creature attacked Hadder with its right hand, Albany Rott flew in from the creature's left, crossing the distance so quickly that he jumped across space, as if several frames were missing from the moving picture. Just as the creature's knife was about to career into Hadder's defensively placed arm, the white comet that was Rott's fist plummeted into the attacker's temple, passing through dirt, skin, bone, brain matter, bone, skin, and dirt again on its journey to the other side of the man's head.

The creature fell instantly, as if its batteries had been removed, crumpling grossly to the pathway's stoney floor. Rott shook his bloody hand, trying to fling off as much gore as possible. "What an unwelcome surprise! And I sense more where he came from." Rott's red eyes peered into the dense shrubbery, seeing things Hadder never could. "Many more."

As Rott carefully removed a silk handkerchief from his suit jacket, and began to clean off his soiled hand, Hadder took a harder look at the corpse below them. It looked like the man had been starved for weeks, with a body and face that reminded Hadder of the concentration camp victims of another world.

On a whim, Hadder knelt down and took the corpse's arm, scrubbing off caked-on dirt with his palm until he found what he was looking for. There, on the inside of the dead man's forearm, clear beneath the too-tight skin, a Slink slowly pulsed, a third of its usual size.

Hadder rose from the body. "Fuck me, Al. Is this what Slink is doing to people here?"

Rott finished removing bits of skull from his hand, and responded. "You tell me, Marlin. Only one of us here has taken that vile slug."

"It was a horrible experience, and something I would never want to do again. Even in Station, only a few truly hardcore partiers did Slink more than once, and, then, it was several months between uses. But here? Who could get addicted to this shit?"

"Trenton said it himself, Krill has been altering the Slink, making it a more profitable product. To do so, I am sure that the first thing the bastard did was make the bio-drug more addictive, carving out a hole in the user that can only be filled with more Slink."

"But does that explain this? A walking skeleton? An animate corpse?"

"Yes, you would think that Krill would produce a less deadly form of the slug, one that could keep users alive and desperate to purchase more. Maybe there is more afoot than we realize. Let us keep moving. I think, in this jungle of death, only the dead can afford to be stationary."

The rest of the afternoon went in much the same way. Hadder and Rott dodged, or stepped over, Slinkers where they could, slapped them aside, when necessary. The companions watched as a constant stream of junkies, rich and poor, disheveled and collected, made their way through the once-beautiful park, each clutching a weapon. Each attempted to wear a brave face as they entered the heavily guarded gazebos, only to exit moments later, dumb smiles plastered onto their lips.

Every drug spot they encountered was managed by the thugs in white, known now as the Risers. Hadder and Rott stayed well out of sight as they observed each, impressed with the military precision demonstrated by the gang. Armed guards surrounded each site, making it impossible to enter without declaring your presence to all. But Hadder didn't need to see inside to know what he would find, an equally efficient method of collecting credits and notes while delivering deadly Slink.

"I have seen enough, Marlin. They are all the same. Professional. Dangerous. Cold. A true reflection of their leader. I am curious about what we will find to the Southwest, closer to that lone gang in black."

Hadder nodded his assent, and the pair moved further through the park, heading towards the lone crack that Rott could see in Viktor Krill's compressed empire.

As they walked, Hadder and Rott spoke in hushed tones, not wanting to murder any more junkies than absolutely necessary. Hadder was about to inquire about what Rott hoped to find in the Southwest, when an impossibly strong arm tipped with a pale hand swept him to the side of the pathway, almost causing him to stumble into the bordering flora.

"What the fuck, Al?"

Rott had also moved to the far side of the walkway. "Silence, you fool! And keep your damned eyes down!"

Hadder did as he was told, but stole a look through his thick eyelashes.

Ambling down the walkway towards the companions, dragging a third leg that didn't seem to fit any purpose, was a giant almost as large as the

Caesars. Hadder's stomach leapt into his throat as dark memories floated once more to the surface, stealing his breath. He kept his head down, but stole more glances.

The behemoth was just shy of seven feet, with green, bubbly skin, and a bald head that looked like it had been pulled from the oven long before the bell. Its mouth jutted out angrily from its face, showcasing bright pink gums that held too-few teeth. On its mammoth, chiseled body, the beast wore loose pantaloons that were complete with a third leg for its extra dead appendage, heavy black boots, and a barely-there tank top that exposed both shoulders and more blister-covered skin.

As the twisted thing drew closer, Hadder could feel his breath draw in as other details clarified. Below the creature's left shoulder, peeking out from the meaty upper chest, was a second face with angry purple eyes and a tiny snarling mouth. While Hadder continued to lower his face, sneaking glimpses of the beast through lashes, Rott met the creature's gaze with his own fiery red stare.

"Who the fuck does this fucking guy think he fucking is, hey Brutto," came the squeaky voice from the shoulder-face, its purple eyes wide with excitement. "Let's eat the fucker, hey Brutto? Eat! Eat! Eat!"

"Shut up," thundered the green giant, its own yellow eyes appraising Rott and the nearly bowing Hadder. Yellow orbs connected with red, and something unsaid passed between the two titans. The green giant merely offered a nod before passing the hunters.

More high-pitched words accompanied the passing. "No fun, Brutto. No fucking fun, at all. You fuckers are fucking lucky, you are. Next time we fucking see you, Brutto's going to fucking eat one of you and fucking feed the other fucker to me. Cause I'm always hungry, fuckers. Your boy Smeggins is always hungry and..."

The words of the tumor-face known as Smeggins quieted as Brutto continued past before becoming completely mute. Hadder gave it a few more seconds before finally raising his head.

"And what the fuck was that, Al?"

Red eyes embers once more, Rott smiled. "Another piece of the puzzle, dear boy. And maybe a key piece. Come. Let us continue to learn before we are forced to act."

Shortly after their encounter with the behemoth Brutto and nasty little Smeggins, Hadder and Rott knew they had arrived at their destination.

All afternoon, the pair had encountered, and skirted, gazebos guarded by small battalions of white-clad Risers. They watched through dense cover as consistent streams of junkies flowed in and out of these makeshift drug dispensaries, which, they discovered, were known locally as dope tanks. They watched as man, woman, and everything in between marched into the dope tank, anxiety and perspiration hanging heavy on their faces, only to exit minutes later with the smile of the lobotomized painted on their dry lips.

But this dope tank was different. Unlike the ubiquitous thugs in white, the charges of this dope tank wore black hoodies with large white Xs on the back. Additionally, almost all of them had dark skin to match their uniforms, wearing both proudly.

The differences didn't end with management; even the drug spot's clients set it apart. While the rest of the fallen park, which was overheard to be called the Jungle, attracted a potpourri of the walking dead, the visitors of this particular tank seemed quite normal, by comparison.

"Well, this certainly seems different," offered Hadder, unable to formulate more insightful commentary.

"I would say that this is the last dope tank untouched by the poison of Viktor Krill and his Slink," said Albany Rott, his red eyes studying minuscule details. "Let us take a closer look."

"You think that's safe?"

Rott cracked a smile, and shrugged. "We have money. We enjoy drugs. Why would we be turned away?"

And with that, Rott walked toward the clearing, leaving his final thought unsaid, but obvious. *And what if it is not safe? Am I to fear these mortals?*

Hadder shook his head, but moved to follow, watching carefully as the guards' eyes swung their way as they entered the unholy grounds of this abnormal dope tank. Although no barrels were pointed the companions' way, the pair observed how the dark hands tightened on the handles and stocks of their guns, ready at a moments' notice to eliminate the potential threat.

Cool faces and itchy hands greeted Hadder and Rott as they neared the partially boarded-up gazebo. When the companions had almost reached the gap that served as the dope tank's entrance, they were stopped by an upraised hand and a deep voice.

"Stop! What you boys looking for here?"

Hadder and Rott looked to the older, dreadlocked man who spoke. He had a long scar that ran down his face, across a left eye that had been rendered white and blind from the attack. Hadder wondered if he and Rott felt a kinship because of their similar marks, but his curiosity was swept aside as Rott responded.

Rott, noticing the guards' preoccupation with his and Hadder's suits, decided to play up that angle. "Whatever you have to offer, friend. My associate and I are in Bhellum on business, and we do not have the time, nor patience, to traipse around town for the party favors that we will require this evening. Thus, we decided to come to the source. Now, again I ask you, what do you have to offer?"

Normally, two idiots who had wandered into the Jungle would be ejected, or executed, with the quickness, but the men in black hoodies spoke quietly among themselves for a moment, chuckling at certain points, before the dreadlocked man, delivering a smile that showcased several gold teeth, answered.

"Goddam, y'all really don't know where the fuck y'all are. We only got Leaf here. If you want something stronger, you'll have to go deeper into the Jungle." He looked Hadder and Rott up and down. "Something I highly recommend that *neither* of you do."

"Thanks for the advice," responded Rott. "Pardon my ignorance, my friend, but we saw some serious-looking men in white as we entered...what did you call this? Oh, that is right, the Jungle. Partners of yours?"

The dreadlocked man turned his head and spit on the moss-covered ground. "Partners? Fuck me, man, you boys are outta your element. We're the Broken Tens, last of the original Muck gangs. We hold our heads high. All those whitewashed muthafuckers are slaves, fuck boys, traitors, and cowards."

Rott cut in with a bow. "My apologies for confusing you for them. As you said, we truly are out of our element here."

"Enough. You want some Leaf or not?"

Rott looked to Hadder, who nodded his silent approval. "Well, yes, we would love some Leaf. How about a quarter to get us through this terrible business trip? Would that be all right, Mister...?"

"The name's Zero. And, no, you don't get to ask how I got that name."

Rott's arms went up in surrender. "Understood, friend. So, do we just go in to complete the transaction?"

Zero studied both men, but Rott, in particular, before responding. "Nah. Something ain't right about y'all two. Wait here."

As Zero ran into the dope tank, Rott leaned in toward Hadder. "He is a sharp one. If the rest of the Broken Tens crew is like this, we may have a shot."

"And what makes you think they're gonna welcome our help?"

Rott chuckled. "It was one of the first lessons you humans learned. *The enemy of my enemy is my friend.*"

"I don't think they're going to be that jazzed about the assistance of two white guys in suits."

"Yes, that is why I am sure they will have us do some horrible errand or...wait, here comes Zero."

Zero appeared in the gazebo's gap, a small bag in one hand, and a hand scanner in the other. He walked up to Hadder and Rott, his gold teeth reflecting the few rays of sun that managed to penetrate the overgrown park. "Here's your Leaf, boys. That'll be one-hundred credits, or eighty notes." Audible laughter could be heard from the crowd of armed Broken Tens.

Hadder and Rott were not brand new to this world and, as such, knew they were being charged double. Hadder looked to Rott, as if to ask, *are we fighting over this?* But Rott waved away his unspoken question. "That sounds great, friend, really great. Credit will be fine."

Zero held out the hand scanner, better known as a dark ream, to Rott, who slowly placed his pale hand on the crystal face, not wanting to spook the other Broken Tens. The dark ream glowed red, then green, as credits were discreetly transferred. When a high-pitched ring emanated from the hand scanner, Zero lowered the hardware and handed Rott the baggie of Leaf.

"And now, white tourists, we must say our farewells. If you need other shit, you gotta go deeper, which I highly recommend that you *don't do.*"

"So, what do you recommend," asked Hadder.

Zero smiled again, this time bringing a glimmer to his light green eyes. "I recommend you boys get the fuck out of here. As fast as you can. And that you go this way." He motioned behind him, towards the Southwest. "This will put you out of the Jungle near Brizo Tower, which the Broken Tens control. If you exit anywhere else, I can't promise the Risers won't skin you alive."

Now it was Rott's turn to return the toothy smile. "What a splendid idea, Mister Zero. I thank you for the Leaf and the sound advice. Marlin?"

Hadder jumped to catch up to Rott, who had already begun to exit through the opposite side of the clearing. As he reached Rott, an explosion of laughter could be heard from the Broken Tens, who were obviously relishing ripping off two square businessmen. Rott joined in their amusement, chuckling to himself.

"What's so funny, Al? We just got ripped off."

Rott shook his head, then smoothed back his dark reddish hair with a pale hand. "Those men will be taking orders from us within the week. So, just consider that a down payment."

"A down payment for what?"

"For war, dear boy. For the war we are about to start."

18

A s the two suited strangers closed in on the large building marked Brizo Tower, the Broken Tens standing guard straightened and fell into strategic position, guns out, but aimed at the ground. Albany Rott smirked as he and Hadder continued to approach, thinking that if all the Broken Tens were this disciplined, they may have a real shot in the upcoming war.

Similar to back at the Broken Tens' only dope tank, Hadder and Rott were told to halt twenty feet from Brizo's entrance stairs. From the group of wary gangsters, a single man in a typical black hoodie moved forward to stand before the intruders. "You boys look like you're lost. Maybe I can help you find your way."

As usual, Rott started the conversation. "Not lost, friend. Looking."

"And what is it that you're looking for, *friend?*"

"The leader of your fine organization."

As if an invisible switch had been hit, guns that had been safely pointed towards the grass and dirt swung up to dance before the suited visitors' faces. The Broken Tens spokesman, the only one who had yet to raise his weapon, responded, his face a mask of barely controlled rage and concern.

"And what do you want with Old Tens? Maybe you want to put a bullet in his head, or draw a knife across his throat? Who sent you? Did Viktor Krill send you? Tell that bastard it's gonna take more than two half-assed whitey assassins to retire Old Tens! If Liquid Tye couldn't reach him, I'll be goddamned if you two sore thumbs are gonna complete the job. Tell Krill, if he wants war, he's gonna have to do it the old-fashioned way, armies spread across the field of battle!"

The man's voice grew louder as he continued, and both Hadder and Rott were impressed with the level of respect and loyalty that this *Old Tens* demanded of his followers. Rott's pale hands went up in a calming gesture. "You have us all wrong, friend. We were not sent by Viktor Krill. He is our quarry."

"Your what?"

"Our quarry. We are hunting him."

Gun barrels swung left and right, up and down, as raucous laughter from the Broken Tens beset the companions. Hadder and Rott stood silently, accepting the ridicule, until discipline had found the armed men once more.

A large smile was still present on the spokesman's face when he said, "Well, shit, man, why didn't you tell us? You're hunting Viktor Krill, that's great to hear. So, why don't you march over to Cyrix Industries, kill the demon, and bring his head back here for us to see and dance around?"

Hadder and Rott's heads swiveled to face each other before both sets of eyes spun to the giant C slowly spiraling in the distant air. While they had heard of Cyrix Industries in their minimal investigation around Bhellum, neither had thought the company was involved in the Viktor Krill business. Perhaps they were wrong. Perhaps Viktor Krill's ascension had been underestimated. Perhaps their mission would prove even more difficult than initially thought.

Rott's eyes found their way back to the lead Broken Tens member. They were now a much brighter shader of red, with small fires buried within each. "We will do what you ask, but we need help."

"Let's just blast these fools and be done with it, Caddoc" shouted a voice from the tightly grouped Broken Tens. Several statements of agreement followed the idea.

To his credit, Sonny Caddoc did not acknowledge the suggestion of his men, instead using this time to study, really study, the strange visitors. "Something's off about you two. Now, whether that works to our favor or detriment, that's not my call."

An angry question was launched from the mob. "You're not really taking these white fools to see Old Tens, are you?!"

Caddoc yelled over his shoulder, his brown eyes never leaving Hadder and Rott. "That's *my* call. And I'll take these white fools anywhere I see fit. Anyone got a problem with that?"

The man called Caddoc's influence was revealed when no further dissension was heard. After a beat, Caddoc rose his wrist to his mouth, and pressed a button on the side of his wristwatch before speaking into the device. "Tennian, are you there?"

Several seconds of silence followed before a voice, simultaneously old, tired, and powerful, emerged from the wristwatch. "What is it, Sonny?"

"Got a couple of strangers out here, real weird muthafuckers, and they say that they're hunting Viktor Krill. Need our help, or some shit. Want me to send them away?"

An even longer silence followed. "And, so, my dream grows legs."

Confusion crossed Caddoc's face before he spoke once more into his wrist. "I don't follow, Tens. You want me to send them away?"

"No. I need to see them. Give me fifteen minutes to put my legs on, and I'll meet you all in the conference room. And Sonny?"

"Yes, boss."

"Treat them with respect. They might be very dangerous men."

"One of them doesn't even seem to be a man, boss."

"Even more reason to be polite. Fifteen minutes."

"Yes, sir." Caddoc lowered his wristwatch and stared once more at Brizo's uninvited guests. "He'll see you both. But we have to wait here a minute." An uncomfortable stillness fell over the dangerous collective of men before Caddoc decided to break the silence. "You boys ain't from around here, are you?"

"What gave it away," asked Hadder.

"You don't smell right."

Hadder's surprise couldn't be contained as he turned to look at Rott, who only shrugged as if to say, *I told you so.*

Caddoc continued. "So, if you boys ain't from Bhellum, then where are you from?"

Hadder laughed lightly. "That's a long story that would require a long explanation."

Now it was Caddoc's turn to chuckle. "You obviously never seen the boss get his legs on. We *got* time, man."

———

As soon as Hadder and Rott were ushered into Brizo Tower's "conference room," which was surrounded by armed gangsters, they understood the joke about Old Tens and his legs.

Standing at the far end of the long, empty room stood Old Tens, or at least half of him. From the waist up, he was all man, with dark skin, salt and pepper hair, a matching beard, and an unbuttoned military jacket. Below the waist, however, he was all military mech, with auto-turrets already out and facing Brizo's newest visitors.

Sonny Caddoc moved between the companions and his boss. "Gentlemen, let me introduce you to Tennian Stamp. He doesn't suffer fools easily, so please, be on your best behavior."

"Enough with the pleasantries," said Tennian. "Why have you come to me today?"

Rott looked around the empty room before responding. "No table. No chairs. Not much of a meeting area."

"If I can't sit, which I cannot, then ain't nobody going to sit. Also, hands can be hidden under a table. I don't like that. Now, tell me, why are you here?"

Rott couldn't help but smile. Hadder could tell that his god-friend immediately liked this seasoned gangster. "We are here, Tennian, to help you end the reign of Viktor Krill. We are here to kill the Devil."

"You are here to kill the Devil, and, yet, there is a devil standing before me."

Rott shrugged once more. "There are many levels of devilry."

"And I assume you are of the highest level?"

"You assume correctly."

Hadder watched as the meeting played out between the two serious entities, unable to tell if Tennian knew the truth of Albany Rott, or if he was simply speaking in metaphor.

"And do the two saviors of the Muck have names?"

"I am Albany Rott, and next to me is my associate Marlin Hadder." Hadder nodded to Tennian at his introduction.

"And what makes you think, Mister Rott and Mister Hadder, that you'll be able to eliminate the scourge that is Viktor Krill?"

"Because I created the bastard."

A long, heavy silence fell over the conference room. Tennian's eyes latched onto Rott's now-flaming red orbs, and ten thousand words seemed to quietly pass between the two kings. It was Tennian who finally spoke, but not to Hadder or Rott.

"Everyone out!"

Sonny Caddoc seemed the most put out. "Certainly you don't mean that, boss? Tens, we don't even know who these crusty white muthafuckers are yet! Let's at least…"

"I said, out," roared Tennian, the strength in his voice sending every man except Hadder and Rott back two steps. The entire collective of armed Broken Tens, after looking to one another, slowly began to file out of the conference room. Caddoc, ever the loyal Second, was the last to remain behind.

"Tens, at least let me take their weapons. We can't…"

"Sonny," interrupted Tennian, his voice now soft, "I'll be perfectly fine. Please leave." Caddoc did as he was told, but not before shooting Hadder and Rott with looks of warning. The conference room door closed behind him, leaving Tennian Stamp alone with his visitors.

The whirr of gears and pistons filled the room as Tennian's mech legs came to life, driving their owner closer to his guests. The auto-turrets adjusted as the man moved, always keeping their barrels pointed at the chests of Hadder and Rott. As he neared, Tennian placed a dark hand on the shoulder of each guest. Up close, Hadder could see the scars that criss-crossed the man's chest. "And so, my deus ex machina has finally arrived."

Hadder couldn't contain himself. "What are you saying?"

Tennian shook his head. "Not here. Let us talk on the roof. I have many things I need to point out."

————

A CHILLY BREEZE came in off the ocean to attack Tennian and his guests as they stood atop Brizo Tower, looking down upon the Muck, now known as the Rising. Both Hadder and Rott remained silent, waiting for their host to lead the conversation. After several minutes of quiet contemplation, he did just that.

"Do you know how I got these scars across my chest? These legs that are not my own?" Tennian waited a moment before continuing. "I got them from running away. Running away from the terrible area that was my place of birth. Running away from the Muck. Back then, the military didn't even care if you had papers; they needed bodies.

"I thought I would find glory across the Great Water, but all I ended up with was a broken body, missing limbs, a one-way ticket back home, and a country that spit at me upon my return. Bitter and angry, I returned to the Muck, resigned to the fact that I could not escape my home, that I was going to have to make the most of this hellish existence. And, so, I did." Tennian spun from the roof's edge to face Hadder and Rott. "I used what I learned in the military, the connections I had made, the skills I had developed, the comfort I had gained with extreme violence, and built something I could be proud of." Both Hadder and Rott could tell that Tennian was speaking from the heart. "My boys are good boys. The product we sell doesn't kill people. I take what is owed to me, and nothing more. I keep promises, and punish liars. It wasn't a perfect life here in the Muck, by any means, but it was a fulfilling life, one carved out over the course of thirty years."

"And then Viktor Krill came," filled in Hadder.

Tennian thought it over before responding. "Things were beginning to go sideways before his arrival but, yes, then Viktor Krill came." Tennian's metal legs came to life once more, driving the Broken Tens leader closer to his visitors. "And he's not from the Muck."

"No, he is not," agreed Rott.

"And he's not from Bhellum, for I have eyes and ears across the city."

"No, he is not."

"And having been in war, having watched men from around the globe fight, I would say that Krill has nothing in common with any of them, either. Which means the demon is from somewhere else, somewhere..." Tennian looked around dramatically. "Not here."

Hadder unknowingly held his breath, unsure of how much Rott would reveal to this, as yet, unsecured ally. "He is from a special place, which has given him special abilities."

"And my two guests, are they from this same place?"

"We are."

"Then tell me, stranger..." All four of Tennian's turret guns escaped their docking stations and pointed their barrels at Hadder and Rott. "Why should I ever let the two of you off this roof?"

Hadder's stomach leapt into this throat, and his hand inched toward one of Higgins's clear handguns that he had tucked into his dark dress pants. Rott, however, remained calm, even smiling at Tennian's question.

"Well, Tennian, you will let us off this roof because you are dead man if you do not. And you know this."

"I'm still here, Mister Rott."

"And why is that? Truly?"

Tennian's dark blue eyes waged a silent war with Rott's increasingly fiery red orbs. After several seconds, Tennian blinked away the standoff and laughed lightly. "Because I know my place, am no threat to anyone, and sell the product that everyone, Viktor Krill included, still loves, despite the influx of Slink."

"And you have no desire to get into the Slink game," asked Hadder, his curiosity for this unique gang leader growing by the minute.

Tennian's smile vanished, and a cold look crossed his brown face. "I sell plants that make people feel better about themselves and life. I don't push poison. I'm a gangster, not an exterminator." The tense moment passed quickly. "Anyway, that is why I am still here, Mister Rott. So, please, tell me, what the hell do I need you two for?"

"Because Viktor Krill will not remain satisfied with controlling four out of the five towers. He is extending his Slink empire now, but do not doubt that his attention will swing back toward the Broken Tens in short order. Now, tell us the tower in which he resides, and we will end his reign of tyranny."

Tennian Stamp looked back and forth between Hadder and Rott before breaking into uncontrollable laughter, his leg turrets returning to their docks as he did. When he could finally regain control of his breathing, he said, "You two great *hunters* really have no idea what's going on here, do you?"

Now even Albany Rott looked confused. "I do not understand."

Tennian's salt and pepper head shook back and forth. "No, you certainly don't, do you?"

Rott looked to Hadder, who could tell that his devil-friend was losing patience, unaccustomed to not being the most informed entity in the room. "Tell me. What is it that I fail to see?"

"What you fail to see could fill a city, Mister Rott."

"Tell me!" Rott's eyes became raging infernos.

Both Hadder's human legs and Tennian's mech legs took significant steps backward from the angry god's forceful words. To his credit, Tennian Stamp recovered quickly, taking in the scene before smiling once more. "Viktor Krill has grown much more powerful than you have assumed."

"I have assumed that he controls the market of the most powerful drug known to mankind."

"That was last year."

Rott looked nervously toward Hadder, who posed the question. "And what has happened this year?"

Tennian turned back to the roof's edge, but, this time, his attention was aimed away from the Muck, toward the West, where a giant building hoisted a large C into the air, its shadow falling over the leaky remains of a massive manufacturing plant. "Your boy Viktor Krill caught the attention of Cyrus Bhellum V."

Hadder's brow furrowed. "You mean..."

"Yes," replied Tennian, answering the question before it was asked. "*That* Bhellum. He controls not only Cyrix Industries, that monstrosity you see in the distance, but the majority of this city, and a good portion of several other cities. And the Muck."

"What interest does a Bhellum have in the Muck," asked Rott, sounding perplexed.

"No idea," responded Tennian, "but before Viktor Krill's appearance, he was already bankrolling another gang in the endless war, even replacing its First with one of his choosing. One that had no previous attachment to the Muck."

"To what end?"

"I told you, I don't know," snapped Tennian at Hadder's repeated question. "Maybe his finances are hurting, and he decided to get into the drug game."

"Doubtful," stated Rott.

"Agreed. So, it must be something greater. Back-end politics at work, weakening Bhellum's adversaries somehow."

"Or maybe it's something much simpler."

Tennian stared hard at Rott, as if seeing the man-god for the first time, as if finally gauging the weight of his guest. He smiled coyly. "Yes, I thought of that, as well. Maybe it's something much simpler." The two seasoned leaders turned their attentions back to the spinning C. "Anyway, it seems that Viktor Krill and his special brand of violence caught the eye of Cyrus fucking Bhellum himself, who replaced his selected First with the shiny new Krill."

"That doesn't explain why he's not in one of the towers," added Hadder.

Tennian Stamp's black and white beard became split by a wide smile. "Why would one of Cyrix Industries' highest-ranking VPs live in the Muck?"

"The Rising," corrected Rott.

"It will always be the Muck to me."

"What the fuck are you talking about?!" Hadder was dismayed, looking upon the colossal Cyrix Industries Headquarters in the distance. "Viktor Krill is a fucking Vice President? Of one of the largest robotics companies in the world?"

Rott answered for Tennian. "It appears so, Marlin."

"So, what does this mean?"

Now it was Tennian's turn to answer for Rott. "It means, Mister Hadder, that your hunt has just become that much more dangerous."

Hadder exhaled deeply. "Fuck. I was hoping it didn't mean that."

———

ALL THREE ON the rooftop now focused their attentions squarely on the Cyrix Industries Headquarters, the intimidating monolith that housed the most dangerous character in history.

Hadder looked to his left and watched Albany Rott as he studied the massive construct, the gears in his head almost audible as countless variables were defined and accounted for. Soon, however, the man-god had learned all he could from mere distant observation. Without taking his red eyes off Cyrix Headquarters, Rott spoke.

"What is in store for us, Tennian?"

Tennian blew his nose into a cloth handkerchief, folded it carefully into a smaller square, and placed it back into one of the many pockets of his black and white camouflage jacket. "Well, the building itself for starters. It's operated by one of the most sophisticated AI security systems, obviously not of Cyrix make. It controls unknown numbers of auto-turrets hidden across offices, conference rooms, and dining areas, guided by the myriad of video cameras that occupy every nook. Not to mention the hundreds of mechs that patrol the hallways, ready to put a hole in the chests of any unrecognized visitors."

"Is that all," asked Rott, his crimson orbs still locked on the faraway target.

"For building security? Not by a long shot. That's just what I *know* is in there. Who knows what kind of secrets are kept by that kind of money and unlimited resources. That's why I think, even in the best of times, you would have a hard time getting in there. Now that Viktor Krill has claimed it as his residence, I'd call it nearly impossible."

"What has changed since Krill moved in?"

"Well, for starters, the lower levels are now swarming with Risers. The Cyrix Industries Headquarters hasn't operated as a true headquarters for decades, with all its cheap manufacturing now done overseas. The regional offices now run everything, and house the vast majority of Cyrix's work-force. What you see before you is the fossil of a once-great command post, occupied by a singular CEO who seems to have recently lost touch with the world."

Hadder cut in. "Wait, you mean Cyrus Bhellum V still lives there? Why?"

Tennian glanced over to Hadder before responding. "You're still young. Your eyes don't look it, and I'm sure you don't feel it, but it's true. It's never easy to vacate your throne, and, as you get older, it only gets harder. The throne becomes a piece of you, oftentimes, the defining piece, and it grows difficult to separate yourself from the chair on which you sit."

"Any other reason," asked Rott, as if from away.

"Possibly. But if there is one, it falls outside my scope of vision."

Rott continued. "All right, so in addition to the corporate security system and Risers filtering in and out of the building, is there anything else to worry about?"

Tennian smiled again, a sure sign that more bad news was coming. "Just the Mech Force."

Hadder beat Rott to the punch. "Mech Force? What the fuck is that? I've never heard of it."

"You're not from Bhellum, so you wouldn't have. For years the Mech

Force was just a myth, a boogeyman to scare criminals. Elite, cutting-edge, military-grade mechs that swoop down from the heavens to make problems disappear. They single-handedly stifled the Great Citizen Revolt almost a decade ago before disappearing into the mist, for years only existing in rumors. Everyone assumed the Mech Force was the premier arm of the city PD, but we were all proven wrong last year."

Hadder leaned in, gripped by the gangster's story. "What happened?"

"Goddam Mech Force fell from the sky one day, showed everyone their big robot dicks, and ensured Viktor Krill's ascension to King of the Muck."

Hadder's mind spun with this new knowledge. "But how does that tie them to Cyrus Bhellum V?"

"Well, for those too stupid to figure it out on their own..." Tennian looked to Rott, and both seasoned leaders shared a silent laugh at Hadder's expense. "The Mech Force, after neatly slicing Krill's predecessor in half with a laser cutter, scooped Viktor Krill up like a goddam taxi fare, and flew him directly to Cyrix Industries."

"Meaning?"

Tennian rolled his dark blue eyes at Hadder's slowness. "Meaning, the fucking Mech Force doesn't belong to the city at all. It belongs to Cyrus Bhellum V, the Mech Force's sole commander. And now that the secret is out, the Mech Force is free from hiding, and is now actively protecting Viktor Krill and Cyrix." Tennian saw Hadder about to speak. "Meaning, what would have been a nearly impossible task has been rendered truly impossible. At least, with the resources currently available." A dark smirk danced on Tennian's mouth and sent shivers down Hadder's spine.

Rott finally tore his gaze from Cyrix Industries and faced Old Tens. "And what resources do we need, pray tell."

Tennian thought for a moment. "My only dreams are nightmares. They fill my ears with the sounds of mortar shells, drone drops, and screams. They fill my nostrils with the scents of burning flesh and gunpowder. They show me images of twisted bodies and loose limbs. But last night, for the first time in decades, I had an actual dream, one that didn't force me upright in the middle of the night. Would you like to hear of this dream?"

Hadder and Rott simultaneously answered in the affirmative.

Tennian's mech legs came to life once more, turning their owner toward the South. "In the dream, I was a boy again. I was sitting on the bluff that overlooks the Muck, but instead of looking down upon the Five Thieves, I was staring out into the ocean. There, in the distance, I watched as a black bird dove into the water, only to return empty-handed, missing many of its feathers. Several minutes later, the black bird returned with two others, one white and one red, and together they dove beneath the water's surface. Several minutes passed before the triumvirate broke from the water once more, their claws digging deeply into the flesh of a massive fish, its golden scales catching the sun's rays, and reflecting them like a disco ball. They had almost raised the leviathan completely into the air when it thrashed violently, ripping free of the three sets of talons, and sending the birds careening into the swirling waters.

"I held my breath, thinking the small birds had drowned as the giant fish dove again into the deep. But then, just as the water's surface grew calm, the three birds, looking worse for wear, broke from the ocean and flew away in tight formation.

"The youthful version of myself sat on that bluff, staring out into the endless ocean, as an overwhelming sadness took over, the failure of the birds feeling like a personal disaster, one from which it would be hard to fully recover. Tears rolled down my unwrinkled black face as I stared into the distance, mourning that which I didn't understand. I rose to my feet, ready to return to my home in the Muck, when something in the air demanded my attention.

"My triumvirate had come once more, and they had another in tow! Joining Black, Red, and White was a bird that looked as if it had been microwaved. With green, bubbly skin, and missing more than a few grey feathers, the group's newest member had difficulty remaining in formation, its flight path jagged and uneven.

"Black, Red, White, and Green dove in unison. After what felt like an eternity in dream time, the four friends broke the water's surface, their claws full of enormous goldfish flesh. The quartet flapped their meager wings with all their might, lifting their quarry from the salty water. The goldfish began thrashing once more, tearing tiny bird tendons, and ripping feathers from thin bird skin. The four birds faltered, but held tight, lifting their prize higher and higher before turning toward to the far side of the coast, where they would undoubtedly drop the fish to the ground and feast.

"The boy-me sat there, watching the scene unfold, as a smile fell upon my mouth, and understanding struck me."

Rott's eyes had grown fiery as Tennian recounted his dream. "And what did you understand?"

Tennian's blue eyes flashed. "That to kill a demon, it would take a team unlike any ever assembled."

Rott nodded solemnly, but Hadder remained confused. "Ok, so, obviously, the black, red, and white birds represent the three of us. I don't get what the green bird personifies. Some kind of poison, or virus, that we have to unleash?"

Tennian chuckled once more. "In a way."

Hadder was beginning to lose his patience. "In what way?"

"Tell me what you know about the Blisters?"

"The who?"

"The Blisters."

"Who the fuck are they?"

"If you end up winning this little war of yours, Mister Hadder, they will be the reason."

"And they will assist us?"

"They will either help you, or eat you."

"Eat us?!"

"That's right."

"And how do we know which approach they will take?"

"You won't, until you make your pitch to them."

"And where are these Blisters?"

"They reside in the Hammers, the old Cyrix manufacturing plant."

Hadder shot Rott a panicked looked, who only returned a shrug. "At least you will not have to revisit the Rising, dear boy. Maybe you can keep that promise to yourself, after all. Tennian, is there anything we need to know about these Blisters?"

Tennian wiped his nose once more with his handkerchief. "Let's lunch together inside. Yes, there is much you need to know about the Blisters. And, yes, not fully understanding what I am about to tell you will most certainly lead to your imminent demise. Both of you."

Hadder shuddered at the statement of warning. "Sounds like a blast."

Tennian laughed loudly. "Come! Everything sounds worse on an empty stomach. A belly full of meat pie will make everything, even the goddam Blisters, a bit more digestible."

19

The sun was racing for the horizon by the time Hadder and Rott finally reached the entrance to the dilapidated Cyrix manufacturing facility known colloquially as the Hammers. The large metal gate that had once served to keep out corporate espionage and run-of-the-mill thieves had been violently removed from its heavy hinges, and now lay half-buried in the thick grass that bordered the entry road. A tall chain-link fence, topped with razor wire and long-deceased auto-turrets, surrounded the Hammers, with giant gaps appearing sporadically where some Blisters lacked the patience to reach official access points.

"I guess the Blisters aren't worried about security," commented Hadder as he and Rott passed the discarded gate.

"You see how that gate was ripped off, Marlin? And those vicious holes in the fence? I would say these Blisters have all the security they need. I think it is us who should be concerned."

"I was being sarcastic, Al."

"Nevertheless, look around you. What do you see, dear boy?"

The long shadow of Cyrix Headquarters fell over the Hammers, draping the entire facility, including several massive buildings, in muted darkness. Hadder looked deep into the gloom, attempting to observe what Albany Rott wanted him to see. "I just see a dead past, Al. The remnants of something once great. What do you see?"

Rott's ember eyes flared to life as he looked around, taking note of things invisible to all others. "I see a cauldron."

"A what?"

"A cauldron. And, in this oversized pot, something truly magnificent is being created."

"I don't follow."

"I am afraid you will shortly, dear boy."

As the companions crossed the threshold into the Hammers, things immediately felt different, sending a shudder through Marlin Hadder. Feeling short of breath, Hadder breathed in deeply, only to exhale through a fit of coughing. "Fuck me, what is that?"

"That, dear Marlin, is poison. The air is thick with it here. Remember what Tennian told us over lunch? When these plants were abandoned, they were left to decay, to leak, and to ferment. And I have a feeling that Cyrix was not the best steward of the planet, using dangerously cheap chemicals, metals, and processes."

Hadder reflexively put his hand to his nose. "But, what man could tolerate this foul air?"

Rott looked to Hadder, small flames now dancing in his eyes. "Who said they were still men? Come, let us investigate deeper. Contact must be made."

The air grew increasingly stagnant and toxic as the visitors made their way between stoic buildings that looked down upon the pair with disapproval. The scampering of feet, and disruption of metal, could be heard between the buildings, where even the weak shadow light refused to go. Small piles of bones, random mixes of dog, cat, rodent, and human, littered the even, paved ground, reminding Hadder of the notorious Blister appetite. Dirty, discolored water ran from each building, directed by weathered gutters, into the surrounding soft ground, polluting the soil for miles.

On the duo marched, and although no Blisters could be seen, their sounds could increasingly be heard from all angles. Guttural laughter sped through alleyways to assault the intruders, while warnings in an unnatural language were issued from rooftops. Hadder's eyes began to water, so he carefully wiped them with a silk handkerchief given to him by Old Tens. The darkness of shadow fell away to reveal the true twilight of night as the sun fell under the horizon.

"I don't think there's as many Blisters as Tennian believes, Al."

"Why do say that, Marlin?"

Hadder removed his hand from his nose, waved it around. "Look around, Al. We can hear a few scuttling around, but the numbers that Old Tens was talking about; I just don't see it. The Hammers should be thick with them; so, where are they?"

"Perhaps they have already collected. Perhaps they wait for us now."

"We do, foolish peddies."

The voice, thin, gravelly, and dangerously close, came out of nowhere, causing both Hadder and the usually unflappable Rott to jump. They looked to the left, from where the voice came, and had to squint to make out the figure against the concrete wall of a factory. Standing at only around five feet, the creature's skin was the same color as the building, but shifted slightly as it moved away from the wall. It took five ambling steps towards the companions before stopping, its smooth, oily skin continuing to adjust until it went from dull grey to vibrant yellow, reminiscent of Station's deadly mimics.

Hadder's face unintentionally twisted in disgust as the lone Blister came into focus, its too-long nose, too-pointy ears, and too-stretched face more suited to a comic book villain than a real-life character. Wearing only rags, and a thin strip of slimy hair, it smiled widely, showing off rows of small, sharp teeth, as if it had traded its mouth for that of a baby shark.

Unsurprisingly, Rott recovered from his shock much more quickly than Hadder. "Greetings, my friend. And how did you know we were here?"

A crackling laugh was emitted from the shark mouth. "Foolish, peddies. We see all that occurs in our Hammers. You peddies think us blind, but it is only us who truly see."

Hadder, annoyed by the little twisted man, cut in. "Where's your bubbly skin, *friend*? I thought you all had bubbly skin."

The creature spun towards Hadder, who, for the first time, made note of the small man's all-black shark eyes. "We Blisters embrace variety, unlike you peddies, who only have room in your miserable, selfish lives for a singular form. Many of my brothers and sisters have been stricken with, as you put it, bubbly skin. Others of us bear alternative marks of our banishment and isolation in this toxic prison."

The little man's anger, and the fierce honesty behind it, tempered Hadder's own irritation. "My apologies, I did not know. We are not from Bhellum."

"Of course, you're not," replied the yellow creature.

"It's that obvious?"

"You both stink of another land."

Hadder pressed on. "And what land is that?"

A stubby yellow finger waved Hadder's way. "Not my question, peddie. That is for Gash to figure out." Hadder and Rott's faces swung to meet each other. Tennian had informed them of the Blister leader, a secretive individual known by his full name of Acid Boy Gash.

"Can you take us to him," asked Rott, his excitement becoming apparent in his smoldering eyes.

"What do you think I'm standing out here for, foolish peddies? Follow me."

"Thank you," said Hadder. "I'm sorry, I didn't catch your name."

Shark eyes stared at Hadder for a moment, perhaps trying to discern any condescension or ridicule behind the visitor's words. None were detected. "You can call me Niblit. Now come, we Blisters are a patient bunch, but only to a point."

The yellow creature called Niblit moved ahead of Hadder and Rott, walking slowly because of the clubbed foot that tipped its right leg. The pair followed, chased by wicked laughter and terrifying growls that were carried on chilly breezes careening through factory buildings.

Hadder put on a brave face to match Rott's, but, inside, his stomach churned, threatening to expel the large lunch provided by the Broken Tens. Shadows danced on the edge of his periphery, similar to his trek through the

Rising alongside the Caesars Cal and Otho, whom he desperately missed at this moment.

Within a few minutes, it became clear that the trio was heading towards the large southernmost factory building. Hadder almost commented when Niblit bypassed the small entrance doors to the building, but remained quiet when Rott placed a pale hand on his shoulder, silencing him. Instead, they walked around the factory, making for the rear of the building. As they rounded the corner, Hadder instantly understood the reasoning behind this choice.

Massive garage doors laid open before the trio as they reached the factory loading dock. A concert of sounds poured forth from the building's open mouth, along with the smell of a thousand unwashed bodies, hitting the visitors' ears and olfactory nerves in equal measure like a linebacker.

Unwilling to scale the loading dock's elevation, Niblit moved towards the side, where a gentle ramp would lead the men up and into the cavernous factory. The companions followed slowly behind their guide, progress hampered by Niblit's club foot.

All three reached the top of the loading dock in short order. By now, even Rott's red eyes watered from the thousand smells and toxins rushing forth from the open bay doors. Niblit spun to face his two guests.

"Watch your fucking mouth in here," he growled. "Gash doesn't tolerate idiot peddies."

Hadder leaned toward Rott. "No one seems to tolerate anything in this goddamn world."

"Agreed. But I think we really need to heed those words in this case."

Foreign sounds and angry voices continued to assault the companions. "What do think's in there, Al?"

"You tell me, Marlin. You visited *Biomass* and the Rising much more recently than I did."

"Fuck, you think it's gonna be that bad?"

Rott inhaled deeply. "Worse. Much worse. But this is a necessary step in ending Viktor Krill's reign of terror. So, let us meet our potential allies. And try not to get eaten in the process."

Hadder sucked in, trying to calm his nerves, and nodded. Together, he and Rott marched forward to follow Niblit, who had already entered the loud factory building.

The companions crossed under the giant metal doors and entered a new world. One seemingly ripped straight from the twisted minds of Jackie Crone, Lester Midnight, and The Krown.

A world invisible to anyone not bearing the label of Blister.

———————

AN EXPLOSION of jeers accosted Hadder and Rott as they entered the defunct factory. That, combined with the overwhelming smell of ammonia, dirty bodies, and unknown chemicals, was enough to bring tears to Hadder's eyes and make Albany Rott twist his face in revulsion.

To the companions' left and right, sitting on inactive conveyor belts, hanging from metal hooks, and looking down from chain-linked catwalks, Blisters could be seen screaming at the unwelcome visitors. Hadder and Rott continued to follow closely behind Niblit, moving easily through the center space that had been kept empty of the riled up citizens of the Hammers. As they passed through the deafening factory that was strewn with unused robotics components, Hadder attempted to swallow his fear and mentally record everything he observed, useful should he not end up inside a Blister's stomach.

Rott was correct, of course. The scene around Hadder was as if the Risers decided to throw a party at *Biomass*, with Jackie Crone leading the dark festivities. Each Blister was distinct in their mutation, something Hadder's old friend Lester Midnight would have found painfully beautiful.

A seven-foot green monster with red lesions covering its green, oily body stared daggers at the two men, its oversized mouth showing dagger-like teeth that looked able to bite through a person's skull. Across from the green behemoth, a gangly woman with bright orange eyes and rough grey skin stood unmoving, her stomach exceedingly swollen and hanging heavy on her small frame.

Everywhere Hadder looked, he identified a new variety of skin, another mutation. Too many arms here, not enough there. Some were oversized, others were diminutive. One poor bastard had several organs on the outside of his body, protected by dirty plastic bags. Despite the horror that he was witnessing, however, Hadder forced himself to look beyond the graphic displays, to find something still human in the beasts that surrounded him.

And find something profound, he did.

As Hadder walked, he looked deeply into the eyes of those throwing vulgar curses his and Rott's way. Moving from white eye to grey to orange to yellow, Hadder found rage, something he knew all too well. But he also discovered pain, a pain deeper than perhaps even he had ever known. And from somewhere even deeper, behind the anger, pain, and sadness, was something else entirely.

Was it hope that Hadder saw within those strangely shaped irises?

Hadder didn't have time to ponder this question, as Niblit had halted his march, moving to the side of a creature who sat on a throne of old robot parts. Niblit waited patiently to the side as the Blister leader studied Hadder and Rott, and vice versa.

The head of the Blisters was of typical human size, but that was where all normalcy ended. He had light blue skin, and dark blue hair that weirdly complemented indigo eyes that vacillated back and forth in place, making it hard to maintain eye contact with the creature. Down the center of its bluish face was the worst scar Hadder had ever seen, neatly cleaving the man's face in two. The scar was wide and deep, as if the wound had never been properly tended. Skull bone, nasal passages, and teeth could be seen where the cut had never fully closed up, giving the Blister leader a permanent terrifying expression.

The noise of the factory continued to rage until the Blister leader finally raised a gloved hand into the air, bringing immediate silence. Rott looked over briefly to Hadder, as if to say, *this man has complete control over these people*. Hadder simply nodded his assent.

With only silence now filling the factory, Niblit dramatically cleared his throat and spoke. "Unwelcome guests! Welcome to the Hammers! May I present Gash, also known as Acid Boy Gash, leader of the Blisters and Keeper of the Prophecy!"

The factory fell into an uproar before Gash quieted it once more with a gloved hand. He looked from Hadder to Rott with vibrating eyes.

"N-n-n-name yourselves, v-v-visitors," said the soft, stuttering voice.

"My name is Albany Rott. And to my side is Marlin Hadder."

"And w-w-what is it that you w-want from us B-B-Blisters?"

Rott's eyes, now lazy fires, met Gash's shaky indigo orbs. "I have a feeling you know already, Mister Gash."

"It's j-j-just G-Gash. We d-don't use c-common honorifics h-here."

"And why is that," asked Hadder.

Gash's disconcerting eyes swung Hadder's way. "B-b-because those are for humans. W-w-we no longer c-consider ourselves m-m-members of that heartless g-group."

"The people of Bhellum have treated you lot poorly, have they not," said Rott.

Gash's face broke into a smile at that, making his old wound appear even more garish.

"W-what m-makes you s-say that?" Gash motioned around with his gloved hands. "L-look at the w-wonderful ac-c-commodations that have been p-provided to us."

"It looks to me like you've been banished here. I hope you know that my colleague and I are not from Bhellum, had no hand in your people's plight."

Gash laughed at this, a wheezing, sickly sound. "Of c-c-course I know you aren't from B-b-bhellum. If you w-were, your m-meat would already be h-hanging up, d-drying in p-preparation for the l-long c-cold season."

"Good. Then you know that we are here to help."

"L-l-liars!" Gash's unexpected outburst sent Hadder and Rott back on their heels. The Blister leader continued. "Y-y-you are here b-because you n-need the B-blisters. Am I w-w-wrong?"

Rott put his pale hands up in surrender. "You are correct, Gash. But that does not necessarily make me wrong, now, does it? It is true, Marlin and I need your assistance. But, and correct me if I am in error, don't the Blisters also need some help?"

A low murmur broke out among the collected Blister audience. Gash snickered. "And w-what would w-we need h-help with, p-p-peddie?"

"The Risers."

Laughter once more trickled from the Blisters. "F-f-foolish outsiders. The R-risers p-pay *us*. H-handsomely, and on t-time. W-why should we n-need help w-with them?"

Hadder had no response to this, but, luckily, Rott was prepared. "They pay you now, Gash. But for how long? The Blisters have survived this long because you, alone, have remained unified. You benefitted greatly from the Muck's many wars. While the gangs waged violent battle with each other, none could afford to be on the feared Blisters' bad side. But that is not the case anymore. Is it, Gash?" The Blister leader hissed angrily, but did not argue Rott's point. "Viktor Krill has consolidated all the gangs under the banner of the Risers. With no enemies left, he will be looking to maximize profits. The easiest way to do that would be to eliminate costs, with the Blisters being the most obvious expense to cut."

"The B-b-broken T-tens still stand," shot back Gash.

"That is true," conceded Rott, "but we come directly from meeting with Tennian Stamp. He admits that it is only a matter of time before the Risers descend upon them and take the final tower."

"Again, th-that is the b-business of the M-m-muck."

"The Muck *is* your business," Rott countered. "Without your interests in the Jungle, where would the Blisters be?"

"W-we have f-fingers in m-many pies, f-foolish outsider!"

Rott raised a hand to concede the point. "I do not doubt that, Gash. But I would wager that none are as profitable as extorting the dope tanks."

"And your p-p-point?"

Acid Boy Gash was playing obtuse, and Albany Rott was growing impatient. Rott decided to up the ante. His crimson eyes, dull fires flickering within, looked through Gash's shaky violet orbs. "I know what you need, Gash."

The surrounding monsters grew even more silent while Gash froze on his throne of robotics. His purple eyes also stopped moving, and now latched tightly to Albany Rott. "W-w-what did you s-say?"

A tight, almost invisible smile crept onto Rott's face. "Old Tens told us how much he estimated the Blisters made from their extracurricular activities. Quite the sum. But what in the world do you all spend it on?" He looked around dramatically. "Certainly not rent." His red eyes continued across the sea of Blisters, most of whom wore literal rags over their bubbly or discolored skin. "Nor clothing." Gash hissed, but Rott continued. "So, why the need? Why the need to acquire such wealth? You don't seem to have extravagant desires and expensive tastes, Gash. None of you do. So, why the drive to accumulate?" Rott paused for effect, narrowed his fiery eyes. "Unless there is something very, very valuable that you wish to purchase."

"You know n-n-nothing, f-fool!"

"I know Tennian Stamp. And he knows you. You two have been secret friends for many years now, keeping your relationship as hidden as you keep your true motives." Gash's blue face twisted in concern. "Do not fret. Old Tens did not betray your confidence. But he did tell me something of the utmost importance and relevance."

"And w-w-what is that?"

"That you are a strong leader, a magnanimous king. Someone who has always kept the long view of life, even when you and yours were struggling to survive the day-to-day."

"S-s-so?"

Rott smiled widely, showing his too-white teeth. "So, what would the great king of a ragtag group that has been exiled to a toxic existence need with the wealth of a nation?"

Gash looked away from Rott, his violet eyes vibrating once more, as if in deep contemplation.

Hadder stepped in to answer Rott's question. "If I were such a leader, I'd be looking to get my people somewhere safe. Somewhere where mankind's greedy hands and judgmental eyes couldn't reach."

Rott delivered his next line just as the pair had rehearsed. "You mean like a city?"

"Not sovereign enough."

"A country," asked Rott.

"Too close in proximity to others."

"An island?"

A murmur spreading through the crowd of Blisters, coupled with Gash's purple eyes going wide, told Hadder and Rott that their educated guess was correct.

The Blisters meant to buy a fucking island.

Hadder continued to play his role. "Yes, you know what, Al? An island would be perfect. A safe haven for this unique community, away from the prying eyes of people and governments who would like nothing more than to see it destroyed."

Rott feigned surprise. "Well, that *would* be perfect, Marlin. What do you think, Gash? It wouldn't be an island in your crosshairs, would it?"

Acid Boy Gash released a wheezing, sickly laugh, followed by a slow, sarcastic clap that was muffled by his dirty gloves. "Well d-done, peddies. We have g-g-grown tired of being Bhellum's discarded c-c-citizens. M-my Blisters will have their ultimate f-f-freedom, or I w-will die t-trying."

Rott's tone grew serious. "I can get you your island."

A hush fell over the poison-soaked factory. Gash's tone matched that of Rott's. "T-tell me how."

"I have a small fortune in credits that you are welcome to, but not nearly enough to buy your island."

"W-what then?"

"Viktor Krill."

"He is a g-g-gangster. He is w-w-without such f-funds."

"Viktor Krill is now a VP of Cyrix Industries, one of the globe's leading robotics companies."

"Do not tell me about Cyrix!"

The anger behind Gash's words, amplified by the fact that he did not stutter, sent Hadder back a step. Rott pivoted to regain control of the conversation. "I know what they did to your people."

"You know nothing!"

Rott held his hands up once more. "Perhaps not. But I know, between my credits, and what we can siphon off Cyrix after defeating Viktor Krill, you'll have enough to relocate your people to somewhere truly safe. An island of your very own."

Gash's anger appeared to wane as his stutter returned. "W-w-what makes you think you c-can t-take Cyrix's money?"

Rott shrugged. "Just a hunch. But even if I cannot, between my credits, your reserves, and the money you will make from taking over the Slink trade..."

"I w-want n-nothing to do with that v-vile Slink?"

Hadder's eyebrows furrowed. "Why's that?"

Now it was Gash's turn to show his discolored, misshapen teeth in a wide grin. "Y-you boys r-r-really don't know w-what's g-going on, d-do you?"

"Inform us, please," responded Rott.

"Krill's v-vulgar d-d-drug is killing all whom it t-t-touches. We h-have no l-love for h-humans, but that d-doesn't mean we want them d-d-destroyed." Gash pointed a gloved finger at this own chest. "Th-th-this is what s-separates us from the peddies. When w-we k-k-kill, there're reasons b-behind it."

Rott sighed heavily. "Very well. Then you will not inherit the Slink business; you will destroy it. This should dramatically increase the sales of other drugs, all of which you will own."

"H-How d-do you f-figure?"

"As I said, I spoke to Old Tens. He's willing to rule the Rising side-by-side with Acid Boy Gash. No more hiding, or extortion. You'll split the profits on all the other drugs fifty-fifty."

"If w-we help you k-k-kill Viktor Krill?"

"That's right."

Gash leaned back in his throne, deep in thought. The surrounding Blisters remained politely quiet as their king rendered his difficult decision. After nearly a minute of tense silence, Gash sat up once more. "V-v-very well, outsiders. You w-w-wish to enter into a p-pact with the Blisters? The t-test of h-heart must be c-c-completed."

At this, the gathered Blisters exploded into applause, as if the opening credits of a long-awaited movie had just appeared. When their ovation had receded, Rott spoke up.

"I accept any test you wish to give me."

Gash laughed again, ushering in shrieks of amusement from his minions. "This is a p-p-pact between m-m-man and Blister. Y-you are n-neither, Albany Rott."

Rott and Hadder looked to each other, surprised by the Blister leader's insightfulness. Soon after, however, Rott's surprise turned to concern as he considered his companion's predicament.

Hadder read the worry on his friend's face and sighed heavily, terrified of what the very near future would bring. "Fuck me," he muttered, but no one could hear his soft words over the Blisters' harsh laughter.

———

THE EXCITED CROWD of Blisters moved further back into the massive defunct factory, pulling both Marlin Hadder and Albany Rott along for the journey. Acid Boy Gash followed shortly behind, taking quick, tiny steps that seemed more at home on child than man. After several hundred feet, the group reached a large clear spot on the loaded factory floor.

Looking down, Hadder could tell that giant machinery once stood where the mob now collected. Impressions in the concrete marked where the feet of heavy equipment once sat. The dark stains of oil told the tale of decades of manufacturing that once took place on this exact spot. Unfortunately, that was not all that was discovered on the factory floor.

Mixed in with the chipped concrete and oil stains were other blemishes. Dark red chips of dried blood could be seen pulling up from larger crimson stains. Evidence of other biological matter criss-crossed the cold factory floor here, telling Hadder that this was the place where Blisters settled their internal disputes.

Blisters aggressively moved to get better views of the upcoming battle-field. Some climbed atop the shoulders of larger Blisters, while others settled into the upper levels, or scaled the numerous catwalks that spanned the high ceiling like a spiderweb.

Apparently, no one wanted to miss Marlin Hadder getting his ass kicked.

In short order, the Blisters had found desirable seats for the show that was to begin, their tight, poisoned bodies forming a large circle that would serve as the arena. Hadder looked around, staring into the snarling faces of the Blister audience, seeing bloodlust everywhere he looked. In their hyste-ria, words came out guttural, as if they were speaking a fantastical language of their own creation.

I can't believe it, thought Hadder as he removed Higgins's twin hand-guns from his waistband, took off his suit jacket, and rolled up the sleeves of his white dress shirt. *I'm back in the fucking Meat Show.*

Rott, sensing his friend's anxiety, tried to offer words of encouragement. "Well, dear boy, at least you have experience in this."

"That was different. Skeelis was about revenge. I don't know what this is about."

"I suppose they want to see if you, and me, by proxy, are worth the part-nership."

Just as Hadder had finished rolling up his second sleeve, Gash lightly stepped into the middle of the circle and spoke. "M-m-my Blisters!" The crowed quieted again on their king's command. "T-t-today is a very s-special d-day. Outsiders h-have appeared, n-n-needing the h-help of the Blisters. They s-s-say that they w-will lead us to Sanctum. Should w-we find out if they are the Shepards of w-w-which prophecy s-speaks?" Another wave of cheers broke over the factory floor before receding back into silence. "V-v-very well. Then w-we shall t-t-test the m-man's heart. Sowler!"

A break appeared in the circle of Blisters, allowing room for a mammoth creature in a metal helmet to pass through and enter the open space that would soon be a battleground. Although he stood about the same height as

Hadder, just over six feet, that's where the similarities ceased. The Blister's soft-looking pink skin covered its barrel body, complete with a thick, powerful chest and short tree trunk legs. Its nose was horribly disfigured, looking more like a snout than anything that would be found on a human. Long upper canine teeth had grown too long and now hung over the creature's weak lower jaw. Wearing a tattered tank top that was more hole than material, Sowler's left arm was impressively large, with blue veins being pushed to the surface by thick layers of heavy muscle. It was an arm that could do significant damage to another.

And that wasn't even the most extraordinary appendage on the creature.

Sowler's right arm was three times as thick and almost twice as long as his meaty left. The skin that covered it appeared dry and hard, and was significantly scarred. Most shockingly, the arm was tipped with an oversized hand that looked to have been calcified into a permanent fist. Sowler hefted his organic sledgehammer into the air, and bellowed out a great cry, sending the other Blisters into a frenzy.

Rott leaned into Hadder to be heard over the cacophony. "You are going to need to use your Rage, Marlin." His voice was thick with concern.

That most uncomfortable feeling called panic began to form in the center of Hadder's chest. He turned towards Rott. "What Rage? I don't know even know this guy."

"It is always inside you, Marlin. You need to find it. *Now*."

Hadder reached deep within himself, but came up empty. "I got nothing, Al."

"Then perhaps our adventure ends here, dear boy."

"Thanks for the words of encouragement."

The companions' dialogue was broken by Acid Boy Gash, who silenced the factory for the last time. "T-t-today we find out if these v-v-visitors are the t-true Shepards, or j-just food for the younglings. M-marlin Hadder. S-sowler. The f-fight is to the d-d-death. N-no hard f-feelings. You m-may begin...now!"

The pig man known as Sowler screamed once again into the air, and tossed his metal helmet at Hadder with his good left hand, revealing a tight skull cap underneath, half of which was stained red with blood. The audience ate up his theatrics and roared their appreciation.

Hadder moved tentatively into the wild circle of Blisters, but not before he heard Rott from behind. "What is under that cap, Marlin? The cap!"

Hadder didn't have much time to digest Rott's words, however, as Sowler came on in a fury. He easily crouched under the first blow of the Blister's hammer-hand, but was nearly pushed off-balance by the wind created by its wake. Just as Hadder recovered, a backhand came at him too low to duck, forcing him to jump straight up, pulling his knees as high as possible.

Hadder almost cleared the oversized fist, but the toes of his high tops were caught by the passing scythe, sending the man tumbling towards the hard concrete. Hadder fell heavily onto his side, driving most of the air from his lungs, but had no time to fully assess his situation as Sowler's gigantic fist was cocked back once more, this time perched high above the Blister's head.

Hadder's eyes went wide, and he rolled desperately to his right, Sowler's hardened hand crashing down where he had just been, leaving cracks to spider across the concrete floor. With no time to lose, Hadder scrambled to his feet and shot forward, determined to get inside of Sowler's primary weapon. As he did, Hadder stepped quickly into an elbow strike, connecting cleanly with the Blister's face, and chipping its long left canine tooth.

Unfortunately, the blow did little more than amuse the pig-man, who smartly stepped back to create space before smiling wickedly at his intended prey. Hadder, undeterred and emboldened by his small success, danced a bit before springing forward once more, well inside the deadly hand-hammer. A self-satisfied smile found its way onto Hadder's lips as Sowler's weak jaw came into focus again, only to disappear a moment later when the Blister's *other* fist, imposing in its own right, slammed into his temple.

The left hook from Sowler sent both Hadder's mind and body spinning. He came to almost immediately, at the edge of the circle of spectators, being held upright by a pair of pale hands. He heard words in his ear, but they sounded far away, as if from a dream.

"The fight is not going well, Marlin. Marlin? Can you hear me?"

Despite an obvious concussion, Hadder *could* hear Rott speaking, but something else had captured his attention. An old acquaintance had returned, one who had played the role of both friend and foe over the course of Hadder's several lives. Hadder reached up and touched the side of his head, saw red fingers upon their return. A shot of adrenaline coursed through his veins.

The Rage took over.

"Marlin, dear boy? Can you hear me?" Rott was about to pose another question, when his friend straightened instantly in his arms. Hadder spun to face Rott, who smiled like a child on Christmas, for it was not his companion who stood before him, but the Rage, that greatest of gifts hiding as a curse. "Marlin, my boy?"

"Yes, Al?"

"You are losing this fight, you know?"

"That's going to change. Right. Fucking. Now."

Rott chuckled gleefully as Hadder waded back into battle. Although he had the fiery red eyes, Rott thought that, at this moment, in this lair of mutants, there was nothing more terrifying than Marlin Hadder's mask of death. And, so, the fight commenced.

Sowler, unaware of the devilish gleam now residing within Hadder's eyes, reengaged quickly, ready to end this battle against a mere "peddie." Once more, Sowler swung his mutated arm like a scythe, desperate to introduce his calcified fist to Hadder's stubbly jaw.

Hadder leapt out of the way of one swing before diving headlong over the next low stroke, his reactions and reflexes maximized by the Rage. He heard a scream as he completed his roll on the hard, stained floor, and turned back just in time to see a small, reddish man with no lips soaring through the air, the unfortunate recipient of Sowler's missed strike. The small Blister landed at the rear of the mob, and Sowler moved to the edge of the circle, barking out apologies to be heard over the din of the fight.

Hadder, seeing Sowler temporarily preoccupied, rushed towards his fellow combatant. Determined to level the playing field, Hadder attacked from the side as Sowler's attention remained diverted, cracking the side of the Blister's knee with the hardest leg kick the man had ever thrown. Unfortunately, it was Hadder who groaned from the blow, and he was immediately reminded of kicking rubber trees in Thailand, or the vile Skeelis in the Meat Show.

Sowler, unfazed by Hadder's attempt to hobble him, spun like a top to his left, executing half a spinning back fist that connected once more with Hadder's jaw. The man stumbled backwards, stars exploding across his vision, and would have collapsed to the dirty floor if not for Blister spectators catching him at the circle's edge. Hadder shook his head violently to clear the cobwebs.

As his vision returned to normal, the picture before Hadder clarified. The mutant Sowler stood across from him, laughing heartily, the Blister's confidence at an all-time high. Hadder took in the scene as time slowed down. Sowler's stupid overgrown canines, deformed arm, and grossly honest laugh painfully picked at something deep within the man who had lived multiple lives. The Blister's amusement at his pain dredged up old memories of violence and blood.

The Rage came on doubly strong.

The situation before Hadder grew clear. A plan came together in fractions of a second. A grim smirk appeared on Hadder's face.

Hadder spat a wad of blood to the floor before moving forward carefully, intent on staying out of range of his foe's bioweapon. The red-stained smile pasted onto Hadder's face was enough to rid the Blister of his own wicked grin. Unnerved, Sowler bellowed into the air as he strode toward the peddie, suddenly anxious to be done with this particular fight. After several tense seconds of feints, Sowler made his move, launching his hammer-fist at the center of Hadder's comparably small chest.

Powered by the Rage, Hadder leaned back at an impossible angle, the giant hardened fist missing his face by inches. Hadder could have struck now, but exercised patience, waiting for the inevitable backhand that was to come. His assumption was proven correct as, moments later, Sowler put his all into a backhand meant to remove head from shoulders.

To those watching, Sowler moved with a speed that should have been impossible for one so large. To Hadder, however, time began to slow, another benefit of the Rage powering through him. Anticipating the back-hand, Hadder was already chest-down on the factory floor as the Blister's weaponized arm passed harmlessly overhead.

Hadder leapt up like a panther as Sowler completed his failed maneuver, quickly moving inside the hammer-fist's range. Sowler's grin returned at Hadder's move. *So predicable,* thought the Blister as he moved to once again crack Hadder's unprotected head with his meaty left fist. As Sowler's scabby knuckles soared for Hadder's exposed face, the crowd held their collective breath, ready to erupt at their champion's victory.

Unfortunately for the gathered Blisters, Marlin Hadder had other plans.

Just as Sowler's left hand was about to shatter his jaw, Hadder dropped his head, causing the incoming fist to meet with this forehead. A sickening cracking sound reverberated across the factory as Sowler's hand shattered upon Marlin Hadder's lone elevation, diamond plating installed just below the skin's surface.

Sowler screamed in agony as he leaned forward, protectively pulling his crushed hand into his massive chest. The Rage, sensing the promise of blood in the air, drove Hadder into immediate action. The former Setter leapt into the air, coiling up mid-flight to drive a flying elbow down onto the blood-soaked cap that covered the Blister's pink head.

The Rage within giggled gleefully as Hadder's pointy right elbow passed cleanly through the crimson-dyed material to slam into spongey matter just beneath the cloth. By the time Hadder's feet returned to the factory floor, the Blister known as Sowler was already beginning to short circuit, his large body shaking uncontrollably before collapsing to the cold concrete, where he continued to convulse like Acid Boy Gash's eyes.

Hadder moved to tower over the large Blister, his face still an unfor-giving mask of death. He unceremoniously pushed back the bloody cap from Sowler's head with a black and white high-topped foot, silently congratu-lating himself for a hunch proven correct. Much of the left side of Sowler's skull was missing, because of either violence or mutation, leaving a vulnera-bility that Hadder was all-too happy to take advantage of during their brawl.

Sowler's eye's glazed over as the Blister laid frozen on his back, shaking violently, a large bruise spreading across its exposed brain. The fight was over in everyone's eyes.

Except for the Rage, who demanded that blood be spilt and a life be lost. Hadder grinned wider as he knelt down beside the paralyzed monster, determined to see the battle through to completion, his body humming with the Rage's power and anger. Drawing back his right hand, Hadder readied himself for the killing blow, desperate to witness the spark of life exit Sowler's eyes. Voices could be heard in the background, including Albany Rott's, calling for Hadder stop the fight.

While Hadder was listening, however, the Rage continued to ignore, never caring much for demands. Hadder's right fist fell like Lilly Sistine's dagger.

Just as he should have felt the soft, wet press of brain matter against his fingers, Hadder was hit from the side by an amorphous shadow, sending him careening toward the edge of the Blister circle. The Rage still coursing through him, Hadder tried to get up to finish the job, but found himself trapped within a smelly, grotesque substance that had him locked firmly to the ground.

Waging a silent battle against his viscous assailant, Hadder looked over to see his Blister escort Niblit standing within the fighting circle, wiping brown wetness from his too-pointy chin. The Rage fought more with its sticky prison, to no avail.

Marlin Hadder had been caught.

As the severity of his situation sank in, the Rage dissipated, leaving Hadder with fears of another impending death, one that may be more permanent. Unable to move his head in the phlegm cocoon, Hadder's eyes followed Gash as the Blister leader, taking his usual baby steps, came upon him.

Gash's indigo eyes vibrated on either side of his grotesque scar, making it hard for Hadder to determine the intentions behind those purple orbs. He looked down on Hadder, a curious smirk on his damaged blue face. "C-c-congratulations, M-marlin Hadder. You have p-p-passed the t-test of the h-h-heart. B-but that d-doesn't mean I w-w-would ever l-let you k-k-kill one my own. R-remember, w-we are n-not one of y-y-you. W-we do not throw away each other's l-l-lives so easily." Gash called out behind him. "F-f-free him!"

Two Blisters came out of the crowd, each holding a bucket of thin chemicals. They both fell to their knees and began pouring the solvent over the mucus that encased Hadder. A hissing sound was heard as the solvent turned Niblit's phlegm into an odorous vapor that threatened to overwhelm the trapped human.

Just as Hadder thought he couldn't take anymore, that his lungs would blacken and die before he was released, his arms and legs once again felt free to move. He leapt to his feet to escape the smell, and looked down to see himself still coated in a loose slime.

"D-d-dont w-worry, H-hadder, w-w-we'll get you c-cleaned up b-b-before the celebration."

Hadder's face was still twisted in disgust. "What celebration? Do we have a deal, or not?"

Acid Boy Gash smiled so widely, Hadder was concerned that the Blister leader's face would split in half along his scar. "F-for us Blisters, a d-d-deal is n-never f-finished until a c-celebration of our union has b-been c-c-completed." Gash's eyelids narrowed. "Y-you d-d-do know how t-to celebrate, d-d-don't you, H-hadder?"

Marlin Hadder looked over to Albany Rott, who was grinning like a schoolboy under his ember eyes. He turned back to Gash, and passed along the smile. "I think it'll come back to me."

20

After Hadder was given the opportunity to shower, and wash off his clothes in the bathrooms, he and Rott were removed from the factory and marched through the manufacturing complex towards another building on the far northwest corner of the property.

As most of the Blisters, including Acid Boy Gash, had gone on ahead while Hadder was cleaning up, their escort was a small one, comprised of Niblit, the grey-skinned woman with the swollen abdomen, who went by Gayle, and the conjoined twins Brutto and Smeggins, whom the companions had run into back in the Jungle. As usual, the tiny shoulder-face that went by Smeggins had much to say on the trek.

"Fucking lucky, he is, Brutto. Fucking lucky fucking guy, eh? Nine fucking times out of fucking ten, Sowler eats that fucking guy's heart for fucking lunch, isn't that fucking right, Brutto?"

"Shut up," was all that Brutto would ever answer.

As the quartet, or quintet with Smeggins, continued to walk, they passed many smaller structures, and one massive building even larger than the factory in which Hadder had just fought. As they neared the immense construct, Hadder noticed the word *WAREHOUSE* in faded white letters across the door. Overtaken by curiosity, Hadder moved to open the door, and steal a peek inside. A grey hand appeared flat against the door, preventing his efforts.

Gayle spoke in a soft, almost sing-song voice. "Terribly sorry, but that building is off limits for non-Blisters. Even for new associates." Orange flecks danced across her orange eyes as she spoke, threatening to hypnotize the lone human of the group.

The high-pitched squeal that was Smeggins ripped Hadder from his trance. "Who does this fucking guy think he fucking is? Hey, fucking guy! That's for fucking Blisters only. You see any fucking *Peddies Welcome* signs, 'cause I fucking don't. You see a fucking *Peddies Welcome* sign, Brutto?"

"Shut up."

"My apologies," Hadder said to Gayle, who simply nodded in return before continuing to lead the group forward.

In short order, they reached their destination, another impressively large building nestled in the back corner of the complex, so close to the ocean that Hadder could hear the waves lapping against the compressed sand not far from where they stood. The building's large bay doors were closed, so Gayle led them around to a small entranceway on the far side. She opened the heavy metal door that read *Testing*, and held it for the group.

"This way please."

Hadder nodded once more, impressed with Gayle's charming ways, and entered the Cyrix testing facility with Albany Rott and the twins on his heels. Once everyone was inside, Gayle took the lead again, taking the males through and past numerous offices and computer rooms before they came upon a set oversized double doors. She pushed open the large barriers with a strength that belied her thin frame. As she did, strange hypnotic music struck the visitors, a more moving welcome than could ever be accomplished by words.

Marlin Hadder and Albany Rott stepped forward and entered the true world of the Blisters.

———

THE TESTING FACILITY was much cleaner than the previous building Hadder and Rott had visited. The air inside smelled clean, as if the Cyrix vents and scrubbers were still working at optimal levels. The only scent that Hadder detected was that of the Leaf smoke that was coiling up towards the high ceilings from groups of relaxing Blisters.

And relaxing they were, a far cry from the snarling, screaming beasts that Hadder had encountered back in the factory. Old couches, love seats, and chairs were scattered across the otherwise empty testing facility, no doubt a collection of discarded furniture that had washed up on the beach. Blisters filled almost every empty seat, calmly talking among themselves as they shared Leaf, memories, and opinions.

To the far right, standing and sitting on the loading area's elevated landing, was the source of the beautiful music that filled the cavernous space. More than a dozen Blisters, each holding a strange instrument that looked to have been fashioned from old robotics components, played their mutated hearts out. Sounds comparable to those of flutes, saxophones, guitars, violins, and heavy drums wafted from the musicians, creating an atmosphere that the hippest bar in the world would be hard-pressed to emulate.

Gayle smiled as she saw the surprise on Hadder and Rott's faces. She placed her rough grey arms across the shoulders of her two guests, and leaned her head in between them. "We only appear to be monsters. An invaluable defense mechanism, wouldn't you agree? Come, Gash is waiting for you to start the celebration."

Hadder looked around at the enchanting ambiance. "Has it not already started?"

Another wonderfully honest smile appeared on Gayle's lips. "No, my friends, *this* is just a normal evening. You'll know when the real celebration begins. Come."

The pressure of Gayle's gentle hands on their shoulders pulled Hadder and Rott from their reverie, and moved them toward the opposite side of the facility, away from the band. Positioned near the back of the building sat Acid Boy Gash on another throne of robotics parts.

"He must have one in every building," whispered Hadder to Rott as they approached.

"I d-d-do," agreed Gash, revealing that hearing was another sense improved by his mutation. "I d-do n-not stop b-being k-k-king just because I enter another b-b-building." He looked to Gayle, and something changed in his vibrating eyes when he looked upon the charming, orange-eyed Blister. "Thank y-you for b-b-bringing them, m-my love."

Gayle, instead of answering, strode forward, gently put her grey hands to either side of Gash's head, and kissed him deeply. When they separated, Gash wore a grin that Hadder knew all too well. It was the smile that one only wore when in the company of a true love. "You are most welcome, *King* Gash."

Gash chuckled embarrassedly, and Gayle moved to the side, quite pleased with herself for flustering her boyfriend-king. Gash overcame his chagrin quickly, and turned his attention back to Hadder and Rott.

"P-p-please sit," he said as he motioned towards the two rusty lawn chairs that had been placed to either side of the makeshift throne. The companions followed instructions, Hadder settling in more gingerly than Rott because of his injuries from the Sowler confrontation. The three shared a quiet moment before Rott spoke.

"Quite the setup you have here, Gash. I see now why you are in no rush to leave."

"I w-w-wouldn't say that, R-rott," responded the Blister king. "D-d-despite the scrubbers s-s-still working in this f-f-facility, our home is s-s-still thick with p-p-poison. B-b-but we will n-not l-leave our home until w-we have f-f-found a n-n-new one. Away f-from human hatred. Th-th-that is m-my d-d-dream."

Rott continued. "I hope you do not mind, but I ran some rough numbers based on estimates of how much you Blisters make from your many enterprises. You are a wealthy people. Why do you still wallow in this toxic prison?"

Acid Boy Gash did not speak for a long while, instead staring out onto his fellow Blisters with his vibrating indigo eyes. Finally, he addressed the question. "Y-y-you c-called us a wealthy p-p-people. B-but we are n-not. W-w-wealthy? Yes. P-people? No. Y-y-your kind m-made it c-clear that w-we are not c-c-considered one of y-y-you."

Hadder cut in. "For the record, I'm not from around here, and Al's not even human."

Gash shifted his disconcerting eyes to Hadder. "P-p-precisely w-why you're still alive."

"And, so, you save every credit, every note, until you can purchase land far away from your abusers," filled in Rott.

Acid Boy Gash nodded, solemnly. "The m-m-moment the humans n-no longer f-f-fear us is w-when we lose all p-p-power. And, s-so, we m-m-must continue to live l-l-like beasts. W-w-which is f-fine. We have m-m-more in common with b-beasts than humans. B-beasts are v-violent, b-but honest. C-c-can we say the s-same about humans?"

"No, I don't suppose we can," responded Hadder, who looked over to Rott, and saw a shadow of pain deep within his crimson eyes.

"M-my people have b-b-been outcasts for t-t-too long now. F-first, they f-f-forced us from our h-homes w-when the Cyrix jobs w-were t-taken from us. Then w-we were ch-ch-chased from the b-beaches by the g-gangs and other f-f-foul groups who b-beat and raped us on a d-d-daily basis. We t-t-took sanctuary in the only p-p-place we knew others w-would be s-scared to f-follow."

"The Hammers," answered Rott.

"Th-that's right. And it w-w-was here that we were ch-ch-changed. It w-was the p-p-price of our s-safety."

Hadder shook his head in disbelief. "I find it hard to believe that the gangs out there terrified your people more than the poisons and toxins of this place."

"W-w-we feared the m-mutations at first, to b-be sure. M-many wanted to l-leave. S-some left to be s-street urchins, always l-living in f-fear of the p-p-police, or n-nasty t-t-toddy gangs. Those who s-s-stayed? They and their offspring b-b-became something m-more than h-human."

"I am surprised that all of your people did not flee once the extreme mutations started," said Rott.

"M-m-many wanted to. Th-then Orrin the Child c-c-came to us."

"Who is Orrin the Child," Hadder and Rott asked in unison.

"He w-w-was the f-first true Blister. He w-was small, his g-g-growth stunted by the chemicals. He had t-t-tiny arms and gnarled legs, b-b-but his b-brain?" Hadder watched as Gayle smiled deeply, enjoying the story of her people's journey. "B-b-by age f-four, he w-was the smartest p-p-person in Bhellum. He s-saw things the r-r-rest of us could not. It was Orrin who was g-g-gifted the prophecy."

Rott's face twisted in curiosity. "Of what prophecy do you speak?"

"Orrin the Child w-w-was convinced that we were God's ch-ch-chosen p-p-people. He s-s-said that God was g-g-going to change us, improve us. Orrin said that we w-w-would suffer much, but, eventually, They w-w-would come. And They w-would help g-g-guide us to Sanctum, far away f-f-from the humans wh-wh-who cast us away."

Hadder, engrossed by the king's story, leaned in. "Who is *They*, Gash?"

Acid Boy Gash smiled wide, the act once again pulling at his garish scar. "The Twin Angels, of c-c-course."

Hadder and Rott looked to each other. Rott spoke before Hadder had a chance to collect his thoughts. "And you think *we* are these Twin Angels?"

"I d-d-do not think, M-M-Mister Albany Rott. I know."

Hadder's mouth hung open, and his shoulders ached as another expectation was laid heavily upon him. Rott immediately recognized the look on his companion's face. "Come now, Marlin. This certainly is not the first prophecy you have been a part of, is it?"

Hadder recalled his role as savior, or destroyer, of Station. He didn't care for that prophecy much, and this seemed even more dangerous and bizarre. "If I'm one of the Twin Angels, then why the fuck did I just have to fight that giant pig-man?"

"His n-n-name is Sowler."

"Then why the fuck did I have to fight Sowler?"

Gash shrugged. "I h-h-had to be s-sure."

Gayle put a grey hand on her lover's chest. "My King, I think our Blisters are ready for the celebration."

Hadder, lost in Gash's tale, looked up to see that hundreds, if not a thousand, Blisters had quietly gathered in the testing facility, their movements hidden under the calming noise of the house band. Several large pigs, roasting slowly over metal barrels filled with coals, had been wheeled into the facility and placed along the walls. Giant vats of a greenish liquid had also been placed around the facility, with Blisters approaching every few minutes to dip metal cups into the concoctions before collapsing onto old couches and lawn chairs.

Rott pointed to one of the spinning pigs. "I had heard that you Blisters were cannibals."

Gash shook his head. "L-l-long ago, my people did what they had to d-d-do to s-survive. N-now, it's j-j-just another story that h-helps k-k-keep humans away f-from us." His vibrating eyes stopped their movement as they shifted towards Rott. "W-w-we very much like the s-same foods as you d-d-do."

As Rott and Gash spoke, Hadder stared out into the sea of Blisters. Despite the odd shapes, strange colors, and irregular textures that filled Hadder's vision, he couldn't help but notice the camaraderie among those gathered before him. Some danced, others made toasts, but all enjoyed the closeness of each other.

As Hadder's eyes swept from one side of the facility to the other, something caught his attention, forcing him to freeze. In the midst of the relaxing Blisters, a tall, lean woman stood, staring directly at Hadder. Wearing only an athletic leotard and ankle boots with bladed metal tips, her skin was impossibly white, and she appeared completely hairless, without eyebrows marring her angular face, or a mop covering her impossibly perfect head. She spent a long time taking in Hadder with her too-bright blue eyes before moving toward one of the barrels of liquid. She retrieved two metal cups from the floor next to the barrel, and dipped them both into the vat before heading Hadder's way with the beverages. The young woman walked with the balance and poise of a gymnast, her gait accentuating her long legs and hips.

"You look thirsty, new friend," said the woman as she handed Hadder the metal cup. She absently held the second cup out toward Rott, her blue eyes firmly fixed on Hadder's hazel orbs.

Rott, seeing the scene play out, chuckled as he accepted the drink. "Thank you, young miss."

The woman ignored Rott's words. "My name is Sheela."

"My name is Marlin. Marlin Hadder."

"I know who you are, Marlin. I hope we can spend some time together during the celebration."

"I would like that."

And with that, Sheela offered a small bow to Acid Boy Gash, Gayle, and Albany Rott in turn before turning about and disappearing back into the ever-increasing ocean of Blisters. Hadder stared Sheela's way long after she had vanished into the masses. Rott and Gash shared a knowing smile.

The soft voice of Gayle finally brought Hadder back to reality. "My dear King, I think it's time."

"Of c-c-course, m-my love." Acid Boy Gash rose from his throne and baby-stepped toward his gathered Blisters. As if by magic, the entire testing facility, filled to the brim with terrifying Blisters, fell impossibly silent as Gash began to speak. "My b-b-beloved Blisters!"

"Our King, Gash," came a resounding cry from the crowd.

"M-m-most of you know w-w-why we are g-gathered here t-today. F-f-finally, after y-years of t-t-torment and p-pain, the w-words of Orrin the Child are c-c-coming true!" Another eruption, before immediate silence. "The Twin Angels have c-c-come to us, j-j-just as our city s-spirals into oblivion. They w-will lead us to Sanctum, f-f-far from the unkind r-reach of the humans who t-t-turned their b-backs on our k-k-kind. B-but we will have to f-f-fight for w-what is owed to us! That is n-n-nothing new to us. This t-time, however, I f-f-fear many of us w-will not r-r-return! But we Blisters are n-n-not strangers to s-s-sacrifice, are w-we m-my friends?!" Another round of raucous applause before quiet. "Let us n-not dwell on that t-t-tonight! T-t-tonight is a celebration. Orinn's w-words were p-p-proven correct, and the appropriate t-t-tests were p-passed. So t-tonight, we celebrate the Blisters of the p-p-past, p-present, and future. For t-tonight m-m-marks the beginning of a new chapter f-for our p-people!" Blisters exploded into a cacophony of hoots and hollers, this time without subsiding. Gash continued over their noise. "Yes! Y-yes! Music! D-drink! D-d-dance! Let us g-g-give thanks for Orrin! For the Twin Angels! F-f-for a future without h-humans!"

As soon as Acid Boy Gash concluded his speech, the testing facility spun out, transforming into a nightclub for the ages as the music changed course, becoming more joyful and frenetic, the lights were dimmed, and the drinks were consumed in single gulps. Gash and Gayle were brought metal cups of their own by Niblit, and the lovers held up their drinks to Hadder and Rott. The quartet nodded silently to each other, words unneeded, before touching metal and downing the contents of their cups.

Hadder immediately felt the effects of the strong drink, his pupils shrinking, and his vision growing full of strange colors and trails, whisking him back to Station, where the Number 3 had brought on similar feelings. He breathed in deeply to calm the butterflies that accompanied all strong drugs.

Gash, seeing Hadder's reaction, commented. "You've n-never partied until y-you've b-been with Blisters. Think y-y-you can handle it?"

Rott looked to Hadder, who smiled in return, remembering similar words from departed friends long ago. "I think I'm going to have fun trying."

A SHORT TIME LATER, Marlin Hadder looked around, his head hazy from the strong Blister concoction, and realized that he had been transported back in time, to a place that held memories both dear and horrifying. The Blister celebration was very much like being back in *The Soirée Noire*, with loud hypnotic music driving partygoers into a frenzy of dance and revelry. Small bundles of herbs were burning in the facility's corners, painting the entire canvas with a layer of sweet-smelling smoke that made the scene even more abstract, bending the room's dimmed light at strange angles. The festive Blisters could just as easily have been Celebration Cluster residents, their strangely colored skin acting as couture clothing, and their mutations taking the place of Elevations.

Hadder wove through the party, dancing with a small group of Blisters one moment, and accepting toasts from another clique minutes later. Hadder was struck by the camaraderie demonstrated by the Blisters, the evident kindness and respect shown among their own. Even those with prior issues with the new companions managed to put things aside for the celebration.

Hadder learned this the hard way, when his knees almost buckled from an unexpected weight thrust upon him. When he looked to his left concerned, he saw that his former opponent Sowler had joined him, mutated arm draped over Hadder's unremarkable shoulders. "Good fight. For a peddie."

Hadder thought it best to make nice with the intimidating Blister. He raised his cup. "Same to you. You would've had me if it wasn't for that pre-existing injury."

Sowler reactively reached up to the blood-soaked cap that covered his pink head. "Not an injury. Born like this. It was a fair fight." Sowler looked up, saw something through the smoky, light-filled haze. "Brutto! You have Leaf? Come!"

The couple soon became a trio, or maybe a quartet, as Brutto and the shoulder-face named Smeggins joined them. As always, Smeggins had much more to say than the imposing Brutto.

"Ahh, fucking look at who it fucking is, Brutto. The fucking Twin Angel, himself. You ever fucking wonder what a fucking Angel tastes like, Brutto. I know I fucking do."

"Shut up, Smeggins." Brutto offered Sowler an already lit joint. "Here."

Sowler put the joint to his lips, and took a deep drag. He exhaled the smoke slowly, his body instantly becoming more upright from its effects. A contented smile appeared on Sowler's face as he handed the joint back to Brutto.

Smeggins spoke once more. "You want a fucking hit? If you're our fucking savior and all, you should fucking take a fucking hit."

Sowler looked over to Hadder. "Careful. Laced."

The Blisters couldn't have known Hadder's past with strong chemicals, so he forgave their low opinion of him. "I think I'll survive."

"Fucking great. Come get it, fucker."

With that, Brutto took a long, deep hit from the joint, burning it down to the roach, and held it in. He then gently cupped Hadder behind the head with a giant meathook hand and pulled his face towards Smeggins, who laughed maniacally while showing piranha-like teeth.

While both, or all three, Blisters had been hoping to freak out Hadder, little did they know that he had accepted smoky gifts from much more terrifying vessels, namely Monty the Mod's Ophidian. Hadder fearlessly leaned in, ignoring the putrid smell pouring forth from the little creature's mouth, and opened wide as the smoke Brutto inhaled was exhaled through Smeggins. Hadder accepted the gift, closing his eyes as the smoky chemicals ran through him, further awakening each of his senses. He stumbled back on uneasy legs.

Smeggins giggled. "It packs a fucking punch, doesn't it?"

"It does," agreed Hadder, a wide smile resting easily on his face. As his vision began to clear, Hadder noticed a vision in white across the testing facility, impossible to miss among the dull skin tones of most Blisters. "Thank you for the Leaf. Now, if you boys will excuse me."

As Hadder began to leave, he heard Smeggins behind him. "Where are you fucking off to? Who the fuck leaves in the middle of a fucking... Ohh, I see where you're fucking going. Wanna fucking take me along for the fucking ride? I can..." Smeggins's words disappeared into the background as Hadder waded through the Blister mass. The music was becoming more intense, driving the partygoers into a craze. Hadder gingerly made his way through the crowd, careful not to bump into any Blisters with sensitive skin, or obvious boils.

Eventually, Hadder reached his destination, the strong drink and potent smoke staining his face with a goofy smile. Sheela grinned in return, showing perfect white teeth behind perfect white lips.

"What took you so long, Marlin Hadder?"

"Strategy session with Smeggins."

Sheela giggled. "Did you get much accomplished?"

"Not really. Hoping our meeting is a bit more productive."

Sheela's blue eyes danced before Hadder, twin storms attracting a Twin Angel. "Only time will tell."

———

ALBANY ROTT, Acid Boy Gash, and Gayle stood on an elevated platform in the testing facility, looking out onto the Blister celebration. The three watched as Marlin Hadder approached the enchanting Sheela. The two began to talk, then dance.

Gayle was the first to speak, showcasing her singsong voice. "Looks like Hadder has found a female friend."

"Yes, he is very good at that," replied Rott.

"Has he had many girlfriends?"

"There have been others."

"And where are they now?"

"Dead. All dead."

Gayle put a grey hand to her chest. "Oh my, such terrible news. Poor Hadder. I hope Sheela can bring him some joy this evening."

Rott laughed. "I think you can count on it."

Gash turned to Rott. "And w-w-what about Albany Rott? D-d-does he not also w-wish the c-company of a g-g-good woman?"

"I do not enjoy sharing my bed with humans."

"M-m-may I remind you that Blisters are n-n-not humans?"

Rott held up his pale hands in surrender. "I understand. What I meant to say was that I prefer the company of synthetics. Spirit Girls."

"Y-y-you tire of earthly c-c-creations?"

"Yes."

"As d-do I."

Rott changed subjects. "Tell me, Gash. Do you really think we have enough to best Viktor Krill? Even with the Blisters, it is us and the Broken Tens going against the collected forces of the Rising, the Mech Force, and

Cyrix Industries. Not to mention, you may have noticed that Viktor Krill is not a normal man."

"He is a w-w-Wakened human."

Rott was unable to conceal the surprise on his scarred face. "How do you know that?"

"M-my broken eyes see m-much, Albany Rott."

"Then you already know the odds we are up against."

"I d-d-do."

"And still, you see victory?"

"I see a g-g-great battle. Nothing m-more."

"But you sense a chance at victory?"

"I d-d-do."

"And what do you see that I cannot?"

"Alphus."

"Who?"

Gayle cut in. "My brother, Alphus. He will return from the sea soon. I have already called to him."

"And you think he can turn the tide of the battle."

"I do," replied Gayle.

Rott shook his head in doubt. "He better be a leviathan."

"He is. My love, I'm going to mingle." And with that, the lovely Gayle pressed a kiss against her king's cloven face, and melted into the celebrating Blisters.

"She is quite the woman, Gash. You are a lucky man."

"Th-th-this I know."

The two kings stood in comfortable silence, letting the music, dancing, and carousing speak in their stead. Finally, Rott broke the peace. "Tell me, Gash, how did that scar come to you. Having one of my own, I am curious about such things."

Gash took a moment to collect his thoughts before answering. "Even among Blisters, m-m-my mutations are ex-extreme. M-my f-f-father thought I w-would never s-s-survive, w-w-would be a b-burden to our p-people. He t-tried to t-t-take an axe to my f-f-face as an infant, b-but was s-stopped by my m-m-mother, who held b-back his h-hand just in t-time. He w-w-was cast out f-from the Blisters for b-breaking the c-c-cardinal rule."

"That being?"

"W-w-we don't hurt our own k-k-kind." Another silence between the two kings followed. Eventually, Gash took another deep drink from his metal cup before continuing the conversation. "And y-y-you, Albany Rott? H-h-how did your scar come to b-be?"

"I was struck down from Heaven."

To his credit, Gash did not miss a beat. "And that s-s-symbol at your neck that g-g-glows?"

"That's a blueprint, Gash."

Now it was Gash's turn to appear confused. "B-b-blueprint for w-what?"

Albany Rott faced Acid Boy Gash, his crimson eyes now small fires that threatened to burn a hole through the Blister king's head. "For you, Gash. For *all* of you."

Gash's indigo eyes halted their vibration and met Rott's twin fires. A grin crept back on his disfigured face. "Then the p-p-prophecy is t-true."

"You had doubts?"

"G-gone. R-r-replaced."

"Replaced by what?"

"Ex-ex-excitement."

"What are you excited for?"

"To f-f-feel human b-blood on my f-f-face. This w-w-war has long b-been my d-dream."

"Careful, my friend. In my experience, dreams can quickly devolve into nightmares."

"B-b-but don't you s-see, Albany Rott? You and me, all of us, w-we *are* the n-nightmares."

Rott left it at that, and turned back to view the celebration. As the music of the Blister band grew increasingly sensual, the revelers danced closer, their bubbly, discolored skins touching as oversized mouths with jagged teeth reached for each other.

Perhaps Gash was right. Perhaps they were the nightmares, willing to unleash Hell to achieve victory over the demon Viktor Krill.

Only time, and blood, would tell.

————

HADDER AND SHEELA held each other tightly. The slow music of the Blister band demanded that Hadder caress Sheela's soft cheek with the back of his hand, demanded that Sheela run her fingers through Hadder's coarse brown hair. Just as Hadder had finally worked up the courage to lean down and kiss the beautiful Blister, the music stopped, and the two separated. They clapped to show their appreciation for the band without unlocking eyes, their applause mixing with the other Blisters in attendance.

Only when the band leader screamed something unintelligible into the air did Sheela finally break Hadder's gaze. She looked around to her Blister family, and they all hollered at the testing facility's ceiling in unison, wide smiles showing beastly teeth in too-big and too-small mouths. After a slight pause for effect, the Blister band launched into a pounding, frenetic song that sent the crowd into a cohesive frenzy, the strange homemade instruments creating sounds that only computers could replicate in Hadder's world. The Blisters threw their arms into the air with the beat, ruined skin showing on many of them, gaining momentum from each other as much as from the music.

It was then that Hadder came to a realization. Despite the smoky haze, the strong drugs, and the strobing lights, this party was unlike those of the Celebration Cluster, where everyone wore a mask of delight and feigned happiness as they hid from themselves and others. What Hadder found himself in the midst of was much more akin to the Great Bash, that final celebration of life and friendship put on by his beloved Setters. That final chance to be together as one. As Blisters draped bubbly arms over twisted shoulders, Hadder wondered if these people understood that this was the end of the road for many of them.

When Hadder returned his attention to Sheela, he saw that she was staring at him intently, as if reading his thoughts. She responded to his unsaid words, leaning in closely to be heard over the drumming music.

"We know that many, maybe all of us, will not survive the coming war, Marlin. But if victory means that our people will finally have a place to call their own, away from the harsh words and mistreatment of the humans, then we are all more than happy to offer up our lives. You are the prophecy that Orrin the Child spoke of years ago. We cannot miss this opportunity."

Although Hadder was moved by Sheela's determination and bravery, a part of him wanted nothing more than to sweep her into his arms, and carry her far from the upcoming madness. Hadder had seen too many lovely women die too soon during his lives, and the thought of another was almost unbearable. "You don't have to do this, Sheela. You could easily pass for a human. A beautiful woman, at that. Why don't you wait out the war, help in other ways? If Viktor Krill proves victorious, at least you'll still have a life to return to, a way to keep the Blisters' memory alive."

Although Sheela laughed off Hadder's suggestion, the cold blue of her eyes told him that she did not appreciate his weak attempt to persuade her to shirk her duties. "Putting a stethoscope around my neck would not make me a doctor, Marlin. Life is too short, even one lived to a hundred, to pretend to be something that you're not, for people you don't respect. As my people go, I go."

Sheela had barely finished her sentence when Hadder pulled her in close, and kissed her passionately, his admiration for her mixing with the smoke and drink to render his usual self-control impotent. Lips met lips, and tongue met tongue as the two became lost in a sea of twisted bones and abstract flesh, as if they were the only true lovers in the Neon City of Bhellum.

The night went on with more food, more drink, more smoke, and more good company. Hadder laughed at the Blisters' humor, which was surprisingly self-deprecating and witty. He teared up at the Blisters' stories, each one more poignant than the one before it. He smiled at the Blisters' camaraderie, a true family in every sense of the world. Hadder joined in their hoots and hollers, gave out hugs, when needed, received embraces, when offered. Although they had little in common, came from different worlds entirely, for this one night, Marlin Hadder was a Blister. And he enjoyed every second of it.

As the celebration wound down, many Blisters began to filter out of the testing facility in pairs and small groups. Others disappeared into doors that lined the far side of the testing facility, opposite from where Hadder and Rott had entered. Hadder and Sheela sat around for a while, talking quietly with Albany Rott, Acid Boy Gash, and Gayle. They spoke not of the upcoming war, but about life and loss, friends and enemies, and the meaning of family.

As Hadder downed one last cup of the Blister concoction, Sheela rose without speaking, grabbed his hand, and led him silently away from the gathered kings and queen. Hadder looked towards Rott as he was being pulled, who only offered a slight knowing smile and a small nod. Gash and Gayle added their grins for good measure.

Sheela took Hadder through one of the facility's side doors, and guided him down a long corridor that was home to several rooms on either side. As they passed these rooms, Hadder peeked inside to find Blisters in various stages of intimacy. In one room, a small female Blister gently rubbed ointment onto the painful-looking cysts and boils of several large men who sat Indian-style in a circle, all humming a foreign tune. Within another, a Blister couple slow-danced to a song that only they could hear. Inside a third room, Hadder was unable to tell which arm, leg, hand, and foot belonged to whom as a mass of bodies rose and fell, entwined in passionate lovemaking.

Sheela led Hadder forward until they reached the final door, which was closed and covered in beautiful drawings of exotic landscapes. She entered without knocking, and Hadder followed behind. Unlike the other rooms they had passed, which were sparsely furnished and without decoration, this one was warm and welcoming, with a large, comfortable mattress on the ground surrounded by posters of beaches and drawings of other Blisters on the walls. Sheela closed the door once Hadder was inside.

"I guess we're lucky this room was still available," said Hadder.

"Of course it would be. We're in my room, silly. Please, sit."

Hadder did as he was told, falling onto the mattress. As soon as he touched the surprisingly soft sheets, Hadder realized how incredibly tired he was, the long day of strategizing, fighting, and carousing finally catching up to him. Sheela kicked off her ankle boots, and joined him atop the silky sheets, the two lying down in silence for a long time, sharing in a moment that would only be marred by words.

"Tell me, Marlin, why do you care about this war? You seem to have nothing to gain, and everything to lose."

Hadder had to think for a while before answering. His chase for Viktor Krill had made him myopic, unsure of his true purpose. "Albany Rott has saved my life four times." Hadder knew *saved* was the wrong word, but didn't want to complicate the issue. "I exist now because of his grace. He needs to rid this world of Viktor Krill to go home. I want to help him with that."

"Are you sure that it was *grace* that made him save you?"

This was a difficult question that Hadder was unprepared to answer, so he shifted gears. "Viktor Krill is a Wakened human, a monster. He came to this world to conquer. To enslave. The place where Rott and I come from created this freak. It's now our responsibility to eliminate him. For the good of Bhellum." Sheela looked away, uncomfortable with something Hadder had said. "What's wrong?"

She continued staring at the decorated wall. "Oh, nothing. It's just that word, *freak*. My people are called that daily. And it makes me uncomfortable."

Hadder kicked himself for his insensitivity. "I'm sorry. I should have chosen my words more carefully." He gently tugged at Sheela's jaw, pulling her back to face him. "Viktor Krill is a villain. His death will not only help Rott get home, but will help the Blisters purchase a permanent home. I don't have much left to fight for in life, so this will do."

Sheela smiled sweetly. "Well, as long as you're not fighting to save Bhellum. This city is rotten, and has been for countless decades. The bright neon lights are there to hide crowded mass graves and lifetimes of unapologetic sins. I want to know that if you're going to die, Marlin, you're doing it for the right reasons."

"How about for the love of a beautiful woman? Would that be for the right reason?"

Sheela giggled lightly. "That would certainly be a step in the right direction." Hadder tried to join her in a laugh, but it came out in a long, drawn out yawn. Sheela softly cupped Hadder's face with her too-white hand. "Oh, Hadder, I forgot what a long day it's been for you. Forgive me. I fear we will all have long days ahead of us. You should get some rest."

With that, Sheela rose and helped Hadder get undressed, tucked him in neatly under the satin sheets. Just as Hadder began to drift off into unconsciousness, he watched through slitted eyes as Sheela slipped out of her leotard, revealing a perfect body devoid of excess fat. Hadder's eyes popped open as his pulse began to race and blood began to run. He cast off the sheets, reached up, and pulled Sheela down onto him. The two strangers from different worlds then became one, working desperately together to achieve a common goal.

As always, rest could wait for death, which was seemingly always right around the corner for Marlin Hadder.

———

ALBANY ROTT SAT ALONE in the testing facility, smoking a Leaf cigarette and sipping on the Blisters' potent brew. Everyone else had retired for the evening, but Albany Rott did not sleep, and, at this moment, could not even enter his usual meditative reverie. His eyes blazed with fires as his mind flashed with uncertainty. Rott was always one to play dangerous games, but never had he cared about the other participants. New, uncomfortable feelings accosted the living god as his inhuman brain raced with thoughts.

Rott took one last drag of his joint before dropping it to the floor and stamping it out. He rose quickly and almost stumbled, not from the drink or smoke, which never compromised his faculties, but from an idea that played over and over again in his mind, threatening to tear him apart.

Albany Rott might win in the coming days, only to lose that which he had grown to appreciate most.

PART III

THE HADDER REVELATION

21

V iktor Krill lounged on an expensive leather couch in his private suite within the Cyrix Industries Headquarters building. Although the Wakened human seemed lost in thought, his attention was fully locked onto the small girl going through the motions of various fighting stances and performing an array of combat maneuvers.

Natthi flowed effortlessly from one pose to the other, her mastery of the movements akin to someone much older and more experienced. As Krill watched the young girl practice, strange feelings swirled inside the king of the Risers. His heart leapt when she smiled broadly after completing a new technique. His stomach lurched when she became disheartened after failing to successfully execute a difficult maneuver.

These new emotions, and Krill's discomfort with them, ripped his attention away from his pupil for a moment, just as she missed a crucial step in a complex combination. Luckily, another in the room was not similarly distracted.

"Natthi! Your left foot needs to be out front. And keep on the balls of your feet."

Natthi halted her movements, and wiped sweat from her small, brown brow. "Shit! Sorry, Miss Mayfly. I think I'm getting tired."

"Language, young lady. Come and get some water. I think that's enough for today. Viktor?"

The mention of his name pulled Viktor from his contemplations. "Yes, of course. Nice job, Natthi. Soon, you'll be able to best any two-bit scumbag Bhellum has to offer. But stay diligent. Life is easily taken from a lazy hand."

"Thanks, Mister Viktor," the girl responded, his words of encouragement bringing a wide grin to Natthi's heart-shaped face.

That foreign feeling raced through Krill once more as the child walked over to Mayfly Lemaire, where she received water and a warm hug. To his left, reclining in an oversized chaise lounge, young Darrin studiously poured through the contents of a dark ream. He must have felt Krill's eyes on him because he looked up and offered a smile to his boss and mentor.

"Our increased output of Slink has sent profits through the roof, Mister Krill. We can finally provide enough supply to meet the demand."

Krill tried unsuccessfully to mask the overwhelming pride he felt in the boy he had once considered eliminating. "That's great, young Darrin, but none of it matters if we are unable to protect our turf and wealth. You also need to stay diligent. Relay that message to your toddy gangs."

"Of course, sir." There was something else Darrin was going to say, but looking around at those in the room, he thought better of it and closed his mouth.

"No talking business in front of the young one," Lemaire scolded.

"Sorry, Mayfly," Krill and Darrin said in unison before laughing at their shared acquiescence to the Bitch-Whore leader. Young Darrin was the head of the largest conglomerate of toddy gangs Bhellum had ever seen, and Viktor Krill was not only king of the Rising, but also a Vice President of one of the world's most powerful robotics companies. But when it came to matters of the child Natthi, there was no question who was in charge.

And her name was Mayfly Lemaire.

Young Darrin returned to his dark ream as Lemaire began to towel off Natthi, who had crawled up to sit in the lap of the gangster queen.

Viktor Krill sat back in his seat and looked around at the scene surrounding him. His black eyes bounced from young Darrin, to Mayfly

Lemaire, to the girl Natthi, each one ushering a torrent of feelings that accosted the notorious killer. The silence of the room sent Krill's mind spiraling into a thousand different directions, with each path emptying into the same place.

Words Viktor Krill had never thought he would need to concern himself with played in his head, making the Wakened human both fearful and hopeful. They were dangerous words, ones that could render a strong man weak, leaving openings through which enemies could attack. The words fell from the sky like icy rain, refreshingly painful on Krill's tan, scarred skin.

The Rising leader's head spun in the face of this new reality, that these new words could force him to reevaluate everything, could pull him away from the plans he had so carefully laid out. Part of Krill wanted to run from these words, wanted to cut them from his chest with one of his infamous knives. But another part, much larger than its negative analogue, demanded that he embrace these words, make them an intrinsic part of who he was, and who he would become.

Love. Family.

There was a weight to the words, and they pulled on even Krill's impossibly strong shoulders. His mind was a whirlwind, tearing through scenarios both good and bad faster than any other living creature could hope to replicate.

Just as Krill could take no more, thinking his heart would punch a hole in his breastbone, Red Texx entered the room, salvation in the form of a giant red-haired man. Texx stopped just inside the door, but refrained from speaking for a moment. Instead, the Rising's second-in-command remained silent for several minutes, taking in the scene with the ghost of a smile on his large, ruddy face.

Finally, he spoke up. "Boss, it's time for me to escort these lovely ladies back to Thoosa Tower."

"Can I stay with Mister Viktor? Please," pleaded Natthi to Lemaire.

"Maybe some other time, sweetheart. Mister Viktor has a full docket today."

The child's little face turned to Krill. "But I can come back soon? I promise I won't mess anything us next time, Mister Viktor."

Another emotion stabbed at the feared king. "Mistakes are necessary here, so we don't make them out there, before our enemies. Never apologize for them. And nothing in this world, or any other, could keep me from hosting you again very soon."

With that assurance, Natthi leapt from Lemaire's lap and ran towards Krill, eventually attacking him with a heartfelt hug. He squeezed back, careful not to hurt the tiny person. "Thank you, Mister Viktor," she said into his chest, and Krill knew the girl was talking about more than their combat sessions.

The intimate moment ended as Lemaire rose, took Natthi by the hand, threw Krill a knowing wink, and exited the room, clapping Red Texx on his large shoulder as she passed. Texx nodded to the two females, and turned his attention back to Krill. "Boss, you wanted me to remind you about your meeting with Cyrus Bhellum this afternoon."

"Thank you, Texx, I won't forget."

Red Texx nodded once more, and paused. He met Krill's black eyes with his own and offered a sweet smile, difficult for such an imposing man, one that contained more than a few thoughts. He nodded to his commander and backed out of the room, readily accepting the duty of protecting Krill's most prized treasure.

As Texx left, another word assaulted Viktor Krill, one that had all the substance of the others that he so feared. One that he never thought to find, especially in the depths of the war zone that was one known at the Muck.

Friend.

As Krill was rolling yet another foreign term around in his mind, Darrin set his dark ream down, looked around to ensure privacy, and spoke.

"Mister Krill, we need to talk. Something's going on. Something terrible."

———

"WHAT DO YOU MEAN, they're just disappearing?"

"I mean what I mean, Mister Krill. Kids keep disappearing."

Krill's tan face scrunched up, unable to process why this was important, or worthy of his time. "Street rats go missing all the time, young Darrin. That's literally what makes them street rats; they disappear for days, months, even years. They'll return once they've worn out their welcome wherever they ran off to."

Darrin grew frustrated, but maintained his composure. "It's not street rats that are disappearing, Mister Krill. I mean, it *is* some street rats. But now, even my toddy gang leaders are starting to go missing. Boys with everything going for them are here one day, gone the next."

"Conspiring against you, perhaps?"

Darrin shook his head emphatically. "No, sir. Some of these were good friends of mine. Loyal to me, and even more loyal to you, Mister Krill. And now they're gone, and more keep following." The rising panic in Darrin's voice grew increasingly apparent as the boy spoke.

The cracks in Darrin's usually unflappable demeanor made Krill realize that he needed to take his mentee's concerns more seriously. "How many?"

"What?"

"How many have gone missing, Darrin?"

"Ten this week."

"That doesn't seem like such a high number."

"Ten toddy leaders, Mister Krill. Friends. I don't have an accurate number for either the lower toddy members or the *street rats*, as you call them. But it's much higher."

Krill's black eyes widened, both at the number of friends Darrin had lost in a short time, and at the anger bubbling just under the surface because of Krill's dismissal of "street rat" lives. Sometimes, even Viktor Krill's Wakened brain forgot key elements of the past.

"What do *you* think is happening, young Darrin?"

"I think someone is taking them."

"For what purpose?"

"I don't know, sir. But it ain't to give them new bikes."

Krill thought for a moment. "The Harvesters? Surely, those dopes wouldn't touch a mosquito in the Rising without clearing it with me first. They have to know that I will gut every fucking one of them if…"

"I don't think it's the Harvesters," Darrin cut in. "That trash sticks out like a sore thumb in the Rising. They can't pick a weed in the Jungle without a Riser knowing about it."

"Who then?"

"I don't know, Mister Krill. That's why I'm bringing it to you, sir. I generally try to hide stuff like this from you…because I know how busy you are. But friends are vanishing, and the gangs are splintering, and business is being threatened, and…"

Krill raised a scarred hand to quiet his upset protégé. "Ok, young Darrin. You have my attention. I will look into it."

Darrin exhaled, as if a burdensome weight had been lifted from his small chest. "Thank you, Mister Krill. That's great to hear. This news should chill out a lot of the boys. I guess I'll take my leave and get back to work. The increased Slink production is keeping us busy across the city."

Young Darrin tucked the dark ream into his waistband, and rose from his seat. He turned to leave, paused, and hurried towards Krill instead. The boy gave the notorious killer a quick hug, the first of its kind, before spinning back and hurrying for the door.

Once Darrin was out of sight, Krill sat back as his mind began to wander. He should have been thinking about the missing children and the culprits behind the apparent abductions. Instead, however, Krill's Wakened mind was fixated on the small hug delivered by the small boy, and the strange feelings that it brought forth. Krill attempted to smother these sensations, to avoid giving a name to their cause. But bubble up it did, injuring Krill in a way that no battle ever had.

Son.

———

ONCE MORE, Viktor Krill found himself passing through the large golden double doors that led into Cyrus Bhellum V's personal office suite. As usual, the inset monitors to his left displayed news from around the world, while the windows to his right allowed him to stare down at his thriving empire.

At the far end of the room, Bhellum and his two-headed Spirit Girl were waiting for the newest Cyrix Vice President. The air in the office was thick with illness and heavy with tension. Viktor Krill's Wakened senses picked up on this immediately, forcing him to raise his guard. Perhaps this wasn't to be a friendly meeting, after all.

As Krill rounded the heavy boardroom table, he realized that Bhellum was waiting not in one of the usual seats, but in an ornate wheelchair. Tubes ran from his left arm to several bags of clear liquid that hung heavy from a metal pole on wheels. The two-headed Spirit Girl stood at the ready, now more nurse than sex doll.

Time had not been kind to Cyrus Bhellum V in the weeks since Viktor Krill had last seen him. His pink skin was now a mottled red, and the few remaining hairs he once had atop his head had joined their brethren in death. Bhellum no longer wore his opulent rings, as his hands and fingers had swollen into hams and sausages. His right hand shook uncontrollably upon his blanket-covered lap. Cyrus Bhellum V was a man on death's door. And dead men were unpredictable and dangerous.

Krill nodded to Bhellum as he approached, but stopped a safe distance away. The Cyrix leader had grown increasingly paranoid about germs in recent months. "It's good to see you again, Bhellum. You look...well."

Bhellum flashed his stained, crooked teeth, a wolf beneath a shawl of inflamed flesh. "Do not lie, Viktor. It does not gel with your personality. But I appreciate your effort."

"Very well. No more lies. How can I be of service?"

Bhellum looked up to his twin-headed Spirit Girl. "You remember Morgan and Morgin, of course."

Krill nodded to each head, in turn. "Of course." Neither acknowledged his greeting, instead shooting the Rising leader with cold stares. Krill looked back to Bhellum. "What's their problem?"

Bhellum coughed loudly into his sleeve before reaching up and grabbing the synthetic's right hand with his bloated left. "Look at them, Viktor. The most sophisticated Spirit Girl ever created, capable of pleasures beyond imagine, now resigned to mere nurse. *That* is their problem. Now tell me, Viktor, what is *your* problem?"

Krill was taken aback. "I don't understand the question, Bhellum. Things are progressing on schedule. Slink production has increased, even beyond my own wildest dreams, and the deaths of junkies are increasing every day. If you don't count my Risers and the toddy gangs, we should reach the critical population decrease you need to sell the land in a few short months."

"Do I look like I have months, you idiot!" Krill almost backed up a step, unused to being spoken to in such a way. His immediate impulse was to rip the fat man's lungs from his chest, but their game was long from being over. "You are abiding by an old schedule, one that means nothing to me anymore. As you can see, things have taken a turn for the worse. I need the Healer, and I need him now!"

Morgin, the head on Viktor's right, spoke up in a silky voice. "Cyrus, you must remain calm, my love. Do not waste your limited energy in anger towards this underling."

Krill raised his black eyes towards the twin heads, and realization hit him like a brick to the face. After many months of interactions, Viktor Krill finally saw Morgan and Morgin for what they truly were. He looked on as their eyes studied his every move, watched as their twin synthetic brains calculated thousands of variables, sizing up the Riser leader, Cyrus Bhellum's leading killer.

Morgan and Morgin were not a Spirit Girl, although he was sure that they could fill that role rather easily. No, this dual-headed monstrosity was a Paladin disguised as a sex bot, one of the most sophisticated synthetic warriors on the planet, dedicated to serving one master, and eliminating all potential threats. Krill noted the risk before his attention was pulled back to Bhellum, who had taken a deep, raspy breath to calm himself.

"Forgive me, Viktor, but, as you can see, I am hardly myself anymore." There was no real apology in those words. "Let's cut to the chase. Everything must be accelerated. Slink production, deaths, paperwork; all of it must be expedited. Time is no longer a luxury."

"Slink production has already been increased exponentially."

A greasy smile appeared on Bhellum's fat face. "But not under your watch."

Krill shrugged. It was true that his new duties as Cyrix Industries VP had forced Krill to relinquish some responsibilities, namely management of the Slink farms, which he had turned over to Levi Lessons and his hand-picked group of Slink Reapers. Under their direction, Slink production had nearly quadrupled in the past month, due in part to the additional farms established in Triton and Hydrus Towers. "The Slink Reapers are doing a good job. But deaths from Slink still take time. Junkies are resilient, if nothing else."

"That is why we can no longer rely on Slink to do our dirty work, Viktor. We must supplement its efforts."

"But, I thought the point of this was for the population decrease to appear natural, even if assisted?"

"I'm dying, you fool! Plans must change! You've never felt death's hot breath on your neck, never known the grip of the unknown wrapped around your heart!" In fact, Viktor Krill had indeed known these feelings, but decided it would be fruitless to argue the point. "Throw away the old schedule, and give me results. I need deaths! Now!"

Viktor Krill took a moment to process this unforeseen outburst. As he did, he watched as Morgan and Morgin coiled their artificial muscles, ready to strike out should Krill make a move on their master. Krill's Wakened mind sped through scenarios, tore through variables, made connections that others could not. His black eyes narrowed.

"Bhellum, your accelerated schedule wouldn't have anything to do with all the children that have gone missing recently, would it?"

The Cyrix CEO's greasy smile grew wider, even more hideous. "One of your Slink Reapers, someone who has been performing at a much higher level than the disappointment standing before me now, made a critical discovery. It seems that the Slink prefer the taste of younger meat, and rewards us with significantly increased production each time we make a childish offering."

Krill's stomach threatened to released its contents; this was too much for even the seasoned villain. His words came out in a loose, quiet stammer. "You're feeding children to the Slink?"

"Well, the Slink Reapers work for you, so it would be more accurate to say that *you* are feeding children to the Slink."

Krill's brain spun, and it became hard to focus on one thought, something foreign to the Wakened human. "But, even my toddy gang leaders are disappearing. Why would..."

"They're all meat, you fool! Just meat. Their lives are only to serve *my* needs. And we need more Slink, more death. Two birds with one stone, you fool." Krill stood in stunned silence as Bhellum and his devilish guardian watched him squirm. "You never struck me as the weak-willed type, Viktor. He appears weak, does he not, my pets?"

"Very weak," the twin heads said in unison.

"I will put an end to this practice, right now," said Krill, nausea making his proclamation sound toothless.

"You will do no such thing, Viktor. You work for *me*. I have given you everything, and I can take it away with a word. With a command, I can have the Mech Force raze your precious Rising to the ground. You will be stripped of your position at Cyrix. I will take everything that you have worked so diligently to collect. I have nothing left to lose, so please do not try my patience, or my resolve." A heavy silence fell over the massive room as Krill's storming emotions prevented him from forming an appropriate comeback. Out of the quiet, Bhellum issued a raspy laugh. "I'll take your silence for agreement, Viktor. No more delays, and no mistakes. I don't have time for either, so neither do you. You are dismissed." Krill remained frozen. "Which means get the fuck out of my office, you fool!"

As Morgan and Morgin shared in a giggle, Krill turned on his heel and walked back towards the golden double doors, only capable of following simple commands as a tornado of emotions tore through him. Only when the office doors closed silently behind him did Viktor Krill finally exhale, desperate to remove the diseased air from his lungs.

Walking down the long corridor that led away from Bhellum's chambers, a grotesque understanding assaulted Krill, one that he was unprepared to embrace.

In this world, Viktor Krill was only one of many monsters, and they were willing to escalate things to places even the Rising leader dared not tread.

———

It was Morgan who finally spoke once Krill had exited the room. "This is not the same killer who strode into your office so confidently not that long ago, my master."

Bhellum sighed deeply, a sickly sound emanating from his chest. "I know, my pets. But I still have need of his services, despite this new, softer side. What have you learned in your observations of the man?"

Morgin answered. "He has been spending significant time with Mayfly Lemaire, the boy Darrin, and the girl Natthi. They visit regularly."

"And he weakens at every visit?"

"It appears that way, my master," responded Morgan.

Bhellum thought for a moment, then looked up at his mechanized caretaker. "You know, my Uncle Tedd wanted nothing to do with the family business, decided to take his small share of the family's money and open a fur farm. The dainty man so loved his furs. I visited his massive farm as a boy one summer. While there, Uncle Tedd showed me how some animals were smarter than the others, how they showed their dumber companions ways to escape, taught them to grow angry at their captivity. When these *smart* animals were identified, they were immediately removed from the others to have their throats cuts, regardless of size or age."

"What would you have us do, my master," the twin voices sang out.

"I need Viktor Krill the way I found him, an emotionless killer who will stop at nothing to get the job done. Perhaps someone needs their throat cut before he is taught too much, before he feels too much." Bhellum looked to the golden doors, as if he could see Krill still standing defiantly on the other side. "Bring me you-know-who. It is time that we help Viktor Krill shed the excess baggage of emotion. And remind him of who is still in charge."

Morgan and Morgin turned to each other, their synthetic noses almost touching, and shared in a grim smile. They loved when their master gave out lessons, especially those that ended in blood.

22

Marlin Hadder, Albany Rott, Tennian Stamp, Acid Boy Gash, and Gayle stood atop Brizo Tower, the cold night breeze drifting in off the ocean to chill even Rott's more-than-human skin. The Neon City of Bhellum sprawled out beneath them, all the colors of the spectrum dancing and mingling across the expanse of sunless dark.

Despite the beauty of the scene below them, all eyes, crimson and orange, vibrating and still, were focused on a singular place — the Cyrix Industries Headquarters building. It, too, was bathed in soft neon light, with a giant rotating C slowly above the tower, a crown waiting to be knocked from a dead ruler's head.

"Are we all clear on the plan," asked Hadder, pre-battles jitters finally making their long-awaited appearance.

"Shit, what's not to get? Not like it's some elaborate strategy," replied Old Tens as the auto-turrets on his mechanical legs moved in and out of their docking slots, the only thing betraying the gang leader's confident tone.

"Simple is better, especially with all these moving parts," said Rott, who seemed surprisingly anxious, especially for one who had lived through the millennia.

"Then w-w-we are d-done here for n-n-now. I d-do not enjoy b-b-being surrounded b-by so many humans."

"How long does your brother need, Gayle," asked Old Tens.

Gayle absently rubbed the dead gray skin on her arms for a moment before responding. "He tends to move at his own speed, but I have conveyed the urgent nature of our request. I would say three days to be safe. Once he is closer, we will be able to communicate more complex ideas, and I can better gauge the exact timing."

"Very well. I need to prepare the Broken Tens. Three days is not a lot of preparation to topple an empire." Tennian's legs roared to life as the veteran made his way towards the rooftop elevator. He stopped midway, turning back towards his unique group of allies. "You all coming? Gash, I know you prefer to use the service elevator."

"Y-y-yes, I am c-coming. Th-thank you, Tens."

As Old Tens and Gash took long metal strides and tiny steps towards the service lift, Hadder, Rott, and Gayle remained where they were on the cold rooftop. Tennian turned to Gash. "You want us to wait for your girl?"

Gash chuckled. "If she w-w-was ready to c-come, she w-would come. D-do not worry, she is qu-qu-quite safe traveling alone."

Tennian simply shrugged, and the two old secret friends entered the lift and disappeared. In silence that followed, Hadder made his way toward the north side of Brizo Tower's rooftop, and stared out at the black sea that stretched out into infinity. After several quiet minutes, Hadder heard the unmistakable sounds of Gayle as she shuffled up next to him. Together, they looked into the beyond, both searching for something that was, as yet, not there.

"Are you sure he's coming, Gayle?"

"Alphus is not one to shirk his duties to his people."

"Then, why is he not here with you now?"

"Everyone must balance the needs of themselves with the needs of others. Alphus is no different."

"Do we really need him to win?"

"With him, we have a slight chance. Without him, all hope is lost."

"He's that good?"

"He's that necessary."

Another long silence. "Gayle, if you believe that we have a slight chance of success, even with Alphus, why join the fight? The Blisters are doing well, and will continue to thrive. Why not wait out this insanity?"

Gayle pondered the question for a moment, staring out into the dark ocean. "Humans tolerate us for now because they fear us. And because we don't have anything they want. Yet. The gears are turning behind the scenes. Things we Blisters don't understand are happening. Strange eyes are starting to turn towards the Muck." She giggled. "I'm sorry, I can't get used to this Rising name. It will always be the Muck to me. Anyway, my point is that the humans will not leave us alone forever. One day, they will come in unannounced, with their guns and their MCEs and their combat bots, and will eliminate us without a single tear shed. We understand this, all too well. If we are going to meet our end, we will rush toward it with gusto, not have it fall upon us while on our knees."

Tears began to roll from Hadder's hazel eyes. Gayle's small speech touched upon one he had given a world ago. It echoed Hadder's passionate words to his beloved Setters on the eve of the Great Battle. Hadder fought the urge to wipe the wetness from his cheeks, instead letting them form icy trails to remind him of the upcoming conflict's stakes.

For some reason, maybe her gentle eyes or mutated appearance, Hadder felt comfortable in being vulnerable around the Blister queen. "Gayle, what if he doesn't come?"

"Alphus?"

"Yes."

"Alphus will come, Marlin. Have faith."

Hadder nodded, attempted to shake off his worry. "Very well. I believe you, Gayle. Tell me, what does his ship look like? We'll station some Broken Tens up here to keep watch for his arrival."

Another sweet giggle. "Alphus does not travel by ship, Marlin."

Hadder's face twisted in confusion. "I don't understand."

"What you don't understand could fill a world, Marlin Hadder. Do not waste good men by having them stare out at a desolate sea. Don't worry, when Alphus nears, I will know." Despite Gayle's words, Hadder continued to look out into the darkness. As Gayle studied the strange human, one half of the Blister prophecy, she began to realize that maybe it was not just the looming battle that was worrying him. "I will leave you now, Marlin. Take care."

With that, Gayle leaned in and kissed Hadder on the cheek. Despite her rough grey skin, it was one of the softest touches that Hadder had ever known.

———————

HADDER DIDN'T KNOW how much time had passed as he stood on the rooftop's edge. Although his eyes were pointed toward the sea, Hadder was looking inward, and what he found within terrified him.

A light appeared out of nowhere and stole Hadder from his dark thoughts. He looked to his right to find that Albany Rott had joined him. His red-eyed companion lit two cigarettes, handing one to Hadder. They smoked in silence for a while before Rott spoke up.

"What's troubling you, Marlin? I've never seen you so distraught on the eve of battle. You tend to thrive in these situations."

Hadder took a long drag, exhaled smoke through his nose. "I'm scared, Al."

"Scared of dying?"

Hadder laughed bitterly. "I've forgotten how many times I've died, Al. I don't fear death anymore."

"Then you fear losing?"

"I fear winning."

"I don't understand."

Hadder took a second to calm himself. "My entire time in this reality has been for one purpose, to destroy Viktor Krill. If that is accomplished, what happens then? The Blisters will have their island in the middle of nowhere, the Broken Tens will take their rightful place as kings of the Rising, and you..."

"What about me, Marlin?"

"You'll return..." Hadder rose his eyes to the stars. "Up there. And I'll be here, alone. My wife and child still gone, no better than the day I entered Station's massive walls. All of this, and nothing has changed. Everyone I love gone, alone once again in a world that seems intent on removing the good-hearted and the innocent."

"You are *not* the same man who came to Station, Marlin. You are so much more."

"Am I, Al? I don't feel it."

Rott did not speak for a while, and Hadder thought that he sensed real discomfort in the almost-god. Finally, he responded. "You'll have much of my credits when I'm gone, Marlin. You can build your new life any way you wish."

"You mean start a new family?"

Another strange pause, as if Albany Rott, who always had the answers, was struggling to find the necessary words. "If you wish."

Hadder looked to Rott, whose ember eyes could be seen even in the night's blackness. "Tell me that everything's going to be ok, Al. Please."

Rott took another long drag of his cigarette before tossing the butt over the side of Brizo Tower with a shaky pale hand. He started to say something several times, but stopped each attempt before words came out. Finally, he simply clapped Hadder on the shoulder, an impersonal act that did not align with their close relationship.

"I'm sorry, Marlin," was all that Rott finally said before heading back toward the service lift, leaving Hadder again with his worries. Hadder finished his cigarette alone, surrounded only by his fears and the cold breeze attacking him from the sea. He looked around and, seeing himself abandoned completely, sighed heavily.

Hadder didn't want to admit it, but, even in possible victory, this loneliness was something he was going to have to make friends with in the near future.

THE SAME CRUEL winds that flashed above Brizo Tower struck Viktor Krill as he casually strolled through the Jungle late in the evening. His mind racing, Krill didn't event notice the icy touch on his scarred body. Slink fiends, each looking as if they had been dancing with death, tore out of the thick brush to score drug funds from an isolated victim. In turn, each recognized the notorious Viktor Krill, even through their drug-addled mind, offered a weak apology, and disappeared back into the Jungle overgrowth. There would be other victims who wouldn't separate their skull-like heads from their emaciated bodies.

Krill paid them no mind, supremely confident in his reputation and abilities.

What the Wakened human wasn't confident in, however, was the current state of his organization, and the recent costs of its immense growth.

Despite the late hour, toddy gangs still roamed the Jungle, ten and fifteen children deep, picking up Slink packages from dope tanks to distribute them across the Neon City and an ever-increasing portfolio of other metropolitan areas. As Krill came upon them, the toddies would snap to attention, lining up along one side of the path to give their leader a wide berth. The dirty faces smiled widely as Krill nodded to each in turn, their little hands up near their heads in tiny salutes, offering their respects to the man who had given many a chance beyond victim and street urchin.

By the time Krill passed the third such group, he no longer saw infantile strangers showing deference. He saw Darrin's round face on the head of one young boy. He spotted Natthi's soft eyes on a dirt-covered girl who was missing more than a few teeth. No matter where Krill looked, he was confronted by the judgmental looks of those he cared about most.

"It's late. Go home!" Krill roared, sending the diminutive gangsters scattering across the Jungle pathway, some offering weak *'yes, sirs'* as they ran. Krill sighed deeply as their little legs carried them away, not nearly fast enough to escape those who would bring them harm.

"Fuck this," Krill said to himself, a decision made. When he reached

Hydrus Tower, he would meet with Levi Lessons and put an end to the Slink Reapers' detestable new strategy.

And if they didn't like it, the Slink would enjoy a gigantic breakfast, courtesy of the man who introduced them to this world.

————

WHILE EVERY TOWER under Riser control was home to one or two Slink farms, Hydrus had become the epicenter of Slink cultivation, with several entire floors being remodeled and dedicated to the dark business. In their sprawling office on the top floor, the Slink Reapers had been gathered under Viktor Krill's late night command.

Levi Lessons stood at the head of a motley crew of Risers known as the Slink Reapers. Chosen for their strong stomachs and weak moral fiber, the Slink Reapers were among the most despicable individuals in Krill's enormous collective of killers, capable of doing the vile work that others could not, or would not, do. Krill had hoped that this would be a temporary job for most, a gross assignment necessary for quick advancement, similar to how Vaskez treated the duty. Unfortunately, looking into the eyes of these Reapers, he feared that many had grown to enjoy their work.

As Krill looked upon these creatures under his command, a tense silence fell over the large room. Levi Lessons shifted uneasily from one booted foot to the other, his trademark mohawk remaining untouched while his Dead Rogues head tattoo had been burned off with a torch, something Krill never demanded that he do.

"Is there a problem, boss? There must be a problem; it's the middle of the night. You need someone to disappear? You've come to the right place."

Laughter filled the room, but immediately stopped as Krill's black eyes stared daggers into every Reaper present. He let the silence hang heavy like a noose over their heads. "Why was I not informed of these new feeding practices?" Krill's voice was thick with anger.

Levi's worn face twisted in confusion. "New practices? You mean Operation Cronus?"

Krill's stomach turned. Even the plan's name was grotesque. "Yes, that is what I am referring to."

Levi's eyes swung around nervously as Krill's anger grew increasingly apparent. "You said you didn't want to be bothered with Slink affairs. That you had too much to do with Cyrix. You said that increased production was all that mattered."

Krill's own words repeated back to him hit harder than a blow from a Caesar. He took a moment to compose himself before continuing. "Is that why you chose to go over my head, and speak directly to Cyrus Bhellum? Some would call that treasonous, Levi." The hidden threat in Krill's words was glaringly apparent to all the gathered Reapers.

Despite Krill's dangerous warning, a ghost of a smile formed on Levi's smug face. "But I didn't, *First* Krill. Mister Bhellum called *me* in; wanted ideas on how to increase production." A dismissive shrug. "So, I shared my discovery."

"You mean your discovery of feeding children to the Slink?"

Levi didn't blink. "That's right. The numbers speak for themselves. It's a no-brainer."

Krill took a deep breath to calm himself. "No, Levi, you're the no-brainer. It ends. Now."

Another confused look. "What? Operation Cronus?"

"Yes."

"I don't think so, sir. My orders came directly from Mister Bhellum. I don't think..."

Levi's words were cut off abruptly as Krill moved faster than lightning, one tan hand appearing around the gangster's throat, as if by magic. "Is Cyrus Bhellum the First of the Risers, Levi?" The Reaper leader attempted to respond, but could not as Krill's rage forced his grip to tighten around the man's neck. Levi's face turned red, then purple, as Krill's dark eyes narrowed. Just as Levi's neck was about to snap under the force, Krill released him, dropping the man to the floor, where he gasped for air through a bruised windpipe. "I'll ask you again. Who is the First of the Risers, Levi?"

Almost a minute passed before Levi could form words. "You are, sir," he said, finally croaking out the syllables.

Krill looked over the fallen man to the collected Slink Reapers. "Operation Cronus ends now! Do you understand me?!"

Without missing a beat, the Reapers answered with a resounding, "Yes, sir," before looking to each other anxiously.

"Any man caught defying my order will be next on the Slink's menu." A swift kick sent Levi spiraling into the other Reapers. "And if you ever go over my head again, Levi, I'll eat your lungs while you still live." With that, Krill spun on his high tops and exited the office, leaving the group of vile killers on edge.

Eventually, Levi Lessons rose uneasily to his feet, now nursing broken ribs alongside his damaged throat. Despite his injuries, Levi looked to his men and managed a smile. His voice came out broken, but coherent. "Looks like Viktor Krill finally learned who's the real head of the Risers." The room filled with laughter once more. "Nothing stops. Business as usual, boys. I'll take care of this."

THE NEXT DAY, back in the small grassy area behind Thoosa Tower, Viktor Krill sparred against Natthi and young Darrin as Noora looked on, her pink eyes hidden behind thick black shades. While Darrin fought with patience and intelligence, Natthi used instinct and rage, her tiny fists and feet always aiming for Krill's crotch, just as he had taught her.

The children spread apart, forcing Krill to focus on one at a time, and attacked in synchronized tandem when an opportunity presented itself. Although neither could land a significant blow on the Wakened human, their skills had improved immensely since Krill's lessons had begun.

With too much on his mind, Krill had trouble concentrating, and decided to cut the lesson short. He faked right, causing Darrin to flinch while drawing Natthi in, before cutting left to scoop up the attacking girl and tossing her gently into the recovering toddy gang leader. As any good brother would, Darrin caught the girl in his arms, and both fell to the soft ground, laughing in defeat.

Krill caught himself laughing with them, and stopped abruptly. He moved to the edge of the clearing, and fell into a lawn chair that had been set up by Noora, who was standing nearby. "Good work," he called to the children. "Now let's see those fighting stances. One hour, at least." The children groaned, but did not argue, instead falling into poses that would strengthen their muscles and toughen their minds.

Krill smiled inwardly as he watched Natthi and Darrin flow from one movement to another, both already technically superior to most Risers far beyond their ages. He closed his eyes as the sun shined warmth onto his tan face, still appreciative from the extended time he spent without its rays.

The wind then shifted directions, no longer coming off the ocean, but rolling in from the Neon City. Krill breathed in deeply, his Wakened senses taking in the multitude of smells that were carried on the soft breeze. The aromas of hundreds of chowsets melded with the exhaust of countless machines to create a wholly comforting mix. This sat in stark contrast to the odor of...

Viktor Krill's black eyes sprung open as his back went rigid. He inhaled once more, tossing aside the smells of food and dirty bodies and smoke and fuel, focusing all of his attention on one particular odor, one that stood out among the others like a human at a Blister party. It tugged at his memory, demanding recognition. It was a smell that he would never forget, one that had been literally implanted into his DNA, as much a part of him as his long-forgotten mother and father. Viktor Krill rose to his feet, his heart racing, and forced himself to believe that which his senses already told him was true.

Someone from Station was here. And Viktor Krill feared he knew exactly who that someone was. "What do want from me," Krill asked no one in particular. "You couldn't just leave me alone, could you, you devil?"

"Did you say something, Mister Krill?"

Krill looked over to see Noora studying him through her dark lenses. "Watch the children."

"Is there a problem?"

"I don't know yet. But I think, yes. A major one." He pointed to Natthi and Darrin. "I want an hour of practice from those two."

As always, Noora knew when it was her place to question or remain silent. "It will be done, sir," said the Bitch-Whore Second.

Krill nodded in gratitude, and began to walk towards the West. A small voice called to him from behind.

"Mister Viktor! Mister Viktor!"

Krill turned to see Natthi running towards him. He knelt to get down to her level as she closed the distance between them. She slid to a stop a few feet away. "Where are you going?"

"You're not supposed to break your pose reverie, young lady."

"Poses, schmoses. Where are you going? Our lessons aren't over."

"I have something important to attend to, dear girl."

"Something bad?"

Krill almost spoke the truth, but held back, not wanting to upset the child. "Something important. You finish your movements, now. Miss Noora is going to tell me how you did."

"Will I see you later?"

"Of course."

A broad white smile appeared on her dark face. "Ok, good."

"Goodbye, for now."

"Goodbye, Mister Krill." Krill began to rise, but before he could, Natthi buried him in a tiny hug, and whispered into his ear. "I love you."

Krill hugged her back and, before he had a chance to comprehend the weight of the situation, replied, "I love you, too." With that, Natthi planted a kiss on Krill's dark cheek, and ran back to join her brother in their exercises.

His head spinning, Krill shot up straight, and turned back toward the West, wiping a single tear from his eye as he did, desperately hoping that Noora didn't notice. But deep down, Viktor Krill knew better. Although Noora's albino eyes were poor, they saw everything.

Which is why he could feel the weight of her smile upon his back as he walked away.

———

MORGAN AND MORGIN looked down upon the Rising from Bhellum's office suite, their twin sets of telescopic eyes zooming in to focus on a scene playing out far below.

"What do you think, Morgan?"

"I think it might be the perfect time, Morgin."

"Should we pull the trigger, Morgan?"

"Yes, let's, Morgin."

"Do you want to make the call, Morgan?"

"No, you do it, Morgin. You have much more patience with these lesser creatures."

"Thank you for the kind words, Morgan."

"Just speaking the truth, Morgin."

"Viktor Krill is going to be very upset, Morgan."

"I know. But he will have to get over that, Morgin."

"And what if he doesn't, Morgan? What if he does something drastic? What if he threatens Master, Morgan?"

"Then we will cut his heart from his chest, Morgin."

A long pause. "Then I hope he does something drastic, Morgan."

A soft laugh. "As do I, Morgin. Now, do you want to make the call?"

"Yes, it is time people learn what happens when you disobey Master."

"Oh, I'm so excited, Morgin. For the first time in a while."

"Save that energy, Morgan. We may need it very soon."

"Good call, Morgin. I'll run some diagnostics to make sure we are tip-top."

"You're the best, Morgan."

"No, you're the best, Morgin."

23

It took Viktor Krill longer than usual to make his way to the Cyrix Headquarters building. Usually, he strolled through the Rising without a care in the world, unable to comprehend a threat that could cause him real harm. But today, Krill found himself carefully peering around every corner, jumping at every Jungle Junkie who stumbled into his path.

For today, there was a new breed of monster in the Rising. And this one wouldn't flinch before the notorious Viktor Krill, or his Wakened abilities.

Eventually, Krill found himself approaching the Cyrix building. As always, the building seemed sparsely guarded, with only a handful of Cyrix security forces stationed on the bottom floor for visitor check-in.

Krill, however, knew that these looks were deceiving.

Krill walked past security without pause, not even acknowledging the multiple salutes he was given as he passed. Executing a retinal scan, he was granted entry into the Executive Lift, and was soon on his way to the top floor of the Headquarters.

When the elevator doors finally slid open, Krill was greeted by one of Cyrus Bhellum's Spirit Girls, the same synthetic who welcomed him during his first visit to Cyrix.

"Good afternoon, Viktor Krill. What a pleasant surprise. I assume you are here..."

"What's your name, Spirit Girl?"

"They call me Nadea, Viktor Krill."

"Ok. I need you to shut up, Nadea. I have urgent business with Bhellum."

The Spirit Girl shuffled out of the way. "As you wish, Viktor Krill."

Krill walked briskly down the never-ending hallway, his thoughts spinning as he tried to find the words to accurately explain this new danger to Bhellum. A few minutes later, Krill pushed open the large golden double doors without knocking, and entered the lair of Cyrus Bhellum V. He quickly spotted both Bhellum and Morgan/Morgin in the back of the cavernous office, the former in his wheelchair, and the latter calmly peeling an apple with a knife, both calmly facing him.

As if they knew he was coming.

Krill strode past the various monitors and giant conference table, and stopped twenty feet from the strange pair. Now that he knew what Morgan/Morgin was, he wasn't about to take any chances. Krill discarded all pleasantries.

"Bhellum, we have a problem. A serious one."

Bhellum's response caught Krill off-guard. "I agree. Don't you, my pets?"

Morgan and Morgin answered in unison. "Yes, a serious problem, Master."

Krill shook off the strange reply. "We have an intruder in the Rising. An enemy beyond comprehension. I'm going to need control of the Mech Force to..."

Bhellum cut in. "Denied."

Krill's tan brow furrowed. "You don't understand the nature of this..."

"No!" Bhellum's anger put Krill on his back foot, forced him to raise his defenses. "There *is* a serious problem going on in the Rising, Viktor, and it has *nothing* to do with our new visitor, whom I'm sure you can handle on your own."

Krill took a deep breath to calm himself. Although he had no idea of the "problem" of which Bhellum was speaking, Krill didn't have time to find out.

Time was of the essence. "Look, Bhellum, this isn't just some gangster who has come into the Rising. It's not some high-level executive. It's a king, like you, and he's here to..."

Bhellum began to laugh in his wheelchair, a wheezing, sickly sound that betrayed the man's confident bluster. When he had finally caught his breath, Bhellum spoke. "I'm sorry, did you just call me a king, Viktor?"

"I did."

"Why?"

Another moment of confusion. "Because that's what you are."

"Really?"

Krill began to grow anxious. "Yes, of course. Look around at all that belongs to you. If this isn't the definition of a king, then I don't know what is."

Bhellum looked up to Morgan/Morgin, and they shared a smile. Krill felt like a child preparing for a magician's big reveal. One that would scare the shit out of him.

Bhellum returned his eyes to Krill. "If I am a king, as you have so clearly stated, Viktor, then why do you go out of your way to disobey me? Why do you spit in my face? Have I not been good to you, Viktor? Have I not made you a... lesser king in your own right?"

Krill's heart began to race. "You have."

"Then why did you try to put an end to Operation Cronus?"

And there it was, the great reveal of betrayal. "We don't have time for this, Bhellum. You don't understand the magnitude of the situation."

Another wheezing laugh. "No, Viktor. It is *you* who does not understand the magnitude of the situation." Morgan and Morgin smiled in turn, twin vipers ready to strike.

Krill's hands began to shake, the first time that had happened since his awakening. "What is going on, Bhellum?"

Crooked, yellowed teeth appeared beneath fat folds of flesh. "I took an interest in you, Viktor, because you were ruthless. You slaughtered your way to the top. And I respected that. The perfect mix of brains, brawn, and steely resolve. I'm afraid one of those things has gone by the wayside."

Krill had a hard time forming the words that came out of his mouth. "What have you done, Bhellum?"

Cyrus Bhellum V went on, as if he couldn't hear Krill's desperate words. "I asked you to do one simple thing, Viktor. And you were unable to perform your duties. My initial reaction was to have you eliminated, but that would have been such a waste. Like tossing away a perfectly good Taragoshi model because one of her eyes was a little uneven."

"What have you done, Bhellum?"

Bhellum continued, as if Krill's words had been lost in transmission. "So, my next thought was to discover why my favorite killer had grown soft, unable to perform his duties."

"Bhellum?"

"And what do I discover? I find that the notorious Viktor Krill, feared across the Five Thieves, has fashioned himself some sort of makeshift family, one that is draining him of his resolve, and weakening his once-iron stomach."

An uncomfortable mix of panic and rage coursed through Krill. "What have you done, Bhellum?!"

"So, I say to myself, what can we do for poor Viktor to show him that family is a weakness? Friends are a weakness. There is only victory, or loss. Life, or death. Giving orders, or taking them."

Krill's voice grew quiet. "Bhellum, tell me what you've done."

"Me? I've done nothing. Wait, that's not entirely true. I've done you a favor by removing the one area that was an open vulnerability in the otherwise ironclad Viktor Krill."

Control was now completely lost. "What have you done, you vile old man?!"

"Nothing! I have done nothing! It is *you* who have committed a crime most foul. *You* are the one who defied *me*! The blood is on *your* hands, not *mine*."

"What blood? What is happening?!"

Bhellum's dark smile disappeared under his blotchy skin, replaced by a look that could almost be described as pity. "Tell him, my pets."

Morgan and Morgin put the peeled apple down on the Bhellum's personal desk, but kept the knife at the ready. The head on Krill's right, Morgin, spoke. "Your Natthi is dead."

Krill spoke in a whisper. "No."

Morgan took up the conversation. "Yes. She was picked up by Levi Lessons soon after you left her. She'll be in the belly of a Slink any moment now."

For the first time since he was a child, Viktor Krill was frozen with fear, unable to speak, or move, or think. He only managed a weak, "No."

Morgin spoke again. "It's for the best, Viktor. There will be sadness, no doubt, but soon you will realize the necessity of our actions. When you are once again free of the chains of family, you will be like yourself once more."

Viktor Krill's Wakened mind reeled, shaken to its core. As understanding began to set in, he felt torn between beating Bhellum to death with Morgin's arm, and rushing to save his daughter.

Bhellum's words reached Krill's ears, but they sounded far away, as if from another reality. "Look, Viktor, I know you are upset. But this really is best for business. Soon, you'll look back on this and understand..."

Krill never heard the rest of Bhellum's empty attempt to calm him. The Wakened human disappeared in a flash, leaving a streak of color across the boardroom that ended in the sound of glass shattering, and a hole in one of the oversized windows that dominated the righthand wall.

Bhellum, Morgan, and Morgin stared at the large opening that was now allowing a cold, hard wind into the office suite. Bhellum was the first to speak after the unforeseen turn of events. "I thought those windows were supposed to be bulletproof."

Morgan and Morgin answered in unison. "They *are* bulletproof, Master."

"Then it seems that our Viktor Krill might be more formidable than we ever imagined. If he comes back hat in hand, we will welcome him with open arms."

"And if he comes back a naughty boy," asked Morgan.

"Then you will use those wondrous arms of yours to carve him up, my pets."

"Oh, I do hope he comes back naughty, Morgan."

"So do I, Morgin. So do I."

———

THE COLD AIR threatened to freeze Krill's tears to his cheeks as he fell from the top floor of the Cyrix tower. Part of him hoped that he would continue to plummet to his death, stopping this horror movie before the terrifying ending could be reached.

Unfortunately, just as they had on a previous occasion, Krill's Verrato high-tops, a gift from his adopted son, sensed the fall and kicked in, slowing him just as he was about to crash to the earth.

Krill landed with a hard thud, but nothing broken. Without a thought, he took off across the Rising, leaving only a smear of color to mark his passing. As Krill ran, his legs pumping faster than they ever had, pushing the limits of his Wakened abilities, one thought dominated his mind.

He had time. He had time.

He had to have time.

Please, God, let him have time.

———

As KRILL rapidly approached the small, grassy area behind Thoosa Tower, the site of so many wonderful memories, his Wakened eyes clearly saw that young Darrin was still practicing his fight maneuvers while Noora looked on. But there was no Natthi to be seen.

There was no fucking Natthi to be seen.

Viktor Krill's sudden stop forced him into a long slide into the grassy area, startling both Darrin and Noora.

The young albino woman was the first to find her voice. "Mister Krill, you frightened me. What is…"

"Where's Natthi," asked Krill, his voice thick with restrained panic.

Confusion crossed Noora's face before transitioning into concern. "Levi Lessons came and picked her up." A slight pause. "As you commanded. Right?"

The little control Krill had over his panic was lost. "Where did he take her?"

Noora began to stumble over her words, the realization of a horrible mistake finally settling in. "He, he said he was bringing Natthi to meet you. That, that your meeting would be a short one, and you had something else to show her. Part of her lessons. I…"

"Where did he take her, woman?!"

"They were walking towards Hydrus Tower the last I saw. Oh my god, Mister Krill, what is…"

Krill pointed at young Darrin, who had ceased his lessons and was now frozen in fear. "You get him into Thoosa with Mayfly. Lock the doors. Let no one in! Now!"

"But I…"

Krill morphed into a blur once more as he sped toward Hydrus, passing open-mouthed Risers on his way. He slowed as he reached the tower's entrance, but only so the guards could recognize him and let him through.

"Levi Lessons come this way," Krill asked the nearest guard.

"Yes, sir. Said he was bringing the girl to meet you later. Seemed a bit strange, but I'm just a grunt. What do I know?"

Krill spoke no more to the low-ranking Riser, and fought the urge to tear out the young man's throat out of desperation. Instead, he raced up the tower steps and through the main entrance that was opened for him. He sped toward the tower lift, ignoring the Riser salutes and bows offered to him. When he reached the lift, he saw that there were two guards stationed there.

They jumped at the appearance of their supreme commander, and snapped nervous salutes. "Sir!"

"Levi Lessons. What floor?"

The seriousness of Krill's tone froze one young guard. The other eventually found his voice. "The lift stopped on seven, sir."

Once again, Krill stamped down the urge to murder the two junior Risers. The *ding* of the elevator tore him from his dark impulses, and sent him into the lift. When the doors shut behind him, leaving Krill with his dread, the Wakened human had never felt so alone. The ride up to the seventh floor took an awful eternity, the kind that Viktor Krill was sure awaited him were he to finally die a real death.

Krill's Wakened muscles coiled as the lift crept toward its destination. He closed his eyes, breathed in deeply, and looked inward, attempting to control the chemicals being released into his bloodstream.

When he opened his black eyes again, just as the lift arrived at the seventh floor, Viktor Krill was a black slate, a killing machine.

Krill ripped the elevator doors apart before they could open on their own. Standing just outside the lift were two Slink Reapers, each with a Stutter in his hands, and a smug smile on his face. But, although the reputation of Viktor Krill was known throughout the Rising, many had failed to see the notorious killer's true abilities at work, had failed to believe the stories that they heard. Therefore, it was to be forgiven that the Slink Reaper guards thought they had an easy kill before them.

So, they had to learn the hard way.

Before their stupid smiles had even finished curling up, Krill was upon them, inside the range of their gun barrels, knives simply appearing in the Riser king's hands. One knife was plunged through the temple of the long-haired Reaper to Krill's left, while his dark-skinned partner magically found himself on the floor with the notorious killer atop him.

The knife danced before the Reaper's wide eyes. When Krill spoke, there was a terrifying disconnect in the man's cold words. "Levi Lessons. Where did he take her?"

"Fuck you."

Wrong answer. With an expert flick of his wrist, Krill plucked out the Reaper's eye with his knife. Ignoring the man's screams, he then took the eye, nerve endings still attached, and shoved it into the man's open mouth. "There's still one more, Reaper. Where did Levi take my girl?"

The Reaper guard tried to form words around the eyeball. "Den Three! Den Three!"

Krill got up, drawing his blade across the Reaper's throat as he did, and rushed towards Den Three, which was down the hall and to the right. He passed one other Reaper on his hurried journey, whose throat was promptly ripped from his neck.

When Krill arrived at Den Three's security door, he discovered that Levi had somehow removed Krill's access to the room. For a normal human, this would have been the end of the road. But like so many others, Levi Lessons had underestimated the powers of a truly Wakened human, especially one as enraged as Viktor Krill.

Half a dozen insanely powerful front kicks was all it took for the security door to be torn from its concrete frame, and sent flying into the Slink den. Viktor Krill's cold, emotionless demeanor was immediately shattered when the image before him finally registered.

Natthi, bound at the ankles with her hands tied behind her back, stood on the edge of the Slink pool, much as Gideon Moon had not so long ago. "Daddy," cried out the girl, tears streaming down her small, brown face.

Relief flooded Krill, threatening to take him off his feet. "I'm here, sweet girl. I'm going to..."

A blade flashed before Krill, driving toward his tan face. Only Krill's unnatural reactions saved him as he turned his head at the final moment, taking a nasty slice across his cheek.

Krill ignored the pain that followed the cut, and caught the wrist holding the knife. Levi Lesson's gleeful smirk quickly turned into a look of horror as Krill's black eyes met his own. That look of horror twisted into a yelp as Krill snapped the traitor's wrist and sent the Slink Reaper to the sticky floor.

Levi spoke through panicked breaths. "J-just did as I was t-t-told. N-not my c-call. Truly."

Krill was unable to hear the man's whimpers through his anger. Instead, he neatly sliced both of Levi's Achilles tendons before slamming a knife through the Reaper's left hand, and deep into the concrete floor, trapping the treacherous Riser. Krill took a second to assess Levi, spotting scratches across his face and bruises along his neck and arms. *That's my girl*, thought Krill.

Threat neutralized, Krill turned back to Natthi to reassure the young girl, but found his words trapped in this throat as a terrifying image assaulted him.

Behind his quivering daughter, risen from the pool's brown sludge like a demon, was the largest adult Slink Krill had ever seen. It swayed gently behind its prey, as if relishing this dark moment.

"Noooooo," screamed Krill, the words torn from the deepest part of his soul, as the Slink struck like lightning, consuming Natthi in one awful bite before falling back into the muck with a sickening sound.

Krill did not hesitate, racing towards the pool's edge, a new knife in each hand. He dove in without a second thought, slipping beneath the dark slime to slam heavily into the monstrous Slink. Krill stabbed out with his knives, carving deep fissures into rubbery skin. After several blows, the Slink turned to the offensive, its razor-like teeth cutting into the Wakened human, tearing apart flesh as it attempted to consume a second victim.

Krill's rage sent him into a frenzy, removing all feeling except that of unthinkable loss. His arms became pistons, repeatedly slamming blades into the Slink's soft skin. He bit out where the Slink had sunk its fangs into his chest and neck, removing chunks of vile flesh.

Other, smaller Slink joined the battle, attacking Krill from behind, slicing up the Wakened human from shoulder to ankle.

Krill ignored them and fought on in a blind rage. When he lost one of his knives, he used his hand, thrusting it into the Slink's body and tearing apart anything he found inside.

After what seemed like an eternity of struggle, the large Slink finally ceased it movements, and the two smaller Slinks abandoned the fight. Krill, using what was left of his breath, swam the Slink corpse to the surface, and flopped it over the edge of the pool.

Taking no time to catch his breath, or clear his eyes, which were burning from the thick sludge, Krill pulled himself from the tub of grossness and dragged the Slink away from the pool.

"Please, please, please," Krill said repeatedly as he took his lone remaining knife and carefully ran it along the Slink's underbelly. As Krill completed his cut, a mass of mess poured forth from the cut, including bones, gore, and the muddy outline of a child.

Krill's hands burned as the Slink's powerful stomach acid began to eat through his skin. He paid the pain no mind, frantically wiping the slime off the young girl's face, arms, and legs.

Eventually, his Natthi finally came into view, her soft skin eaten away by the Slink's harsh insides. In many places, the acid had eaten through to the bone. Gone were the girl's sweet eyes, replaced by empty sockets that sent an icicle through Viktor Krill's heart.

"Natthi! Natthi! I'm here, sweet girl! Can you hear me?!"

"Daddy?"

Krill laughed desperately through the tears that poured down his face, and the bile that had risen in his throat. "Yes! I'm here, sweet girl. You're safe now. I promise, you're safe."

"Why can't I see, Daddy?"

Krill fought to find the words. "You just have some gunk in your eyes, darling."

"Ok, Daddy. I'm tired."

"Go to sleep, sweet girl. It's ok. It's ok. It's ok."

And go to sleep Natthi did, her small head lulling to the side in death, held by the first adult that ever cared for her. The only father the young girl ever knew.

Viktor Krill let out a primal scream, one that shook the pillars of Hydrus Tower, and put the Rising on notice that something especially dark had formed in the shape of a man.

Krill cradled the small body, rose, and made his way toward the opening of the Slink den. He stopped just before the hole in the wall, remembered something, and turned back, his black eyes finding the trapped Levi Lessons.

"No, no, no! Viktor! Mister Krill! Please! Just doing as I was told!" Levi began to cry, a pitiful sound made more offensive by the man's grotesque soul.

As Krill approached Levi Lessons, he carefully shifted the body of his daughter to one shoulder. He then reached down with his left hand, caressing the condemned traitor's tear-soaked face. "Poor Levi. I forgive you."

"You do?"

"Yes, but Natthi does not." And with that, Krill plunged his hand into Levi's abdomen, coming out with a handful of intestines. While Levi's face twisted in a silent mask of pain, Krill's remained unchanged, as if a human no longer inhabited his Wakened body.

Krill calmly tied the intestines around his belt and slowly exited the Slink den, leaving Levi Lessons to gape in horror as his insides unraveled before him. As Levi Lessons slowly, painfully died, Slinks began to slither towards him, hungry for another meal.

Natthi once again cradled in his arms, Viktor Krill stepped into the hallway of Hydrus Tower, where a crowd of Risers had gathered. To a man, eyes dropped as Krill stepped forward covered in slime, and bleeding from dozens of deep gashes that appeared across his white suit. But it was not the blood that scared the men; rather, it was that it was no longer their First who stood before them, but something lesser, more frightening. A darkness made more terrifying through loss.

The Risers remained respectfully silent as Krill slowly made his way toward the lift, his dead daughter held close to his chest.

Levi Lessons' intestines following his every step.

"No! No! No!"

The heartbreak in Mayfly Lemaire's screams carved holes in Viktor Krill's damaged chest as he was forced to relive Natthi's death.

Krill had placed the young girl on the desk of Lemaire's office, where young Darrin and Noora had holed up per Krill's command. As Lemaire wept over the small corpse, Krill looked over to Darrin, who sat quietly on the leather couch, knees pulled up to his chin. Although the boy had seen his undue share of death, this was different. For the first time, young Darrin was experiencing the loss of family, the parting of a little sister. And his young mind was unable to process it.

Mayfly Lemaire was also struggling. After nearly ten minutes of open weeping, her own defensive mechanisms kicked in, brought on by a lifetime of pain and hardship. Lemaire looked up, rage in her amber eyes, and sought a target for her pain. Noora stood against the wall, her pink eyes studying the marbled floor at her feet.

"You! You foolish idiot of a girl! You did this! You!" Lemaire sprung at Noora, and accosted the young albino with desperate, open-handed slaps. Noora, lost in her own grief and guilt, sank to the floor, accepting the blows.

After almost a minute, Krill spoke up. "Mayfly. Mayfly. Mayfly!" The Bitch-Whore queen looked up, anger still present in her eyes. "It isn't Noora's fault."

"Then whose fault is it, Viktor? Yours?"

"Yes."

Lemaire wasted no time in shifting her violent attention toward Krill. She ran at the Riser king, raining fists down upon him. Like Noora, Krill accepted the hits. Although he could tell that his skin was bruising and his face was swelling, he felt nothing. Soon, Lemaire's yells and grunts became deep, heaving sobs as she collapsed into the notorious killer's arms.

"I'm so sorry," was all that Krill could say, empty words for a grieving mother.

"Who did this," asked Lemaire into Krill's blood-soaked chest.

"Bhellum. Cyrus Bhellum."

Lemaire's sobs stopped almost immediately as a target of her rage came into focus. "Then he needs to die."

"He does."

"I want to be the one to do it."

"No. He is protected by something you don't understand. I will do it."

Lemaire's water-filled eyes looked up to Krill in desperation. "I *need* vengeance, Viktor."

"And you shall have it. Everyone is in danger. Everyone. I need you stay here with young Darrin. You remember Darrin, don't you? Our son, Darrin?"

Something snapped back into place for Mayfly Lemaire, a reminder of other duties and responsibilities. She looked over to Darrin, who remained frozen on the couch. "Of course, I remember my dear Darrin. Come here, my boy."

As if he had been waiting an eternity to hear those words, Darrin jumped off the couch and into Mayfly Lemaire's strong arms. They held each other tightly, as if they were the only two souls in the universe.

Krill wanted to take comfort in their closeness, wanted to take solace in a family still together. But he could not. There was a hole inside him that could not be filled with love or devotion.

So, Viktor Krill decided to fill it with rage.

Krill turned to leave the grieving mother and brother huddled together in the office. As he neared the door, Lemaire's voice stopped him dead. Her words were ice, full of promised death.

"I need my vengeance, Viktor."

Krill did not turn back around. "I'll send Red Texx and Renny around soon, Mayfly. You'll have your revenge."

"Are you going to see Bhellum, Viktor?"

"I am."

Krill reached for the door, but was stopped again.

"Viktor!"

"Yes, Mayfly."

"He needs to suffer, Viktor. He needs to suffer like no one before him."

Viktor Krill finally turned back to face Mayfly Lemaire. His black eyes shone with a power she had never noticed before. "I promise. The brutality of his death will ring out across the ages."

Krill then exited the office, leaving Lemaire, Darrin, and Noora behind on a soggy carpet of tears.

"Do you believe him, Miss Lemaire? Will he be able to make Bhellum pay," asked Darrin into the Rising queen's chest.

"Yes, dear boy. And if he doesn't, I'll kill the bastard myself."

RISER, toddy gangster, Jungle junkie, Bitch-Whore, and chowset worker alike remained silent, and gave Krill a wide berth as he slowly made his way across the Rising. Anyone with a functioning sensory system could tell that it was not Viktor Krill who now walked among them.

It was the shadow of death.

Krill walked with this head down, moved at a deliberate pace. As he progressed toward the Cyrix Headquarters building, his mind turned inward, completing necessary tasks.

Krill dammed up the chemicals that accompany grief, compounds that could dull his senses, slow his reactions. He quarantined thoughts of Natthi, put them away for safekeeping, promised to revisit them many times at later dates. Krill barricaded all unnecessary emotions, anything that couldn't directly help him in this time of vengeance.

Leaving only focus and rage.

"HE'S ON HIS WAY BACK," said Morgan as she stared out the office window with her too-sharp eyes.

"How does he appear," asked Bhellum from his wheelchair between wheezing breaths, anxiety thick in his voice.

"What do you think, Morgin?"

"He looks like a broken man to me, Morgan."

"I would agree, Morgin. But could it be a hoax?"

"Humans cannot control their emotions so easily, especially after tragedy. It's just one of their infinite weaknesses, Morgan."

"So, you're saying he looks broken, my pets?" There was real desperation in Bhellum's words, proof that his condition was worsening by the day.

"I would say so. Morgin?"

"Yes, I would concur, Morgan."

Bhellum let out a visible sigh of relief, one that almost brought upon another coughing fit. "Good. He took his medicine like a man. Let us welcome him back. I will need him in the coming days."

"And then, my Master," asked Morgin.

"And then you can kill him."

Morgan and Morgin looked to each other and smiled, a demon admiring its reflection.

KRILL KNEW THAT HIS "DEFEATED MAN" ruse had worked when he was granted immediate access into Cyrix.

Or maybe Bhellum was simply confident that his Paladin was *that* good at killing.

As he had done a few short hours ago, hours that felt like a lifetime, Viktor Krill meditated as the Cyrix lift took him to the top floor, home of Cyrus Bhellum V's office suite. Krill controlled his breathing, slowed his heart rate, coiled his muscles, and became the harbinger of death.

When the large elevator doors finally slid open, Krill was once again greeted by the Spirit Girl known as Nadea.

"Mister Krill, another pleasant surprise. My master will be thrilled to see you."

Unfortunately, it was not really Viktor Krill to whom Nadea was speaking, but, rather, the shadow of death.

And it didn't have the same soft spot for Spirit Girls.

"Ahh, Viktor, it's so good to see you, again. Listen, I'm truly sorry how this all went down, but you needed a serious reality check, a jolt to the system. I know you're feeling down now, but in a few years, when you're relaxing on your very own tropical island, this will appear but a blip on your journey to greatness."

Viktor Krill didn't respond to Cyrus Bhellum V's words, remaining silent with his hands behind his back and his head down, a good underling taking his punishment like a man.

"Come now, Viktor, I can't bear to see you like this. You know what, let's have a conversation about your payout at the end of this crazy ride. In my experience, every dirty job is tolerable when there is a clearly defined prize waiting at the end. Tell me, what is it you really want, Viktor? Power and riches? That's a given. But what is it that your dark heart truly desires, Viktor? I can make it happen. I can make anything happen."

Viktor Krill finally raised his black eyes. When they met Bhellum's silver orbs, the Cyrix leader was forced to lean back in his wheelchair, so angry, focused, and purposeful was the look being shot his way. Instead of offering words in response, Krill simply tossed something towards Bhellum and Morgan/Morgin. The object landed heavily on the large conference table and rolled forward, stopping perfectly just before it was to fall off the far edge.

Bhellum let out a wheezing sigh of disappointment as he was greeted by Nadea's lifeless eyes staring out at him from within her decapitated head. "That was a two-million credit Taragoshi sex unit, you fool! Its synthetic vagina was worth more than that whore girl of yours!" Bhellum paused to calm himself. "And I had such high hopes for you, Viktor. Do you think this changes anything? Do you think I don't have a dozen contingency plans? Do you think I will even remember your name a year from now?"

Krill spoke, his voice cold and removed. "I know you won't remember my name in a year. Ten minutes from now, you won't know anything except pain."

"I don't take well to threats, Viktor."

"You asked me what I wanted, Bhellum."

"I did."

"I want to see your insides. I want to play with them, remove them one by one. I want to see your tears darken the blood stains that will soon cover your floor. I won't take any pleasure in it, but it will be done."

"Enough of this! Who are you to speak to me in this way?! You are no one! I am Cyrus Bhellum V! My family has gone through countless killers such as yourself. Congratulations, Viktor Krill, you will soon be erased from history. Kill him, my pets. And make it hurt."

Krill turned his attention from Bhellum to Morgan/Morgin, who were once again looking at him like a cornered mouse. With their too-white teeth showing, all they were missing were the viper's eyes. "Are you ready, demon bitch?"

"Oh, Morgan, did you hear what he called us?"

"I did, Morgin. That wasn't very nice."

"I think he needs to learn another lesson, Morgan."

"I agree, Morgin. Seems like feeding his baby to the Slink wasn't enough."

The Paladin's words were an obvious attempt to distract Krill, to drum up emotions that would confuse his senses, dull his movements, and usher in mistakes. Unfortunately, Krill had already isolated those feelings, insulating them from the rest of himself. At least for now.

Right now, there was only one feeling. A desire to kill.

"Talking is done, Paladin bitch."

"Oh, he won't engage in some harmless pre-fight banter, Morgin."

"What a shame, Morgan. But he always was a dullard, wasn't he?"

"Always, Morgin." To Krill, "Rules of engagement, dullard? Guns?"

A knife appeared in each of Krill's hands, as if by magic. He slowly shook his head, his long hair trailing behind to tickle his shoulders.

The Paladin heads spoke in unison. "Good boy." Morgan/Morgin then stepped forward, creating space between themselves and Bhellum, and began to subtly vibrate. Its hands doubled back, as if on hinges, and long blades slowly extended from the holes that were exposed. As if that wasn't off-putting enough, two more arms unfolded from the Paladin's sides, hidden until now. They, too, extended long blades from where hands should be, creating a wholly frightening creature.

Viktor Krill stared at the Paladin, Shiva in the synthetic flesh, and grinned. "I'm going to take your parts and make cleaning bots out of you. You'll be sucking up cum in VR porn theaters for the remainder of your existence. I want you to know that."

"Oh, he so has a way with words, Morgan."

"I *really* don't like him, Morgin."

"Then let's show him what happens to lowly humans we don't like, Morgan."

In unison, they spoke. "Come, Viktor Krill. Time to get carved up."

Krill moved as if he was shot from a canon. The Rising leader leapt onto the conference table and ran forward in a blur. As he neared the table's end, he kicked at Nadea's head, sending it flying towards the Paladin's chest like a bullet.

Although Cyrus Bhellum's human eyes could not make out what was happening, Morgan and Morgin had no such difficulties. Both right arms chopped at the head, cutting it neatly into four harmless pieces that flew to either side of the Paladin.

Their computations, however, did not account for the speed, or gall, of Viktor Krill, who soared in on the heels of the head. As the Paladin's right arms dispatched Nadea's head, Krill came in right behind, his left arm coming in over the top to cut a deep chasm into Morgan's face, while his right plunged a knife into the creature's chest.

Krill backed out just as quickly as he had entered, a testament to how fast Morgan and Morgin recovered. The foes took a moment to stare at each other, six eyes filled with nothing but death.

"He cut my face, Morgin."

"Yes, but you're still beautiful, Morgan."

"Thank you, Morgin. But now I really want to get even."

"That makes sense, Morgan. Let's cut his heart out. What do you think?"

"I think that's a wonderful idea, Morgin."

And with that, the unnatural adversaries engaged once more, six arms and six blades moving in a blur. The Paladin's four arms stabbed and slashed impossibly quick, in perfect harmony with each other, cutting unimaginable angles that should have been impossible to defend.

But Viktor Krill moved faster.

Outnumbered two to one in every way, Krill, for perhaps the first time, maximized his Wakened abilities, his mind seeing six moves ahead of even the Paladin's extreme processing power. Krill ducked, leaned, and pivoted, the Paladin's blades always narrowly missing the killing blow. He stabbed out where he could, scoring hits to Morgan/Morgin's chest, arms, and shoulders.

And still, the Paladin came on.

Bhellum's sick grin slowly morphed into a frown as he watched Viktor Krill move like a god, giving his beloved killing pets everything they could handle. Bhellum had heard the stories, had watched some video, but neither adequately revealed the speed, skill, and ferocity with which Krill could fight. Bhellum wasn't scared for his Paladin, but he was growing concerned.

On and on the warriors fought, working their way around the conference table and toward the front of the office suite. When it became apparent that Krill's various hits would not stop, nor even slow, the twin demons, the Rising king decided that he would have to take some more serious wounds to deliver those of his own.

Krill took a nasty slash on his left forearm, but cut a deep gully in Morgin's neck. He almost lost the pinky on his right hand, but buried his left knife into the Paladin's chest. Krill was taking damage, but he was dishing out even more. Eventually, he would land a substantial hit on the mechanized killers.

No one understood this better than Morgan and Morgin, who began to speak silently to each other.

He's good, Morgan.

Yes, he's very good, Morgin.

We're taking too much damage, Morgan.

I agree, Morgin. What should we do?

I think it's time we show this human what we can do, Morgan.

You mean break the rules of engagement, Morgin?

Do we have a choice, Morgan?

It appears we do not, Morgin.

Then melt him, Morgan.

Ok, Morgin.

Krill fell into a fighting rhythm unlike any he had experienced before. He saw all the Paladin's strikes before the creature could make them, and continued to score major damage on the demon mech. So engrossed was Krill in the fight, he almost didn't notice Morgan's mouth slowly opening, creating an outrageously large hole in the synthetic woman's head.

As Krill parried two blows with one swipe of his right blade, he finally took the millisecond needed to study the void that had appeared in Morgan's face.

And there the notorious killer saw his demise.

In the back of Morgan's throat, hidden to all but the most observant, Krill spotted the dull flicker of a pilot light.

Krill immediately dropped both knives and executed a double back hand-spring, just as a geyser of flames erupted from Morgan's open maw. Extreme heat attacked Krill's left side as he was consumed by the fire. Ignoring the pain, Krill continued to flip, eventually exiting the searing flames after three complete revolutions.

When Krill finally came to a stop, he heard the soft laughter of Morgin as her twin continued to shoot flames into the air next to her. "Sorry, Viktor Krill, but we can't let you win this one. Our programming overrides any gentlemanly rules of engagement. Now, come die, foolish man."

Krill looked down to see his entire left arm coated in angry bubbles from his burns. The side of Krill's white suit, his only prized possession from Station, had been melted into his skin, a testament to the power of Morgan's flamethrower mouth. But Krill locked away the pain, forced nerves to react to his will. He looked back up to Morgin, his black eyes showing no sign of surrender. "Wakened human."

"What did he say, Morgan?"

"I said, I'm not a man. I'm a Wakened human, you stupid bitch. The first in history across the realities. They make you twats on an assembly line."

"Oh, but I want to you to barbecue him, Morgan."

"Come get it, whore."

Both Krill and the Paladin waded forward, each now wary of the other's abilities. Spears of flame continued to shoot out from Morgan's too-open mouth, testing distances, as Krill moved lightly in and out. As Krill appeared weaponless, Morgin/Morgan grew bold, taking big swipes at the vulnerable human.

But anyone who truly knew Viktor Krill knew that he was never without a dozen blades hidden on his person, tucked into his belt, strapped under his shirt, and waiting in the pockets of his jacket.

Krill waded into the fray, accepting nasty wounds to each of his sides, and flicked both wrists just before diving back as another heat wave covered him and bubbled more skin. Through the flames, his knives flew at Morgan. One ticked harmlessly off Morgan's brow, but the other found purchase deep within the demon's left eye, exploding the synthetic orb found there.

"Oh, Morgan, your poor eye. We'll make him pay for that one." Morgin, unable to speak while in flamethrower mode, nodded her desperate agreement.

The Paladin flew into a rage.

On came the twin demons, all four arms spinning like tops as fiery lances led the way. Krill continued to spin and dodge, always retreating, never attacking. This went on for several minutes before Morgin spoke again. "Oh, it looks like he's out of those dirty little knives of his, Morgan. I think it's time to end this charade. Thanks for the practice, Viktor Krill. You've been a real peach. Cook him, Morgan."

Krill ducked low as the largest pillar of fire yet soared just over his head, singing his hair. As Krill came up, he retrieved a small blade from his right Verratto high-top, palming it like a magician, before diving once more onto the conference table.

As Krill rolled, rose, and ran along the table, he was chased by the fountain of fire. "You've got him, Morgan," screamed Morgin, showing emotion unnatural for a Paladin, exposing how much the twins truly wanted to see Viktor Krill burn.

Just as the flames had caught up to Krill, just as he could feel the cold heat on his back, the Riser king dove once more, snapping his right wrist behind and over his back as he did, sending the small blade soaring through the air. With the fire being used as cover, neither of the twins spotted the diminutive knife as it flew straight and scored a direct hit, exploding Morgan's remaining good eye and sending the head into a craze.

Unaware of what had just happened, Morgin called out in delight. "Burn him, Morgan," she cried as Krill landed on the marbled floor in a roll and kept running, circling around to the left of the Paladin.

Krill continued to move impossibly fast. As he came around to Morgin's side, he called out, doing his best impression of Cyrus Bhellum V. "Fire hard left, my pet! Now!"

The blinded Morgan, enraged and in pain, reacted immediately to what she thought was her master's command, releasing the full power of her flames.

Right into Morgin's shocked face.

The 4,000-degree fire slammed into Morgin, melting the synthetic flesh from her metallic skull and rupturing her telescopic eyes in their sockets.

Now completely sightless, the Paladin devolved into a fury of off-balance movements and blows that caught nothing but air. Morgan, her mouth normal once more, spoke first. "What happened, Morgin?"

"You burned me, Morgan. You burned me good. I can't see."

"I can't see either, Morgan."

"Keep fighting, Morgin."

"Ok, Morgan."

True to its word, the Paladin kept fighting, swinging wildly as it danced around the room, one blow almost taking the head from a petrified Cyrus Bhellum.

Viktor Krill kept his distance from the increasingly malfunctioning Paladin, relishing the moment. As the twin demons made their way around the room, Krill waited, understanding the perfect time to strike.

That moment came almost a minute later, when the Paladin finally circled the conference table and stood before the office suite's large bay windows, its four arms swinging in literal blind fury. Moving quietly across the room, Krill easily hefted one of the conference table's large chairs and closed the distance to the Paladin.

Clearly a novice to real battle, it was now that Cyrus Bhellum decided to call out to his failing guardian. "Paladin! Look out!"

The voice of their master cut through Morgan/Morgin's desperation, giving them pause, stopping the motion of their bladed arms for a second.

Just long enough for Viktor Krill to swing his chair like a Louisville Slugger, putting all of his hatred, grief, and rage behind the blow. It connected cleanly with the Paladin's chest, blasting the creature back and through the office window's bullet-proof glass, sending it hurtling towards the concrete below.

The sounds of shattering metal bounced up from the ground floor and into the office, riding on a cold wind that now swept through the office from two broken windows. Krill looked out and down to admire his handiwork, but was pulled back by the sounds of a wheelchair whirring to life.

Cyrus Bhellum V accelerated toward his secretive back room, but was stopped cold as another of Krill's cursed knives flew in to pierce the wheelchair's small engine. Bhellum tried to manually advance the wheels, but was spun unceremoniously around by his biggest fear.

Viktor Krill's unforgiving black eyes again stared deeply into Bhellum's tear-filled grey orbs. "Viktor! Viktor! Listen to me, listen to me." The fat pig-man spoke through panicked breaths. "It was just business, just business. Nothing personal, Viktor. We can get past this, we can, I tell you." Bhellum's eyes darted back and forth as he searched for a solution that didn't exist. "Half! You can have half of all Cyrix holdings! That would make you one of the richest men in the world, Viktor! You can't imagine the power that brings! You can buy anything with that kind of wealth! Anything!"

Viktor Krill began to shake, the viselike control over this emotions beginning to wane. "Anything, you say?"

"Yes! Yes! Anything!"

"Can it bring my daughter back, you fucking pig?"

A deep gulp was followed by a wheezing breath. "Well... no. But you can always make another. Viktor! I don't even know most of my kids' names, Viktor! You have the money now. You can make as large a family as you want, Viktor. Viktor!"

But Krill was no longer listening to the invalid in the chair. He spoke to himself. "So, you can't bring my daughter back. Then you'll have to give me the other thing that I want most."

"Yes! Yes! Anything! Name it!"

"I told you already. I want to see your insides."

At this, Cyrus Bhellum V, supreme leader of Cyrix Industries and bane of the Neon City, began to openly weep, tears and snot running down his fat, pink, blotchy face. "Please, Viktor," the man begged. "I don't want to die."

Viktor Krill leaned in, kissed the crying Bhellum on his oily head, and remembered the words he had spoken a lifetime ago, when he was a different man, a different Wakened human. "Poor, Bhellum. I'm not going to kill you. Not yet, anyway. You're just going to wish that I did. In fact, you're going to plead for it."

Bhellum shook with fear and released his bowels, filling the office suite with a sickening stench. Viktor Krill wanted to gloat over the pathetic man, wanted to smile in his terrified face as he carved him up.

But Viktor Krill reached down deep. And found that he had no more smiles left to offer.

24

Marlin Hadder watched in horror as carts piled high with the emaciated dead were pulled from the Jungle by Broken Tens members. Tennian Stamp looked on, as well, absently smoking a cigar that was now little more than a stub.

"Fucking hell, Tennian. So many bodies. So much death."

Old Tens adjusted one of the settings on his mechanical legs before responding. "You get used to it. To be honest, this is the fewest number of bodies we've pulled out in some time."

"Why is that, do you think?"

Old Tens looked at Hadder as if he had asked if fire was hot. "Because everyone's already dead. Because of this new Slink, the Jungle junkies are a dying breed. Literally. I would say two out of three are already deceased. If I were a betting man, which I am, I would say they're purposely killing off their original consumers." Tens motioned towards the Jungle. "I mean, look. The fucking Risers just leave the bodies lying around to rot, as if to say *get out and stay out*. If it wasn't for my boys, you'd be able to walk from one end of the Jungle to the other atop corpses."

If Hadder was confused before, he was now totally confounded. "I don't understand. Why would you let your best customers die off?"

"They're not *letting* them die, Hadder. They're *causing* them to die."

"But why?"

"Looks like Viktor Krill and, by proxy, Cyrus Bhellum V are trying to thin the herd here in the Muck. For what reason? Hell, Hadder, even I don't know that."

Hadder, full of questions, pressed on. "But such a strategy seems so counterintuitive. The whole point of a criminal enterprise is to maximize profits. And here they are, killing off demand."

Old Tens chuckled at Hadder's ignorance. "Oh, are they?"

"Aren't they?"

"Here? Yes. But you're being myopic. The world's much bigger than the Muck." Hadder respected Tennian's refusal to call his home by its new name. "And outside the Muck, the Slink business is booming. It's already made its way across the Neon City, and is now threatening to become the leading drug in half a dozen major cities. Deaths are up, yes. But profits are up, too, Hadder. And they will continue to climb, regardless of what happens here."

A silence fell as the two men watched a cart of bodies roll past. The Broken Tens manning the cart nodded to Tennian as they made their way to the large pit that had been dug in the eastern corner of the gang's controlled territory. There, the bodies would be dumped and burned, leaving nothing behind of the men and women who had perished because of Slink.

As the scent of burning flesh rode in on a shifting wind, Hadder decided to change the subject. "How are preparations coming on your end?"

"My boys are ready. We've been sleeping on the edge of a knife for long enough. We're ready to either rid our home of the pestilence that is Viktor Krill, or die trying. How about the Blisters?"

Hadder thought for a moment. "They're pretty upbeat for a group that's about to walk into a buzzsaw."

"That's because they think you and Rott are their messiahs. They think victory is preordained, regardless of how many of them die in the trying."

"And they do not fear death, Tens?"

"Not as much as they fear letting their people down. Not as much as they fear not fulfilling their destiny."

"And what is their destiny, Tens?"

Tennian Stamp looked coldly at Marlin Hadder before tossing what remained of his cigar to the cold ground and crushing it with a metal foot. "To get as far away from the trash that is humanity. To get as far away as possible from people like me and you." With that, Old Tens spun on noisy legs and began to head back to Brizo Tower. He spoke as he walked. "My boys will be ready. The Blisters were born ready. You better make sure you and your fellow messiah are ready. Otherwise, all is lost."

———

RED TEXX AND WESS DEY, two of the largest, most distinguished gangsters in the Rising, held each other for support as they entered the Cyrix Headquarters' office suite. The large room looked as if it was home to a battle between titans. Blood spotted the marble floor, carpets, and walls. Scorch marks covered the expansive conference table. Broken glass twinkled on the ground where it lay, the remnants of two shattered windows. And on the back wall...

Wess Dey turned his head, leaned down, and vomited into the wastebasket that had been placed beside the gold double doors. When the contents of his stomach had finally emptied, he rose, wiped his mouth with the back of his hand, and ran a palm over his yellow reverse mohawk. "Sorry, Texx. That's a first."

Red Texx didn't take his eyes from the far wall, couldn't tear himself from what he saw there. "It's ok, Wess. If I hadn't skipped lunch, I'd be right there with you."

"What the fuck happened here, man?"

"Looks like our leaders had a difference of opinion."

"That's putting it delicately."

Red Texx finally looked away, and studied the rest of the office suite. "This place could use a little delicacy right now."

Wess almost spoke again, anything to fill the horrific quiet, but shouting from behind a sealed door at the office's rear caused him to hold his tongue.

The words were muffled and indecipherable, but clearly Viktor Krill was back there, speaking loudly with another. Red Texx and Wess looked to each once more and shared a look, one that said, *this is why we don't gun for the top spot.*

Eventually, the arguing stopped, and all went silent again. Texx, refusing to look away from the rear door, said to Wess, "Remember, someone he loved just died." Texx's voice began to break. "Someone we all loved just died. If he's not himself, we must forgive him."

"Of course," responded Wess, as if this was already understood.

Minutes later, Viktor Krill limped out of the secretive room, nursing what looked to be a hundred wounds, including a left side that was rife with second and third-degree burns. Red Texx wouldn't have believed it if he hadn't seen it with his own eyes, but Krill's usually dark face was pale, as if he had just completed a meeting with a ghost. Or something worse.

To this credit, Wess Dey found his voice first. "Are you all right, First Krill?"

"No. No, I am not," replied Krill as he fell into the large leather chair that used to belong to another. He motioned weakly toward himself. "Come closer, my friends."

Texx and Wess shared another look before moving to the back of the office. Krill had never called either of them "friends" before. The men didn't know whether this change was a good thing, or an omen of terrors to come. As the two Riser leaders approached the desk, they did their best not to glance up at the wall above them and to the right.

Now it was Red Texx's turn to speak first. "Boss, we're so sorry about what happened to Natthi. She was..." His voice crackled with sadness. "A good girl. With a spirit unlike any other."

"Everyone liked her, First Krill," added Wess.

Krill looked back and forth between his two lieutenants, his black eyes void of their usual sparkle. "Not everyone, apparently." Texx and Wess shifted uncomfortably as more silence filled the room. "You need orders."

"Yes, sir," the two men answered in unison.

"The Slink Reapers... at least those that still live... I want them taken...

alive, if possible. Use as many men as you need. Take them to Mayfly Lemaire and follow her orders. A mother needs her vengeance."

"And you, boss," dared Red Texx.

Krill smiled weakly. "A father already has his."

The two Risers reflexively glimpsed to the back wall and swallowed down their rising bile. "Anything else, boss?"

Krill's voice sounded far away, as if he was still with his adopted daughter. "Yes. There's a fractured Paladin at the base of Cyrix Headquarters, just below that window." All three men turned their heads to stare at one of the two missing window panels. "Get your best robotics men..."

"Uhh, the Bitch-Whores are much better than anyone we have, First Krill," cut in Wess.

"Fine. Collect the Paladin pieces and take them to Noora. Tell her I want them recycled into cleaning bots, and then sold at the lowest sex shop she can find. And if she can, I want its memories reinstated. I want the Paladin to remember its prior life of entitlement as it sucks up spilled cum. A promise is a promise, after all."

Texx and Wess knew nothing of this *promise*, but did not press the issue with their off-kilter leader. Both men nodded. "Anything else, boss?"

"Not right now, Texx. But, thank you."

"Then I have something. There's been unusual activity detected in the Hammers. The Blisters are up to something."

Krill laughed lightly before speaking, as if to himself. "Of course he would rally the Blisters to his cause. The devil refuses to run out of tricks."

Both Texx and Wess could feel their faces twist in confusion. "What's that, First Krill?"

"Oh, nothing, Wess." As if it were possible, Krill sounded even farther away.

"Would you like us to prepare a preemptive strike, boss?"

"That won't be necessary, Texx. Thank you for the intel." A pause. "You both are dismissed."

Red Texx and Wess Dey turned to leave, but Texx stopped himself, took a deep breath, a spun back to Krill. "And him?"

Viktor Krill looked up surprised, as if he already forgotten that his men were there. "Him?"

"Yes, boss. *Him*." Texx motioned towards the back wall.

Krill shifted in his chair to look at the wall behind him. "Oh, *him*. Don't worry about him for now, Texx. We still have some memories to make together."

"Yes, sir." With that, Red Texx spun on his heel and grabbed Wess by the arm. The two killers leaned on each other as they crossed the blood-soaked office, stepping over random pieces of head that were laying in their path. When they were safely in the hall, with the golden doors closed behind them, both men exhaled deeply.

Wess pointed back at the doors. "That's not Viktor Krill in there, Texx."

"You're right, Wess. The Viktor Krill that we knew is gone. But who will take his place in that magical body of his. Will it be someone better, or someone much worse?"

———

VIKTOR KRILL SAT in the office suite in silence, staring at the closed door to the secretive back communications room, ignoring the occasional moan that emanated from the wall behind him.

An old ally had resurfaced, his soul darker and more twisted than Krill, even at his most homicidal, could have ever imagined. The Viktor Krill who had carved out the heart of a Caesar, scaled Station's impenetrable wall, and found his way out of the trackless desert would have laughed at the absurdity of it all. He would have welcomed the carnage that was to come, relished the opportunity to partake in the madness.

But that Viktor Krill was dead, gone long before his beloved Natthi met her untimely end. That Viktor Krill disappeared when words like *son, daughter, family,* and *friend* wormed their way into his thoughts, taking hold and growing roots before he could safely pluck them from existence.

Now, the madness that was about the envelope the world no longer excited him. In fact, he found it grotesque, an abomination that needed to be stopped.

Krill's mind whirled with the horror of what was to come. Families would be ripped apart as more daughters were taken from fathers, as wives turned on their sons, and vice versa.

The unfathomable pain that Krill felt as Natthi died in his arms would be experienced around the globe, shared by all in the insanity that was to come. And no one could see it coming.

It was at that moment that Viktor Krill was accosted by another new emotion, one that he had prided himself in avoiding for the past few decades. *Guilt.*

Viktor Krill didn't create the hell that was to come; two others were much more culpable than he. But neither was Krill without blame. He had assisted in drafting the blueprint for what was possible with the human construct. He had shown the power of the body's full potential. He had deciphered the code that turned men into minor gods.

And he had shown his notes to something truly evil.

Now, it was Viktor Krill's turn to face the music. He had sins to answer for, and hoped that he lived long enough to right some wrongs.

Viktor Krill was going to atone. Or die trying.

A SMALL SMILE appeared on Gayle's grey face as she closed her eyes. When she finally opened them, her orange eyes sparkled especially bright in the dimness of dusk.

"Alphus is almost here."

Hadder looked out to the sea, but saw only endless water under the smooth line of the horizon. "Are you sure?"

Gayle smiled sweetly at her ignorant new friend. "Yes, I'm quite sure."

"Then we attack tomorrow?"

"Y-y-yes. T-tomorrow we shall m-m-meet our d-destiny."

Hadder looked to Acid Boy Gash, who was not looking out at the ocean, but was instead staring intently at the Cyrix Headquarters building. "You feeling confident, Gash?"

Gash thought for a moment before responding, his violet eyes vibrating in their sockets. "I f-feel nothing. Only the w-w-weight of inevitability. The p-power of p-prophecy. We w-w-will crush the p-peddies. Or m-m-meet our m-maker trying."

Hadder was unable to control his curiosity any longer. "I keep hearing this word — *peddie*. What the hell does it mean?"

Gayle answered for Gash in her gentle tone. "It's short for *pedestrian*, Marlin. A derogatory term for those that work to oppress our people. It means they are normal, boring. Without the uniqueness that defines, and is embraced, by our kind. They are sheep. Sheep with guns that torment those different from themselves."

"And now all your hopes and dreams are riding on a peddie."

Gayle and Gash, two lovers who controlled a kingdom, shared a knowing look. As usual, Gayle spoke for them both. "You are far from a peddie, Marlin Hadder. You are one of the Twin Angels that Orrin the Child prophesied would save our people. But, even without that, you still would not be a peddie. You see past the open sores, the extra limbs, the..." Gayle looked down at herself, and a shadow of sadness fluttered across her face before disappearing. "... Grey, rough skin. You see folks for who they are, not what they appear. It is for that reason that the term does not apply to you."

Gayle's kind words wrapped in an honest tone caused a lump to appear in Hadder's throat. Unable to form an adequately eloquent response, he simply said, "Thank you, Gayle."

The three stood in silence for a while, appreciating the strange peace and quiet that had fallen over the Rising, a place that would soon ring out with gunshots, explosions, and screams of the dying.

After soaking in the moment, Gayle spoke again. "Where's Albany Rott? I would love to hear his thoughts on the upcoming battle."

"He's off strategizing," lied Hadder. The truth was that Rott had spent much of the last few days alone, battling something that Hadder could not see nor understand. The fallen angel was battling his own demons, and that greatly concerned Hadder.

For if something was enough to worry Albany Rott, then it should terrify the rest of the world.

———

ALBANY ROTT SAT ALONE with his dark thoughts, unable to shake them from his inhuman mind. He finished cigarette after cigarette, hoping that smoky lungs would prevent him from looking inward, and discovering what lay within.

It was not supposed to be this way, thought Rott as he considered the tail end of his millennia in this existence. He was quickly approaching his moment of triumph, about to punch his ticket home. And, yet, all he could think about was those who would be left behind to wallow in the absolute darkness that he helped create.

Darkness that he *did* create.

Rott flicked the butt of his cigarette into the night, watched as the cherry smoldered before blinking out of existence, a foreshadowing of what was to come.

Albany Rott sighed deeply before rising to his feet. He reminded himself that this was the way of things, the fruition of careful planning. This was all an elaborate game, and there were only two players. The rest were mere pieces to be added, removed, or manipulated as he saw fit. They were nothing. They meant nothing. It was time to finish this thing and head home.

As Rott walked alone back to where his "friends" were finalizing plans, a mantra formed in his head. *Ants have no name; they are simply ants, oblivious to the world beyond their nest. They have no name; they are unimportant.*

These words he repeated over and over again, hoping that repetition would lend them strength, make them believable.

But they rang empty in his mind.

———————

MAYFLY LEMAIRE STORMED into the Cyrix office suite with Red Texx, Renny, and Wess Dey in tow. Despite her golden prosthetic leg, she walked with power and sensuality, displayed a confidence that few others possessed.

"Enough of this, Viktor. We need to..." Her voice trailed off as she took note of the garish exhibit on the back wall. "My god, Viktor, what have you done?"

Krill, sitting behind the small desk, much as he had the majority of the past few days, looked back and shrugged. "I told you I would make him pay. This is what that looks like."

Lemaire fought hard to lift her jaw from the floor, forced herself to study the grim scene before her. Fastened against the office's back wall, held several feet above the marbled floor by metal spikes that had been driven through his wrists and deep into the concrete behind, was Cyrus Bhellum V. Or what was left of him.

Bhellum's right hand had been cut off, and the stump cauterized. The man's right eye had been unceremoniously removed, leaving long nerves to dangle from the socket. A quick glance toward Krill's newly claimed desk showed a mason's jar that was now home to the detached orb.

Unfortunately, that was not where the horror stopped.

A neat incision had been had made down Bhellum's shirtless chest, allowing the epidermis, dermis, and subcutaneous fat that once covered the area to be pulled back and pinned to the wall to either side of the man. His glistening organs were exposed to the world, some still throbbing or moving as they worked to keep their owner alive.

"Fuck me, Viktor. He's still alive?"

Krill responded, but the power in his voice had vanished. The fire in his too-black eyes had been extinguished. "It hasn't been easy. I have to squirt his organs once an hour, so they don't dry up. I give him an IV bag every two. Do you like it? I must admit, I stole the idea from an artist friend of mine. Well, he wasn't really my friend, but that's beyond the point." Viktor looked back at Bhellum. "I doubt he feels much of anything anymore. Which is a pity."

"My god, Viktor, just kill him already."

"Can't. Not yet, anyway. I'm consolidating Cyrix's assets and old Bhellum here has made that possible. Fingerprint recognition. Retinal scans. Even voice detection. Everything I need is here. Isn't that right, Cyrus?!"

"Kill me. Please. Kill me." Lemaire's amber eyes went wide at Bhellum's weak words, so surprised was she that the man could still speak.

"Ahh, he doesn't mean that," said Krill coldly.

Lemaire shook her attention from the macabre display. "Enough of this, Viktor. We have to talk."

Krill spoke, as if he had not heard Lemaire. "And how are the Slink Reapers?"

Lemaire snorted angrily, unused to being ignored. Regardless, she answered Krill's question. "I gave them the option of being fed to the Slink, or punished by me. They all chose me. Those that still live now beg to visit the Slink den."

Krill laughed lightly. "Then we are not so different. The lengths we will go to hurt those that harmed our daughter." At this, Texx, Renny, and Wess stared down at the marble beneath them, as if trying to see through to the floor below.

"Yes, Viktor, but I do not have them out as some kind of grotesque show."

"Maybe you should."

"Enough! I'm not going to argue about dead men. Tell him, Texx."

"The Blisters are preparing to move on you, boss. And they're not alone. They've aligned with the Broken Tens."

"Who the fuck could've seen that coming," added Renny.

Red Texx continued. "They've all collected at the Hammers, boss. I'd say they're looking to attack in a few hours, around midday."

Wess Dey cut in. "My boys are Loaded and ready to march, First Krill. When these freaks attack, we'll sweep in from behind and trap them in a vice, put the squeeze on them. They don't stand a chance. I don't care how scary these mutants look from the outside, they all bleed red."

Back to Red Texx. "Preparations have already begun, boss. How many units of Risers do you want to defend Cyrix? I can have them here in an hour."

"None."

The Bitch-Whore queen and three Riser leaders all responded in unison. "What?!"

Viktor Krill smiled weakly. "None. I don't want any Risers here."

Mayfly Lemaire's amber eyes flashed dangerously. "What are you about, Viktor?" There was no response. "Leave us," she said to Texx, Renny, and Wess, who obeyed her command without hesitation. The golden double doors closed behind the three men. "Viktor, look at me," she said softly. "What's going on? I know you're upset about Natthi; we all are. But that..."

"Our daughter."

"What's that?"

"She wasn't just Natthi. She was our daughter. And she's gone. Because of me."

Lemaire wiped the single tear that had escaped to run down her dark face. "Yes, she was our daughter. And, yes, she's gone. But, come now, Viktor. Self-pity does not suit you. There are..."

"It is not self-pity, Mayfly. It is the truth. For perhaps the first time in my lives, I am naked and confronting the cold truth. My daughter is dead because of my ambitions and actions. And many more will suffer a similar fate."

Lemaire's eyes narrowed. "What are you getting at, Viktor?"

"It doesn't matter. The Blisters and Broken Tens are not alone. They have with them a man of unimaginable power. And he's coming for me. They are coming for *me*. Not the Rising. Not the Risers. Not the Bitch-Whores. This isn't about power or position. This is personal. And I am finished letting those I care about die because others want to see me gone."

It took Lemaire a moment to find her voice. "I've never heard you talk like this, Viktor."

"I never thought like this. Before young Darrin. Before Natthi. Before *you*."

Lemaire wiped away more wetness. "Enough of this foolishness. We need a plan. With the united efforts of the Rising and Cyrix Industries, we can eliminate this threat."

Krill stared down at his burned left arm, which was already beginning to heal at an uncanny rate. "You're probably right, Mayfly. We could win this battle. But at what cost?"

"Who cares about the cost, Viktor?!"

"I do!" Krill's outburst sent Lemaire back on her heels. He collected himself. "I do. No one else dies because of me."

"You are a king, Viktor. The Risers are counting on you to lead them. You can't do that as a dead man, as some kind of fucking martyr!" No response. Lemaire softened her tone. "Viktor, I know you are broken-hearted. I am, too. I also lost a daughter. But I have a whole gang full of girls that are looking to me for guidance."

"Which is why I need you to follow my orders."

"Orders?" That classic Lemaire anger flashed to the surface. "Who the fuck are you to give *me* orders? I am *not* one of your Riser lackeys, Viktor. I am Mayfly fucking Lemaire, queen of the Bitch-Whores. I was royalty long before you found your way to this shit hole. And I'll be here long after you're gone." She immediately regretted the words.

Krill smiled softly. "That's what I am trying to ensure, Mayfly."

Lemaire could feel the pressure mounting in her sinuses, the prequel to an emotional breakdown. "Fuck you, Viktor Krill," was all she could muster before she turned and thundered out of the office suite.

Krill sighed deeply. *That went about as well as expected*, he thought. He called out. "Texx, you all can come back inside."

The three loyal Risers reentered the office and stood at attention before Krill's desk, each trying their best to not stare at the filleted man on the wall. As usual, Red Texx spoke first. "Orders, boss?"

Krill's black eyes met Texx, Renny, and Wess's in turn. "I want you all to know how much I appreciate your service and loyalty." A pause. "And friendship." The men glanced sideways at each other. "I know I may seem a bit off to you, but things have clarified for me in the past few days. As never before. I need you all to trust that this is true. Do you trust me?"

"Yes, sir" called out the three voices.

"Good. Then my orders are this — stay away. Keep all the Risers away from this fight. As I said, this battle is not for control of the Rising. It's not to take over the gang, or to assert some kind of dominance over the Risers. This is personal. And I will not have my Risers die over a personal beef. Not a single one." The men remained at silent attention. "Instead, I will rely solely on the defenses of Cyrix Industries to choose my fate. Red Texx, if I die, you will take over the Risers. You're a good man, and a better leader. The men will die for you."

"You cannot die, boss. We've all seen it."

"Kind words, but trust me, I *can* die, Texx. And die, I might. And if I do, I need to know that you'll take up the mantle of Riser First."

A slight hesitation. "It would be an honor, boss."

Krill turned his attention to Renny and Wess Dey. "Gentlemen, will you follow Red Texx in my absence?"

There was no hesitation this time. "It would be an honor," they answered together while flashing small smiles to Texx.

Krill didn't realize that he had been holding his breath until he exhaled. At least one thing went smoothly. "Thank you, gentlemen. The honor has been all mine. You are dismissed." The three Risers turned to leave. "Texx, stay a moment. Please." When Renny and Wess had exited the room, Krill continued. "Texx, I need to know that you'll follow my orders and stay away from this fight."

"You have my word, boss."

"Good." Krill opened his shirt to show a small device connected to his scarred chest. "As I said, with Bhellum's help here, I have been able to consolidate all of Cyrix's liquid holdings into one account. I'm talking billions of credits. Upon my death, this little thing here…" He tapped the device. "Will detect my demise and automatically disperse the funds within that account. Mayfly Lemaire will receive a large chunk. Young Darrin will be taken care of. And you, Texx, will receive the rest. I trust you to do right by the gang."

Red Texx fought down a choking sensation. He spoke around the lump in his throat. "You have my word, boss."

"Of course, it won't be a direct transaction. The funds will travel around the globe for a few days, hopscotching from one account to another, getting cleaner by the jump. By the time it reaches you all, it will be as if the funds came straight from a dark ream."

"That would be one hell of a dark ream."

"It would, wouldn't it?" A heavy silence fell between Red Texx and the world's first Wakened human. "Texx, if I die, I want you to reform the gang as you see fit. I was always the darkest shadow in an unlit world. But you, you are a beacon of light in that same world. Don't try to follow some bullshit lead of mine. Redefine what Riser means."

"You have my word, boss."

Krill slapped both hands down onto the desk. "Good! One last thing. A personal favor."

"Anything, boss."

Krill handed a sealed envelope to Red Texx. "I need you to give this to young Darrin. I then need you to have someone drive him to Sespit. Someone you trust with your life. I've learned that no one is safe around me. And I learned that the hardest way possible." A pause as Krill collected himself. "Anyway, tell young Darrin that I'm proud of him. Tell him, I'm sorry. Tell him that this is for the best. Will you do that for me, Texx?"

Red Texx nodded solemnly, the large man's eyes growing glossy with tears. "It will be done."

"Thank you, Texx. Dismissed."

Red Texx crossed the long office suite, his mind whirling with a thousand thoughts and fears and questions. Just before he reached the large double doors, Krill's voice rang out once more.

"Texx?"

"Yes, boss?"

"Tell him, I love him? Young Darrin, that is."

"It would be my honor, boss."

"Thank you, my friend."

"You're welcome, boss." Red Texx left the office without turning back. No one had seen the giant redheaded man cry since he was thirteen years old. He wasn't about to break that streak now.

25

The Hammers was a hive of activity, with Broken Tens checking guns and ammunition while Blisters unloaded items from various buildings, including rolling defensive barricades that had been fashioned out of unused metal that littered the area. Acid Boy Gash and Gayle roamed among their followers, offering soft words of encouragement and gentle advice, where appropriate. Tennian Stamp was also present, stomping around the old manufacturing facilities on his military-issued legs, barking orders and shouting quotes to inspire his men before battle.

After speaking to several groups of Broken Tens, and the occasional Blister, Tennian joined Hadder at the edge of the Hammers, facing the Cyrix Headquarters building. Without exchanging words, the two men simply nodded to each other as Hadder accepted another offered cigarette. They smoked in silence for several minutes, both envisioning the battle ahead, both working up the courage to remain optimistic.

It was Old Tens who finally broke the peaceful moment. "Where's Rott? I haven't seen much of him?"

Hadder pointed his chin to the North, where Albany Rott could be seen in the distance, sitting alone on a discarded crate, and staring out at nothing as he absently fingered the sparkling symbol at his neck.

Tennian studied the strange man-god for a long while before turning back to Hadder. "Is that something we should be worried about?"

Hadder shrugged, attempting to play off his concern. "He'll snap out of it once the blood starts flying."

"Any chance of him snapping out of it *before* that happens?"

Another shrug. "He's gonna claim his share of scalps. Don't worry, he'd never miss this fight. It means more to him than you could ever know."

"His reputation precedes him. Can he live up to the hype?"

"Can we win if he doesn't," asked Hadder.

Tennian stared once again at Cyrix. "Depends on what surprises Bhellum and Rott have in store for us."

Hadder joined in, returning his gaze to the giant C that rotated slowly in the air. "What do you think is gonna come out of there, Tens?"

"Men, for sure, but I don't know how many. Cyrix Headquarters has been operating with a reduced staff for a while now. I'd be surprised if there were a thousand armed humans that come out to face us."

"And non-humans?"

Old Tens grinned. "Well, now, that's the more important question, isn't it? Cyrix was once the world's leader in robotics. At one point, no one provided more AI-based machines of death to militaries around the globe. Their quality has fallen off, no doubt, and their designs have become shit, but I bet they still maintain a large stock of something in that cursed building."

"Any ideas which models?"

Old Tens laughed aloud. "Damn, son, you want to know the endings of movies before you see them, too?"

"This isn't a movie, Tens."

"Yes, it is. Your friend Rott knows that better than anyone." A brief pause. "Look, I don't want to guess what's coming out because it could be anything. We need to stay nimble, prepared to react to anything that gets thrown at us. *They* move, then *we* move."

Hadder finished his cigarette, and tossed the butt towards Cyrix. "Then I ask you again, can we win if Rott doesn't live up to the hype?"

There was no hesitation in Tennian's response this time. "No." He crushed his cigarette under a heavy metal foot. "Albany Rott better fight like a man possessed."

"He won't."

"Come again?"

"He won't fight like a man possessed. In fact, he won't fight like a man at all. When you watch Albany Rott kill, you'll finally understand what it means to be a devil."

Tennian studied Hadder's face, waiting for a punchline that never arrived. Finally, he let out a great laugh and slapped the suited man's shoulder. "Then perhaps some of us will be able to see tomorrow after all. Cheer up, Hadder! It's always a good day to die!" Tennian's brown eyes flashed to something behind Hadder, and he grinned knowingly. "And with that, I'll leave you to your dark thoughts." Old Tens spun on loud legs and began to walk away, his heavy steps leaving deep prints in the dirt beneath. "Sonny! Sonny! I told you, we're going to need some small munitions. What's gonna happen when..."

As the voice of Tennian Stamp faded into the general cacophony of battle preparation, Sheela approached and stood next to Hadder. "Well? What do you think, Marlin?"

Hadder lost the ability to speak for a few seconds as he studied the beautifully exotic Blister. While Sheela still wore the metal-tipped ankle boots, she had traded in her skimpy leotard for a full black bodysuit and military vest. Strapped at her hips were two wakizashi swords, one hanging from each side. Sheela's sky-colored eyes bore holes into Hadder's heart as she awaited his reaction.

"I think if someone had to cut me in half, I would want them to look like you."

Sheela giggled. "Oh, Marlin, you have such a way with words."

Hadder pulled on the enchanting Blister woman's vest, using it as an excuse to bring her closer. "I don't see many Blisters with these."

"That's because we have very few. And, anyway, lots of my people have very thick skin, better than any stupid old vest."

Hadder fingered one of the blades at Sheela's sides. "And these?"

The woman smiled coyly. "You never know where the battle will take you."

"Why do I feel like everyone knows more about this upcoming battle than I do?"

Another soft laugh. "You only feel like that because it's true."

The two slowly drew closer, their noses almost touching. "And what else is true that I'm unaware of?"

Sheela's coy smile became a wide grin. "Did you know that it's true that they've finished emptying Storeroom 6?"

"The one right around the corner?"

"That's the one."

"I don't believe you."

"Want me to prove it to you?"

"More than anything."

With that, Sheela took Hadder's hand and the two lovers slunk off towards the recently emptied storeroom, looking like cats who had small mice between their teeth.

Albany Rott watched as the pair rounded a building's corner and disappeared. He tossed the butt of his umpteenth cigarette and immediately lit another. Two thoughts assaulted Rott as he pulled smoke deeply into his lungs. First, he was delighted that his companion would enjoy one last moment of intimacy before the fighting began. Second, a small part of Rott, and not for the first time over the last few days, hoped that his dear friend, his only friend, would meet his final end in the looming battle.

Saving Marlin Hadder the indignity of discovering Albany Rott's darkest secret.

———

As Viktor Krill sat behind his desk in the Cyrix office suite, he stared open-mouthed at the inset screens that lined the lefthand wall, all tuned to the same channel. A cold breeze blew in from the man and Paladin-sized holes in the large windows that sat opposite the televisions, but Krill didn't even notice. He was too busy trying to process what he was seeing as belief and fear began to replace suspicion and concern.

Krill shook his head as pieces started to click into place, as previous threats and half-baked plans started to look like promises being fulfilled. The horrifying road ahead grew increasingly clear the more Krill thought on it, going back to his Station days, and the words of an obviously delusional madman.

Or, perhaps not so delusional, after all.

The desk's internal intercom buzzed loudly, ripping Krill from his terrible remembrances. He pressed the small button just under the lip of the desk, and spoke into the air. "Yes?"

An unfamiliar voice greeted Krill from a hidden speaker. "Uh... Mr. Bhellum, sir?"

"This is Viktor Krill. Bhellum is..." He looked up at the butterflied man on the wall behind him. "Hung up with a meeting. What do you need? Who is this?"

"Oh, Mister Krill, sorry about that. This is Jon Wallace, Head of Security. We seem to have, uh, a situation, sir."

A situation, thought Krill. *That is putting it mildly.* "What's the situation, Wallace?"

"Uh, there's a bunch of Blisters who seem to moving towards the building, sir. And they're wheeling forward a bunch of makeshift cover. It's real DIY stuff, but looks effective."

"Effective at what, Wallace?"

"Uh, effective at stopping bullets, sir. It looks like they mean to storm the building."

"Anything else, Wallace?"

"Uh, yes, sir. Looks like they got a bunch of gangsters with them, too, sir. Some of them are Loaded, but all are armed. I don't think they just want to have words with us, sir."

Krill was getting grim satisfaction in hearing the Cyrix Security Head squirm. "Well, what do you need from me, Wallace?"

"Uh, I was, uh, hoping you could call some of your, uh, *friends?* You know, the ones from, uh, the Muck?"

"You mean the Rising?"

"Oh, uh, yeah. Sorry, sir. Maybe you can, uh, call some of your friends from the Rising to lend a hand?"

"I cannot."

"Uh, what's that, sir?"

"I said, I cannot, Wallace."

"Uh, ok. Uh, why not, sir?"

There was a pause as Viktor Krill's anger began to spike. "First, Wallace, it's because this isn't their fight. And, second, Wallace, why am I explaining myself to you? If you can't do your job, I'll replace you with someone who can. And, I promise, you won't like your severance package."

"Oh, no, no, I can handle it, sir. Sorry, sir. Didn't mean anything, sir."

"Is there something else, Wallace?"

"Uh, yes, sir. It's just that, uh, there's a lot of them, sir. And they, uh, look real serious. Do you think we could, uh, wake the stock?"

"By all means, Wallace."

"Ok, good. And, uh, do you think you could make the Mech Force available, sir."

"If it comes to that, Wallace, you'll probably be dead already. But, yes, I'll make them available, if necessary."

"Uh, great. Thank you, sir. Uh, one last thing. Any chance that we could, uh, make use of the Emergence-C system? You know, uh, if it comes to that?"

"Fucking hell, man, *you're* the Head of Security. Use whatever you can, just don't ask me to bring in outside resources to do *your* job for you. Understood, Wallace?"

"Uh, yes, sir. Uh, thank you, sir."

"We're finished here. Don't call me again unless you've succeeded, or you're dead."

"Uh, how would I...?"

Krill cut the man off with a push of the hidden button. The more that

Krill had learned about Cyrix Industries, its murky finances, and its countless dirty dealings across the globe, the more he had grown to despise the company and its complacent employees.

Despite his dislike for Cyrix and its arrogant staff, however, Krill had to admit that he was curious to see its stock and Emergence-C systems put into action. Krill glanced to his left, and looked through the wall of glass. He rose to his feet and walked to stand before the large hole that greeted him. From this vantage point, Krill would be able to see the entire battle play out. He would have the best seat in the house.

But before Krill could enjoy himself, before he could watch the one thing that would take his mind off the loss of his daughter, if only for a short time, he needed answers.

No, not answers. He feared he had those already. Viktor Krill needed confirmation. Any only one...person...could give that to him.

Krill turned away from the soon-to-be battlefield and crossed the office suite. He took a deep breath before entering the office's small back room, unprepared for the conversation he was about to have.

WHILE DOZENS of massive Blisters manned the mobile cover units that now dotted the space between Cyrix and the Hammers, most of the mutants waited patiently in the rear, mentally preparing themselves for the call to attack.

The Broken Tens, however, were at the forefront, filling the spaces behind and between the wheeled metal obstructions. Their guns were loaded, their sights had been checked, and their barrels pointed unwaveringly at the large monolith that was before them.

Marlin Hadder looked from Blister to Broken Ten, from Acid Boy Gash to Old Tens, from Brutto to Loaded Sonny Caddoc. He smiled to himself, realizing that this was an army torn from the pages of a nightmare, ripped from the mind of insanity.

Win or lose, this day would echo across the Neon City for eternity.

After several minutes of uncomfortable silence, the giant sliding doors of Cyrix Industries Headquarters opened, and men dressed in yellow and navy-blue jumpsuits streamed out, all holding submachine guns outfitted with banana clips, the makes of which were foreign to Hadder. As they poured out onto the lawn, the Cyrix security force fell into defensive formations, aiming their guns toward the Broken Tens, while turning on energy shields that sprung to life from bulky gadgets that sat on their wrists. Although the round shields were only three feet in diameter, their versatility and lightness made them effective defensive tools. The Cyrix men held their energy shields before them, making the outlines of their upper bodies appear disconcertingly wavy, as their gun barrels peaked around the sides.

The first two groups of Cyrix men settled into four positions, displaying surprising discipline for hired guns. And then... nothing.

Hadder turned to Albany Rott, who stood between himself and Tennian Stamp. "What's going on? That can't be all there is."

"It is," answered Old Tens for Rott.

Hadder's face twisted in confusion. "But there can't be more than three hundred men out there. Four hundred, tops."

"Sounds about right," responded Tens.

"I don't understand."

Tennian shot his brown eyes over at Hadder. "We've known that Cyrix has been operating on a skeleton crew for years. The place is basically a ghastly monument to the greatness of the Bhellum family. Nothing more."

Hadder had difficulty comprehending what was going on. "I thought you were exaggerating about the reduced staff. I was sure that the building had to be full. I thought this was going to be a dogfight."

"It is full, you fool. It's just not full of humans. It's full of the ghosts of decades of sin. And other things..."

"What other things, Tennian?"

"Patience, Hadder. I think we're both going to find out. Let's just enjoy this first part of the fight, which is looking to be in our favor."

Just as Old Tens finished, a security officer began speaking into a megaphone from the rear of Cyrix's meager forces. "This is Jon Wallace,

Head of Security here at Cyrix Industries Headquarters. I demand that you all cease and desist with your obvious incursion. Turn away now, and this can all be forgotten. No one's fathers, sons, or brothers will have to die here today."

"Sexist much?"

Hadder turned around to grin at Sheela, who was fingering her twin blades behind him. She offered a sweet smile in return, making his heart jump much more than the weapons pointed in his direction.

The Cyrix speaker continued. "You have no idea what is in store for you if you insist on pursuing this course of action. Turn around and go back to your homes. This is your first, and only, warning."

Old Tens looked to his right, past Hadder, to Acid Boy Gash, who stood holding hands with Gayle. Gash nodded to Tens, who nodded to Sonny Caddoc, who nodded back to Tens. Sonny, one of the few truly Loaded Broken Tens, peered through the scope of his shoulder-mounted sniper rifle. Several seconds later, without taking his eye from the scope, Sonny stuck his left thumb into the air.

"Please," was all that Tennian had to say as a single gunshot rang out over the silent battleground. A minuscule beat later, Jon Wallace's brains flew out the back of his head, painting the Cyrix building with splashes of crimson.

All the Cyrix men turned in surprise before facing the invaders once more, much of the confidence now lost from their once-proud faces. Their energy shields began to waver as arms started to shake, making them appear as if they were standing on the opposite side of a desert mirage.

"Attack." At Tennian Stamp's singular command, the Broken Tens opened fire, raining bullets down upon the outnumbered security force. After hiding behind their shields for almost a minute, with several bullets finding their way through the jungle of shields to tear through flesh, the Cyrix men recovered and began to fire back, their machine guns ringing out like a concerto of violence.

Shots were traded for many minutes, with most bullets being caught, or deflected, by energy shields and constructed cover. However, many shots still found their home, with two Cyrix men being dropped for every Broken Ten that was lost.

Slowly but surely, the Blisters maneuvering the mobile cover units inched forward and out, systematically encircling the outmanned security forces. As most of the Broken Tens fired haphazardly at the mass of energy shields, a few elite soldiers, including Sonny Caddoc, carefully took aim at the periphery of the action. Loaded with shoulder-mounted rifles, these men consistently discovered gaps in the Cyrix defenses, punching a hole in a man's heart here, entering the eye of a man there. Little by little, the Cyrix forces began to dwindle. As they did, the balance of losses tipped heavily in the Broken Tens favor.

And then something appeared to rebalance the equation.

Marlin Hadder felt their arrival before he saw them. The earth beneath him bounced subtlety in perfect cadence, the precursor to a well-tuned unit. They came from behind the Cyrix building in a trot, in perfect lockstep with each other. They swung wide around the building, and moved to take positions in front of the beaten down Cyrix men, protecting their allies' weak fleshy exteriors. A silence fell over the battlefield.

"What the fuck is that," asked Hadder aloud to no one in particular.

"That," replied Tennian, "is a theory proven fact."

"But what are they?"

Old Tens couldn't keep the grin from his dark face. "I always thought the Bhellums kept them around, but that bastard Cyrus V managed to keep them close to his chest."

Hadder was losing patience. "Tens! What the fuck are they?"

"What do you see, Hadder?"

"I see a shitload of fucking beefy androids." And that was the only way Hadder could describe them. They were humanoid, with two legs that held up a body, two arms, and a head. Their bodies were made of too-thick metal that fell to cover knee, hip, and elbow joints, leaving very few areas of obvious vulnerability. The androids had no faces to speak of, just slabs of metal with two small holes for eyes. In all of their metal right hands were alloy batons itching to be coated in human blood. "But I have no idea what they are."

Old Tens spoke not to Marlin Hadder, but to Acid Boy Gash. "I never thought we'd live to see the day, Gash."

"I d-d-did."

Tens turned back to Hadder, motioning toward the hundreds of still androids before them. "*That* is the original Mechanical Enforcement Squad. They were going to revolutionize law enforcement around the globe, make Cyrix the most powerful company in the world. Instead, they proved the beginning of the end."

By now, even Albany Rott's curiosity had peaked, tearing a neat hole in his recently dour demeanor. "How so," the red-eyed god-man asked Old Tens.

Tennian continued. "The Mechanical Enforcement Squad was basically invulnerable, at least to normal citizens. That thick-ass metal you see couldn't be punctured by anything back then. Even now, only the most powerful military-grade weapons can pierce that shit. Because of that, they were able to arm the androids with only..." Old Tens made air quotes. "*Non-lethal* weapons such as batons, tear gas, and bean bags."

Hadder cut in. "So what went wrong?"

"What went wrong is that they were glitchy as hell. Cyrus Bhellum IV tried to cut corners, buying motherboards from non-compliant countries to save boatloads of cash. Because of this, the Mechanical Enforcement Squad became a crew of straight killers. Their *non-lethal* batons routinely caved in the heads of protesters, or petty thieves, or, hell, even hoverboarding teenagers. Cyrix made them too strong, for too cheap. For several years, they terrorized the city, killing hundreds, if not thousands, of people. The citizens were up in arms, called them Muggs. That began the Neon City's silent war against the Bhellums."

Hadder was astounded. "What?! They didn't immediately pull them off the streets?"

Old Tens laughed at Hadder's ignorance. "There was a lot of rich people's money at stake, Hadder. And rich people don't like to lose money, no matter the price."

"So, what finally changed things," asked Rott.

Tennian shrugged. "What always changes things? The wrong person's white son died at the Muggs's metal hands, some headstrong young man protesting for immigrant rights. Had his head smashed in at a *peaceful* rally. The Muggs were off the streets within a month. The Mechanical Enforcement Squad was dead."

"And, yet, here they stand," remarked Sheela from behind.

Old Tens only offered a shrug. "If nothing else, the Bhellums were always cheap pricks. It doesn't surprise me that they've held on to these monsters for decades, waiting to unleash them on some unsuspecting dissidents." Tennian lit another cigarette before continuing, as if there wasn't an imminent war zone surrounding him. "Anyway, in the fallout, the Muggs were replaced by another company's much more docile Bobby Bots, which are, until now, a running joke in criminal circles such as ours. Easy to fool, easy to destroy, easy to reprogram; the Bobby Bots have allowed our businesses to flourish for three decades." He exhaled a giant plume of smoke. "God, I love those idiot hunks of metal."

"And the Muggs," prompted Hadder.

"Right," Tens went on. "Bhellum IV was supposed to melt them down, but obviously, he simply socked them away for a rainy day. He also petitioned the city to allow him to build a small, covert, *very lethal* special unit. You know, in case the city was invaded by aliens, or some shit."

"The Mech Force," said Sheela, filling in the blanks.

Old Tens nodded appreciatively at the beautiful Blister. "That's right. The Mechanical Enforcement Squad program was reborn, on a much smaller scale, as what we now call the Mech Force. The last quality work that this god-forsaken company ever produced. And don't think those muthafuckers aren't floating around somewhere, waiting to make a grand appearance."

"Ok, ok, ok," cut in Hadder, starting to grow concerned about their predicament. "We'll worry about the Mech Force if it comes to that."

"It will," interrupted Rott, but Hadder ignored his companion.

"What are we going to do about these... fucking Muggs. You said they were built to withstand bullets. What are we supposed to do? Launch insults at them? Chuck our shoes?"

"I'm not giving up my shoes," stated Sheela, and Hadder almost laughed out loud despite the dire scenario.

Acid Boy Gash stepped forward, his left hand still holding Gayle's right. "Th-th-that's where m-my Blisters c-come in."

————

On Gayle's command, which was a loud whistle that pierced the frigid air, the Blisters tore across the grassy space between Cyrix Industries Headquarters and the Hammers. The stampeding mutants appeared to have stepped straight out of a nightmare, twisted maws topping multi-colored, oversized bodies that were covered in sores, tumors, or a variety of other skin ailments.

Those Blisters with too-thick skin ignored the bullets being sent their way, belting out deep, scratchy laughs as they ran. Others held homemade shields out before them as they rushed toward their human and android enemies, giggling as projectiles were turned aside by the thick metal in their powerful hands.

As the Blisters closed the distance, coming up on the right side of the Cyrix forces, the Muggs turned in unison to face the new threat, batons held high. As the Muggs shifted position, the Cyrix security force was left exposed once more, allowing the Broken Tens to open fire and tear through the distracted men. Many fell before the men had a chance to recover and bring their energy shields back up and angled correctly. Even after they did, the Broken Tens maintained, sending a constant barrage of bullets to pelt the security force, preventing them from assisting their mechanical allies.

The roaring Blisters crashed into the line of Muggs, sending an earsplitting *bang* to echo across the Rising, as if two Goliaths had rammed unbreakable heads. Metal batons came down and across, sending smaller Blisters flying through the air to fall in motionless heaps. Monstrous Blisters let fly their own homemade clubs, knocking Muggs off balance and denting their thick, shiny hides. In short order, a chaotic mass of flesh and metal was all that could be seen by the viewing audience.

"Is this more of what you had in mind, Hadder," asked Tennian, almost giddy with excitement.

Hadder's pulse began to race as old feelings and memories began to bubble up. He looked over to Old Tens, whose smirk turned into a smile upon seeing the twinkle in Hadder's hazel eyes. "Yes, this is much more like it."

"What do you say, everyone! Who wants to get some," cried out Old Tens, and his men echoed the call. As a unit, they marched forward into closer combat, Tennian's military legs tearing up the ground beneath him as he progressed forward.

As the Broken Tens began to engage the Cyrix forces, Hadder looked to Acid Boy Gash, who looked to Gayle, who looked to Sheela, who looked back to Hadder, all wearing smiles that read, *it's a good day to die.*

"What do you say, my King," asked Gayle, her voice as calm as the night Hadder first met her.

"Y-y-yes, my Queen. L-l-let's show these f-fools who really r-runs the M-m-muck." Gash and Gayle, still hand-in-hand, then waded into battle, appearing no different from a couple searching a green park for the best place to set up a picnic.

Sheela moved to follow them, but stopped next to Hadder on the way. "If I fall, I want you to know that I've enjoyed our time together, Marlin. Don't mourn me, just make sure my people get what they deserve. Can you do that for me?"

"Don't talk like that. You're just as likely to survive as I am."

Sheela looked briefly to Rott before turning back to Hadder, looking at him as if he were but a child. "You're one of the Twin Angels, Marlin. I'm just a Blister, nothing more."

"A beautiful Blister."

"Maybe. But just a Blister, nonetheless. Promise me?"

"I promise."

With that, Sheela pulled Hadder in and enveloped him in a long, passionate kiss before pushing away and following her king and queen into battle. Hadder's head swam with the desperation of that embrace, and it took him a moment to gather himself. When he did, he looked over to Albany Rott, who was still simply watching the battle unfold.

"Are you ready, Al?" No response. "Al? Al?!" Finally, after what seemed like an eternity as death floated around the companions, Rott turned to acknowledge Hadder. Gone were the flickering embers and crimson highlights of Albany Rott's eyes, replaced by the roaring fires that Hadder had grown to appreciate all too well.

For those fiery eyes meant much. They meant that things were about to get colorful. They meant that shit was about to get fucked up. They meant that the Devil had appeared, and he wanted to get paid in blood.

Rott said nothing, but sprinted forward faster than any man could move, drawing his two crystalline hatchets out as he ran.

"Oh, he's ready," said Hadder to himself as he, too, took off to once again dance with death. To dare it to finally take him.

———

HADDER CAUGHT the attention of one particularly aggressive Mugg, which swung its baton at his head as if candy would pour forth from the shattered vessel. Hadder easily ducked the first swing, but had to roll away to escape the downward backhand that almost crushed his spine.

As Hadder rolled away, a dark shadow passed just above him, slamming into the Mugg and sending it sprawling onto the blood-soaked ground. Before the android had a chance to recover, Sheela was atop it, sliding her right wakizashi up into the slim opening between the Mugg's head and neck. The Mugg shook uncontrollably as the beautiful Blister's blade sliced through wires, cables, and silicon before neatly dissecting the robot's motherboard. With an angry twist of her slim wrist, Sheela rendered the Mugg a useless piece of scrap metal. She looked back to smile at Hadder before leaping from her defeated foe and diving back into the chaos.

A twisted hammer of a hand appeared before Hadder as he still laid on the ground. He looked up to see Sowler offering him his calcified fist to help him up, the Blister's shattered, wrapped left hand still useless. The pig-man smiled has he hefted Hadder to his feet.

"Be more careful, Angel. We can't win without you," said Sowler through crooked teeth.

"You just worry about that hole in your head, Sowler. It's begging for a Mugg baton."

"Not before my Mitt downs a dozen metal demons," laughed the Blister.

"Very well, my friend. Thanks for the... hand."

Sowler roared in laughter before swinging his giant arm in a backhand, sending a Mugg who had retreated too deep into his killing zone flying away. "Might not be there next time, Angel. Up your game."

———

MARLIN HADDER SLIPPED around the battlefield like a wraith, slipping in behind Muggs that were engaged in combat with Blisters, shoving one of his two clear handguns between small gaps in the androids' thick metal armor and unloading. One Mugg's knee gave out, dropping it to the increasingly wet ground, and allowing a giant Blister to remove its featureless head with a mighty swing of a thick pipe. Another Mugg was completely immobilized as Hadder managed to sneak a barrel under the back of its unprotected neck and fire a dozen shots directly into the awful creation's circuit-filled head.

As the Mugg fell before Hadder, a familiar voice cut through the cacophony of death. "Hey, Brutto, look! It's the fucking Twin Angel. This fucking guy, Brutto. He's not so fucking bad is he, Brutto? Maybe I won't fucking eat him after all."

"Shut up," was all that the mammoth Brutto said before turning to Hadder. "Good job, Angel. Now duck."

Hadder didn't think twice, dropping to the ruddy ground just as a Mugg baton whizzed over his head. Brutto caught the metal arm by the wrist as it ended its failed swing, and grabbed the android's bicep with his other massive hand. Letting out a great bellow, Brutto brought both hands towards him as his giant head thrust down, ramming his forehead against his metal foe's arm, breaking it cleanly in half at the elbow, which bent the wrong way before snapping apart with a loud crack.

Smeggins cackled with laughter. "You fucking see that, Angel? Fucking Brutto, man. My fucking brother, man. Fucking killing machine, he is."

"Go," was all Brutto said before he went back to work on the armless Mugg, tearing it apart piece by piece.

Farther up the battle, Hadder finally found Albany Rott. Despite knowing his companion's capabilities, Hadder's mouth fell open as he watched Rott's dance of death. The red-eyed god-man spun like a top, his twin crystalline hatchets leading the way, intercepting a baton here, removing a metal leg below the knee there.

As Rott faced off with three deadly Muggs, Hadder was never more sure of an outcome. Each hatchet strike was impossibly precise, finding the smallest openings in a Mugg's thick armor. A metal hand was removed at the wrist. A metal leg reaching for his scarred face was taken off at the hip and sent soaring away. A painfully beautiful pirouette neatly cleaved a Mugg's cable-filled neck, separating its metal head from its metal body.

As Rott completed his spin, he looked around with fiery eyes and found that no foes remained, at least none standing. During his search, he found Hadder, and the two friends shared a knowing look and a nod before Hadder raised his right hand and fired his gun towards Rott.

Rott's bright eyes went wide for a moment as the gunshot rang out, but the sound of flesh falling onto wet earth told him the true story. A Cyrix security officer had made his way through the battling nightmares, and was intent on putting a bullet in the back of Rott's head. Instead, *his* brains were now rushing out to feed the worms and grubs that called the dirt home.

Rott nodded once more in appreciation before diving back into battle, where many other Blisters were having less success against their armored enemies.

On the opposite side of the field, the Broken Tens were slowly decimating the Cyrix security ranks. Most were pinned down, and while most bullets were turned aside by their energy shields, the sheer number of projectiles that were being sent their way from the Broken Tens were dropping men by the minute.

Slowly, but surely, the Cyrix men retreated toward the building's main entrance, where they formed a united barricade before the large sliding doors. Several of the men actually went inside the building, closing and locking the entrance firmly behind them.

That doesn't look good, thought Hadder as the Cyrix men shouted orders to each other through the bullet-proof glass doors. As Hadder looked around, a few things became obvious. First, although the Muggs were injuring or killing three Blisters for every mechanical that was destroyed, the invaders simply had the numbers to keep this up. Coupled with the fact that the Broken Tens had lost very few in decimating the Cyrix security force, Hadder could only reach one conclusion.

Victory seemed a certainty, if things continued like this. A much too easy victory, at that. Which is what brought Hadder to his next observation.

The Cyrix security force, despite cowering beneath a hail of bullets, weren't panicking. They were scared, unquestionably, but Hadder did not see the hysteria that usually accompanies certain death. Which means they still had a hand, or two to play.

That hand was revealed moments later when the deafening sound of engines overhead cut through the battle. Hadder closed his eyes and muttered a curse under his breath as his biggest fear, and Old Tens's prediction, had come true.

The Mech Force had arrived.

———

THE MECH FORCE appeared on the horizon like disciplined hellions, flying in perfect formation, freshly recalled from whatever evil mission Cyrus Bhellum or Viktor Krill had them executing. As the Blisters and Broken

Tens looked up in fear and astonishment, they left themselves open to attack, receiving baton strikes to misshapen heads, and bullets that ripped through black hoodies.

Nearing the battle, the Mech Force split into two groups, one targeting the Broken Tens, and the other heading toward the battling Blisters and Muggs. They flew lower as they approached, and Hadder could see heavy rotary cannons hanging from each android as demon-like features were etched onto face screens.

"Shields," Hadder could hear Tennian scream above the roar of the descending assassins, seconds before the Mech Force strafed the battlefield with oversized bullets. Screams ripped through the air as Mech Force bullets found their way around, over, and through the mobile metal cover to cut down Broken Tens members.

And they were the lucky ones.

The Blisters who were fighting the Muggs had no such cover, and fell by the dozens, their sore-covered, discolored skins offering no protection against the missile-like projectiles. Caring not for their design forefathers and android-brethren, almost as many Muggs were struck as Blisters, their thick metal casings no match for the rotary cannon bullets.

The Mech Force swept over the battleground like a scythe, dropping man, Blister, and Mugg, alike, soaking the ground through with blood, causing it to collect in areas like tidal pools. When the flying killers completed their first wave, they swung around in perfect harmony and returned, bringing even more death to the area. By now, even the Muggs had taken notice, and halted their attacks in an attempt to dodge the next Mech Force assault. Hadder did quick math in his head and reached a terrifying conclusion.

A dozen more sweeps by the Mech Force, and all would be lost.

Just as Marlin Hadder prepared to make his peace with the god he once offended, something wondrous happened. Something that convinced the cynical man that magic did exist, even in this cold, artificially lit city of neon.

As the Mech Force completed their second pass, and flew off into the distance to execute another turn, Acid Boy Gash, still hand-in-hand with

Gayle, baby-stepped his way into the center of the battle, surrounded by a massive security force of Blisters. Protected from Mugg attack on all sides, Gash took a moment to kiss Gayle deeply before stepping forward within the empty ring.

Hadder watched in awe as Gash's body began to vibrate as his lavender eyes were known to do. As the Blister king did this, Gayle sucked in deeply, her already swollen abdomen growing immensely, as if she were with octuplets. This went on for almost a minute as the Mech Force reversed direction in the distance, and prepared for another wave of terror.

Then, Gash's vibrating stopped, and Gayle's abdomen grew no more. And the two lovers showed why they were King and Queen of their people.

Gash opened his mouth wide, and exhaled a thick green mist high into the air. He did this multiple times, growing and thickening the cloud with each breath. After the seventh of these massive ejections, Gash fell to his knees, completely spent. It was then Gayle's turn to astonish.

The air within the grey-skinned queen came out in a rush, pushing the green cloud up and out. Over and over again, mighty winds emanated from Gayle's open mouth, propelling and dispersing, until the entire left side of the battle was canopied by a thin sheet of muted green. When Gayle also fell to the ground, her air exhausted, several Blisters ran forward to collect their royals, carrying them both back to the edge of the fight.

The Mech Force pressed on, oblivious to what had just taken place, unconcerned about their place on the killing food chain. They swept in just as they had before, determined to end this fight without suffering a single blemish to their shiny liquid metal exteriors. Just as the awful rotary canons commenced with their ear-splitting spins, the Mech Force entered the thin green cloud. The emerald mist disappeared into Mech Force air intakes, coated liquid metal exteriors, and slipped into the thousands of nooks and crannies that covered each metal killer.

Hadder watched in astonishment as rotary canons halted firing, jetpacks sputtered, and the Mech Force's perfect dual formation faltered. Seconds later, individual Mech Force members began to fall from the sky like wasps sprayed with insecticide.

One by one, they all crashed to the ground in the middle of the battle, sending groups of combatants to one side or the other, splitting the field roughly into two halves. By the time Mech Force XX fell heavily onto the bloody ground, sending a spray of red into the air, Blisters and Broken Tens had surrounded the metallic special unit.

All went quiet for several minutes as both sides attempted to comprehend the new state of the fight.

Marlin Hadder finally realized that his jaw was open, and closed it with effort. He looked up to the sky, which was now much less green than it had been moments ago.

"Why else did you think we call him *Acid Boy*," asked Sheela from beside Hadder, causing him to jump. Hadder looked over to find the beautiful Blister still vey much alive, although she had a nasty knot on her bald head, and now sported one swollen eye.

"I thought it was maybe for his acerbic way of speaking," Hadder joked, calling forth a musical laugh from enchanting Blister.

"How are you, Marlin?"

"I'm alive. How about you, Sheela?"

"Alive. And still hungry for more. You?"

"I'm not dead yet."

"Good." Sheela stepped closer, her unswollen eye shining brightly with mischief. "Do you like me, Marlin?"

"More than anything right now."

"You want to die with me, Marlin?" Hadder didn't have a chance to answer before Sheela enveloped him in a deep kiss before trotting off to the front lines that faced the crippled Mech Force.

"I could die with you," Hadder said to no one, although he was starting to worry that God would no longer take him.

———

UNFORTUNATELY, the Mech Force was not nearly as crippled as they initially appeared. Although all had lost the use of their jetpacks and rotary cannons, the remainder of the metal demons' functionality varied greatly in damage from member to member. Several, like Mech Force III, VII, and XII, shook violently in place, key operating circuitry having been eaten away by Gash's acidic expulsions. Others, including Mech Force II, IX, XIV, and XVI appeared operational, although they moved jerkily, and seemed to have lost the ability to manipulate one or more of their eight limbs. The rest of the Mech Force, however, seemed unfazed and ready to kill. They waved their weapon-tipped, multi-jointed arms threateningly in the air and danced in place on their spider-like legs.

Mech Force I stepped forward, his devilish LED face shifting into a childish smile. Its emotionless electronic voice, staticky and loud, fell across the battle from tucked-away speakers. "You are denied entry to Cyrix Industries. Turn over the leaders of this incursion and evacuate the area immediately. Do this, and the vast majority of you will be allowed to live. Failure to do so will result in..."

Something flashed in the air seven feet above the ground, forcing Mech Force I to cut off its threat mid-sentence. It bent backwards incredibly fast at an impossible angle, allowing the object to pass safely overhead, only to plunge deeply into the plasma face of Mech Force VII, which was shaking in place just behind android leader. The crystalline hatchet was thrown with such force that it nearly sliced completely through the mechanical demon's head, with half of its clear blade jutting out from the back of the metal skull. Mech Force VII halted its shaking, and stood dumbly in place for a moment before falling over onto its side, quite dead.

Mech Force I rose back to its full height and spun its torso 180-degrees to view its fallen comrade. It then rotated back to face the fools who had dared defy a Mech Force order. It spoke again, smiling face twisting into an evil scowl.

"You have chosen death. And it shall be delivered."

Once again, Old Tens's voice demanded attention as it boomed across the field. "I fought your kind at Azar's Crossing, you mechanical cunt! Lost my legs, but that was a small price to pay to see your kin melted down into cufflinks! Broken Tens! Blisters! They're just hunks of metal held together by silicon, and controlled by mediocre circuitry! Fuck them, and fuck their soul-less bodies! Burn 'em all!"

An explosion of sound rang out from the surrounding Broken Tens and Blisters, a unified exhalation of anger, desperation, and determination. Enough to wake the dead.

And enough to finally wake the Rage in Marlin Hadder.

As he had during the Great Battle for Station, Hadder mentally removed the reigns, allowed the Rage to course through him, gave it permission to control his actions, encouraged it to feed on destruction.

And, thus, Hadder found himself taking off towards the Mech Force, leading a group of hysterical Blisters who had fallen in step just behind him. As he neared Mech Force I, another hatchet flew past, tickling Hadder's left ear and catching the unsuspecting android leader in the chest, burrowing itself to the hilt, and forcing the metal beast back a step on its spidery legs.

Hadder tucked his right handgun into his waistband as he ran, diving forward as he came upon the retreating Mech Force I. While mid-air, Hadder managed to grasp the hatchet handle and rip it clear from his foe's metal chest while passing just beneath the android's twin laser cutters, which swung in his direction.

Hadder hit the sticky ground in a heavy roll, sprung up onto his feet, and continued forward, driven by the Rage and the bellows of his comrades. He fired round after round with his left hand, while his right cut down and across with Rott's hatchet, severing several Mech Force arms at various joints.

Then all went red as the Rage demanded more.

The next half-hour went by in a blur of images that were punctuated by injuries to himself or others.

Sheela ran behind Brutto, who hefted an enormous, thick shield of folded metal that blocked even bullets from Mech Force arm canons. Sheela sprung out as Brutto passed Mech Force VI, her muscled right leg shooting up to thrust the metal tip of her ankle boot into the enemy's face screen, sending deep cracks to spider across the glass. The metal creature attempted to bring its two lower arms, both tipped with automatic guns, around to cut down the belligerent Blister woman, but Sheela moved just as quickly, knocking each gun wide with a strike from her two wakizashis. As each gun was forced out, Brutto came around, swinging the giant metal shield over his head and down, crushing Mech Force VI as if it were nothing more than an actual spider before the gargantuan Blister. Steam poured forth from the broken android, narrowly missing the spinning Sheela but catching Brutto directly in the face. The fearsome Blister screamed in agony as his eyes sizzled in their sockets. Smeggins spoke over his best friend's agonized screams.

"Oh, fucking, no! You okay, Brutto? Did that fucking robot get you, buddy? Don't fucking worry, Brutto. I'll be your fucking eyes. Come on, buddy, let's fucking go."

On the opposite side of the grouped Mech Force, Tennian Stamp tore into their ranks on his military-issued legs. Missiles soared from hidden compartments while gun turrets unfolded from each leg to rain terror down onto each grounded demon. Old Tens smiled crazily as he accepted a bullet in the shoulder while leaping high into the air, coming down directly atop an already compromised Mech Force XVI. The killing machine collapsed under the heavy weight of Tennian's legs, and folded in on itself as the irate ex-soldier stomped down with oversized mech feet, relegating the fifty-million credit machine to scrap metal. Old Tens howled in delight, taking another bullet in the arm before stomping away to find his next mechanical victim.

In other places, the Mech Force was having more luck, using laser cutters to slice through flesh and bone while arm-cannons picked apart Blisters preoccupied with battling the "refuse-to-die" Muggs.

One such green laser almost cut Hadder neatly in half from behind, but was blocked at the last second by a thick calcified arm that took significant damage before ultimately turning the four-foot beam aside.

Hadder turned around at Scowler's pained howl and launched into an attack, repeatedly swinging Albany Rott's unnatural hatchet into Mech Force II's face. The crystallin blade carved through the thick glass as if it were warm butter, and Hadder launched a parade of obscenities at the metal creature, repeatedly coming down with the axe and an accompanying curse until it was nothing more than an inanimate heap of insectile metal at his feet.

Hadder spun around to face Sowler. "That's *twice* I owe you."

"Just kill more, Angel," replied the ever-direct Blister.

As Hadder nodded his agreement, he noticed another group of robots rounding the corner of Cyrix Industries to join the battle. Although he spoke to himself, Sowler heard his words.

"Oh, shit."

"GRIT-12s. A lot of them," answered Sowler to Hadder's unspoken question.

Hadder's shoulders, despite the Rage still being present, fell a bit in discouragement. "Then we are fucked, Sowler."

Sowler's deep laugh tore Hadder's attention from the two units of GRIT-12s. "We are Blisters, Angel. We never trust a single plan, or a single ally, to be sufficient." After finishing his words, the Blister whistled loudly and waved his giant arm in the air, catching the attention of Acid Boy Gash, who had retreated to the Hammers to recover.

"What are you doing," asked Hadder.

"Getting our own reinforcements, Angel."

———

JUST AS THE GRIT-12s moved into position, their giant central wheels tearing up the soft ground beneath them, and readied their large guns at the warring Blisters, Broken Tens, Muggs, and Mech Force, a hive of activity could be seen erupting from the Hammers.

Combatants stopped in mid-swing, mid-shot, and mid-cut, their attentions drawn to the symphony of metal sounds that began to sweep down from the Hammers to blanket the blood-soaked field. Seconds later, the cause of the raucous came into clear view.

Thousands of small robots, each uniquely cobbled together from throwaway parts and mismatched components, scrambled toward the Cyrix building. Covered in thickly hammered scrap metal, and outfitted with an array of blades, guns, and other instruments of violence, the robot saviors rolled forward on wheels, tracks, and wobbly legs, cutting a direct path to the GRIT-12s.

Marlin Hadder, unable to contain himself, laughed hysterically as wave after wave of misfit, repurposed bots poured forth from the Hammers. All the "off-limits" warehouses now made sense to the man from another world. He wondered how many decades the Blisters had prepared for this moment, when humanity would be forced to recognize those that they tried to leave behind in a pool of toxins.

"You see now, Angel," asked Sowler, a wide grin of his own pasted on his piglike face.

"I see now," responded Hadder.

"Then let's win this thing," roared Sowler as he went back to work, swinging his giant Mitt to send Mech Force IX sailing away to disappear among a group of Broken Tens.

Both GRIT-12 units turned to focus on the stampeding Blister-bots, and opened fire. Their large-caliber weapons tore through the small robots, dropping line after line of the diminutive helpers. But like waves in the ocean, there was always another right behind the one before. For every Blister-bot that fell, three more took its place and progressed, moving ever closer to the despicable military-grade GRITs.

Hundreds of Blister-bots fell before reaching the GRIT-12 lines, but Hadder soon realized that the Blisters had not brought thousands of reinforcements, but tens of thousands. They advanced like an army of ants, moving around and over their fallen comrades without regard. There was only the target, and the mission.

The GRIT-12s didn't stand a chance.

The Blister-bots rolled over their giant cousins as insects would a large carcass. Their small circular saws sliced into large central wheels. Miniature flamethrowers attacked wires exposed by movement, melting them away and cutting off necessary internal communications. Small-caliber bullets reached for optical sensors, blinding the massive killing machines. Dozens of

Blister-bots fell for each GRIT-12 that was taken down. And yet more came on — fearless and tireless, an innexhasutive supply.

Tennian Stamp screamed in joy from across the field as the miniature reinforcements completed their destruction of the GRIT-12s, and joined the more massive foray. Rockets soared from his mech legs, each catching a Mech Force member or Mugg squarely in the chest, driving them to the scrambled ground.

Albany Rott used the distraction to wreak even more havoc on their robotic enemies. His remaining crystalline hatchet found home in several Muggs' blank faceplates, sending the artificial creatures to their metal knees, before cleanly slicing a leg from Mech Force III, rendering it a teetering mess.

Sheela's twin blades danced in the air, finding the tiniest of openings in the Muggs' thick armor, and carefully plucking the laser cutters from Mech Force members. She smiled widely as she spun from android to android, oftentimes attacking Muggs who found themselves stuck in Niblit's thick phlegm. Her face had become splattered with dirty lubricant that ran down into dozens of bloody wounds on her muscled body. Hadder thought she had never looked more beautiful.

Everywhere that Hadder looked, a Broken Ten fell, a Blister was chopped down, or a reinforcement bot was destroyed. But the feared Muggs were also dropping, as were the nightmarish Mech Force. Death had its arms around the melee, but the good guys had the sheer numbers to come out victorious.

Marlin Hadder dared to believe — *we are going to win this fucking thing*.

And then the Cyrix Headquarters building came to life, extinguishing that hope.

———

HADDER HAD JUST FINISHED UNLOADING a fresh clip into the exposed circuitry just above a Mugg's thick metal breastplate when a deafening groan began to emanate from the Cyrix Headquarters building, demanding his attention.

Looking up, Hadder watched in surprise as the gigantic C hovering atop the building began to increase its spin-speed, causing bright blue lances of electricity to surround the letter, now and then escaping to attack the building roof beneath. As the C rotated faster, the building's groan grew louder, shaking the earth under the combatants' feet.

Several seconds later, the Cyrix building revealed its biggest secret.

Unbelievably massive gun turrets unfolded from the corners of the Cyrix building, each large enough to find placement on a military destroyer. From between floors, thick metal barrels slid out from hidden cubbies and bent downward to aim at the surrounding grounds. On the building's ground floor, just above the blood-soaked earth, a thin veneer of stucco that covered the first three feet of the outer walls peeled away, revealing a complex system of vents just under the fine plaster.

And then the Cyrix Headquarters building attacked.

The oversized turrets fired round after round of mammoth bullets, ripping through man, Blister, and robot alike. The projectiles ripped through the mobile metal cover as easily as they passed through the Blisters' bubbly skin.

From the thick metal barrels, one of two horrors shot forth. Some released thick arms of fire to attack the soldiers beneath. Others discharged impossibly long, wide laser beams, dragging them across the sticky ground to carve away at anything in their paths.

The vents just above the ground began to issue plumes of thick, toxic smoke that soon covered the battlefield like a shroud. Although most of the Blisters seemed immune to this poison, the Broken Tens doubled over in coughing fits.

Death rang out like a dinner bell, and everyone was invited.

Hadder hit the ground, and began to crawl around to escape the carnage. Soda can-sized bullets exploded into the surrounding area, shooting red-stained earth high into the air. His lungs burned as toxic smoke filled them, wreaking havoc on the sensitive bronchioles within. Screams ripped through the air, melding with the sounds of scorched earth and gunfire to create a symphony of slaughter.

As Hadder scampered along the ground, narrowly avoiding the ray of a giant laser cutter that was sliding along the turf, he came upon a large body that he was horrified to discover was Brutto. Hadder climbed atop his friend's unmoving figure to discover that the Blister's torso was home to three gaping holes, curtesy, no doubt, of those accursed gun turrets. Choking back tears, Hadder forced closed his friend's eyes when another voice cut through the mayhem, breaking his heart all over again.

"Hey, is that fucking you, Angel? Hey, can you fucking tell fucking Brutto that we have to get fucking moving? Can't fucking lay here all fucking day, you know?"

Hadder looked down to find Smeggins looking up at him, denial of the situation thick on his tiny, jagged-toothed face. "I'm sorry, Smeggins. Brutto is gone."

The little shoulder face remained silent for a moment before twisting into a snarl. "Don't fucking lie to me, Angel. Brutto's always fucking sleeping on the fucking job. Wake him fucking up, Angel!" A long pause. "Please, Angel. Please fucking wake up my friend."

"I'm sorry, Smeggins." Hadder wanted to say more, but found that he could not. Instead, he reached over and pulled the remnants of a broken Mugg on top of Brutto's corpse, hopefully giving Smeggins a bit of protection, although how long the little guy could survive without his host's body was anyone's guess. "Stay here," Hadder said to Smeggins, and felt foolish as soon as the words escaped his lips.

Hadder continued moving, although he had no idea where he was going, or why. To move was to survive; to stay put was to invite death. He cut down Muggs where he could, pushing one from behind into the path of a beam cutter, taking grim satisfaction as it was sliced neatly in half. On he ran and crawled, helping where he could, mourning where he could not. While Marlin Hadder did not know what he was looking for, he recognized when he found it.

Sheela, despite the chaos surrounding her, remained engaged in combat with Mech Force I, her blades knocking mechanized arms aside before they could do damage to her too-white skin. Hadder took a second to marvel at the beautiful warrior Blister who was willing to tongue-kiss death to accomplish her goals. As Sheela was fully focused on the battle at hand, however, Hadder watched in terror as a Cyrix gun turret fired repeatedly into the ground next to the combatants, cutting a clear line toward the fighting pair.

Hadder took off in a sprint, caring nothing for his safety. Only Sheela mattered, and she needed his help. It was a race between himself and the strafing turret to see who would reach the entangled duo first. Hadder closed his eyes as the distanced narrowed, expecting his head to be blown off at any moment.

Finally, after an eternity folded into seconds, Hadder reached Sheela. He crashed into the Blister woman from the side, driving her to the ground. As he did, a bullet struck the side of his forehead, tearing a deep gash in his skin and nearly knocking him unconscious. Adrenaline driving him, Hadder was able to quickly clear the cobwebs, looking behind as he and Sheela took cover on the ruddy ground. The Cyrix turret had found a new target, blasting holes in Mech Force I's chest and cutting the feared android leader down to scrap metal before ending its barrage, no doubt to reload.

Sheela giggled under Hadder has he shifted to let her up. "Oh, my hero. What would I do without you, Marlin?"

The lovers laid in a pool of blood together, her too-blue eyes locked onto his hazel orbs. "Well," Hadder finally answered, "You probably wouldn't have found yourself in this mess, dancing with death and narrowly avoiding the abyss."

Sheela softly giggled again. "Oh, Marlin, we're always dancing with death. And the abyss is nothing to be avoided. Now come here." With that, Sheela grabbed Hadder behind his head and pulled him in close, enveloping him in a kiss that seemed to heal all his wounds and refill his energy. When they separated, Sheela caressed Hadder's face, wiping away some blood that was running from his forehead and into his eye. "Now, let's..."

Sheela's words were cut off, and her blue eyes went wide as she noticed something terrifying above Hadder, in the direction of the Cyrix building. Suddenly, Sheela flipped Hadder over and covered his body with her own just as a pillar of fire came down to bathe them both in icy heat. Her beautiful face inches from his own, hovering like an angel, Sheela shook atop Hadder, her small body blocking the flames for several seconds before they moved on to other victims.

"No, no, no, no," repeated Hadder as he slid out from under Sheela, pushing down the bile that rose in his throat as he looked upon the woman's back, where skin and muscle had been burned away to reveal her spinal cord. An audible wail escaped his lips. "No, no, no," Hadder begged, the dark images of Reena Song, Lilly Sistine, Coral, and his beloved Emily accosting him from the grave. He gently rolled Sheela over to stare at her shocked face. "Why? Why? Why," Hadder demanded to know through the tears that were streaming down his face.

Sheela smiled weakly. "It's ok, Marlin. You're our Angel. Small price to pay."

Hadder was now openly sobbing. "Please. Not again. Not like this. You'll be all right, Sheela."

The beautiful Blister shook her head slightly. "No. It's over for me, Marlin. Oh, but what an ending. To save the Angel on my way out; I couldn't ask for more. Promise me something, Marlin?" She fought to get the words out, but continued. "Two things, actually."

"Anything."

"Win this war for my people. They deserve some peace."

"Done. What else?"

Sheela smiled sweetly, and tears ran down her temples from her painfully blue eyes. "Kill me, Marlin. I can't move and it hurts. It hurts so much."

Hadder wept as Sheela pushed one of her wakizashis into his chest. He took the blade and gripped it by the handle, the metal's point aimed at Sheela's small chest. "Thank you for everything. I'll never forget you."

"Thank *you*, Marlin. We Blisters have been without real hope for too long. Remember your promise. Now kiss me."

Hadder dropped his head. As his lips touched Sheela's, the point of the wakizashi found her heart. They remained locked together as Sheela's final breath exited her mouth to enter Hadder's, the two becoming one as darkness took another of Marlin Hadder's loves.

An overwhelming sense of loss, of unbelievable sadness, threatened to overtake Hadder as he looked upon the still face of the incomparable Blister known as Sheela. But Hadder shifted the pain, redirected its power, channeled it toward another destination.

Marlin Hadder used it to feed the Rage.

Hadder rose without concern for the toxic smoke, passing laser cutters, strafing gun turrets, or incoming waves of fire. He walked across the battlefield, his clear handguns tucked into his waistband alongside Rott's hatchet, Sheela's twin wakizashis in his hands, and welcomed death. His heart was broken, his Rage was full, and only violence would satiate him.

As Hadder moved to engage a trio of Muggs, he was pulled to the ground unceremoniously by powerful pale hands. They forced him behind one of the Blisters' mobile metal covers before slapping him hard across the face.

"What are you trying to do? Get yourself killed?" Although Albany Rott was bleeding from a dozen wounds, the god-man's eyes were filled with infernos. "Answer me, Marlin!"

"Sheela's dead," responded Hadder, his voice thick with the Rage. "She saved me. Another death placed at my feet, as if there's still space there. I want to avenge her, but all is lost. I can only take as many with me as possible before I go."

Rott slapped Hadder across the face again, sending stars cascading across his vision. "You fool, do you not see what is happening? Take your mind off your grief and Rage for a second and look! Gayle's brother has come!"

Hadder shook his head to think through the Rage. "Alphus?"

"Who else, you fool? Look!"

Hadder looked to the North, where the far end of the battlefield was now dominated by a hulking figure that almost completely blocked his view of the ocean. Alphus had come, and he was everything that Gayle had promised. And so much more.

From his decades in the water, where Alphus had continued to grow, mutate, and adapt, Gayle's brother no longer resembled either man or Blister. Instead, he had become something usually reserved for mythos. Looking to be almost 65-feet in length, Alphus walked on all fours, and appeared to be a mix of human and Mosasaurus. His body had flattened, thickened, and stretched, and was held above the ground by two giant arms and two massive legs that were indistinguishable from each other, ending in webbed, clawed hands and feet.

Alphus moved like a nightmarish crocodile across the field of battle, his elongated head plummeting to the ground to scoop up Muggs and Mech Force members in oversized, fang-filled jaws, crushing them with impossible strength. The Cyrix building focused on the encroaching terror, firing round after round at the overgrown Blister. While Alphus howled in pain, Hadder could see that even the Cyrix building's large bullets could not pierce the leviathan's thick, shark-like skin.

Marlin Hadder looked to Albany Rott, and the two companions shared a knowing nod. They now had a chance.

"What should we do," asked Hadder, hoping Rott would have a plan.

"Look closer, Marlin."

Hadder followed Rott's orders, and his breath caught when he finally recognized what his companion wanted him to see. Atop Alphus, no more than a flea on a dog, sat Gayle, her eyes closed as she transmitted orders to her aquatic sibling. Hadder flashed back to Rott. "She can control him."

"That's right."

"What do we need him to do?"

Albany Rott didn't speak, but simply lifted his fiery eyes to the top of the Cyrix building, where the hovering C spun like a top, feeding power to the building's defenses.

Hadder looked up briefly before returning his gaze back to Rott. "I got it. We go together, Al?"

Rott shook his head in the negative. "You go up top. Shut this fucking building off. I'll get through down here. We'll meet at Viktor Krill."

Hadder laughed through his Rage. "All of this just to get to the most dangerous man in history."

Rott shrugged. "It wouldn't be much fun if it was easy. Now go!"

Marlin Hadder tossed Rott's hatchet back to him, and took off across the battleground. With so much attention on Alphus, it was easy for Hadder, driven by the Rage, to cross the pandemonium unscathed. As he approached his leviathan ally, Hadder saw that the Blisters had circled around Alphus, using his mammoth form for cover while offering protection in return. Hadder slid to a stop just as Sowler, standing twenty yards aways, took the metal head from a Mugg with one of his patented Mitt backhands.

"Sowler! I need you!"

The pig-man turned to face Hadder, one of Alphus's giant limbs shifting just behind the Blister. "You still live, Angel?! But, of course, you do! What do you need?"

"I need to speak with Gayle," Hadder shouted over the din of combat.

"But she's..." started Sowler before realizing what Hadder was asking. "Haha, no problem! Run to me!"

Hadder, the Rage deepening its hooks with every heartbeat, didn't question Sowler's directive, driving straight at his former adversary. Just before Hadder reached Sowler, one of the Cyrix building's laser cutters appeared and moved toward the Blister, leaving scorched earth in its wake.

Sowler held his ground, refusing to move, and waited for Hadder's swift arrival. The laser beam got there first, but Sowler simply held his calcified arm out as a shield, blocking the death ray. Sowler screamed in agony as the beam slowly burned through his mutated arm, but dug in deeper as Hadder approached at a dead run.

Hadder leapt at Sowler just as the Cyrix beam finally carved its way through the thick layers of arm skin, but not before the Blister was able to catch the Twin Angel's foot with his relatively normal, but shockingly powerful, broken left hand. Sowler screamed in pain, but managed to boost the man of prophecy high into the air to land softly onto the manila-colored back of Alphus.

Hadder could hear Sowler cry out below him as the Blister's calcified arm fell free from its owner to splash loudly on the ground beneath. Hadder looked down, and was emboldened to see that while the laser cutter was gone, obviously needing a recharge, Sowler remained upright, his large stump neatly cauterized.

Sowler looked up and waved Hadder forward with his remaining arm. "End this, Angel! Don't let them take my arm in vain!"

Hadder nodded, and began to climb atop Alphus, adding Sheela and Sowler's arm to the list of things that had been taken on this dark day. When he reached the top of Alphus's shifting back, he found Gayle, who had tied herself down with large hooks that had been pierced into the leviathan's thick shark skin.

As always, Gayle wore the face of a Buddha statue, and greeted Hadder with an honest smile, as if the world was not melting around them. "Marlin, so happy to find you alive, although I'm not surprised in the least." She motioned downward. "Marlin, please meet my brother Alphus, whom I love dearly." Gayle raised and lower her small foot gently. "Alphus, this is Marlin Hadder, one of the Twin Angels. Let's follow his commands, shall we?" Alphus let out a roar from his giant maw as he swept three Muggs aside with one of his webbed claws. Gayle smiled sweetly, and said to Hadder, "Alphus says, *yes*. Where to, Marlin?"

Hadder ran behind Gayle, and swallowed her in a bear hug. "Up, Gayle. Please tell Alphus to go up as far as he can."

Gayle turned back to face Hadder, her rough grey skin scratching his stubbled cheek. "Easy enough. I would say, *hold on tight*, but it looks like you already got the memo." Gayle spun back forward, and closed her orange eyes, communicating to Alphus in ways that Hadder could never understand. Within seconds, the behemoth known as Alphus pushed forward, ignoring the Mech Force members attacking his heavy legs, and the pillars of flame that reached down to merely tickle his thick, water-logged skin. Alphus marched through the warring armies, paying them no more attention than a gorilla would gnats, now and then pushing a Mech Force member aside, or stomping a Mugg under a webbed foot.

In short order, Alphus had reached Cyrix Headquarters and began to climb. The leviathan's long claws dug into brick and mortar, and shattered bullet-proof windows as Alphus steadily ascended the building, forcing

Hadder to wrap his legs around the secured Gayle to avoid falling to his death.

When possible, Alphus would rake a webbed claw along the corner of the Cyrix building, removing several turrets and countless metal barrels as he progressed. Sometimes, the great Blister would cry out in pain as a laser cutter or bullet touched an especially sensitive area. But still Alphus climbed, Gayle urging him on telepathically.

Hadder buried his head against Gayle's rough-skinned back, and tried not to look down as the sounds of battle drifted off beneath him, growing increasingly removed by the minute. Soon, they reached a point where even the gun turrets had stopped appearing, and the only thing that accosted the strange trio was the cold breeze coming in off the sea.

Hadder looked around Gayle to see that the roof's edge was quickly approaching, and not a moment too soon, as his arms and legs were starting to shake from exertion. Just before cresting the building, Hadder noticed two gaping holes in a series of large windows that passed under Alphus's belly. Something inside clicked, and Hadder knew that he would return to that room shortly.

With a great heave, an audible grunt, and a desperate kick from his back legs, Alphus flopped onto the roof of the Cyrix Headquarters building. Hadder looked around quickly, expecting to find a small army waiting, but there was only emptiness and the twirling C to greet them.

Gayle turned her head. "What now, Marlin?"

"I think that C is powering the building munitions. We have to destroy it."

Gayle nodded, frowning as she looked upon the electrically charged monstrosity before her and her brother. "Then it shall be done. Marlin, is that the rooftop lift over there?"

Hadder looked to confirm Gayle's suspicions, but was struck in the chest and found himself falling backwards off Alphus. He struck the pebbled rooftop hard, driving the air from his lungs. When his breath had returned, he scrambled to his feet and called up to Gayle.

"What are you doing, Gayle! No! You don't have to do this! We can figure out another way!"

Gayle smiled sweetly at Hadder from atop Alphus, as only she could. "Only I can control my brother, Marlin. There's no reason for us all to die."

"Gayle! Please, listen! You *don't* have to do this!"

Her too-orange eyes flashed, the setting sun catching them just right. "To die for the Twin Angels is my destiny, Marlin. I've never been happier." A single tear ran down her grey cheek. "Tell Gash that I love him. That I will love him forever. Do that for me?"

Hadder was unable to find the appropriate words for the woman's sacrifice. "Of course."

Another genuine smile. "Thank you. Brother, let us end this." Gayle closed here eyes once more, and Alphus moved forward toward the giant C. Bolts of blue lightning shot out from the spinning letter to strike Alphus and his female rider. Hadder scooted back on his elbows, and threw a hand to his eyes to protect them from the explosions of color.

Still Alphus pushed on.

The leviathan roared into the dusky sky, but refused to pause, lifting his mammoth body into the air and pushing his front arms out far to bear hug the hovering letter. Long talons wrapped around the C, and a too-wide maw snapped shut atop its curve, stopping its rotation and redirecting the built-up electrical power into the unwelcome visitor.

Hadder's eyes narrowed as thick channels of electric current ran from the C to Alphus and Gayle, flashing white into the air and showcasing the dark bones of the Blister siblings. Alphus shook violently as the voltage attacked the soft tissue of his muscles, and yet he refused to release his hold on the symbol of Cyrix's dominance and abuse of the Neon City.

Gayle's long hair danced in the air as she, too, absorbed an impossible amount of power into her slight frame. But she did not cry out. Instead, she remained silent, and her orange eyes stayed closed as she pushed her brother forward, demanding every last ounce of his unnatural gifts.

Alphus twisted and ripped at his sister's commands, the long blue fingers of electrical release tearing at his manila skin and boiling organs within his giant frame. Still, he fought, until the hated C in his grasp was finally pulled free of its invisible moorings, releasing a shockwave from the pedestal that struck Alphus in the chest and drove the Blister back, driving him and his sister along the rooftop and over the edge, sending both to their imminent deaths.

Hadder cried out for Gayle, and feebly held out his hand, yet again unable to play a role in a battle between titans. He ran to the edge to confirm that she and Alphus had plummeted to the bottom, and spotted a large crater that now marked where the Blister pair had landed. Hadder's anguish was tempered by the fact that, as he looked down, he noticed that the Cyrix building had grown quiet once more, its last line of defense broken by the sweetest woman in history.

Once again, Marlin Hadder took the physical and emotional pain he was feeling and funneled it toward the one constant across all of his lives, feeding the Rage that never left his side, even as all his family and friends passed on.

The Rage swelled once more, a clear target now in close proximity. As Marlin Hadder walked to the rooftop lift, the Rage reminded him of those who had fallen before its power — namely, the fiend Skeelis and The Krown. It whispered things in his ear that gave him confidence. It massaged his ego and loosened his muscles. It suggested that he take out his twin handguns, let them feel at home against his palms. It high-fived him as he entered the lift and pressed the lone button that would take him one floor down.

Where he would finally kill Viktor Krill. And be done with this awful world, and this awful life.

26

Viktor Krill sat behind his office desk, his chair turned around to face the back wall. Up and to his right, the corpse of Cyrus Bhellum V remained pinned several feet off the floor. Krill did his best to extend the despicable man's suffering, but he had eventually succumbed to his injuries. Bhellum was now no more than an exhibit, one that would have been right at home in Lester Midnight's *Biomass*.

To his left, Krill's eyes couldn't help but wander back to the secretive rear door, where his last conversation with an old acquaintance had frightened him more than anything ever could, save the thought of harm coming to his adopted children. The man he had spoken with in that small comms room no longer resembled the person he once knew; he was something else entirely. Something that was going destroy this world.

The old Viktor Krill would have applauded his efforts, would have shrugged and said that life's a competition, that only the strong should be allowed to survive. But that Wakened human was dead. He died the moment Natthi disappeared into the mouth of an adult Slink. The person who continued on had too many things he cared about in this world, too many people that tugged at his heartstrings. The Viktor Krill that now sat in the most prestigious seat in Cyrix Industries gave a shit, so he decided it was up to him to end this encroaching madness.

But things here first demanded his attention.

The sounds of battle continued to rage on beneath him. Krill had watched much of the fight, was truly impressed by the courage and resolve of the Blisters and the Broken Tens. Had he not had so much on his mind, Viktor Krill would have been thoroughly entertained.

Krill knew the Cyrix Headquarters building's secrets, knew that it would more than likely have the capability to turn aside the invaders. Regardless of who was ultimately victorious, however, Krill knew that one character, in particular, would never be defeated by these conventional means. The Devil was coming for him, had crossed worlds to find him. And no gun turret, laser cutter, or flamethrower would be able to stop him.

When the giant mutant from the sea scaled the building, passing right in front of the office suite windows, Krill was unable to see who rode on its broad back, but he knew.

Albany Rott — the puppeteer, the deceiver, the heretic — was coming for him.

After the commotion on the roof, Viktor Krill had begun counting the minutes. He closed his eyes, coiled his muscles, and calmed his nerves. Krill had claimed to be nearly a god. It was time to test his skills against a real one.

Krill's Wakened ears heard the lift at the far end of the building open its doors. He could sense the footsteps as they grew closer. He could feel the tension as the man at the office suite entrance slowly pushed open the golden double doors.

The odor of Station hit Krill as if he had just walked into a bakery. He smiled faintly, remembering his time in that strange, sunless city that he had grown to hate over time. The uninvited guest walked halfway into the office and stopped, waiting for Krill to break the painful silence.

"So, you have come to catch the one who got away, is that it," asked Krill, his black eyes still squarely on the back wall.

"No. I've come to eliminate the killer who's been terrorizing this world."

Viktor Krill's eyes went wide at the unfamiliar voice. He spun in his chair to face the unforeseen stranger. He quickly took in the suited man who looked like he had been through a war. Although he appeared a normal man, there was something behind his hazel eyes, a power fueled by extreme anger. "Who the fuck are you?"

"I'm Marlin Hadder," said the man as he raised two handguns in Krill's direction. "I'm here to kill you."

Krill chuckled at the bravado, was impressed by the rage-induced confidence. He should have ended the man where he stood, but Krill's curiosity was overwhelming. "You stink of Station. Why?"

Both barrels remained pointed squarely at Krill's head. "Like you, it was my last place of residence."

Krill was confused, but hid it well. "And how is my old stomping ground?"

"Gone."

"What?"

"Gone. Sunk into an ocean of sand."

At this news, even Viktor Krill was unable to hide his surprise. He forgot where he was for a moment, spoke out loud to himself. "Then this *is* it. The wager has concluded. The end is really here."

Hadder struggled to hear Krill's words. "What did you say?"

Krill ignored Hadder's question. "And the residents? Station's residents?"

"All dead."

An uncomfortable mix of emotions swam within the Wakened human. His black eyes narrowed. "Except you, that is."

"Except me."

Krill rose suddenly, and slowly made his way around the desk before leaning back against it. An elaborately decorated gun peaked out from under his white suit jacket. To his credit, Marlin Hadder's hands did not shake before the notorious killer. "And what makes you so special, *Marlin Hadder*? Why do you alone stand before when so many others have died?"

Hadder laughed, a sad, desperate sound. "You know, I ask myself that same question all the time."

"And have you come up with any answers?"

"I have not."

"Then maybe you're asking the wrong question."

Hadder licked his lips nervously, his eyes flashing to the hanging corpse momentarily before returning to Krill. The Wakened human could move like lightning, could be on him in the blink of an eye, but something told Hadder that Krill wanted something else. "What *is* the right question, Viktor?"

"There are several... Marlin. But one is most pressing."

"And that is?"

"Why are you here right now?"

"To kill you."

"And why is that?"

Hadder took a moment to collect his thoughts. "Because you're unnatural. You're a monster. And you're terrifying a world that had nothing to do with you, had no hand in whatever made you become the nightmare that you are."

Krill laughed dryly, and shook his finger at the foolish man. "Those are Albany Rott's words, not yours." Hadder's eyes shifted again, showing discomfort. "Yes, I know Rott's here, too. I've known for some time." Krill pushed off the desk. "So, since you're regurgitating Rott's words, let me rephrase the question. Why is Albany Rott here? Here in the Neon City?"

Hadder's face twisted confusedly. "To kill you."

"But why?"

"Because you're a monster."

"No!" Krill's outburst caught Hadder off-guard, forcing the man to shift where he stood. Krill calmed himself and restarted. "No. Why is Albany Rott so intent on killing me, Marlin?"

Hadder hesitated, but something in the Wakened human's black eyes made him want to speak the truth. "You have to die for him to return to... Heaven, I suppose."

A look of dismay fell over Krill, and for a moment it looked like even the world's most dangerous man would lose his balance. "What? Say that again." A silent beat passed. "Say it!"

Hadder responded on reflex. "Rott can't return to Heaven until you're dead."

Krill's dark eyes dropped to the marbled floor and danced back and forth as thoughts spun through his too-sharp mind. Finally, he looked back up at Hadder. "What was Station, Marlin? What did Rott tell you?"

"That doesn't matter now, Viktor."

"Tell me," Krill roared.

"Don't you already know?"

Krill took a deep breath, regained his composure. "Talk to me as if I am a normal idiot. Like you."

Hadder ignored the barb. "Station was a wager between Rott and God."

As Hadder spoke, Krill had turned to look out of the nearest shattered office window, as if readying himself for a blow he knew to come. "And what was the bet, Marlin? What did *he* tell you?"

Hadder knew he should simply pull the triggers, put two bullets into the side of Viktor Krill's head, ending this murderous tale. Instead, something made him hear the notorious man out. "The bet was, despite being given a utopia, humanity would still fuck up, would still be miserable, would still destroy everything around them. And he was right. We did."

Krill's eyes remained staring out onto the Rising. "Well, Marlin, what you say about humanity sounds about right." His head swung to face Hadder. "But that is *not* why Station was created."

The pistols began to feel heavy in Hadder's hands. "You're saying it wasn't made for a wager between gods?"

Krill moved closer to Hadder, keeping his tan hands out wide. "Oh, there was a wager, all right. But, not that one."

Hadder swallowed hard, attempting to push down the lump that had appeared in his throat. "Then what was the bet?"

Krill paused for a long while, trying to find the words. Eventually, he responded tersely. "An Antichrist-like figure."

"Come again?"

"Ahh, such an inaccurate description, but it's the best I could come up with."

"Explain."

Black eyes met hazel for a long while. "Fine. But, please, put your weapons down. Not only do they have to be getting heavy, but I could take them from you anytime I desired."

"Don't be so sure about that."

"Marlin, you're not the first person to point a gun at my face."

"I don't doubt that, Viktor."

"And, yet, none have killed me."

"Maybe they don't know how to lead the receiver. I do."

Krill laughed aloud, honestly. Against his better judgment, he had to admit that he liked this man from Station. "Fair enough. But let us speak like two old friends from Station. If you want to try to kill me after, no hard feelings."

Once again, Hadder knew that he should unload both his clips into the scarred man's chest, ending this here and now. And yet...

Hadder lowered his weapons, nodded for Krill to continue, which he did. "God, or whatever you want to call Him, or Her, or It, has taken an interest in these worlds of ours."

"I know this."

"Then you know that He, or She, or It, can be a bit of a prick. Upon learning of the manmade, completely ridiculous prophecy of the Antichrist, of a figure who will be deified even as he destroys the world, God became curious."

"Curious about what?"

"Curious if it could really happen, Marlin. Curious if such a person could be... Not created, that's not the right word... Could be nurtured, trained, coached." Krill began to pace across the room. "So curious was God about this, that he gave his naughtiest pupil a way back into his good graces after millennia of banishment."

"You can't mean..."

Krill stopped walking. "Oh, I mean it, Marlin. Station, for all of its utopian bullshit, its talk of second chances, its stated goal of ultimate happiness, was made for one purpose — to incubate the creature that could destroy a world."

"And that creature is you."

Viktor Krill laughed out loud once more. "Me? No, no, no, dear boy. I appreciate the vote of confidence, but I am just a villain. A competitive villain who has recently begun to question his place in the world."

"The Krown?"

Krill looked legitimately surprised. "The Krown? You mean Ronald Cronowski?" Krill was struck by a fit of laughter. When he collected himself, he continued. "That pile of oversized muscle couldn't think his way out of a wet paper bag."

"He was one of the principals involved in the destruction of Station. Along with you, Viktor."

Krill shook his head sympathetically. "Oh, Marlin, there was only one person involved in the Fall of Station. And it happened precisely when he wanted it to happen. When his wager demanded that it happen."

Hadder was growing impatient. The Rage was slowly moving forward. "Who then?"

Krill turned to the wall of inlaid screens, which were all black. "Maybe it's better that I show you, Marlin." Krill spoke into the air. "Office! Play the Flowers Institute commercial." Back to Hadder. "Hold on to your sack, Marlin."

The wall of screens came to life, forever changing Marlin Hadder's thoughts on the world.

The commercial opened with a suited white man speaking into the camera, with the label *Brayden Yorsaf, President of the Centrus Affiliation* beneath. "My daughter had no chance at survival, was given six months to live. We had given up hope. Then Doctor Milo Flowers came to us, was sent from Heaven. After a week of treatment, she was given a clean bill of health."

An Asian woman, denoted as *Xioxian Chan, CEO of Taragoshi Robotics*, spoke next. "My son was resigned to a life in a wheelchair, left quadriplegic by an unfortunate car accident." She took a moment to wipe tears from her face. "Yesterday, he ran a half-marathon, without the use of implants or robotic support. Doctor Milo Flowers saved our family. He is a gift from God."

Marlin Hadder's stomach turned as a familiar face flashed on all the screens. He wore the same white doctor's coat and yellowed dress shirt that Hadder had seen at Rott Manor. His too-blonde hair was still parted neatly over his beady too-pale eyes, which remained behind circular glass frames. His blotchy skin was even more pronounced under the camera's lights, and the Rage that only Marlin Hadder could see swam across his otherwise smiling face.

The camera followed Milo Flowers as he walked through a forest path, a gang of followers dressed in white in tow. As a voiceover spoke of something called the Flowers Institute, stating how it would change the world, Hadder watched the little man that he had met briefly in another world, and came to a conclusion.

That was not a man who appeared on the screens before him, but a nightmare masquerading as a savior.

The commercial ended with vast numbers of influential men and women dressed in white, celebrating the small, vile man who sat on a dais above them. He looked down on them and offered a weak smile, holding up a milk-white hand as the commercial ended with final words from the unseen speaker.

"If you or a loved one is sick, Doctor Milo Flowers is here to help. Death is not an inevitability. The Flowers Institute will get your life back on track. Now with Petal Offices in fifteen cities around the globe. Accept Doctor Flowers, and watch as life blossoms before your eyes."

The screens went dark, and Krill turned to face Hadder. "What do you think, now, Marlin?"

Hadder grew dizzy as a thousand thoughts raced through his mind, including conversations he thought he overheard as he lay dying in Rott Manor after Lilly Sistine's attack. "But Rott said..."

Krill cut in. "I would remind you to consider the source, Marlin Hadder. The Devil is known for many things. Honesty is not one of them."

Hadder leaned against the large conference table for support. "If that's true...what *am* I doing here? Why is your death so important?"

Krill shrugged, feeling legitimately sorry for the confused man before him. It was never easy to watch your world get upended. Krill knew from experience. "It probably isn't, Marlin. But Rott needed time. It took time for Milo Flowers to win over humanity's elite, and longer still to begin destroying it. Rott needed to stall, to prove that Flowers was enough of a nightmare, enough of an Antichrist, to win his precious bet with God."

"And so..."

"And so, this hunt for me was a simple diversion, something to do while he waited for his hand to play out. And do not doubt that this, all of this, is his hand." Krill held up his hand in concession. "Now, I don't want to mislead you. Albany Rott dislikes me. He doesn't like that I prematurely escaped his mousetrap. And he certainly dislikes that I discovered how to waken my hibernating human abilities. He wants me dead, no doubt. But he does not *need* me dead."

"And me?"

Krill shrugged again. "He probably just likes you, Marlin. He probably needed someone to pass the time with."

"The Devil needed a friend," said Hadder, echoing the words he told Rott so long ago.

"That's right." Krill could see the war being waged within the man called Marlin Hadder; it was as apparent and real as the battle taking place just below them.

After several seconds of inner turmoil, Hadder looked once more to Krill. "How do you know that Milo Flowers can do these things? How do you know what power he has or hasn't?"

Krill smirked. "Who do you think helped me awaken my abilities?"

And there it was, the truth laid bare before Marlin Hadder, a dark revelation. The words stumbled out of his mouth like drunken sailors. "So, if he can do it for you..."

"That's right, Marlin. He can awaken anyone he wants. And do so much more."

"Oh god, then he can..."

A familiar voice interrupted from the office suite's large double doors. "Marlin, do not listen to this monster." Both Hadder and Krill turned to see that Albany Rott had appeared in the entrance, bleeding from countless wounds, an oiled-stained crystalline hatchet in each hand. "Move away from him. Now!"

Hadder, compelled by the power in Rott's words, did as he was told, stepping away from the tan villain. Krill began to clap slowly.

"Mister. Albany. Rott. So glad that you could join us. My new friend Marlin here has some questions that he would like to ask you."

Rott's eyes blazed with fire. "You don't have friends, Krill, only victims."

Viktor Krill's black eyes flashed in anger. "What do you know of my life here, Rott?! What makes you think that the man who escaped your prison is the same that stands before you!?"

Rott nodded toward the broken windows. "A cemetery worth of bodies out there tells me."

The glint in Krill's dark eyes dulled a bit, his voice grew weary. "Is the monster Viktor Krill not entitled to personal growth, Mister Rott? Can he not change?"

Rott took several dangerous steps forward. "Right now, you are only entitled to one thing, Krill. A quick death. Marlin, get ready."

Hadder looked from Rott to Krill, but did not raise his guns. Krill, having put both hands in the air in surrender, spoke. "It's too late, Rott. The truth has been spoken, the proverbial cat is out of the bag."

Rott took another step forward, danger flashing in his fiery eyes. "*Your* truth, Krill."

Krill's hands began to lower. "*The* truth, Rott. Already, young Marlin here is mulling it over, rolling the sounds of it across his tongue. And with each repetition, the veracity of my words becomes more apparent as your lies weaken, begin to crack under examination." Krill's hands slipped farther toward his waist. "He knows the truth of your *wager*." A look of panic, one that Hadder had never seen previously, crossed Rott's scarred face momentarily before he recovered. "And he knows that this mission is a farce, a time-waster, a boys' night out. My death is inconsequential in the grand scheme. It will change nothing, especially your ability to return to your precious Heaven."

Rott began to circle forward, his body coiled like a viper. "Maybe. Maybe not. But I'm still going to kill you, Viktor Krill. Because I *do not* like you."

Krill addressed Hadder without looking over, keeping his black eyes locked onto Albany Rott. "See, Marlin? I told you he didn't like me." Back to Rott. "But that seems like a poor reason to kill someone, does it not?"

"You have killed for much less," retorted Rott.

"But that doesn't make it right."

"Ready your weapons, *Riser*."

A grim smile appeared on Krill's face. "Then we're really going through with this?"

"We are."

"Very well." Krill spoke again to Hadder without turning to face the man. "Marlin Hadder. You seem like an impressive fellow. You made it out of Station, which no one has ever done save Milo Flowers and yours truly. You made it to the top of the Cyrix Industries Headquarters building, which should have been impossible. I truly respect you, and I don't throw that word around lightly." There was a strange pause. "I *respect* you, Marlin. But I don't *know* you. And if I don't *know* you, then I can't *trust* you. I can't trust you to stay out of this fight. You still have some misplaced loyalty to this deceiver. And while I understand that, I cannot tolerate it. And so, Marlin Hadder, *this* must be done. Perhaps you'll cheat death once again."

As soon as Viktor Krill finished, his hands flashed before him, impossibly fast, appearing only as a streak of color. In one fluid motion, the notorious killer pulled a handgun from his jacket holster and spun. As Albany Rott called out in slow motion in the background, Krill aimed and fired. So fast was the Wakened human that Hadder only had time to widen his hazel eyes in shock before the released bullet struck him in the center of his forehead, dropping him where he stood, and leaving a second corpse to decorate the office suite.

Krill didn't watch Hadder's body fall. In fact, he had already dropped his handgun, withdrawn two of his infamous knives, and completed his rotation to face a charging, very irate Albany Rott.

The battle between demigods was on in full.

Rott roared in anger, the fires in his crimson eyes threatening to reach out from their restraining orbs to attack their black counterparts. His crystalline hatchets moved in a blur, too fast for the human eye to see.

Unless the eye was that of the Wakened human Viktor Krill.

Krill's infamous blades matched the speed of Rott's axes, intercepting blows and knocking them wide before initiating their own attacks. To an observer, the combatants would have appeared to be on fast-forward, their too-quick movements leaving streaks of color in the air as if the viewer were on an acid trip.

The adversaries' ferocity matched their skill, each strike thrown with deadly intent, desperate to score a killing blow. A crystalline hatchet wasn't knocked aside far enough, and came down to tear a deep gash in Krill's upper arm, leaving blood to run off both blade and white suit. A knife darted forward and found space between the spinning axes to nick Rott's neck, leaving a red line just beside his shimmering tattoo that was the blueprint for humanity.

After another round of attacks, parries, ducks, and dodges, the two men began to speak through their bloodlust. Krill spat onto the marble floor before he spoke, sending blood mixed with saliva to the cold floor. "How could you do it, Rott? Do you miss your home so much that you would destroy the homes of billions to return there? Is there no heart as part of your human costume, your great facade?"

Rott snickered. "Who are you to lecture me about heart? The great killer, Viktor Krill. You've left more families in grief than most in history."

"A great regret, to be sure. And something I plan to rectify." Krill jabbed out with his left knife like lightning, hoping to catch Rott preoccupied with thought.

Rott easily knocked the blade aside before responding. "Tell me, Krill, how do plan on rectifying three lifetimes of murder, mayhem, and carnage?

No time machine exists, that I know of. And I know all. So tell me, how will you *rectify* your misdeeds?"

"By saving this world." Krill's words gave Rott pause. He sensed no falsehood in the villain's assertion, only determination, rage, and... contrition. Clearly upset by Krill's announcement, Albany Rott launched into a blinding attack, simultaneously coming in high to the right and low to the left, forcing Krill to conjure some magic of his own to avoid being decapitated or disemboweled.

After completing yet another dance of death that claimed no victims, Viktor Krill began to lose his cool. "Why! Why! I demand to know before I send you back to your limbo purgatory. Why would you do this? Why would you create a nightmare, and then set him loose on this world, knowing that he will destroy it?"

"I do not have to explain myself to a human! You know, a Wakened human is still a human. And humans were my third draft. Right after monkeys!"

Krill grew dangerously quiet. "I demand to know why."

"You know why."

"I need to hear you say it."

A terrifying tension settled over the room, as if a strand of metal had been pulled tightly over a sharp edge. Eventually, Rott answered. "It is my only way home."

Krill sneered. "Is it? Or is it simply the easiest way home." A heavy silence fell as Rott had no response. "You're condemning this world to a literal Hell. The people here will only know horror before humanity is completely stripped away, making way for a land of nightmares. Why?!"

"Because it is my right, you fool!" Rott shook with rage, his hatchets vibrating in his too-white hands. "It is *my* world. These are all *my* worlds. I can do with them as I wish! And you *humans*? You think I owe you something? I owe you nothing! You were mere specks of energy floating around the multiverse before me! You were lumps of clay without shape! I gave you all form! I gave you all purpose! I gave you light in an otherwise dark place!"

Rott took a deep breath, calmed himself a bit before continuing. "I owe this world nothing. They made this choice, I did not make it for them."

Krill black eyes narrowed. "I spoke to Milo Flowers, Rott. You know, your protégé, your creation. The good Doctor shared with me his plans, mistaking me for a kindred spirit. He's completely insane. And purely evil."

"That was the point, was it not?"

"There's still time to right this wrong, Rott. To hell with your wager."

Rott stepped carefully around Krill, the two men staring at each other like gunslingers preparing to draw. "The wager has already been won, Krill. There is no going back. Several weeks ago, this world's top leaders pledged their undying loyalty to their new deity, Doctor Milo Flowers." Rott smiled grimly. "You know, it is amazing the lengths of depravity humans will go for the possibility of immortality. I have *lived* for millennia, and I can tell you, it is an overrated experience."

"Fine. You have won your all-important bet. Now help me stop him. I beg you!"

"What has happened to you, Krill? The horror that is to be unleashed on this land should be right up your alley. Did you not become a Wakened human to become a harbinger of death?"

A sadness fell over Viktor Krill's dark face. "Not anymore, Rott. I've seen things, experienced things. Met extraordinary people. This world has embraced me in ways that my old world, and even Station, did not. I need to save it. And it sickens me to say it, but I need your help to do so."

Rott paused once again, struggling with Krill's surprising words. "I'm sorry, Viktor, but I cannot. The humans of this world have made their choice. They now have to live with it. It is out of my hands. Top-level decision."

Krill's knuckles went white as his grip tightened on his knives. "You know, you remind me of my father, Rott. He, too, hid behind a lack of control. He, too, was apathetic of pain. Your apathy is noted, Rott. Now, fuck off. Leave me to my attempts to save this misguided world, regardless of how futile they may prove to be."

"No."

"Why not, damn you?!"

"Because I dislike you, Viktor. Now, die!"

With that, Albany Rott became a tornado of blades, each impossibly fast strike aimed to kill. Krill matched Rott's intensity with his own, his attacks faster than ever before, powered by deep grief for the lost, and a deeper love for those still alive. Blood began to fly as the battle intensified. Crimson lines appeared on Krill's cheek, on Rott's wrist. An axe dug deep into Krill's hip. A knife took a chunk out of Rott's shoulder. Both warriors ignored the pain. Both danced with death. Each needed the other to make a mistake.

Krill and Rott danced around the Cyrix office suite, each narrowly missing the fight's endgame several times. Sparks flew where crystalline hatchet met knife, as if the heavens themselves were cheering on the combatants. On and on the two most dangerous men in the world fought, neither giving the other an inch. Neither making an error.

Until one finally did.

Krill backhanded Rott's looping blow, sending it out wide with his right knife while intercepting the lower axe attack with his left. Krill's right hand recovered quickly, and began to shoot forward in a jab, launching a strike that should have been knocked aside by Krill's righthand hatchet as it recovered from its unsuccessful low attempt. That hatchet, however, by sheer luck, had its head caught in the small knife guard for a fraction of a second, delaying its cross-body parry.

That fraction of a second might as well have been an eternity for Viktor Krill. The villain smiled inwardly.

Krill's right knife shot forward like a serpent and, in his mind, the Riser king could already see the blood spurting out like a geyser from the killing blow. Krill threw his entire shoulder into the attack, had already begun to scream in delight.

Then Viktor Krill's world flashed white, and he fell to the marble floor unconscious.

As Krill fell, a crimson-masked Marlin Hadder was revealed to be standing directly behind the notorious killer, Sheela's wakizashi in his right hand, the end of its handle red with Krill's blood. Between Hadder's eyes,

Krill's compressed bullet remained stuck in the man's forehead, stopped by the diamond-plated Elevation.

Albany Rott's eyes fiery eyes went wide before he exploded in joy. "Marlin, dear boy! I should have known! Now, if you'll excuse me..." Rott rose his right hatchet into the air, readying it to finish off the defenseless Viktor Krill. As he began the killing blow, the barrel of a gun appeared before his scarred face, stopping him mid-swing.

"I don't think so, Al."

Rott stared dumbfounded at Hadder. "What are you doing, Marlin?"

Although the Rage surged through Hadder, the gun pointed at Rott's face did not waver in the least, as if it was sitting on concrete. "You know, the thing about dying a bunch of times, it makes it easy to *pretend* to be dead. I heard everything, Al."

Albany Rott, his body previously taught with adrenaline and anger, sank. "Marlin, I..."

"Don't bother, Al. You want to leave this world to the scourge that is Milo Flowers, that's fine. You've punched your ticket home already. I wish I could say that I was happy for you." Hadder struggled to find the words, swallowed down threatening tears. "I *was* happy for you. But it was all a lie, wasn't it? Station. This quest to kill Krill. Our friendship."

"That was real, Marlin."

"Maybe. Maybe not. I don't know what to believe anymore. But I do know this. You *will* step away from Krill. Or I *will* put a bullet through your fucking head, sending you into limbo, and delaying your precious return."

"But Marlin..."

"We're done here, Al. Your personal war with Viktor Krill is over. Now walk away." Hadder's eyes grew misty as the gun finally began to waver. "Please."

The fires in Rott's eyes had disappeared, leaving only smoldering embers. "Ok, Marlin." In one smooth movement, Rott slid both hatchets back into his waistband. He turned and began to exit the office suite. Just before reaching the large golden doors, Rott turned back to face Hadder. "I am sorry, Marlin. I have been sorry for some time now. I am unused to... friends."

"Well, you don't have to worry about that any longer, Al. You have none left."

Rott nodded solemnly and walked out of the double doors, his sunken shoulders looking not like those of a god, but those of a man. A man who had just harmed the only person he had ever cared about.

27

"Y ou are sure he is safe?"

Red Texx nodded. "My man dropped him off precisely where you told us. Made sure no one was around when he did. Darrin will seem like just another toddy walking the streets. The richest toddy in the history of the world."

Viktor Krill found himself smiling thinking his son safe, armed with every opportunity that that notorious killer could provide him. She would make sure that Darrin grew into the man that Krill envisioned he could become. The man who could change the world... given that Krill could ensure that there would be a world to change.

Krill noticed Red Texx's hesitancy, and felt his smile grow wider. "Try it out, Texx. You've earned it."

"It's just that..."

"Texx." Krill's voice still held sway over the new Riser leader, forcing Red Texx to fall into the soft leather of the black, high-backed chair. When he had settled in, Krill asked, "How does it feel?"

A grin snuck onto Red Texx's face, breaking out into a full-fledged smile. "It feels good. It feels... empowering."

"Good. Never forget this feeling. It can be wielded like a scythe for good, or bad. I leave the choice up to you. But remember, it can be taken from you, and many will try."

Red Texx's face grew serious. "I have seen firsthand the chaos that those in this position can wreak. I will not let that happen."

"I know you won't, my friend. What are your plans, wise Riser king? You control more money than all but a handful of men in the world. What will you do with this power?"

Texx thought for a moment. "First, I will rid us of the Slink Farms. They have destroyed enough lives."

A pang of guilt attacked Krill. He swallowed the bile that rose into his throat. "An intelligent move. And then?"

"I will work with Old Tens to consolidate the rest of the drug trade. The corporate world will not accept me, and I want nothing to do with them. Our men still need to eat, still need a reason to wake up in the morning. We will break them up into business units, put guys like Sonny Caddoc and Wess Dey in charge. Over time, we'll transition into legitimate businesses, become legal entities that help the poor and target the upper classes. And then we'll become truly dangerous."

Krill's black eyes became damp upon hearing his former Second's plans for the future. "And Cyrix Industries? The Rising?"

Texx ran an oversized hand though his red afro. "Let that wretched place decay around the body of its previous owner." Both men's minds flew back into the Cyrix Industries Headquarters' office suite, where Cyrus Bhellum V's body still hung from the back wall. "We'll start moving out of the Rising soon. The Neon City is sprawling, and it's long past time for the Risers to spread our legs. I'll work with Mayfly Lemaire on the logistics; she's much smarter than me."

Another shot of guilt needled through Krill. He cleared his throat, which was growing tight. "Then it sounds like the Rising, wherever it may end up, is in good hands. Lemaire received her share of the funds, I assume."

"She did, boss."

"You're the boss now, Texx."

"I consider you Boss Emeritus."

Krill chuckled. "Very well. Then I will leave you to it. I will not be leaving for a few days, Texx. Let me know if you need anything."

"Where are you going, boss? We would all rather you stay here and lead us."

"You are already twice the leader I could ever be, Texx. And there is something else that demands my attention."

"Something more pressing than leading the Risers?"

"Yes, my friend. Something much more serious."

Red Texx sighed before nodding, always one to accept that there were things in this world that he was unequipped to understand. "Then I wish you luck, boss. The Risers are here if you ever need us. Although I am now called First, you will forever be our king."

"Thank you, my friend." Krill spun and began to exit the large room that sat atop Triton Tower. Just as he reached the door, he was stopped by Texx's voice.

"Are you going to say goodbye to her?"

Krill refused to turn back, his dark eyes filling with water. "What's that now?"

"Mayfly Lemaire. Are you going to say goodbye? She's been asking about you."

Krill thought for a moment, the knot in his stomach growing larger by the second. "No, I do not think I will. That poor woman has lost enough. She was better off before me. She'll be better off after me." He spun back to face Texx. "But give her my love. No, not that..." The notorious killer seemed flustered for the first time. "Tell her I love her. Tell her I am sorry. Will you do that for me, Texx?"

"Of course, boss. It would be my honor."

———

"ARE YOU SERIOUS! WHAT GREAT NEWS!" Marlin Hadder threw his arms around Gash, careful not to squeeze any acid from the Blister king.

"Y-yes, Alphus b-b-broke Gayle's fall. And her th-thick s-s-skin blocked m-most of the electricity. She's r-r-recovering now, and hopes to s-see you b-b-before you leave."

"Of course. And Alphus?"

"He'll s-s-survive. P-poor thing was t-t-terribly damaged, b-but he was able to c-c-crawl back into the s-sea, where his w-w-wounds will h-heal. The n-next t-t-time we s-see him, he'll b-be the s-s-size of a warship."

Hadder chuckled. "Glad he's on our side."

"M-m-me too."

"And Viktor sent you the funds?"

"Yes. Enough to p-p-purchase our island th-th-three times over."

"I'm happy for you, my friend."

"I am h-happy for m-m-my people. Too long h-h-have we suffered."

Hadder looked around the Hammers. "And Albany Rott?"

Acid Boy Gash's joyous demeanor was shattered momentarily. "He is w-worse than b-b-before. He s-stays down by the s-sea, staring out into n-n-nothing. S-s-smoking cigarette after c-c-cigarette." Gash looked at Hadder with his vibrating violet eyes. "Y-you should t-t-talk to him."

Hadder shook his head coldly. "He knows what he's done. And he knows that words will not change it. Best to forget him." Hadder's smile returned. "I'm happy you and Gayle made it, Gash. I only wish that Sheela..." His brave facade broke, and a horrible fit of sobbing threatened to overtake him. Only Gash's hand on his shoulder held the tears at bay.

"Sheela d-d-died so our p-people could p-p-prosper. As sh-she would h-have wanted. We w-w-will sing s-songs of her b-b-bravery."

Hadder collected himself. "Thank you, Gash. I'll see you and Gayle before I leave." Hadder turned and began to walk away, but was stopped cold by Gash's words from behind.

"Orrin the Child h-had another p-p-premonition."

"What was that?"

"T-together, the Twin Angels w-w-would save the w-world. B-but forced apart, the w-w-world would shift."

"Shift into what?"

"H-horror. Chaos. H-hell."

Hadder did not respond, instead choosing to continue his walk through the Hammers. He had enough on his plate without the added weight of more prophecy.

———

"Did you take care of everything, Viktor?"

"Everything I meant to take care of? Yes, Marlin."

"Then we are ready to leave?"

"I am. Unfortunately, you are not."

"What do you mean, Viktor?"

"Marlin, right now Milo Flowers is not only awakening those minions around him, but he is transforming them into something entirely not human. What are you going to do to these monsters? Curse at them? Fire your guns at them? They would rip the head from your shoulders before you had the chance to utter one of your witty one-liners."

Hadder's stomach began to churn. "What are you saying, Viktor?"

"I'm saying you are worthless to me like this, Marlin. Actually, you are worse than worthless. You are an active liability."

"Albany Rott didn't think so."

"Rott was marching into the Rising. We are marching into Hell. Big difference."

"What are you saying, Viktor?"

"We need to awaken you, Marlin. Which means, you need to speak with Rott."

"Why?"

"Because I do no want to do it alone. I could try it myself, but there is a fifty-fifty chance that you end up a corpse. A corpse without a Station as a safety net."

"You didn't need Rott to awaken your abilities."

Krill raised his shirt, showing jagged scars criss-crossing his chest and stomach, blurring a tattoo that read *Station's Son.* "But the pain almost killed me, Marlin. I know you are tough. I didn't think you were stupid, too. Talk to Rott."

"We're not exactly on speaking terms."

Krill sighed deeply, an obvious exaggeration. "Then I will talk to him. But do not act surprised if another fight breaks out."

"Ok, ok. I'll ask him. But I don't know why he would help us."

A strange look passed across Krill's tan face, almost as if he pitied Marlin Hadder. "He will help you, Marlin. Because somehow, some way, you made friends with the Devil. And I doubt that he has had many of those over the millennia. He's fucked us. He's royally fucked us. But that does not mean that he will not gift you this last token of friendship."

Hadder thought for a minute, trying to formulate an adequate response to Krill's logic. He could not. "All right, Viktor. I'll ask. But if he refuses?"

Krill laughed out loud, an honest sound. "Then we drink ourselves to death instead because it will be just as productive."

MARLIN HADDER LAID naked on a cold metal table in the abandoned medical wing of the Cyrix Industries Headquarters building. More than a half-dozen large surgical mechs surrounded the nude man who was slowly beginning to panic. Viktor Krill stood near his head, checking off items from a list as Albany Rott could be heard readying tools near his feet.

Hadder spoke through worried breaths. "And why can't you put me to sleep, again?"

Krill looked down at the patient. While Hadder didn't think it was possible for black eyes to express empathy, these certainly did. "You need to be fully aware for your Wakened abilities to take. Otherwise, they will simply slip back into the recesses of your being." A long pause. "I *am* sorry, Marlin, but this is the only way."

Hadder's chest rose and fell quickly in fearful anxiety. "Tell me again, Viktor. Tell me this is the only way."

Krill pressed his hand against Hadder's chest, as if forcing his breathing to slow. Surprisingly, it worked. "It is the only way, Marlin."

"Tell me it will be worth it."

"Do you want to save this world, Marlin."

"Yes."

"Then it is worth it. Now prepare yourself."

Just then, several of the surgical mechs whirred to life as Rott approached Marlin's waist holding several scalpels. He handed one to Krill without looking at his nemesis. Rott shot a look at Hadder that could have read as an apology, or nothing at all, before turning his attention elsewhere.

Krill leaned forward, his face inches away from Hadder's. "Marlin, listen to me. I will not lie to you. This is going to hurt more than any pain you have ever felt. Nerves you never knew you had will explode to life. You will want to die... again. But you will not. And when you next open your eyes, you will no longer be a man. You will be a human. Only the second human in the history of all worlds. Are you ready?"

Everything within Marlin Hadder screamed in the negative, begged him to put a stop to this unnatural act. But Hadder ignored those calls, thinking only of the billions of wives and daughters who would perish without his sacrifice. "I'm ready."

"Then we begin. Soon, you will be a digital man in an analogue world. Remember that." The last thing that Hadder saw was Viktor Krill nodding to Albany Rott.

And then Marlin Hadder's world exploded in pain. Unimaginable pain.

———

"It's been almost a week. How do you feel?"

"My head still rings from where you shot me, you bastard."

"I've told you numerous times, I spotted the metal through that gash on your forehead. I knew you had protection there."

"But you weren't sure it would stop a bullet."

Krill sighed heavily. "Nothing is sure in this twisted world, Marlin.

Educated guesses are the best we can do. Mine seemed to turn out all right. How are you feeling other than that?"

Marlin Hadder stood outside Cyrix Industries, the sun feeling different on his skin. "My mind moves faster. I can view things four, five steps ahead. I see stuff I would have missed before, like that rat pulling a pizza crust into the sewer four blocks down, across Cyrix Boulevard. I'm still sore as shit, but I feel powerful in a way that I've never known. In a way that not even the Rage could offer me."

Krill nodded. "As your wounds heal, and you become accustomed to your abilities, that power will only grow. Coupled with this... Rage of yours, you are going to be quite formidable, Marlin." He slapped Hadder on the shoulder, drawing a pained groan from the man. "Sorry. But I am glad to have you on my team. Together, we may be able to save this undeserving world."

"And Rott?"

Krill looked away. "I'm sorry, Marlin. He left while you were recovering. No doubt to collect his ticket back home. But, at least he gave you one last gift before his exit."

"Is that what this is, Viktor? A gift?"

Krill mulled the question over. "For you? For me? No. But for the billions that we could save? Yes, it is a gift. The sooner you reconcile that, the better."

Hadder thought for a moment. "Very well. Have you said your goodbyes?"

A shadow of pain crossed Krill's face before quickly passing. "Yes. All that needs to be said has been."

Hadder understood that pain all too well, and left it at that. "Then let us be off. Everything hurts like a motherfucker, but perhaps some walking will loosen things up." Krill began to laugh. "What's so funny?"

"Marlin, my strange friend, a week from now, you will find walking the hardest thing to do. Restricting your abilities will be more difficult than letting them loose. I look forward to seeing your face when that realization hits you."

Hadder chuckled, thankful for Krill's words of support. The two men began walking down Cyrix Boulevard, ignoring the auto-taxis that were honking in an attempt to catch their attention. After several minutes, Hadder was unable to hold back the question that had remained on the tip of this tongue for the past week. "Viktor?"

"Yes, Marlin?"

"I am unable to understand something. How does someone, let's say you..."

"Yes, let us say..."

"How does one go from being the world's most eminent killer to its sole savior?"

Krill did not answer immediately. In fact, the pair walked for several hundred yards before the Wakened human responded. "I've been thinking a lot about that myself."

"Reach any conclusions?"

"Only one. The loss of a child. It can turn the good evil. We've all known that. But, apparently, it can also force the evil to become good. The bright mirror that loss holds up before us is a powerful thing, Marlin. Don't you agree?"

Hadder did not answer. In fact, Krill's response had unwittingly pulled him back into a time that he had worked hard to forget. The losses of Emily and Mia remained ever-present, despite his best efforts. Their sweet faces tormented Hadder, along with those of the others he had lost since his first death. For several minutes, Hadder remained lost in that deep well of despair. Finally, Krill's voice ripped him to the surface.

"Marlin? Marlin?!"

Hadder snapped back to attention. "Sorry, Viktor, my mind was wandering."

Krill's black eyes shot over to Hadder as they walked. "Careful, Marlin. The wandering mind tends to lean toward darkness."

Hadder snickered. "Toward darkness? Aren't we already in the darkness, Viktor?"

Krill laughed dryly. "I'm afraid you haven't begun to see darkness, my friend. Soon, you'll see true nightmares. And you'll be glad for the pain that you have endured. For without it, you would crumble in fear."

"You need to work on your motivational speeches, Viktor."

Krill chuckled. "I'm sorry, Marlin. I'm tired, and sad, and lonely. And I am not ready for another adventure, quite yet."

A smirk found its way onto Marlin Hadder's face. "I know of a good Spirit House just a few blocks away. Supposed to be the best in the Neon City. I'm sure our mission can wait a day or two."

A smile, honest and true, cracked open before Krill was able to hide it. "Yes, that might just do the trick. After all, you are of no use to us all banged up as you are."

"My thoughts exactly."

The new companions moved forward with renewed vigor, both concealing boyish giggles under scowls. Both understanding what was to come. Both knowing one inexorable truth.

They would laugh today. But cry later, in the dark days to come.

EPILOGUE

D arrin knocked on the blood-red door and waited for an answer as the camera above focused on the dark-skinned boy. As he waited, Darrin looked around and fingered the ornate handgun tucked into his waist, a habit of a lifetime of street living.

Almost a minute later, the door rose silently on well-greased bearings, and a small woman in large digital glasses appeared in the doorway, a genuine smile painted onto her honest face. At least the part of her face that was showing.

"Young Darrin, I presume," asked the woman, her soft voice immediately putting the boy at ease. "But of course you are. Who else would you be? Come here and let me get a good look at you." The visor-clad woman put her hands on Darrin's shoulders, and pulled him in close. The digital glasses made strange noises as they studied the child before them. "Yes, yes, our mutual friend was right about you. A real diamond in the rough. Come, come, let's show you to your room, dear thing."

Darrin hesitated against the woman's pull. "I'm not looking for a hand-out, ma'am. I can handle not only myself, but a crew should you deem me worthy of managing one. I know you were asked to take care of me, but that's only half the story. I was also told to take care of you. I'm more than able, and have my own money."

If Sammie Tott was capable of forming tears, she would have. Instead, she choked back the lump in her throat. "I understand, Darrin. Then let me show you to your... office. Together, we'll create a Spirit Girl empire the likes of which Sespit has never seen. How does that sound?"

Darrin exhaled, happy to have successfully broached the difficult subject. Happy to have found an adult that would be half mother, half business partner. "That sounds perfect, Miss Tott, ma'am."

Sammie Tott giggled. "I'm not Miss Tott. And I'm certainly not a *ma'am*, although I appreciate the respect. You can call me Sammie."

"Of course, *Miss* Sammie."

Sammie laughed again, but pushed the issue no further. "Well, come on in Darrin... Sorry, do you have a last name, dear?"

Darrin thought for a moment, and his small brown eyes began to quiver with a thin coating of water.

"Krill. My name is Darrin Krill."

THANK YOU

Thank you for taking the time to read The Rott Inertia. I can't put into words how grateful I am that you chose to spend your valuable time in the world that I created. If you enjoyed the book, it would be most helpful if you could leave a rating or review on any of the various retail channels. It is truly insane how much of an author's success is predicated on these reviews.

If you're curious about the music that drove this novel, please visit my website and check out the book soundtracks for both Station and The Rott Inertia. There, you can also hit me up with questions or to chat.

www.JarrettBrandonEarly.com

ABOUT THE AUTHOR

Jarrett Brandon Early is an emerging author of contemporary sci-fi thrillers. He lives with his wife Natthicha and daughter Alexandra Beam. The Rott Inertia is Jarrett's second book and sequel to Station.

Jarrett is currently hard at work on Ill Messiah, the exciting conclusion of the Station Trilogy.